HOMEFRONT

Also by Chuck Logan

After the Rain
Vapor Trail
Absolute Zero
Big Law
Price of Blood
Hunter's Moon

For Jean and Sofie

HarperCollins books may be purchased for educational, business, or sales promotional use. For information, please write: Special Markets Department, HarperCollins Publishers, 10 East 53rd Street, New York, NY 10022.

FIRST EDITION

Designed by Joy O'Meara

Printed on acid-free paper

Library of Congress Cataloging-in-Publication Data
Logan, Chuck.
    Homefront / Chuck Logan.—1st ed.
        p.   cm.
    ISBN 0–06–057020–2 (acid-free paper)
    1. Broker, Phil (Fictitious character)—Fiction. 2. Undercover operations—Fiction. 3. Ex–police officers—Fiction. 3. Minnesota—Fiction. I. Title.
PS3562.O4453H66   2005
813'.54—dc22   2005046054

05 06 07 08 09 ❖/RRD 10 9 8 7 6 5 4 3 2 1

CHUCK LOGAN

HOMEFRONT

HarperCollinsPublishers

Acknowledgments

Dennis P. Moriarty; commander (retired), Washington County Sheriff's Department; Washington County, Minnesota.

Patrick Olson; sergeant, Narcotics, Washington County Sheriff's Department, Washington County, Minnesota.

Heather Nelson; principal, Stonebridge Elementary School, Stillwater, Minnesota.

Jennifer Kern; school psychologist, Stonebridge Elementary School, Stillwater, Minnesota.

Marybeth Rosell; assistant coach, St. Croix Swim Club, Stillwater Minnesota.

Jane Duncan; former NCAA national swimmer, Stillwater, Minnesota.

Rick Chapin; Tractor Authority, River Falls, Wisconsin.

Don Schoff; Schoff Farms, River Falls, Wisconsin.

Deborah Durkin; health studies coordinator, Minnesota Department of Health.

Craig Nagel, stonemason in the Socratic tradition, Pequot Lakes, Minnesota.

HOMEFRONT

Prologue

Broker was looking at women's long underwear in the J. P. Asch Outfitters store in downtown Stillwater when he got the call.

Outside, at the curb, a seven-foot spruce was encased in plastic netting in the bed of his Toyota Tundra. Last night Nina and their daughter, Kit, had raided the local Target store for a cart full of lights to string on the house and the tree. The boxes of decorations had been dusted off, opened, and laid out in the living room. It was going to be the first real Christmas together in four years that didn't involve Nina or Nina and Kit flying in from Europe.

He was debating which color lightweight Capilene to buy; the Red Chili Heather or the Purple Sage Heather. Either color would complement Nina's ruddy freckled complexion, her green eyes and amber-red hair. She had been making steady progress with the rehabilitation on her shoulder, and he had purchased new cross-country ski gear for the family. Nina thought her shoulder might be good enough to lightly hit the trails up north by the middle of January. His eyes drifted out the window at the black iron girders of the old railroad lift bridge that spanned the St. Croix River. The top of the structure feathered off in the haze of an unseasonably warm drizzle.

Hopefully the snow would hold up north, he was thinking.

Then the phone rang. He flipped it open and hit answer.

"Mr. Broker. This is Brenda from the office at Stonebridge

Elementary. Your daughter has been waiting for someone to pick her up for over forty minutes . . ."

Huh? "I'm on my way. Be right there."

What the hell? Rain, shine, or snow, Nina walked Kit to school and then ran five miles every morning. Every afternoon she trekked the six blocks to the school and walked Kit back home. Hadn't missed a day since they'd enrolled her in September.

Broker jumped in his truck, fought his way through the congested downtown traffic, drove past the festive streetlights hung with wreaths and Christmas decorations, half heard the carols piped from the busy storefronts. He drove up the North Hill, and when he wheeled into the deserted parking circle in front of the one-story school building, Kit was waiting at the front door with a teacher's aide.

"Hey. Where's Mom?" she asked, as she hopped in the backseat of the extended cab. Tallish, broad-shouldered, narrow-hipped, and cougar-cub lean at eight years old, she'd learned to be a stickler about punctuality. From her mother. She also had Nina's hair, freckles, and deep green eyes.

"Let's go find out," Broker said as he drove home faster than usual. He'd purchased the house on North Third as an investment; a large white duplex on the bluff overlooking the river. His address of record remained the Broker's Beach Resort in Devil's Rock, north of Grand Marais, on the Lake Superior shore. The needs of his reconstituted family had obliged him to migrate from the remote north woods. Nina insisted on dance lessons, piano, and most of all, access to a fifty-meter pool; her daughter would be a competitive swimmer.

Like her mom.

Broker pulled up the long driveway and parked his truck in back of a rusted Honda Civic. A square, powerfully built man with a graying ponytail and a Pistol Pete mustache squatted behind the car, replacing the license tabs. As Broker and Kit got out of the truck, Kit called to the guy, "Dooley, you seen Mom?"

Dooley stood up and shook his head. Kit jogged toward the back door. Following her, Broker yelled over his shoulder to

Dooley, "Could you take the tree outa the truck, strip the plastic sleeve, and lean it against the garage?"

Dooley nodded and headed for the truck. He was a steady ex-con who'd helped Broker out of a few jams back when Broker was in law enforcement. Broker gave him an efficiency apartment in exchange for yard work, maintenance, and general watchdog duties. He was a good man to have around, except for his tendency to talk up born-again Christianity to Kit . . .

"Daaaddddd!!!"

Galvanized by Kit's shrill yell, Broker sprinted over to the door. "What?"

Kit stood in the open door, glowering, clamping her nostrils together with a thumb and index finger. She pointed with her other hand into the all-season porch. Broker went in and immediately saw and smelled a thick stratum of cigarette smoke hanging in the air.

Broker had been off tobacco for three months. Nina had agreed never to indulge her cigarettes inside the house, a rule she hadn't violated since they took up residence in late August, when she cleared the base hospital at Fort Bragg. He followed the smoke to where it was thickest, through the open door into the kitchen.

Major Nina Pryce, U.S. Army, nominally "retired" and on extended sick leave from government service, sat at the table, still in the sweat suit and New Balance shoes she wore on her morning run. She leaned forward, elbow braced like someone arm-wrestling an invisible opponent. An inch of ash dangled from the end of the American Spirit jammed in the corner of her mouth. A breakfast bowl on the table held four or five butts mashed into the Total cereal and milk. Another cigarette butt floated in a coffee cup.

And then he saw it, in her right hand.

Broker reacted instantly. He gently shoved Kit back into the porch, closed the door in one swift movement, and lunged into the room. Nina, staring straight ahead, seemingly unaware of his presence, was raising and lowering her right arm, in the manner prescribed to strengthen the damaged muscles. But instead of the two-pound weight she always used, this afternoon she was raising and lowering her .45-caliber Colt semiautomatic—in which he saw no vacant cavity in the handgrip.

Jesus! The pistol had a magazine in it.

Immediately Broker snatched the weapon from her hand and dropped out the magazine, which smacked down on the polished maple tabletop like an exclamation point. For a fraction of a second he stared at the top stumpy bullet spring loaded in the magazine like a fat round tombstone. Then he racked the slide. No round in the chamber. Locked, not loaded. He exhaled audibly, only then realizing he'd been holding his breath.

"For the weight," she said in a thick, labored voice.

Broker reached for the breakaway hideout holster on the table and was about to slide the pistol into it when he saw the unfolded note tucked inside:

"Went out for coffee with Janey. Be back soon." A sensual open-mouthed lipstick blot marked the note by way of signature.

Broker took a step back and placed the pistol on the counter next to the stove. Deep breath in. Shaky coming out.

She drilled him with a look that spiraled with palpable self-loathing and hair-trigger rage. With difficulty, he held her fierce gaze as he mentally tracked back five months to that North Dakota morning.

She'd left the note for Broker on the table in their room at the Langdon Motor Inn next to her holstered pistol. She'd decided not to take the gun when she went out with her partner, Janey Singer, for coffee. Then they'd taken a detour to the Missile Park Bar. Northern Route, their undercover mission to Langdon, North Dakota, had apparently been based on faulty intelligence. They had selected the wrong smuggler. Nina felt an obligation to say good-bye to her target in the misguided sting, Ace Shuster.

Broker gauged the turmoil in Nina's eyes, glanced at the note on the table, and instinctively understood the source of her despair. She'd torn her shoulder to shreds fighting for her life.

But that wasn't it. That was later. No, it was leaving her weapon behind that morning.

She had become imprisoned in three seconds of her life . . .

Because Nina was not your ordinary ex-Army Stillwater housewife getting ready to trim the tree.

She was a "D-Girl," attached to the Army's elite Delta Force. She was also one of the few women to qualify for the Army Marksmanship Unit. Under extreme real-world pressure, she had reliably demonstrated the ability to get off an accurate shot with a handgun in under three seconds up to fifty yards.

It was all there in her eyes.

A split second before everyone else, Nina saw it was a trap. She saw Joe Reed appear through the back door of the bar with his big Browning automatic coming up in a two-handed grip. She yelled a warning, her hand flashing in a lightning reflex for the small of her back.

I can beat you . . .

But she came up empty. She'd left the pistol back at the motel on the table next to her sleeping husband. All she could do was watch.

"Janey!"

"I'm here, girl," Janey yelled back, swinging around, yanking her Baretta, turning . . .

Too late. Reed shot her twice in the chest at a distance of ten feet. Lieutenant Janey Singer went down, and Reed came on another two steps and put the last one in her head.

Then Reed swung the gun, and Ace Shuster took the bullets meant for her. That's when Ace's crazy brother Dale stepped in front of Reed and stabbed her with the syringe of ketamine. The last thing she saw, as the paralyzing anesthetic dragged her into the black, was the contempt in Joe's cold eyes. And blood. Ace's blood on her chest.

Her eyes rolled up. Dread was mocked by the sinking euphoria in her veins. The thought that she'd never see her daughter again.

◆ ◆ ◆

The pain, loss, and guilt had taken a freaky rebound; twisted around and got caught in her head. She'd let her buddies down. Worst thing in the world for a soldier like Nina Pryce.

No way she could have known . . .

Didn't matter. She was stuck on those three seconds. If she hadn't left her weapon behind, Operation Northern Route would have ended in that barroom. Janey would be alive, and Ace and Holly—Colonel Holland Wood. There would have been no attack on the Prairie Island Nuclear Plant.

He'd never seen her like this. Ever. Sure, he knew there was a downside to her job. He'd spent his time in special ops in the old days. He knew that killing people—or losing people—leaves a harsh sudden vacuum in the world. And sometimes *this* could rush into it. But you never thought about it, and you never voiced it. Now. Jesus. He was numb, blindsided, like he'd lost his place. His voice shook, searching for reference.

"Nina, hey kiddo . . ."

"Fuck you, Broker. Leave me alone."

He studied the conflicted stranger who now occupied his wife's body. Her taut face had lost its tone and aged ten years since breakfast, now just a clay mask of melancholy and fatigue. He could smell the rank sweat. More than fear; hopelessness, dread. Most of all he saw her shattered eyes, green splinters of pain jammed inward.

She took the cigarette from her lips and dunked it in the coffee cup, in the process scattering ash across the black type that spelled ARMY on the front of her sweat suit. Then she got up from the table, walked past him, went through the living room and up the stairs. As the bedroom door slammed shut upstairs, Kit cautiously stepped through the kitchen door and dropped her backpack on the floor.

"What's wrong with Mom?"

"She's just tired, honey; her arm is hurting her."

Kit arched up on tiptoe, absorbing the tuning-fork tension still vibrating in the smoky air. She arched up more when she spied the pistol on the counter and the loaded magazine on the table. She measured the distance between the forced calm of her dad's words and the hard, controlled look in his eyes, the way his body had changed. Then she regarded him with a wary cynicism no eight-year-old should have. She knew what it meant when her mom or dad adopted this physical tone. Stuff happened fast. Bad stuff. They sent her to stay with Grandpa and Grandma.

Seeing her rising alarm, Broker put his hand on her shoulder. "It's all right . . ."

Kit shook off his arm and fought a rush of tears, forced them back down, and shouted at him. "You said it was going to be normal. It was going to be Christmas. You lied. *People are gonna die and go to hell!*"

She ran from the kitchen. Broker let her go as reflex kicked in. *Deal with it.* He snapped the trigger lock back on the .45, removed the key, and jammed it in his pocket. Up the stairs, past the two tightly shut bedroom doors, into the den closet, back down again with the other guns in the house. Out the back door. He was loading the guns in the heavy diamond-plate toolbox in the back of his truck—to which he had the only key—when he saw Dooley come out of his apartment doorway.

Seeing the guns going in the lockbox, Dooley walked over, leaned against his rusty Civic, checked Broker with his quiet brown yardbird eyes, and asked, "This something I should know about?"

"Nah. Housecleaning," Broker said evenly as he snapped the lock on the toolbox. Too calm. Hurricane-eye calm. Standing dead still, his insides struggled for balance. A palpable sensation churned in his chest that his life had uprooted and was starting to rotate around him.

"Uh-huh," Dooley said.

Still smarting from Kit's outburst, Broker stared at his tenant, standing there next to the Civic with the weathered *Bush/Cheney* sticker on the rear bumper. Dooley, a felon, couldn't vote, but he flew the sticker to keep bleak faith with the Christian Man in the White House.

"One thing," Broker said. "Go easy on the religion stuff with Kit, okay? You got her spooked about people dying and going to hell."

Dooley shrugged. "We were raking leaves last month. She's a smart kid, she asks questions."

"Whatever," Broker said. "Look, Dooley, do me a favor."

"Sure, what?"

Broker pulled two twenties from his jeans. "Go up to Len's and get me some cigars, those Backwoods Sweets."

"Light brown pack. Uh-huh. How many?" Dooley looked at Broker and then at the Toyota, as if to say, You forget how to drive, or what?

"All they got."

Back inside, he scanned the kitchen calender scrawled with holiday commitments. He picked up the phone and canceled their dinner plans with his ex-partner, J. T. Merryweather, and his wife. He ordered pizza and paced the backyard, smoking one of the cigars Dooley had fetched for him. He checked on Nina, sleeping upstairs. More pacing and smoking, aware that Kit was watching him from the back porch. When the pizza arrived, he set Kit up in front of the VCR. In the middle of her second *Harry Potter*, she fell asleep. He carried her upstairs and put her to bed.

Not wanting to disturb his wife's sleep, he spent the night on the floor at the foot of the bed, awake half the time, listening to her troubled breathing.

The next morning Nina was still in bed. Broker sat down with his daughter at the kitchen table. One of Kit's favorite expressions, which she'd learned from her parents, was, "Say what you mean." Broker was direct.

"This is just between us. Mom might be a little sick, she might need a lot of rest," Broker said.

Kit stared at him; the sickest she had ever been was a couple colds and an ear infection.

"We might have to make some changes," Broker said. "If anybody asks, just say Mom isn't feeling well. Understand?"

Kit nodded obediently. She had spent the last two years living on the fringe of the special operations community in Italy. Usually it was the dads who went away; the moms and kids did not talk about it to outsiders.

Christmas came and went, a wreckage of canceled play dates and parties. No one visited. The kids down the street Kit played with were not invited into the house. The new skis leaned in a corner, barely unwrapped. Without water, decorated halfheartedly by Broker and Kit, the magnificent tree dropped needles and shriveled to brown tinder. Nina stopped running in the morning, quit her exercises. She ate and talked little. Mainly she slept.

Broker hovered. He monitored the pills in the bathroom cabinet and the knives in the kitchen. Finally, Nina surfaced through the oceans of exhaustion long enough to tug his arm and say, "We gotta talk."

They sat down on a chilly gray overcast afternoon bundled in fleece and parkas at the picnic table in the backyard, overlooking the color-drained St. Croix River valley. Kit stood motionless, hugging herself on the back porch. Watching them through the windows.

They made up their minds in less time than it takes to play a game of checkers. Broker did most of the talking. Nina, in the grip of the thing that had captured her, refused to speak its name.

"You trust me on this?" Broker asked. She nodded and continued to nod as he frankly ticked off the signs. They both had been brushing up on the relevant chapters in the *DSM-IV*. She had lost interest or pleasure in nearly all activities. He saw insomnia, decreased energy, and fatigue, along with a diminished ability to think or concentrate, irritability, and guilty preoccupations with past failings. And she'd basically ignored her daughter and her husband. He finished up by saying, "We gotta get you away from—"

She nodded again and said, "People."

"What about the doc at Bragg you check in with?" he asked.

Nina shook her head vehemently. "Not a word about . . . this thing. He knows how serious the shoulder is. Time's not a factor. I'm not exactly under discipline anymore, am I? I'm technically a 'contractor.'" She managed a bitter twitch of a smile.

"Okay, so we agree," he said.

"We agree. No doctors, no drugs, no hospital," Nina said flatly. "If anything goes on the record, I'll never work on the teams again. I'll do this on my own."

Broker understood. He had once dated an FBI shrink, a profiler. She had diagnosed him as a fugitive from modern psychology whose emotional development had been arrested when he read *Treasure Island* at age eleven. But he recalled her observation that an otherwise healthy person could tough their way through severe depression, given enough time and seclusion.

"We should send Kit to stay with your folks. It'll be hard on her to lose dance class, swimming. At least with them she can keep up with piano," Nina said, grimacing.

"No." Broker was adamant. "She'll handle it. We'll all three go away. Up north. Someplace safe where no one knows us. It's better if we work through it together."

Too weary to argue, she nodded; then she got up and went into the porch and tried to talk to Kit. Broker watched Nina through the windows, saw her struggle in silent pantomime, head downcast; saw Kit embrace her mother, face upturned, nodding encouragement. Christ. It was almost like they were switching roles.

He took a deep breath, still having difficulty seeing Nina as . . . fragile. But she was right. She had to beat this thing with a minimum of interference.

Still . . .

He'd been around cops for over twenty years and watched as

some of them peeled off and started to descend into themselves, drifting down this dark internal staircase. Usually it was the dead little kids—butchered, starved, abused—they encountered on the job that put them over the line. The main cop taboo was to show weakness, so they medicated with alcohol and hung tough till the pension kicked in. But once in a while a guy would find the dead kid he was trying to forget waiting in the basement at the bottom of those dark stairs, and he'd eat his gun.

Broker resolved to position himself on those stairs for her. Whatever it took.

On this one, he had to reach way back, to someone he'd known before he entered police work, or the odd string of adventures that followed his early retirement from the Minnesota Bureau of Criminal Apprehension eight years ago. After he got involved with Nina Pryce.

He flipped open his cell and called Harry Griffin, his old Vietnam buddy. He'd hunted with Griffin just last November . . .

Way up in Glacier County.

Chapter One

It was another March surprise. Yesterday the kids were playing in long sleeves and tennis shoes. Then the storm moved in last night, riding on serious cold that knocked everyone's weather clock for a loop. Now there was a foot of fresh snow on the ground. The air temperature stuck on 18 degrees Fahrenheit, but the windchill shivered it down to 11. School policy put the kids out in the snow if the thermometer topped zero. Ten-thirty in the morning at Glacier Elementary. Recess.

The new kid was a snotty showoff, and it was really starting to bug Teddy Klumpe. Especially the way a lot of third-graders had gathered on the playground to watch her.

Just like yesterday, when she was doing skips on the monkey bars. Not just swinging, flying almost. And everyone big-eyed, checking her out, like *wow*. See that? Three-bar skip. Except today it so was so cold—ha—that her gloves slipped on the icy bars and she dropped off, the heels of her boots skidded in the snow, and she fell on her skinny rear end. But then she got up and studied the stretch of steel bars over her head; studied them so hard these wrinkles scrunched up her forehead. Slowly, as her breath jetted in crisp white clouds, she removed her gloves.

Boy, was that dumb. It was just too cold . . .

But it didn't stop her. She mounted the wooden platform and carefully placed her gloves on the snowy planks. She blew a couple times on her bare hands, took a stance, gauged the distance, bent her knees, swung her arms back, and sprung. Parka, snow pants, bulky boots. Didn't matter. Smoothly, she caught the third bar out.

Yuk. The thought of his bare skin touching that frozen steel made him wince. Along with the fact he was too heavy to propel himself hand over hand. But when she dropped back to the ground. Then he'd show her. Skinny, red-haired, freckle-faced little bitch.

The Klumpe kid was almost nine. Naturally powerful for his age, he packed an extra ten pounds of junk-food blubber in a sumo-like tire around his gut and his wide PlayStation 2 butt. Biggest kid in the third grade. Most feared kid. Knew the most swear words. King of the playground.

Screw her.

Teddy scouted the immediate area.

Mrs. Etherby, the nearest recess monitor, was watching the kids sliding down the hill on plastic sleds. The other monitor was on the far side of the playground, where some fourth-graders were building a snow fort.

Ten of Teddy's classmates were standing over by the slide next to the monkey bars, making a winter rainbow of fleece red caps and blue and yellow Land's End parkas against the oatmeal sky. All of them curiously watching Teddy and the new kid. They should be watching him take his snowboard down the hill. And repairing the bump jump when he smashed it apart. Instead, they were watching to see what he would do.

The new kid swung from the last bar, landed lightly on her feet on the far wooden platform, and blew on her chapped hands. Teddy eyed the gloves she'd left on the opposite end. As she leaped up and grabbed the bars for the return trip, Teddy walked over casually, snatched up her gloves, and stuffed them in his jacket pocket.

"Hey!" the kid yelled, swinging hand over hand.

Teddy ignored her and kept walking, around the back of a small equipment shed near the tire swings.

"Hey," she said again, dropping to the snow and trotting after him. "Those are my gloves." Her breath made an energetic white puff in the air. Two brooding vertical creases started between her eyebrows and shot up her broad forehead.

Teddy angled his face away from her but let his eyes roll to the edge of his sockets. Kinda like his dad did when he was getting ready to get really mad. He took a few more steps, drawing her farther behind the shed, out of sight from eyes on the playground. Then he spun.

"Liar," he said.

She balled her cold hands at her sides and narrowed her green eyes. The creases deeper now, pulling her face tight. "Thief," she said in a trembling voice.

Teddy saw the tension rattle on her face, turning it red. He heard the tremor in her voice. Little bitch is scared. Encouraged, he surged forward and pushed her chest hard with both hands. She went down on her butt in the snow. Then he yanked her gloves from his pocket and tossed them up on the roof of the shed, where they stayed put in a foot of snow.

"Yuk," Teddy wiped his own gloves on the front of his jacket. "Now I got girl cooties all over me."

She was starting to get up, working to hold back tears.

"Now you're gonna cry. More girl cooties," Teddy said with a grin.

"No, I ain't," she said in a trembling voice as she drew hard, pulling the tears back inside her eyes. She pushed up off the snow.

"Crybaby girl cooties," Teddy taunted, and he rammed her with his shoulder and hip. Ha. Hockey check. She went down again.

"Leave me alone," she said in the shaky voice. "I mean it, that's two." This time she was up faster, bouncing kinda . . .

Two? Teddy laughed and shoved her again. "Loser," he taunted. It was one of his dad's favorite words. Then he blinked, surprised because this time she surged against him, kinda strong for a girl, and kept her footing. Doing this dance thing on the balls of her feet.

"That's three," she said, still moving away from him but her small fists swinging up; tight, compact miniature hammers. Red with cold.

"Oh, yeah?" Teddy sneered, opening his arms, palms out, elbows cocked to shove her again. As he charged forward, he realized she wasn't moving away anymore.

Thirty yards away, Mrs. Etherby started when she read trouble in the blur of red and green jackets that lurched around the side of the shed. Uh-huh. Definitely trouble. She'd need some help. The big kid in the green was Teddy Klumpe. She whipped off her glove better to thumb the transmit button on her playground walkie-talkie.

Then she hesitated and lost her breath . . .

Jesus. The smaller kid—the new girl, hat knocked off, red ponytail streaming—planted her feet and whipped her whole upper body around behind a rigid right-hand punch that landed smack on Teddy's onrushing nose.

Fat droplets of bright poppy red blood splashed the snow. More red dribbled down Teddy's chin as he dropped back on his rear end. Aghast, he began to sob.

Running forward, breathless, Etherby got her call off to the office receptionist:

"Madge, you're not gonna believe *this*."

Chapter Two

When Broker leaned down, the material of his tan work jacket tightened across his shoulders, stretching the pyramid logo and the type, "Griffin's Stoneworks," on his back. The jacket Griffin had loaned him was a touch small. He wrestled a heavy oak round up on the chopping block next to the woodshed in back of the garage and grinned; never thought he'd be chopping firewood at the end of March again. He'd been splitting oak since they'd moved into Harry Griffin's lake rental. The hardwood didn't grow up here, pretty much it petered out in the middle of the state. Griffin imported the oak by the truckload to heat sand and water so he could mix mortar for winter work on his stone crew.

If anybody asked, Griffin would say the new guy in town was working on his crew. Mostly Broker stayed home and split wood for exercise. Stayed close to Nina. Going on three months.

But the geographic cure was working. She was slowly climbing out of the black pit. So he picked up the twenty-pound monster maul, hefted it, getting his stance, swung it up using his legs, hips, and shoulders to transfer the weight in a powerful arc over his head. Then he brought it down. The wood parted with a clean snap that echoed into the surrounding trees, out across Glacier Lake.

He put down the maul and yanked another hunk of oak from the pile next to the chopping block. Seventy degrees yesterday down in the cities. Fifty-five degrees up here. Then in midmorning the temperature nosedived, and he noticed the nuthatches and chickadees mob the bird feeder in a feeding frenzy . . .

Sensing the onrushing storm.

Now, a day later, Broker picked up the maul and raised his eyes to the clouds still coming in rolling gray ranks from the northwest. The clipper had roused out of the Yukon, roared across Canada, and dumped fourteen inches of snow on Glacier County just after lunch yesterday. Almost as if the Canadians were sending a cold wish of censure across the border.

On the day Dubya rolled the tanks into Iraq.

As he bent to lift the heavy round, he heard a low, shivering moan. He paused and listened carefully. Okay. Got it. Wolves. An acoustic bounce, rippling in their baying on the wind from the big woods up north. He was sizing up the knot in the wood on the block when Nina came out on the back deck and held out the cordless phone. "Can you take this?" she said.

He looked at his wife, leaned the splitting maul next to the chopping block, removed his gloves, and walked to the porch steps, raising his thick eyebrows and heaving his shoulders in a questioning gesture. Then she grimaced and darted her eyes north, sensing more than hearing the wild sigh on the wind. She narrowed her eyes. "Is that . . . ?"

"Yeah. The pack up in the big woods, sounds like they're active in daylight. It's the new snow freezing last night. Crust on top makes it hard for the deer to run," Broker said, matter-of-factly.

"Cool. Now we have wolves day and night," she said, staring into the distance, listening to the faint rise and fall of the eerie baying. Then she recovered and thrust the phone at him. "Something happened at school." Still no help, doing a quick handoff.

He took the phone. "Hello?"

"Mr. Broker?" said a calm but controlled voice, "this is Trudi Helseth, principal at Glacier Falls Elementary. We met when you registered your daughter, Karson."

"Kit. She goes by Kit," Broker said as he stared at Nina, who stood on the deck, huddled in her robe and slippers, puffing on an American Spirit. Oblivious to the cold, her green eyes flitted up to the gray clouds with apprehension, as if they were a messy ceiling about to collapse. She yanked her eyes from the sky and fixed them on the edge of the tree line where the woods started, eighty yards away. The wolves howled again on the errant shaft of wind, and she hugged herself.

Broker was watching Nina closely as he listened to the phone. Past the worst of it; now, the way she had started to key on the weather had him thinking—could be a swerve in her condition toward seasonal affective disorder. The overcast sky meant she'd have a bad day . . . Then Principal Helseth commanded his full attention when she said, "There was a playground incident involving Kit this morning . . ."

His heart sped up. "Is she . . . ?"

"She's fine. Just skinned her hand a little. I have her here in the office. Is it possible for you to come into the school to talk?"

"What happened?"

"I really need to see you in person. This is not something we can handle on the phone." When Broker didn't respond immediately, Helseth continued. "We'll be sending Kit home with you for the rest of the day, Mr. Broker."

"I'll be right there." He switched off the phone and went over to Nina, who was stuck, her tired eyes anchored to the snow-draped pines behind the house. He put his arm around her shoulder and gently guided her back toward the patio door. "C'mon. It's cold out here."

Jeez, Kit?

Galvanized by the understated urgency in the principal's tone, he stayed in his work clothes, went straight to his truck, and drove toward town. The plows had been through, but there was still a hard undercoat of icy snow on the roadbed. After he skidded through a curve a little too fast, he eased off the accelerator, leaned back, and took a deep settling breath through his nose.

Center down. Wait and see. Don't jump to conclusions.

So he let his eyes track the snowy landscape to either side of the road. Glacier County was aptly named; a white place on the map, just this long skinny ditch the last ice age had gouged into the map and filled with moraine and melt. Wedged between Thief River Falls and the Red Lake Rez. It had always been remote, and now it had pulled ahead of Broker's native Cook County as the least populated county in the state. In the winter. The population quadrupled in summer. Broker smiled ruefully when he came around a bend and saw the construction site of another lake house going up. The flimsy yellow sticks thrusting at the pines and snow. A bundled work crew swarmed over it. *Hola.* Mexicans, by the swarthy faces peeking from their headgear and the amused grins. Yesterday they had been wearing shirtsleeves. But they were swinging their nail guns, working like hell. Even up here they were starting to build the fast Pac Man houses that ate the woods.

He took another deep breath. Up ahead, over the tree line, he saw the town water tower pinned against the gray sky. The city council had tacked a tinny round cupola on top and painted it red and white like a fishing bobber to promote their main resource, the chain of Glacier Lakes. The tower stood like a wish, to lure the tourists to come with their boats to fish in summer. And the snowmobile crowd in the quieter winter.

It was an uphill fight; Glacier County was off the main track. North of the lakes it consisted of a long stretch of jack pine barrens. The barrens led to the spooky Washichu State Forest and the Canadian border, where no one lived but the wolves. After Labor Day you couldn't get a cup of Starbucks in the whole sparsely populated county. No local newspaper. Hardly any cops. The two gas stations closed at 8:00 P.M. in the winter, so you had to mind your gas gauge. Which suited Broker just fine and was, in fact, the reason he'd brought his family here.

He came into town south on County 12. Crossed the railroad tracks and went past the population sign: 682. He paused for the town's single stoplight near the old railway depot, where 12 intersected Main Street. Turned right. The elementary school was on the west side, past the two blocks of business district; a durable two-story cube of Depression-era redbrick. Just a traprock driveway and the traffic circle that he'd wheeled around this morning when he'd dropped Kit off.

Decided to drive her every day. Didn't want to put her on the bus.

A brown extended-cab Ford F-150 was parked skewed at the curb by the front door. Stylized cursive type in white on the door: "Klumpe Sanitation." Same colors as the local garbage truck. Broker braked his Tundra halfway up the drive, more alert when he saw the green-and-white Glacier County Sheriff's Department Crown Vic parked behind the Ford. No one behind the wheel, it idled empty in a low cloud of creeping exhaust.

Another deep breath. Coincidence? Flags going up? Forcing himself to approach very slowly, he parked behind the cop car, got out deliberately, walked to the school, opened the front door, and—

"Little bitch attacked my Teddy, that's what!" The shrill voice came from a woman whose gaunt beauty was almost painful to look at; early thirties, dark eyes flashing, long dark hair in motion. She wore snow boots. A ski parka lay on the floor behind her.

Biiig diamond ring.

Oh-kay. Easy does it. Broker's eyes swept past her, taking in the fact that even undernourished, she'd up the temperature in a room. But his gaze faltered, snagged on the broken intensity of her eyes, the way they seethed in the sockets like two nests of bluebottle flies, feeding off something ugly. Her eyes buzzed at him, her facial expression flitted. Her carefully applied mask of cosmetics barely kept up.

She held a digital camera in her right hand.

The husky cop who belonged to the car outside wore green over brown. He had short-cropped sandy hair and wore wire-rimmed glasses that seemed to emerge naturally out of the tired lines of his oval face. He stood patiently, arms loosely extended, palms out; but a little up on the balls of his feet too, like he got stuck with trying to cover a particularly nasty point guard who was way too fast.

"Now, Cassie, just calm down here," the cop said. Then he saw Broker come through the door, sized him up fast, and waved his arm to get someone's attention in the office. Broker, having been announced, turned left, opened the office door, and went in.

There was a counter with three desks behind it, storeroom at the back, three doors on the left. A TV bolted to the wall was tuned to the Weather Channel.

The room was full of women and one tall, thick blond guy wearing a brown jacket; color and white type on the chest matching the truck outside. He seemed not all the way awake, with a stubble of beard gilding his red cheeks and jaw and his short hair sticking up. Broker made his own fast assumption and figured the guy belonged to the woman in the hall; they both had the same manic twitch to their eyes. His blue eyes were several notches lower in velocity than the woman's; about the ratio that separates a bluebottle from a hatched larva. Both of them unpleasant to the touch.

Okay.

So let the hick games begin. First the cop, now this guy checking him out. Broker held the guy's sticky scowl for a fraction of a second; enough to absorb the murky heat of someone barely under control. Then the guy jerked his attention into the far door. The one with "Nurse" printed on a sign over the top. Broker anchored down on another slow deep breath. Way more tension poisoning the air than an elementary school office deserved at ten-thirty in the morning.

Then, like the next cue in a choreography the cop in the hall had set in motion, one of the women broke away and approached. She was a tidy fast mover in faded jeans, a snug white sweater, and Nikes. Wheat brown hair cut in a pageboy swung clean above her shoulders. She took his arm with quiet urgency as her direct brown eyes stated simultaneously and emphatically, "I'm here to help, so don't mess with me."

"Mr. Broker, right?" Perfectly timed bright smile, expertly smoothing an edge. He nodded. She pressed his arm and guided him toward the other office door to the right. "Kit is fine, she's in the conference room with a teacher's aide. Could you come with me, please?"

Broker was led from the office down a side hall, but not before he saw the group move away from the nurse's office. The guy in the brown jacket had his arm around the shoulder of a stout little boy who raised his arm to wipe tears from his eyes.

He had a spray of fresh blood stippled down the front of his beige SpongeBob T-shirt.

"Oh, honey, look at you. Does it hurt?" said the woman in the hall. She raised her camera and started snapping pictures. Then the end of the hall blocked Broker's line of sight, and he turned to face the women who'd escorted him from the office and eyed her left hand on his arm. She removed her hand. Out of old habit he noted: no wedding band. As her fast eyes gauged him, the angry female voice started up again around the corner.

"At least this time you're not blaming him, that's a switch. You know how they're always trying to trip him up. You should have more help on the playground to watch out for sneaky little bitches who like to hit people. This is *not* the end of this."

"Sneaky little bitch, huh," Broker said in a neutral tone.

"Hold on. We wait until *they* leave the building."

"Uh-huh. So why the cop?"

"That's Cassie Bodine you hear out there."

"I see 'Klumpe' written all over everything?"

"She's married to a Klumpe, but she'll always be Cassie Bodine. The last time we had a scene with her, she threatened the principal . . ." She knit her smooth forehead. "It's a special needs case."

Broker stared at her, and her cheeks colored slightly. "I'm sorry." She extended her hand. "Susan Hatch. I'm the school psychologist."

Broker's hand hesitated. "Psychologist?" He glanced around. "This place rates a psych?"

She shook his hand firmly. "Relax. I'm on a co-op schedule.

Mostly I work next door, in Thief River Falls. Her kid's on my list. Your isn't. We're a cluster school. We have all the special-ed students in the county. So I travel here two, three days a week."

A fifty-something woman stuck her head around the corner and said with a touch of inflected drama, "All clear. *Cassie has left the building.*"

"Thanks, Madge," Susan said. "Okay, let's go." They started toward the office.

"You gonna tell me—" Broker started.

"Sorry, you have to talk to the principal first." Susan Hatch was all cool and professional now that her delaying action had been successful. As they approached the office, Broker was aware of two small, quiet bodies creeping along the hall, all eyes and ears. Susan turned on them. "Why are you not in class, Mr. Wayne Barstad?"

"I gotta go to the bathroom."

"In the hall?"

The boy darted away. She turned to the next kid. "Billie Hatton?"

"Ah, I'm getting a drink of water. My mom says I gotta drink eight glasses of water a day." His voice sped up. "Is the new girl gonna get expelled for decking Teddy?"

"Scram," Susan said.

Trudi Helseth, a raw-boned, striking woman in her fifties, stood in her doorway. She was almost as tall as Broker and clearly in charge of her turf. She did not offer to shake his hand; instead she indicated her office with a practiced tilt of her head. "In here, please, Mr. Broker."

Broker went in and saw Kit sanding behind a chair, her arms folded tightly across her chest. Her face blazed with stubborn fire that was an miniature cameo of her mother. It had been months since he'd seen Nina's eyes as on fire as Kit's at this moment.

Helseth stood back a moment, observing. Broker moved forward and put his hand on his daughter's shoulder. "What happened, Kit?"

She shook his hand off and stared straight ahead. "He stole my gloves, and then he pushed me."

"And?"

"And he's a bully. All the kids are afraid of him. He gets away with stuff." Eyes narrowing, lips bunched.

"Stick with what happened," Broker said.

Kit clamped her arms tighter, then released them. She held out her right hand, peeled back a Band-Aid and showed two raw skinned knuckles. "He took my gloves and threw them up on this roof, then he started pushing me *hard*. I backed away and warned him three times, like I'm supposed to . . . and then when he kept it up, I hit him. Once. In the nose." Her voice was level but her tone and her hot eyes were unrepentant.

Like I'm supposed to.

Broker showed no expression, but his eyes settled on Trudi Helseth. Clearly she didn't like the sound of that.

"Please sit," Helseth said, standing behind her desk.

As Broker and Kit settled into two chairs in front of the desk, Helseth pushed a sheet of paper across her blotter. Broker scanned it fast.

Notice of suspension . . .

"This is to advise you that the above-named student has been suspended from school . . ."

Farther down the form, under "Grounds," he saw a check next to:

"Willful conduct that endangers the pupil or other pupils, or surrounding persons, or property of the school."

Under the heading, "The facts have been determined as follows," Broker scanned the handwritten notation:

During morning recess Karson P. Broker and Teddy Klumpe got into an argument over Karson's gloves. Teddy said Karson had thrown her gloves at him and that they flew over his head and landed on the toolshed roof. Karson said Teddy had taken her gloves and tossed them on top of the shed. No one witnessed this event. Jackie Etherby, playground monitor, did observe Karson and Teddy when they came around the back of the shed having an argument. Etherby then saw Karson punch Teddy in the face causing a bloody nose."

Helseth motioned toward the doorway. A ruddy woman in jeans and a pile jacket entered. "This is Jackie Etherby. She was the playground monitor who witnessed the incident," Helseth said.

Broker sat resolutely still, willing himself to look humble and respectful. Inside he felt his defensive hackles start to raise. Moving toward pissed.

Helseth continued, "We expect a certain amount of roughhouse from time to time during recess. But this incident was extreme. Jackie?"

Etherby shifted from foot to foot and peered sincerely at Broker. "Well, like it says on the form there, I saw Teddy Klumpe and your daughter come running around the toolshed out by the monkey bars. They were yelling at each other, but I was too far away to hear. But I started toward them, and then she . . ."

Etherby licked her lips, shifted from foot to foot again.

Broker started to open his mouth, paused, looked to Helseth, who nodded. He continued, addressing Etherby. "What about the other kids? What did they see?"

Etherby shrugged. "None of them were behind the shed, where it started."

Kit lurched forward in her chair. "They all saw him take my gloves and run behind the shed. He's got 'em all scared."

"Kit," Broker said quietly, firmly. She settled back in the chair and clamped her arms over her chest again.

Etherby waited a few seconds, then she said, "The thing was the way she did it. Like she really knew what she was doing. She really hit him a hard one."

As Etherby's words sank in, Kit squirmed on her chair and stared straight ahead. Helseth thanked Mrs. Etherby, who left the room and closed the door behind her. Broker waited a moment and then asked, "So where does this go next?"

Helseth pointed to a second sheet of paper on her desk and said, "A readmission conference is scheduled for tomorrow at ten A.M. Here in my office. We'll go into it all then, when we've had some time to settle down."

Broker stood up, collected the forms, and motioned for Kit to get up. "Thank you," he said. "We'll be here."

Helseth raised her hand, "Kit, could you wait in the office, just outside the door, please?"

Kit looked to her dad, who nodded. "Yes, ma'am," Kit said, then exited the door and closed it behind her.

Helseth then opened a manila folder on her desk. Looked up at Broker. "I just have a few questions, if you can take a moment."

"Sure."

"This is Kit's prior school record. She's a very bright student. The only thing we've noticed is really minor, how she really keeps to herself. Not that unusual for a transfer into a new school. But the record jumps around a lot. She started third grade in Stillwater, here in Minnesota, before she transferred to us. Before that it mentions tutors in Lucca, Italy, and she attended a military school at the Aviano Air Force Base in Italy, for first grade. But she attended preschool in Devils's Rock, Minnesota, and kindergarten in Grand Marais." Helseth closed the folder and studied Broker. "Were you in the Air Force?"

"No."

Helseth cocked her head, waiting.

"Her mother was in the Army," Broker said finally.

"I don't believe I've met Mrs. Broker," Helseth said.

"No, you haven't."

"Will she be coming to the meeting tomorrow?"

"Does it require both parents?" Broker asked.

Helseth shrugged but continued to study him. "No, not at all."

"Then I'll be here. Is there anything else?"

"No, we're through for now. And thank you for coming in so promptly on short notice."

Susan Hatch was waiting in the office with Kit's coat and book bag, which she handed over with a curt smile, no words. Broker walked Kit outside, and he asked her where her gloves were. Kit pointed to the toolshed on the playground. He noted that the brown Ford was still parked at the curb, its black-tinted windows and opaque mirrors full of reflections of the gray churching clouds. Another reason to hate tinted windows. He could feel the mom and dad and the kid in there, watching.

A little more aggravating was the presence of the county cop car, still parked idling in back of the Ford. The cop stared over his steering wheel, his creased face composed in an unreadable professional mask. He did not make eye contact as Broker and Kit walked past.

Then Broker heard the trouble start behind him.

Chapter Three

The driver's-side door on the Ford tore open too fast, springing on the hinges. Broker spun and heard a burst of unintelligible words, like profanity; a taunting back and forth between the man and woman. He could actually see the spat rise in a cloud of frosted breath over the top of the truck cab. The door slammed. Klumpe stalked around the back of the truck.

Broker shoved with his right arm, pushing Kit away. "Kit, go stand by the side of the school. Now!"

"Don't yell at me." Kit bristled.

"Move!"

Klumpe stepped between the back of the truck and the front of the Crown Vic and came onto the slippery school sidewalk. The cop sitting in the car bowed his head and swung it slowly from side to side. Through the windshield, Broker could read the pained silent grimace that formed on the cop's lips: *Aw goddamn . . .*

Kit was clear, but Klumpe, in his face now, swung up his right hand, pointing his finger like a no-neck Uncle Sam. *I want you.*

"You owe my son an apology," Klumpe stated.

Broker took it in fast: the window on the passenger side of the truck zipped down, framing the wife and kid, a glowering gallery. The cop heaved from his car, calling out, "Now, Jimmy, take it easy . . ."

Some parts of Broker, the old street parts, were going on automatic; other parts were stunned, treading on new ground, not sure what the rules were. He'd had custody of Kit when she was a toddler; Nina had her in Europe after kindergarten. He had handled a lot of pissed off, drunk, and just plain crazy people in his life. But he'd never dealt with an infuriated parent who was mad at *his* kid.

Hopefully the cop coming up behind Klumpe would chill it out. So he smiled, hands extended, palms out, reasonable. "Hey, fella; like the officer says, take it easy . . ."

The smile only infuriated Klumpe. The wife yelling—all her makeup curdling to war paint—"Don't take any shit, Jimmy," didn't help.

"Sneaky little bitch sucker-punched my son, and you owe us an apology," Klumpe yelled as he set his feet and balled his beefy hands into fists. A puff of angry white breath crossed the short space between their faces. Broker smelled the pancakes and syrup Klumpe had for breakfast. And, more significantly, caught a sour curdle of alcohol over syrup. Felt it actually in an angry spray of his spit. Broker did a fast shuffle between street rules and the new world of parent etiquette.

Okay, this Klumpe asshole was getting ready to hit him.

And he'd had just about enough of this "sneaky little bitch" routine.

Street won.

Klumpe had forty pounds on Broker, went 220 maybe, but he looked out of shape and puffy. But also a little nuts, like his wife. As he cocked his right fist back to throw the punch and charged, Broker instinctively closed the distance, his left hand drifting up, extending, palm still open to trap the punch before Klumpe could power it forward. Simultaneously, he fended Klumpe's left hand away with his right hand, clamped down on the wrist, twisted, and levered the arm straight into a come-along hold.

The effect was to rotate Klumpe a half turn. When the bigger man was off balance, Broker stepped in fast behind him, whipped his right arm around Klumpe's neck, scissoring the biceps and the forearm on either side of the throat. Now Broker lowered his forehead and pressed Klumpe's head firmly into the V formed by his arm. His left hand came up and applied crushing pressure to his right hand. Smooth, pure reflex; it took less than two seconds.

Klumpe struggled briefly, then started to fade as the blood supply to his brain was cut off. The instant he felt the resistance cease, Broker loosened the restraint and stepped back. Klumpe staggered, flailing around. Lost his footing.

Broker backed away, hands up and fingers spread open. Klumpe fell face forward, unable to get his flailing hands up to break his fall. Red stippled the snow-packed concrete under his dripping nose.

Big Klumpe and little Klumpe had both caught some nose-bleed action this morning.

As Klumpe went down, he was replaced by the cop, who now stood over him pointing his finger at Broker.

"You. Move away."

"Yes, officer."

The cop removed a green bandanna from his jacket pocket and thrust it in Klumpe's face. "Here, Jimmy; hold this on your nose. Then get up and go sit in the front seat of my car. You hear? I mean it, Jimmy."

Klumpe shook his head back and forth, blinked, took the hanky. "Okay. Okay."

The wife yelled from the car, "Keith, you gonna let him get away with that!"

Keith Nygard. Broker read the name tag on the cop's chest. And the word under it: *Sheriff.*

Nygard ignored her, bellying up to Broker. Broker asked, "Am I in trouble here?"

Nygard looked him over, his eyes doing a fair imitation of two tired ball bearings. "I seen it all. Jimmy was out of line, and I'll give him a talking to. So, officially, no—" Nygard narrowed his gray eyes. "But—between the lines—watch yourself. This ain't the ideal way to meet the sheriff. What's your name?"

"Phil Broker."

"Where do you live, Mr. Broker?"

"I'm renting Harry Griffin's place south of town off County Twelve. On the lake."

"Uh-huh." The tension loosened a bit in his face. Maybe Broker detected a faint glimmer of curiosity in the gray eyes. "I know Harry. That's one of his jackets you're wearing?"

Broker nodded. "I work on Griffin's stone crew."

Nygard studied Broker's clothing; jeans, work boots, and a tan Carhartt jacket smeared with dirt from manhandling the oak. "You work this morning?"

Broker shook his head. "I work part-time."

Nygard's eyes lingered on Broker's face for a few more seconds, and then he said, "Okay, collect your daughter and go on home."

Broker pointed to the playground. "I got to get her gloves off that shed by the monkey bars."

"Fine. Make it quick."

Broker motioned to Kit, who was waiting obediently next to the school, keeping her face blank with some effort. As she joined him, Nygard called out, "Broker. This ends here. Clear?"

"Clear," Broker said. He took Kit's hand, and they walked to the playground.

"Dad, there's a bunch of teachers and the principal watching from the door," Kit said under her breath.

"Don't stare."

"How'd you do that? Knock him down?"

"Shhhh."

"You gonna show me?"

Broker's voice stiffened. "I think I showed you too much already. This isn't funny one bit. You better start thinking about the C word."

"Consequences." Kit lowered her voice, deflated.

They walked to the toolshed on the playground next to the monkey bars, where Broker spotted one of Kit's green mittens peeking from the snow on the roof. He lifted her by the knees, and she was able to reclaim her gloves.

Then they walked back to the truck, got in, and fastened their seat belts. Broker started the Toyota, pulled away from the curb, and checked the rearview. Cassie Bodine and her son stood stolidly in the cold a few feet from the sheriff's car, where Jimmy Klumpe sat, head on his chest, in the front seat with the sheriff. Exhaust from the police car and Klumpe's truck swirled in a gust of wind, cloaking them like smoke over wreckage.

He turned to his daughter. "We'll talk to Mom about the fight with that kid. But we won't mention what happened here, in front of school. You understand? She's got enough on her mind, okay?"

Kit blew on her hands, rubbed them together. Then she sucked on her skinned knuckle. "Yes, Dad."

Chapter Four

After Keith Nygard finished up his lecture, Jimmy got back in his truck, still holding the hanky to his nose; he turned the key, put the Ford in gear, and pulled away from the curb. Cassie sat next to him, arms crossed, knees crossed, face working.

"You got any more smart ideas?" Jimmy mumbled through the hanky.

"You let him make fools out of us in front of everybody," she said back.

"Some old guy from the cities, you said. Back right down."

"Gonna be all over town."

"I tripped and fell down on the ice," Jimmy said.

"Bullshit. He spun you around and dropped you on your ass and got away with it, just like his fucking kid punched Teddy—"

"Mom, don't swear. Dad tripped. Me too." Teddy spoke up from the rear seat, where he pressed the ice pack the nurse gave him against his nose.

"No, I'm the one who tripped when I had to marry your dad," Cassie muttered. And suddenly she had trouble breathing, as if the air they were taking in changed in their lungs and came out poison. She jammed her finger on the door panel controls and opened the windows, flooding the cab with icy air.

"Mommm," Teddy protested.

"For Christ's sake," Jimmy said, and he hit his controls. The windows started up. Cassie jammed on hers again and sent the windows down again. An electric whine cycled as they both hit their controls and the windows jumped up, then down, then froze, stuck in their tracks.

They glared at each other.

Then Cassie relented, took her finger off the controls, and crossed her arms across her chest again. Jimmy closed the windows. They drove in silence for a while, no sound except the tap of Teddy's GameBoy in the backseat.

Cassie spoke first. "So, what you gonna do?"

"Drive the speed limit home." He craned his neck to check the rearview mirror, dabbed at his nose with the hanky. "Seeing how I got Keith on my tail."

Another glum interval of silence. Then Cassie started in again. "He was a lot older than you, too. I saw some gray in his hair, over his ears."

"Not now, Cassie. Please." He sighed, seeing how no way she was going to back off; she was getting that feral Bodine vendetta fix in her eyes.

"I heard Keith talking to him," Cassie said. "His name is Phil Broker. He rents Harry Griffin's place, the one on Twelve, across the lake from us. Works for Griffin part-time."

Jimmy grimaced, inspected the blood on the hanky, put it down, and tested his nose with the fingers of his free hand. The bleeding had stopped. He turned to his wife. "Part-time on the stone crew won't pay much on that new Tundra he's driving, or the freight on that house. Not after all the work Griffin put in fixing it up to rent to summer folks."

"What's Griffin pay his laborers?"

"About ten, fifteen bucks an hour."

"Don't fit, does it?" Cassie said.

"So? Maybe he's got some money."

"Then what's he doing working labor part-time for crazy Harry Griffin? See, it doesn't fit. Plus how he had you so fast. Like he's used to putting men on the ground. Another thing. The way Keith was talking to him, kinda like two dogs sniffing each other out . . ."

"What are you getting at?"

"Dunno, just something," Cassie said. Then she turned to the backseat. "How you doing, hon?"

"Okay, I guess." Teddy was hunched over, preoccupied with the GameBoy in his free hand.

"No, you're not okay. You're in pain. And that's what you'll tell Ed Durning at the clinic. We're gonna get you X-rayed for your neck."

"Huh?"

"Your neck, it hurts, don't it?"

"Ah? I don't—"

"It hurts, honey. You tell Ed it hurts."

"Okay, Mom."

"She'll apologize for hitting you. In front of everybody. I insist on it. We'll make them pay."

Jimmy accelerated around a bend and checked the mirror again. "Can you believe this shit? Fuckin' Keith. He's gonna follow us all the way home."

"Dad, you said the F word. You and Mom both."

"Don't swear around Teddy. You know how I can't stand that," Cassie said in a strict voice.

Jimmy sighed. "Yeah, right. Teddy, I apologize for using bad language. Now, look, Cassie—Keith gave me a warning, says to back off this thing."

"'Keith says,'" Cassie pronounced with mincing sarcasm.

"He's the sheriff, for Christ's sake."

"They don't look after him like they should . . ."

"Cassie," he said patiently, "we don't need Ed Durning in on this. I want you to start cooling down now before it gets—"

She cut him with a look. "Gets what? Out of control. *Don't you talk to me about things getting out of control.*"

Jimmy winced and looked away from her seething voice, and they drove in silence for a minute. Then he said, "Just take it easy, okay."

"I just worry," Cassie said.

"I know you do." He dropped the subject, fixed his eyes ahead on the road. "I'll drop you home. I have to get back to the garage."

♦ ♦ ♦

It took Jimmy and Cassie fifteen minutes to drive to the east end of the big lake where they lived in Jimmy's dad's house on the ten acres of prime real estate Jimmy had inherited. When they moved in three years ago, the woods had screened them. When Cassie was growing up, it had been the biggest house on the lake. Now there were new log homes dripping balconies and gables a hundred yards off on either side. Cassie stared at the bright new houses, all that glass and stonework. Lodgepole pine—they'd build the houses in Colorado. Take them apart, truck them cross-country, and put them back together. Like the summer people were mocking the older place where Cassie lived, boarded up in tired brown cedar siding . . .

The first thing Cassie did after Jimmy dropped them off was wave to Keith as he drove away in his police car. Keith was a sweet man. Her guardian angel.

But waving to Keith was one thing. Listening to him was another. The morning churned in her chest, dredging up gobs of anger, fear, and self-consciousness. This called for a response. No way she was going to back off on that guy and his snotty little kid.

Teddy drifted to his room to change out of his shirt and play his computer games. Cassie went for the kitchen phone, tapped in the number for the school office, and got Madge.

"So who are they, Madge?" she asked by way of hello.

"Honest, Cassie, I don't have the slightest idea. New people. They showed up in January," Madge said in a hushed tone.

"You gotta know something."

"Well, there is one thing. Nobody's ever seen the mother, just the dad. He registered her, drops her off, and picks her up every day."

"That's a little weird," Cassie said, pausing slightly to furrow her brow. "Thanks, Madge." She ended the call abruptly.

No-show mom—that didn't fit either. The thing was taking a suspicious shape in her mind. She went to the living room, where they kept a tripod telescope to look out over the lake. Slowly she focused the lens and searched the west shore. Griffin's was the narrow green house with the wraparound deck, cedar siding, a rusted tin roof, and a newer kitchen addition thrusting toward the shore.

She found it, between the Nagel place and Chris Johnson's. She squinted, straining her eyes. She had never been in the house and could only guess at how the rooms were laid out. Some people liked their kitchens facing the water; others, herself included, liked the living room on the lakeside.

"Mom?"

Cassie turned and saw Teddy standing behind her. He'd washed his face and changed into a fresh T-shirt. She brushed a dark curl of hair from her eyes and studied him. "Is anything wrong?"

"Ah, no . . ."

"Don't worry about that snotty little girl, honey. We'll fix her."

Teddy shrugged. "Only reason she knocked me down is I slipped on the snow."

"I know. They pick on you . . ."

"Mom," he said with a slight edge of irritation in his voice, "I want some lunch."

After lunch she let him ride the ATV around the backyard to take advantage of this last snowfall. She was tidying up the kitchen when she noticed the crumbs from Teddy's tuna-melt sandwich on the linoleum under his chair. Must have missed them when she cleared his plate and loaded it into the dishwasher. She immediately stooped, plucked up the crumbs, and then wiped down the area with a dish rag and lemon-scented 409. When she was finished, she took the soiled dishrag and some towels into the laundry room. That's when she saw Teddy's shirt on the floor under the laundry chute.

With the blood on it.

The sensation that she was being watched came slowly as she methodically took the shirt to the sink, poured Shout on the stain, and worked it into the material. The red stain foamed up and covered her fingers. Got under her nails. Grimacing, she flung the shirt into the washer, put the dial on hot/hot, added Tide, and turned it on. When the rush of steaming water poured into the washer drum, she thrust her hands into it, blasting away the scum of foam.

But a tiny residue resisted the scalding water and still clung under her fingernails, and the sensation was coming stronger now, almost a glow in the walls. When it got bad like this, she actually believed that a presence inhabited the house. She could even smell it sometimes, no matter how hard she cleaned. A smell like old Tommy Klumpe's lingering pipe tobacco smoke that permeated the walls.

The presence shifted around in her mind. Sometimes it was old Tommy himself, sitting at the kitchen table, telling Jimmy straight out, right in front of her, like she didn't count.

"Nothing good will ever come of marrying a fucking Bodine."

Other times it got weirder. And she felt she was under scrutiny by a vague judgmental figure who demanded to be pleased. Sometimes she pictured this presence as a bizarre nexus between Martha Stewart and Jesus Christ.

One night this watchful presence had chosen to speak through her husband. Jimmy didn't even know he was the vessel of an angry house god; he was just being Jimmy, half loaded, making one of his nasty passive-aggressive cuts. But his spiteful voice had echoed like thunder in Cass's ears: "*Since you're not working anymore, the least you can do is keep this fucking house clean!*"

It had started again; the bad carnival ride that turned the big dump they lived into a fun house with distorted mirrors, eyes in the walls; the craziness getting ready to jump out of where it nested in the bathroom closet . . .

Cassandra Bodine always tried to fight the crazy.

Dutifully, she filled her bucket with hot water, grabbed the Comet cleanser, her scrub brush. She carried the bucket up the stairs and down the hall to the unused storage room past the master bedroom. Went in. The shades were pulled. A throw rug filled most of the floor space. She could hear the engine on Teddy's ATV grinding in circles in the snow below the window as she rolled back the rug, kneeled, and began to scrub.

Jimmy had put in a new floor.

Didn't matter. It was still there.

An hour later Teddy was back in his room playing Doom instead of doing his homework. Cassie squatted naked in the tiled corner of the shower stall. The master bath was Jimmy's one concession to fixing up the place. Didn't help. She cringed under the stinging needles of hot water.

She was boxed.

The trap they had built for themselves was so cunningly designed that there was nobody she could really talk to. Except the one person who built the box. No other way to go. Because they were out there planning to hurt her son. Hurt them all.

She stood up, turned off the shower, stepped from the stall, and took a fresh towel from the wall rack. She wiped the steam away from the broad vanity mirror and, seeing her compulsively trim body, got a flash of the loathing that drove the young girls to cut themselves.

Her eyes traveled around the bathroom, every surface sparkling, the towels arranged just so. No matter how hard she scrubbed, she couldn't stop the crazy. It whispered to her now from its hiding place in the closet next to the sink, where it nestled, waiting, among the carefully folded towels and washcloths. Like church back when she tried that; like communion. An altar call. Her hand trembled as opened the closet door and snuck through the clean folded cotton until she felt the dirty crumple of tinfoil. She withdrew her hand and studied the way the foil winked dirty silver gray in the soft vanity mirror lights . . .

. . . like a lump of anti-meteorite that had not fallen from the sky . . .

That had blasted up from hell.

Carefully she peeled back the foil, expecting a chunk of yellowish crystal the size of her thumbnail. Aw, man, musta lost track.

Nothing left but a few pebbles, some dust. And there was only one place for her to get it now . . . and he never gives me enough . . .

. . . and it never came easy. Always the old undercurrent.

Carefully, Cassie shook the residue of the crystal meth into her mouth, then probed the fissures in the wrinkled foil with her tongue, licking up every last speck.

Not enough.

Still, like a catechism, she recited the ground rules: Just never smoke the stuff.

Nibble a little, to keep your weight down, to zoom through housework on jet afterburners. Smooth out the day.

To turn down the volume on the loud goddamn world . . .

Cassie swallowed the last dot of crystal, sat down at her vanity table, and tried to concentrate, putting on fresh eye shadow. Could tell by the way her fingers shook.

Wasn't going to be a real boost. Waiting. C'mon. Then . . . *Almost.* Just a small caress of pre-rush foreplay. Her perfect lover trying to do it from the inside. Then fizzle.

Get more.

The sensation clamoring now. Flushed, her face out of balance, with a streak of the makeup breaking down her cheek like a black crack, she jerked the towel around her. She paced down the hall, passed the sounds of cyber carnage on the other side of her son's door, then went into the grim bedroom with its turgid blue wallpaper. Christ, the room where old Tommy and Adele made Jimmy. At least they got a new bed before . . .

She sat on the bed and stared at the phone. Caught herself digging nervously at her cheek with her fingernails.

Only one way to make it stop. And for that she needed more than Keith, her guardian angel. She needed her guardian devil.

Jimmy wouldn't like it. But then Jimmy just got knocked on his ass. She'd lost the last hope of the mini rush, so it was with faint nausea that she picked up the phone and called her brother. It was her brother, after all, who had taught her to keep an eye out for people who didn't fit.

Especially now.

Chapter Five

"Okay, Cassie; calm down," Gator Bodine said as he patiently listened to her lament about how little Teddy had been mistreated at the hands of a girl with a red ponytail.

"Hey, Cassie, get a grip. It's just kids at school."

She didn't hear. Just kept going. Now she was saying how Jimmy had been put on the sidewalk by the kid's father. An older guy.

Gator thinking: *Jesus. Like father, like son. Serves them right. The fat spoiled faggots . . .*

"They made him bleed," Cassie said.

Aw, shit. When Cassie got to talking about bleeding, it could turn into a long night, and it was still morning. "They, huh?" Gator asked, putting some concern in his voice.

"The girl's dad, after he knocked Jimmy down, he looked smug, like he was happy he did it . . . like it was easy. The way he looked, the vibes he put out; remember how you said to Jimmy and me to keep an eye out for people who stick out, who don't fit. Well, this is that kind of guy . . ."

"Oh?" Gator became a bit more attentive. His sister lurched around on her own personal drugged-up roller coaster right now; hitting all the swoops from manic to paranoid. But she always did have eyes like a hawk. "What about the way he looked?"

"The way he got on Jimmy, he looked *trained*."

"Trained like what?" Gator was now paying full attention.

"I don't know what, like he's used to knocking people on their ass, that's what. And he don't look local. He was wearing one of Harry Griffin's crew coats. Everybody says Griffin has some dark bullshit in his past. Maybe this guy is part of that. Point is, he don't fit up here. Making laborer's pay, paying the rent on a lakefront cabin, driving a brand-new green Tundra."

"Okay, okay; slow down, back up. Who is he? Where does he live?"

"I heard him talking to Keith."

"Oh, great, Keith was there. Wonderful. What'd Keith do?" Cassie had paused to organize her thoughts. So Gator read between the lines and said, "Jimmy tried to get smart with the guy, right?"

"He was upset seeing Teddy all bloody," Cassie said.

"C'mon, Jimmy bit off more than he could handle." As usual. When she didn't answer, Gator said, "Cassie, who wound up sitting in Keith's car afterward?" Still no answer. "Never mind. So where does he live, again?"

"It's the old Hamre place, off County Twelve on the west side of the lake. Griffin bought it way back and fixed it up."

"Gotcha. I know the property. You got a name?"

"Uh, his name is Phil. Phil Broker. Another thing. I called Madge Grolick at the school, and she said nobody's ever seen the guy's wife. He brings the kid, picks her up."

"You ask how long they been here?"

"Transferred in January, right in the middle of the school year." Having delivered the information, Cassie's voice launched into her basic global plea. "Gator, I could use a little help here to make it stop, you know how hard I try . . ."

Gator smiled, loving her palpable need vibrating in the cell phone. Damn. It was like . . . fan mail. "Jeez, Cassie, you gotta back off on that stuff. Don't want to use too much, know what I mean."

"Please, Gator, What do I have to do, beg or . . . what?"

Gator shut his eyes and listened to his sister's voice, like she was right there with him, shrunk down and imprisoned in the oblong Motorola slab of cell phone plastic in his broad hand.

Locked in and pleading to get out, his own private genie in a bottle, all mixed up in with the tiny jit-jit lights and chips and shit. Like she was under a spell. Yeah, he could see that. So he let the ambiguity dangle on the connection for several delicious seconds, and then he said, "Okay, I'll check this guy out, now you just calm down. It'll be all right. You did good." Then he paused, letting the stress compound on the other end of the connection. When the silence was closer to snapping, he soothed. "I'll bring you something. But you gotta treat me right, understood." Then he ended the call before she could blubber thanks. He set the cell phone aside. He leaned back against his workbench, arms thrust back for support.

Gator stood five feet ten and a half inches in his stocking feet. He weighed 185. Once a month he went into town and had old Irv Preston run clippers over his scalp so his hair resembled a dark cap. Excess hair could get caught in moving parts.

Get him out of the greasy work overalls into decent clothes, and he'd be handsome in a saturnine way. His blue eyes could have a devilish Gallic twinkle. Had métis in his blood; his people sprang from the nomadic mix of French and Cree out of Canada. A lifetime working with machinery had given him a taut, dense body. His hands were square and powerful, with at least one signature mashed fingernail in evidence.

When he was in the Navy, a woman in a Pocatello, Idaho, barroom told him once he had a Steve McQueen look going for him, but darker, and he could see that—if McQueen packed more muscle, from a year lifting weights in Stillwater Prison after getting busted for transporting a kilo of cocaine with intent to sell.

Gator Bodine looked around his shop. Years back he'd had dreams of crashing the mechanic elite; getting on a pit crew at NASCAR or the Indy. When that goal proved out of reach, he had to face the facts. The most he could hope for was a berth at an auto dealership with a benefits package. Or start his own shop. And that required capital. His first attempt at alternative financing had fizzled when the cops kicked in his door.

He had tried real hard to learn from his mistakes. Brooding

in jail, he'd realized he was sitting on a modest gold mine. All the antique tractors his dad had pack-ratted into the big junkyard behind the shop for forty years.

His eyes traveled to the wall where he had a centerfold page taped up out of a slick color Minneapolis Moline coffee-table-type book: looked like a hot rod with the distinctive flared tinwork, the fender sloping over the big rear wheels, grill, and cab. It was a rare 1938 Moline Model UDLX. Painted in an orange they called Prairie Gold. Gold was right.

Barnie Sheffeld, who displayed one of Gator's restored tractors at his implement lot in Bemidji, told him a UDLX, restored to mint, would bring a hundred grand.

The stripped-down tractor sitting in the shop under the picture on the wall didn't look like much now. He had the rusted cowling and the gas tank pulled off. Had unbolted the front half, legged it up, and pried it away from the rear section. Took out the engine. The cam and crank. Had the back end up on blocks and bottle jacks and had spent the day pulling the clutch.

But it was a vintage UDLX, and when he got done, it would look exactly like the one in the picture.

As perfect as he could make it.

Then he'd paint it the same color—Prairie Gold.

Methodically, he shook some Boraxo into his hand and worked it into his hands and forearms. Scrubbing up to the coiled green-and-red alligator tattoo that ran the length of his left forearm. When he wiggled his fingers, the bunched muscles rippled and the tattoo moved.

He shook his head and used a rag to worry the deeply ingrained grease from his thick fingers. As he cleaned his hands and arms in the work sink, he glanced out the window, at the sign planted in the yard in front of his shop. Next to a red 1919 Fordson with giant steel-treaded wheels.

Bodine's Old Iron.

The corner of his lips tipped up slightly as he imagined an invisible hand coming down out of the restless gray sky and painting a letter Y at the end of the sign. *Bodine's Old Irony . . .*

Except for the dark perpetual four o'clock shadow that stubbled his cheeks and dimpled jaw, Gator Bodine resembled the garage bay in which he stood. On the outside, he was a compulsively tidy, meticulously organized man. The inside was more difficult to chart.

He had always loved machines. Loved taking them apart, putting them together. Loved puzzling out how they worked. Could spend hours watching the moving parts.

Sometimes he wished he could take people apart and put them back together. Be nice if he could see the moving parts behind their eyes. His own eyes. His sister's . . .

Thing about Cassie; she'd just keep working on a guy. It was like some wacko relentless religion with her; in the beginning God created pussy. He shook his head, took a fresh towel from the rack by the sink, dried his hands.

She'd been just about the most perfect-looking women he had ever seen in his life. Until she opened her mouth.

Until she fucking moved . . .

. . . toward some man . . .

Gator, make it stop.

He shook his head. Gotta fight her battles for her. That turd she married sure wouldn't. And besides, he needed Jimmy to make the plan work. And he needed Cassie to keep her mouth shut. And, who knows, maybe she'd actually spotted something out of line with this new guy.

Due diligence dictated that he go see.

———

He was Cassie's twin, born eighteen minutes after her. He always joked, half serious, about that. He always thought he should have been first.

Not born really, more like hatched.

He had seen this show on the Discovery Channel about how baby alligators get born in a swamp, and the trick was not getting devoured by their daddy. By the time he was a junior in high school, he had no doubts that he was living in his own private

Everglades set down in the middle of the glacial lake country of northwestern Minnesota. He had come to view his father as a reptile subspecies of the Bodine strain of jack-pine savage white trash. Mom was no help at all; hell, she was outa the same stagnant pool, the old man's first cousin.

So the main challenge for him and his sister right from the start was how to survive their parents.

In fact his father, Irv Bodine, looked like an alligator. He was thick in the trunk and stubby in the arms and legs. He was glint-eyed, scaly, and always lying in wait with his long snout half submerged in a slop of cheap whiskey. And Mom never even put up a fight. She just went along until she was so leached out by the booze she resembled a shrieking caged swamp bird, bouncing off the walls.

It came as no surprise to the neighbors, to the teachers, or to the sheriff when their branch of the Bodine family went all to hell. It happened in October, the night of a hard frost; with half the hay left to rot in the fields, with Irv's machine tools sprouting orange whiskers of rust amid the cobwebs in his repair shop. A colony of rats had taken over the sprawling tractor junkyard behind the shop.

Junior year in high school. Before he got the gator tat on his arm. Back when he was just Morgun, Morg for short.

Morg came home from his after-school job at Luchta's Garage in town, heard the feeder calves bellowing, starving in the barn, went in the house, and smelled more gas than usual. And not the gas in the coffee cans on the mud porch where Irv had tractor parts soaking. This was propane, in the kitchen. He went in and saw a bread pan full of raw meatloaf sitting on the kitchen table. His mom's thick fingerprints still squished in the red mush. He saw the oven door open. And he saw the box of Blue Tip matches for lighting the pilot, just sitting there on top of the stove. Which was as far as his mother got with supper before she wandered into the living room and passed out drunk on the couch with raw hamburger smeared on her fingers.

Then he heard the racket down the hall; Cassie screaming, the shower going. And he just knew. Knew before he kicked open the door—the old man still had enough bar whiskey prod going for him to corner Cassie in the shower again.

But this time he'd gone too far. Usually when he got to drinking and started feeling up his daughter, he kept his clothes on. Not tonight. There, in the steam from the shower clouding the tiny bathroom, he saw the old man grappling with Cassie in this mist, saw he had his overalls down around his knees as he bent her dripping wet over the sink.

"Ain't you slippery," the old man was howling and giggling over and over. He was trying to hold her steady with one burly hand and aim his business with the other.

There was the shower gushing, there was the smell of gas, mildew, mold, whiskey breath. And there was this single lightbulb over the cabinet above the sink. Just the bare bulb, no shade on it. This cheap little chain jiggling down from the commotion. The weird split image of them there in front of him and coming at him again from another direction in the mirror. In the raw light Morg saw the old man's spit sprayed among the water droplets on Cassie's squirming back muscles. Gas, water, the mirror, and these raised blisters dotted with tiny bubbles. Maybe it was seeing the tiny air bubbles popping in the spit that set him off.

Set him off so he finally reached in through the years of this bullshit that had been going on since Cass started wearing a bra. He grabbed a fistful of his father's greasy hair and slammed his head down on the hot water faucet. Irv collapsed into a fetal butt-mooning heap at their feet, out cold.

She had turned and clung to him. And it was him in the mirror now with Cassie as she hugged him and cried, "Make it stop."

"I will."

He watched the shock drain from her eyes and get replaced by a hot mindless idle, like she had a runaway motor chugging deep in her guts that, once it got turned on, just kept going and going . . . maybe some jealousy mixed in there.

Maybe a lot.

And they were still holding on to each other past the point

*where she should be thinking about standing there naked. And
Morg was caught up for a few seconds remembering the really
interesting way they said it in the Bible, talking about the tempta-
tions of flesh and blood.*

Cleave.

*Sharp knives. Room-temperature raw meat out there on Mom's
lax fingers. Pictures like that coming to his head.*

*And Cassie, eyes wide open; mouth open; her tongue moving in
there arched up, this soft red question mark . . . like it had been the
hot July afternoon last year, standing barefoot in the cowshit of the
loafing shed behind the barn when she lured him into making her
virginity stop . . .*

*The shower and the gas and the naked light and Cassie still all
wet and first trembling then melting against him and the old man's
head shifting on the warped linoleum floor and beginning to snore
between their feet.*

*And she said, like real perplexed, "Ain't our fault that the two
best-looking people in the eleventh grade have the same last name."*

*He'd been halfway there, again, till she said that. Then she
totally sobered him up with her follow-up line, tonguing the words
into his ear: "You were first at something, remember."*

*It was just possible her head was so empty because her brain
had crawled down into her mouth, where it took up residence in her
sucky tongue. It was enough baggage having Cassie permanently
in your life as a sister. You'd have to be completely nuts to compli-
cate it by doing the doggie in the bathroom with the shower running and the old man snoring on the floor.*

Morg could have a weak moment, but he was not nuts.

*It was plenty just to feel the cannibal gene slither up and load
in his blood. It didn't have to go off, not at the exact moment.
Cassie was the perpetual rain-check girl. Count on her to stay wet.*

But she was right about one thing. It had to stop.

*So he yanked a towel off the hook on the back of the door, cov-
ered her, and said, "You ain't thinking too clearly right now. Get
dressed. We're getting out of here, over to Nygard's."*

She studied him, and it wasn't so much that the moment passed.

More like she slowly folded it up and tucked it in her pocket. Except she was out of pockets right then. "You smell gas?" she asked as she carefully stepped over the snoring heap on the floor.

"Yeah. Stay away from the kitchen. Use the back door. Go out to the barn and feed the damn calves. Sounds like they're starving."

They didn't take anything with them when they left and went over to the Nygards' house, because when they usually showed up—because Irv and Mellie Bodine got themselves outrageously drunk—they never brought anything. But the last thing Morg did, after he made sure no windows were open, was close the door tight behind him.

And not turn off the gas.

It was like that gas was meant to be, and Morg wasn't going to interfere with destiny. Uh-uh, not him. And the stove was working off a fresh tank, because he'd hooked it in two days ago.

No one was surprised when the sheriff went out the next morning and found the Bodines with their lungs soaked with propane and their blood testing off the chart with alcohol. The medical examiner and the sheriff agreed, it looked like the kind of stupid accident that would happen to a couple drunks; passed out, pilot light on the stove unlit. Irv falling down getting off the toilet, bruising his head on the sink, and breathing the slow creep of the rising gas. Hell of a sight, with his bibs down around his ankles. And nobody was surprised when Cassie and Morgun didn't cry at the pine-box funeral.

The day after he buried his parents, he buried Morgun when he drove to Bemidji in his daddy's truck, to a tattoo parlor there, and got the alligator tattoo on his left forearm.

Chapter Six

They came through the door and immediately smelled the cigarette smoke. Kit rolled her eyes, made a resigned face, ran up the stairs, and slammed the door to her room. Broker took the long view and accepted it as the exhausted breath of insomnia that inhabited the house. Along with the TV blaring in the kitchen.

Part of the healing process.

He made a signal of shutting the front door forcefully behind him, telegraphing their arrival. Then, methodically, he removed his coat in the living room.

Give her some time . . .

Didn't matter. She barely noticed him come into the kitchen; still in her robe and slippers, one of his old T-shirts she'd slept in. Hair askew, her face puffy with backed-up caffeine, nicotine, and fatigue; she slumped at the kitchen island, worrying at her cigarette with her thumb. She stared at the TV he'd installed in the corner above their one houseplant, a hardened snake plant that thrived on her erratic watering regimen of dumping cold coffee cups, many containing soggy cigarette butts.

The television screen flashed an image of military vehicles coated in that signature third-world red dust. Some breathless embedded reporter riding in a Bradley, yelling about taking small-arms fire . . .

Day two of the War in the Box.

"How're the Crusades going?" Broker nodded toward the TV.

Nina slowly shook her head, and a spark of interest sputtered in her eyes. "Looks cool on the tube. Road race to Baghdad. But

I got a feeling they shoulda listened to Shinseki, going in light like this. Those Army kids are going to wind up taking up the slack for the politicians again."

Broker nodded. "Let's hope the fix is in." She saw the war as inevitable. He thought it was a mistake. They agreed on one point; during the run-up to the invasion they'd assumed that the Iraqi generals had been bought off, that they'd resist symbolically to preserve their honor, then turn over Saddam and his inner circle. So far that hadn't happened. Any other plan was just too dumb, given Iraq's history and ethnic composition.

"Nina," he said softly, "give it a break." Did she really miss it? Want it more than being with him and Kit? Did she feel left out, flawed because she'd been left behind? He found the remote among the unwashed breakfast dishes and thumbed off the TV. He faced her and said, "The thing at school—Kit got into a fight. This kid wouldn't stop pushing her, so she punched him. One-day suspension. There's a readmission conference tomorrow."

Nina stared at him, and he could almost see his words methodically crawl over her face, searching for a way to get inside. Finally she focused and said, "Did she get hurt?"

Broker shook his head. "Skinned her knuckles. But the boy she hit wound up with a bloody nose."

Slowly she nodded. Then she dropped her cigarette into the sink. "I'll go up and talk to her." The words had no force, seeping out like a last puff of smoke.

"Let's wait, do it over supper. Maybe, ah, you should take a shower and try a nap," Broker said gently.

Nina slowly raised her right arm and touched her fingers to her right temple in a smirk of a salute. She let the arm fall back to her side and walked from the kitchen.

Broker smiled. Two months ago she would be wincing with the effort when she hit the painful range of motion at shoulder level. Would be trembling by the time she got her hand up to her forehead. The ROM therapy had made slow but steady progress rebuilding the shoulder. She was healing. The shoulder faster than the rest of her. But healing.

He turned the exhaust fan on over the stove. Then he opened the patio door to the deck and the side windows and turned on the ceiling fan. To air the place out.

Next he emptied the dishwasher, put the plates, glasses, cups, and bowls away. Then he rinsed off the dishes in the sink and started loading the washer.

Kit came down the stairs and into the kitchen carrying her school backpack. "Mom's taking a nap," she said.

"How's your hand?"

Kit looked at her raw knuckle. "Don't think I need a Band-Aid anymore. Mom put some hydrogen peroxide on it."

"Stung, didn't it?"

"A little." She held up her hand so he could see the white residue of disinfectant etched into her knuckle. Then she stared at him.

So he debated whether to address the unsaid question hanging over her. Should he do it now, or wait? Whatever he said would be tempered by the fact that he'd knocked the kid's dad down. "We'll talk about the fight at dinner," he decided. "Put on your stuff. We'll go outside so we don't wake her. Maybe you could put some wax on the skis."

Kit brightened when he said that, walked to the patio door, and studied the thermometer fastened to the deck rail. "Twenty-two degrees. Purple wax."

"Sounds about right," Broker said.

As Kit worked with the skis in the garage, he took a white package of venison round steak from the freezer and set it on the counter to thaw. Then he checked the pantry and the refrigerator to make sure he had all the ingredients he'd need. Satisfied, he put on his coat and went outside.

As he pulled on his cap and gloves, he checked the overcast sky and the surrounding woods. Griffin bought this parcel of land with frontage on the west shore of Glacier Lake twenty years ago, when it was cheap and the lake was almost totally uninhabited. Broker had spent part of a summer helping him put the kitchen addition on the gutted house. Not much older then than Nina was now, not long out of his own war.

Broker returned to his maul and chopping block, knocked apart a few armloads of kindling, took it into the kitchen, and stacked it in the wood box next to the Franklin stove. When he came back out, he saw Kit come out of the garage, lean the skis against the side of the building, and use a cork to smooth out the long stripes of wax she'd applied. His were the long skinny Nordic racers. Hers were shorter, combos for both Nordic and skating.

Kit came back with the ski poles. Lined everything up, then turned to him and held up her hands, palms up, in a question. In addition to being quiet, the west end of Glacier was only a couple hundred yards from fifty winding kilometers of some of the best cross-country ski trails in the state.

"After lunch," he said. She went inside, and he went back to his wood.

As the maul rose and fell and his woodpile grew, he went back over the morning. The tiff on the playground didn't concern him that much, and his first impression was that the principal and that chubby kid's mom were overreacting. Kids had to learn how to work out problems for themselves. Should think about that, though. How maybe his approach was too old-fashioned for the current social climate.

More to the point was the fact that he had to keep explaining to an eight-year-old that, as a family, they didn't need to draw extra attention to themselves right now. Explain it in a way to make it stick.

After a fast grilled cheese sandwich, tomato soup, and a glass of milk, they changed into long underwear and wind pants and laced on their ski boots. During the three months they'd been on the lake, the quarter Norwegian in Kit's blood had taken to the skinny skis with a single-minded intensity some people might find scary in a kid her age.

They'd hit the ski trail a lot. What Kit had this winter instead of friends.

Back outside, he watched her toe into her ski bindings, grab her long skating poles, and power off into the woods on the connecting route they'd blazed to the groomed trail. He stayed a few yards behind her in parallel tracks as she swept left and right in the athletic skating technique that he, the die-hard purist, rejected. She'd learned the rudiments last year, when she was living with her mom in Italy. And now her initial clumsiness had fallen away with the last of her baby fat.

Broker dug in his poles and pushed off. They met a family plodding in fat waxless skis and snowmobile suits. Passed them.

A moment later two athletic high school boys powered around them, wearing orange camo hunting parkas. Locals by their dress. Out taking advantage of the new snow.

The confrontation with Jimmy Klumpe still replayed in Broker's muscles, a not unpleasant afterglow. Dumb to dwell on it. *Put it behind you.* He tried to lose himself in the rhythms of the kick and glide. The crisp air bit into his lungs, and the sweat froze on the tips of his hair as they swept through the silent forest.

Chapter Seven

Gator closed the door to his shop and stood for a few moments looking across the empty fields and into the woods beyond. The eighty acres was fifteen miles north of Glacier Falls, at the edge of the Washichu State Forest. He'd signed it over to Cassie when they both turned twenty-one, when he was in the Navy.

Spent three years at the Idaho National Engineering Lab by Idaho Falls. Nothing but razor-sharp black basalt fields, used nuclear fuel rods, unexploded ordnance, and a Navy facility that trained submariners on nuclear engines. Mechanic/machinist mate. Never did get to see the ocean.

Cassie had tried renting the place out. Didn't have much luck. People didn't like it up here in the big woods, said it was too spooky.

He'd moved in when he got out of prison two years ago. He liked it just fine. No people, and lots of machines that needed fixing. His parole officer had remarked how Gator had cleaned the place up considerably. People grudgingly admitted he was a local success story. No small accomplishment for a Bodine.

So he stood for a few minutes looking over his domain; uninhabited—now—for a ten-mile radius. The low clouds almost scraped the crowns of the pines, going off forever like the bottoms of a million gray egg cartons. He sniffed the crunchy air. March in Minnesota. It would snow again.

He cocked an ear, listening. Earlier today he'd heard the pack. Nothing now.

He approved of the way the snow carpeted the fields and

frosted the evergreens. Was up to him, he'd have winter all year. Liked the way it imposed a kind of order; compressed the colors into manageable whites and grays. Covered up all the crud.

Made the big woods even more inaccessible. Kept people away. The wolves coming back helped, too.

Going in the farmhouse, like now, sometimes he missed his dogs. The two big shepherd pups he bought had been poisoned last year by some uptight citizen who didn't like homeboy felons moving back into the neighborhood. He'd brought in some geese for lookouts but got rid of them because he couldn't abide the green crap everywhere. Decided the isolation was security enough.

There were no animals on the farm now. The land was in the crop rotation. Just him and his tools and the quiet.

The farmhouse was pretty much the way it'd been; just a lot cleaner now. Same old furniture covered with blankets. He'd hung a few tractor posters on the wall. His ribbons from high school cross-country. A framed certificate that announced that Morgun Bodine had finished twelfth in the Bierkebinder Cross-Country Ski Marathon five years ago, in Hayward, Wisconsin. A souvenir German battle flag hung on the wall that his dad had brought back from Europe, when he was the best mechanic in four counties, before he went on the booze. A good sound system.

A 5,000-piece puzzle was half constructed on the kitchen table.

He heated some water and put on a Johnny Cash CD, the one recorded at Folsom Prison. When the water boiled, he made a cup of Folger's instant coffee, lit a Camel, and got out his maps and refamiliarized himself with the ski trail loop that followed the east shore of the lake, where the old Hamre place was located.

He picked up the phone, checked down the list of numbers taped on the wall, and called Glacier Lodge. The clerk told him, yeah, they'd run the tractor on the ski trails this morning—what the hell, probably the last chance to ski this season.

Gator thanked the clerk, ended the call, and returned to his maps. One loop of the trail skirted the Griffins' rental. He thought about it. Go in fast, scout the place, mess with the guy's stuff. Get out. Just enough to keep Cassie happy so she didn't bounce weird.

The other thing toyed with him. Cassie said he didn't fit? Like a puzzle. Something to figure out.

Cassie had always expected him to attend to her dramas, large and small. Like he was on this open-ended retainer because she'd talked Jimmy into bankrolling the repair shop. When he got out of the joint. Back when she had her nose in the air, when they were flush, all full of plans.

That was almost two years ago, and he'd owed them. Gator grinned and knuckled the bristle of spiky growth on his chin. Yeah, well, now—the way it worked out—they owed him. Big-time. And now he had the plans.

But he had to keep them in line, on task. Especially Cassie, who had boundary issues when she got herself all worked up and got wired and got to talking too much. So she wanted to see her brother teach the guy a lesson, country style. Like he had learned last year, the accepted way around here to send a message was to kill an animal. Okay, if that was the price of keeping her quiet.

Kid's stuff. And messy. He put on a pair of old rubber gloves, went to the icebox, poked around, and found half a pound of hamburger starting to turn brown. Quickly he packed the meat into a squishy ball, eased it into a Ziploc bag, then stepped onto the mud porch and carefully lifted a liter of Prestone, took off the twist cap, and sloshed antifreeze into the plastic bag. Leaned it gingerly on a workbench against the vise. Let it stew. One green greasy meatball slurpy for Rover.

Gator made a face. *So what if the guy doesn't have a dog?*

He went back in the kitchen and dug in the utensil drawer next to the sink until he found the skinny ice pick. *I know he's got a vehicle.*

He placed the pick in the narrow side pocket of his backpack. He thought for a moment. *Probably have to do some creeping.* He went to the shelf on the mud porch and selected a pair of old oversize felt boot liners. Then he selected his small bear-paw snow shoes. After he loaded the footwear in his pack, he nestled the meatball baggie in among the boot liners.

Okay.

Next he changed from his work clothes, pulled on long underwear and lightweight Gore-Tex winter camo. He yanked a ski mask over his head and down around his neck like a muff, so he could pull it up if he needed to hide his face. He put a bottle of water, an energy bar, and his smokes in a small backpack. After he laced on his ski boots, he checked the thermometer on the porch.

Twenty-two degrees. Blue Kleister.

Carefully, liking the routine, he waxed his Peltonen racers.

He put his cell phone in his chest pocket, then loaded his skis and gear in the back of his battered red '92 Chevy truck and headed out. He slowed five minutes from the farm to check the intersection of County Z. The crossroad was all fresh undisturbed snow, no tire tracks. He continued on County 12 south through the deserted jack pine barrens, going slow, inspecting the deserted houses scattered along the road for signs of recent activity. Half an hour later, he arrived at the trail head at the north end of the lake.

Most mornings when there was good snow, he skied the north 20K. He unloaded his skis and stepped into his bindings, shouldered his pack, and poled through the woods to the trail. When he got there, he saw that the tractor from the lodge had been through, just like the clerk said. Fresh-groomed trails. He pushed off and fell into the powerful rhythm, heading south.

Twice he skied off the trail, letting other skiers pass. This time of year they'd be local people, and he didn't want to be spotted out here. Allowing for the detours, it took just fifteen leisurely minutes to come to the yellow No Hunting sign that posted the back end of Griffin's land. Could see the green cabin peeking through the trees, the lake beyond it. He saw they'd been skiing, probably last night just after it snowed. They had worked a connecting trail. He scouted in closer down the connecting trail and settled on a slight rise that overlooked the backyard. He got out of his skis, hid them in some thick spruce, strapped on the paws, and went to the knoll, where he made a place to sit against a tree. Then he tested the wind, which was gusting from the northeast, and figured he could get away with a smoke. So he lit a Camel and settled in to watch the house. First off, he spotted a snow-covered doghouse in back of the garage. Uh-huh. Okay. Keep an eye out for the dog. Then he saw a pile of kindling next to a chopping block. Oak, from the bark and grain. Must be three cords stacked up in the long shed along the garage. Then he remembered that Griffin trucked in oak, used it to heat sand and water to mix his mortar. On that winter job at the lodge.

Then he noticed two sets of skis and poles set out against the garage. One set shorter, for a kid. He finished his smoke and stuffed the butt deep out of sight into a crevice of pine bark, wiggled his toes in his boots, drank some water, ate half an energy bar. A dedicated bow hunter, he was stoic about the cold. He figured he had about half an hour of cooldown before the sweat he'd worked up on the trail started to freeze.

Another half hour passed. Still no sign of a dog. Then he heard voices and saw a man and a kid come out the back door in skiing duds. Where's Mom? Now that he'd come this far, he was getting curious; just who were they? What was it like inside that house? How come nobody had seen the woman? What did Cassie mean? *He didn't fit.*

Now they were putting on their skis.

Okay. He was up fast, made his way back to his own skis. So which way are they going to go? Assume they're good citizens and will follow the arrows posted on the trail. Go the direction he'd come in. He lashed the bear paws to his pack, got back into his skis, and worked hard, backtracking up the trail. When he'd poled up the approach to the first big downhill, he paused and peered back through the trees. He'd been right. Eagle Scouts, following the rules. Coming this way. The kid wore green and was on the skating path, the guy was in red and stayed in the Nordic tracks.

He pulled up his ski mask and adjusted it. Okay. *Time it so you meet them at max speed when you rocket back down the hill. Get a feel for this guy.*

Chapter Eight

Ten minutes into the trail Broker caught a blur of movement up ahead through the trees, shooting over the top of the first big hill. A skier coming down the tracks in a downhill tuck, poles back, hands braced on his bent knees. Some daredevil cowboy. Really pushing it.

"Watch yourself, Kit. That guy up there. He's coming pretty fast," Broker called out. Kit slowed her stride, reacting to the alarm in Broker's voice. She swung her head, her eyes flashing, uncertain.

"Don't look at me, Look at *him*!" Broker yelled at her.

She glowered at the anger in his voice, wasting seconds she needed to react. And all he could do was watch. He was helpless because the guy was coming so fast, and he was hard to see in gray-and-white hunting camo and a black face mask. Onrushing like a puzzle piece catapulted out of the winter pattern of the forest. Jesus. Too fast.

"Kit, goddammit! Get off the trail!" Broker shouted.

"You don't have to yell," she shouted back.

Time and distance. Broker did the quick gut math and realized he could not reach her, thirty yards ahead of him, before the oncoming skier . . .

"GET OFF THE TRAIL!" he shouted again, waving his poles.

The guy came out of his tuck nearing the bottom of the hill and executed a snappy sidestep, and now he was ripping down the skating path, straight at Kit.

Kit was stepping to the right as fast as she could, but the guy was on top of her.

"Watch it, asshole!" Broker shouted as he struggled on the skis to gain the distance. Wasn't going to happen. He did his best to step out into the skating path, instinctively gripping one of his poles with both hands like a pugil stick and menacing it forward in an attempt to warn the guy away.

The guy came straight ahead, streaked past with a swish and clatter as one of his poles banged on Kit's poles. Not even seeing them, it seemed, his hooded eyes fixed ahead on the trail. Kit was flung in his wake and fell sideways into the parallel tracks ahead of Broker. In seconds he was bending over her. She sat up, removed her glove, and put her fingers to her cheek.

A thin red stripe started next to her nose and went across her cheek almost to her ear. Gingerly she touched it, and her finger came away with a tiny dot of blood.

"He must have raked you with his pole as he went by," Broker said, helping her to her feet and inspecting her face. "Just a scratch."

With an exaggerated indignant expression and in a very dramatic voice, Kit protested, "You didn't have to yell at me."

"Hey, he almost squashed you flat."

"Did not. He missed."

Broker stared, perplexed at the touchy coiled springs of mood sprouting out of her. "I'm sorry for yelling, but I was scared for you," he said.

She thought about it and said, "I was scared, too. Just a little." She furrowing her brow and stated, "He was going the wrong way, Dad,"

"I know, honey. Some people are like that. And they just don't see kids. You all right?"

"No problem," she said deadpan, delivering the line with a nonchalance she'd overheard hanging out with Nina's Army crowd in Italy. Seeing him a make a face at her language, she grinned. Perhaps encouraged by the encounter with the speed demon, she said, "Let's go. Race you down the first hill."

Broker looked off through the silent trees in the direction of the asshole skier. The guy had vanished. The small crisis passed. "You're on," he said.

Kit took the lead, and he made a production of staying just behind her, goading her faster, as they herringboned up the incline. He watched her breath surge in tight white bursts next to her green cap as she half ran the hill. Broker was reminded of something he'd learned long ago; how the Vietnamese wrote their prayers on slips of paper and burned them. Because the ghosts of their ancestors could only read smoke.

They reached the top, and a minute later the trail forked; beginners to the left, advanced to the right. Without hesitation Kit dug in her poles and plunged toward the steep downhill they'd nicknamed Suicide One. Broker double-poled to catch up, tucked into the slope, and heard Kit's exhilarated squeal echo in the trees. Her breath streamed over her shoulder, and in that exuberant white cloud Broker, giddy with the rush downhill, read a happy answer to a long prayer.

The journey that had brought them here was terrible, but finally the long separation had ended and they were together, living under one roof. Then Kit came down too fast on the steep bend at the bottom of the run and misjudged shifting into her step turn. Her left ski wobbled out of control, and she lurched in front of Broker, who was on her too fast. He tried an impossible hockey stop. No way. They tumbled together into a snowbank in a tangle of poles, skis, and laughter.

Chapter Nine

Gator put a few hundred yards of twisting trail between him and the man and the kid and then slowed, stopped, and leaned on his poles. He panted, catching his breath after the near collision at the bottom of the hill. That was fun, but now he was more than a little intrigued. Not so much the way the guy called him an asshole like that. He could let that pass under the circumstances. He'd gone by too fast and nearly creamed the kid. But he managed to get a good look at the guy. And there was something about the way his hard eyes peeped out from his gaunt face and thick Ernie Kovacs eyebrows. Suspicious, judgmental, a little too in charge. Cop's eyes, his gut told him.

Like Cassie said, something that didn't fit.

So maybe go in a little deeper, see what these folks are about. He figured he had about an hour, maybe more, if they skied the whole loop.

He skied back and turned in at the connecting trail, stepped into the parallel tracks, and skied up to the trees at the edge of the yard. He watched the house for five minutes. No shadows moved in the windows. His eyes went back and forth between the house and the new Toyota truck parked in front of the garage.

Go in, see if you can get a look at the wife.

But stay practical. Think. The house invaders he'd met in the joint always said, first, you look for the dog. Gator looked again. No piles of crap in the yard, no evidence of tracks. Just the green Toyota Tundra in the drive. He stowed his skis and pack out of sight and pulled the roomy felt liners over his ski boots.

He walked in crooked on the tracks already in the yard up to the garage, peeked in the side window. No other car. Maybe the wife was out on errands? He crossed to the back deck, went up the steps, and knocked on the sliding patio door. Waited a minute. No one came. He tried the door. It slid open.

Okay, dude. This is what's called a threshold for a guy with a parole officer. And home invasions had never been his thing. So take some precautions. He knocked again and called out. "Anybody home?" If the wife appeared, he'd ask to use the phone. Say his cell phone battery went dead. Say he fell on the ski trail, hurt his knee, needed to arrange a ride.

No sound, no wife. Gator went in silently on his felt booties and—shit!—froze when he heard a tinkling bell. A black kitten appeared in the doorway at the end of the kitchen. Gator vibrated alert, straining his ears. All he heard was the bell move off into the next room. Then go silent.

He stopped, perplexed. He could see killing a dog if there was a reason. But a kitty? He'd have to think about that. He smiled. Starting to enjoy the thrill, he went deeper into the house. Past the kitchen there was a small room that held bookcases and a desk with a fax machine and stacks of envelopes, a checkbook, stamps. Paying the bills, it looked like. He studied a stack of cardboard boxes piled next to the desk. The top one held an old high school yearbook, some books, and a few frayed manila folders. Some kind of paperwork. Like they weren't really unpacked. Not really settled in.

He continued into the living room. Christ, more piles of boxes against the wall. Renters, Cassie said, so all this stuff was Griffin's. Futon couch and chairs. A quilt hanging on one wall was interesting; a pattern of black, red, and white stitching that Gator found appealing.

But he wasn't a thief. And, besides, they'd miss it right off. He continued through the living room and paused at the foot of the stairs to the second floor.

"Hello," he called again, looking up the stairs. "Your back

door was open, and I wondered if I could use your phone . . ."

No response. Dead quiet here.

Come this far, might as well go up and have a look. Probably no one home. *God, I love this shit.* Stepping carefully, he climbed the stairs. A tiny hall, two doors. The door to the right was open. Where the kid slept. Yellow comforter on a twin-size bed, a gallery of stuffed animals arranged above the fold. Not much on the walls for a kid's room. More cardboard boxes spilling toys and clothes.

Gator turned to the other bedroom on the left. The door was ajar.

And there she was, asleep at one in the afternoon, flung face down. A redhead. Hard to tell what she looked like, with her face flattened out on the tangled sheets, surrounded by a frizz of hair that needed a wash. Her ass made a tidy swell in her purple pajama bottoms, but the effect was spoiled by the dark bath of sweat that pasted her gray T-shirt to her shoulder blades. He tiptoed into the room and stared down at her. He made a face when he heard her labored breathing and saw the sheets under her head soaked with sweat. Beads of it like a wet headband, starting at the roots of her hair. His eyes moved away, and he noticed a stack of books on the bedside table.

Darkness Visible by William Styron. *A Memoir of Madness.* And a fat red volume: *DSM-IV.* He squinted, his lips moving as he read the subtext on the thick spine: *Diagnostic and Statistical Manual of Mental Disorders. Fourth Edition.*

Hmmmm. Real fun folks Cassie had run into here.

Oh-oh! The woman shifted on the bed. Gator froze as he watched her twist at the waist, one arm flung above her head, turning, the other arm coming across and flopping on the edge of the bed, the limp fingers almost grazing the pant leg of his camos.

He started. *Jesus!*

Not her face, which he could see now and which was not half bad as far as he could see, eyes still clamped shut in troubled sleep. Shit, no, it was the faded type printed across the front of shirt, like a sweat-soaked pennant stretched between the mounds of her tits:

EAST METRO DRUG TASK FORCE.

Sonofabitch! What have we got here?

Gator reeled as his mind tacked out, going from zero to sixty in a second flat. Had to concentrate to keep his balance. He backed quietly from the room, rocked by a weird hilarity that alternated with a pure spooky sensation. In the hall his eyes traveled over the kid's bed, and he had an inspiration. Riding the impulse, he entered the room and plucked a worn blue-and-white-striped bunny from among the toys tucked into the fold of the bed. Then he hurried down the stairs, wanting to get out fast . . . but couldn't resist shuffling through the paperwork on the desk next to the kitchen door.

A Visa statement . . . his eyes stopped, reversed.

Drawn on a bank in Hong Kong? What the hell—$10,000 cash advance. Credit limit a hundred thou? He looked up at the sheet of paper on the fax that had printed out a log of calls. Devil's Rock, Minnesota. Stillwater. St. Paul.

Fort Bragg, North Carolina?

Huh?

He rifled through the envelopes, and a return address jumped out:

Washington County Sheriff's Office.

Whoa, what's this? He opened the envelope and took out the top of a pay voucher. A handwritten note bearing the letterhead of John Eisenhower, Sheriff, was clipped to the form.

Broker,

Here's the balance of the Special Projects money. Sorry as usual it took so long. I could only swing a few hundred to help defray the cost of your truck getting wrecked on the Saint thing. I heard your

*insurance didn't cover it. I'd look into suing that nutcase
Cantrell. He finally resigned the county.*

Hope all is well with Nina and Kit.

Best, John

Gator looked around, bouncing, giddy—damn Cassie, well no shit! *They don't fit. Gonna put something extra in your stocking. . . . Some kind of cop.*

He listened carefully and decided he could chance only a few more minutes. But this was too good to pass up. It only took a few seconds to figure out the fax's copying function. Okay. He smoothed out the Visa statement and the pay voucher and aligned them into the feeder. Hit copy. The machine grumbled, and seconds seemed like an eternity until—Yes!—they printed out. Then he took the note, copied that. He rolled the sheets of paper carefully and inserted them into the wide webbed inner pocket of his jacket.

You should really get the hell out of here.

But now he was staring at the stack of boxes. On impulse he reached into the top one, snatched a manila folder at random, and stuffed it under his jacket.

Enjoying himself immensely, clutching the bunny comically with both hands to his chest, he cakewalked through the kitchen, having some fun but making sure he wasn't leaving any trace. He didn't worry too much. The floor was dotted with pools of melting snow that the guy and the kid must have left going in and out.

Going past the sink he paused, tucked the bunny in his jacket, and selected a brown glazed bowl from the countertop. Somebody just had some tomato soup. He slipped out the door, down the porch, and crossed to the truck. Knelt, listened. Quickly he fingered the ice pick from his pack, felt the deep tread on the left rear tire. New. Blizzak. Good snow tire.

He thrust the pick deep into a crevice of tread, heard a whoosh of rubbery air escaping. Up quick, skirting around the garage, where he stopped and set down the bowl next to the doghouse. Carefully, he slung off his pack, opened it, withdrew the Ziploc, and dumped the meat and antifreeze into the bowl. Tucked the bag back in the pack.

Dog or not, if this guy had half a brain, he'd get the message.

Then he caught Christmas-tree colors in the pines, moving red and green. A second later he heard their breathless chatter, coming in fast.

Shit! They didn't ski the whole loop.

Gator ducked along the side of the garage, keeping it between him and the trail, slipped around the front, hurried in through the front door. Christ, if the wife was up and looking out the living room window, she could see . . .

The voices, louder now.

Looked around fast. Found a cranny in the corner behind a table stacked with boxes, backed into it, and squatted in the dark as the back door opened.

Oh, shit, oh shit! They were right there. Seeing the steam from their breath rising in the half-light over the top of the boxes, he pulled the mask up over his mouth. Clatter of skis, c'mon. C'mon. Go inside.

Then the guy, Broker, told the kid to shovel the back deck. Not good. Then he went through the door that attached to the kitchen, leaving the goddamn kid out back scraping at the snow on the back porch. Gator didn't want to chance heading out the front—too open, and his stuff was back in the woods.

Sonofabitch. He got up to a crouch, listening hard. Had a chance heading out the front. Gotta go now. He left his cover, starting to head for . . .

Jesus Christ. The kitchen door opened, throwing an oblong splash of yellow light across the floor and far wall.

Gator scurried back to his hiding nook. Now what?

He listened as he heard Broker move to the back of the garage, go outside, talk to the kid. Then the soft scrape of his slippered feet went back into the house. The door closed.

Something. A tinkle. A bell. Hey, kitty. Why not. A souvenir. Moving swiftly, Gator tiptoed from hiding, did a little dance to cut the cat off, and snatched it up, carefully easing it into the deep side pocket of his hunting parka. Zipped it down, leaving a little opening so it could breathe.

He froze in place for another minute until he heard the shovel stop scraping. Heard the kid tramp across the back deck, go in through the patio door to the kitchen.

Finally.

On the way out he grabbed one of the short ski poles from the stack along the wall. He stepped out onto the deck, flattened himself against the outer wall of the garage. Looked up. Wonderful. Stuck out his tongue, let a snowflake melt on it. The snow started driving down. Hell, in minutes it would obliterate his faint tracks on the deck. Like he was never here. He slipped over the deck rail and, keeping the garage between him and the lights of the kitchen, headed for the tree line. Once he got into the woods, he could work his way back to the trail. Get his skis and gear.

Wow. What a kick.

Chapter Ten

After stowing the skis in the garage, Broker told Kit to shovel off the back deck and think about what happened today at school. Then he took off his ski boots and went into the kitchen. He heard a fast hell's-bells jingle too late—shit—and tripped, almost losing his balance as the demon kitten ran a crazy zigzag between his stocking feet.

Cursed under his breath. "Goddamn cat."

Griffin had brought the kitten as a housewarming present for Kit after they moved in. By the third day it was in the house, with Nina keeping the TV on, Kit had named the cat Ditech. It was everywhere underfoot, like the mortgage commercials.

Broker put on the slippers that were by the door, leaned down, swept up the handful of black fur, opened the door to the garage. Carrying the cat, he went to the back door, opened it, and spoke to Kit.

"When you're finished, come in though the patio door. Keep this door closed. I'm putting the cat in the garage while I cook dinner."

"She's just a kitten—it's cold out here," Kit protested.

Broker lifted the cat by the scruff of her neck. "It's an insulated garage, and this black stuff she's made out of is fur. Just till after we eat. Now, you shovel." He closed the door, put the kitty down, and went back into the kitchen.

Broker finished thawing the meat in the microwave, then sliced it in long strips, poured some canola oil into his big stewpot, started the burner, and added the venison. As the meat browned, he sliced onions, mushrooms, and green peppers, added them to the pot, and started unscrewing four jars of Paul Newman pasta sauce. He raised one of the jars and eyed the contents for carbs and sugar. Hmmm. The late Dr. Atkins would probably not approve of the high-fructose corn syrup.

Kit came in, took off her coat, boots, and gloves, and went upstairs.

Broker cocked his head when he heard the pipes in the wall of the downstairs bath rattle. Good. Nina was in the shower. He'd wait till she was done before he started the dishwasher. As he was wiping down the island, he looked up and saw Kit standing in the kitchen doorway.

"Mom's taking a shower," she said.

"Yep."

"I'll pick out some clothes for her to wear."

"Hey, that's good, honey."

Up on tiptoe, peering at the pot. "Ah, what's cooking?"

"Spaga," Broker said, using her baby word for his venison spaghetti.

She grinned, turned, and ran up the stairs.

Kit in motion: this house they rented from Uncle Harry was small, half the size of their home up in Devil's Rock. But Mom didn't want Kit going to school in the woods, so they'd moved into the Stillwater apartment. Then Mom got sick, and they were back in the woods again. Because people here didn't know her up and couldn't tell that she was different now. Just for a while, Dad said, until Mom's arm got better. When her arm was better, the rest of her would be better too.

Kit was used to her mom being real strong, bossing whole platoons and companies in Italy, so sometimes it scared her, seeing the way she wandered around smoking cigarettes in her pajamas and robe all day. Most of the other kids at school had their moms coming in, picking them up, talking to the teachers. Helping out. With her it was always her dad. And he never came in, just waited out in the truck.

Kit went into the closet next to the room where Mom slept and dug through some boxes. Up on tiptoe, she searched through some clothes on hangers, picked a few, then came back into her room and plopped them on her bed. Then she opened the door to the bathroom. Mom was standing at the sink, drying herself with a towel. She put the towel aside, opened the cabinet over the sink, and took out a jar of skin cream, removed the top, and dabbed some on her face.

That was a good sign.

Fresh from the shower, wreathed in steam, Mom had some color to her face. Mom was smoother now. She used to be too thin, laced tight with dents and veins. Could see the muscles sliding back and forth under her skin when she moved. Now she was filled out all around. Still sort of skinny, but not the way she used to be skinny. Kit understood she was not like other moms; but, of course, Kit hadn't seen other moms naked in the bathroom.

———

Nina Pryce peered into the steamy bathroom mirror. At thirty-six she still looked fit, for a civilian.

Five-nine. One hundred and forty-five pounds. She'd gained ten pounds on the disabled list. She was getting breasts, a suggestion of fullness creeping into her hips and rear end.

Curves, for Christ's sake.

The nagging thought: did Broker like her this way; ripening like a pear . . . ?

Dependent on him.

A lot of moms were in shape. Gym-rat skinny, Dad called it. But not like Mom used to be. For instance, other moms didn't have the kinda purple gouge in their left hip and a bigger glob of purple scar on their butt. Where the E-ra-kee shot her during the war in the desert, the war before the one that was on TV now. The one before Kit was born. Didn't have a big grinning skull-and-crossbones tattoo on their right shoulder.

Kit entered the bathroom cautiously, feeling her way into her mother's mood. In a general way she understood that Mom wouldn't get on her about the fight at school. She knew Mom didn't have the strength for that right now.

"It's okay, Little Bit," Nina said, turned her warm green eyes on Kit, smiling in real life.

Kit brightened and smiled back. Mom only called her "Little Bit" when she was feeling pretty good. Auntie Jane had called her Little Bit. And Mom's smile was only a little bit sad.

"So what's this boy like, you got in the fight with?" Nina asked.

Kit made a face. "He's a bully. He swears more than all the other kids put together. He knows the F word."

"Hmmmm," Nina mulled.

Kit tilted her head. "Can I say . . . hell?"

"Okaayy . . ." Nina drew it out, curious.

"Hell is a swear word. But no one says, 'The H word.' Why is that? And what's the big deal about the F word?"

Nina fingered a snag in her hair and studied her daughter. "What do you think it means?"

"Don't know. But it's cool, because the older kids say it a lot."

Nina put down the comb, wrapped a towel around her middle, came into the room, and sat on the bed. "Well, it's complicated," she said.

"That don't sound like an answer. Sounds like another question," Kit said.

"I don't think you're ready for this. You sure you really want to know?" Nina asked.

"I want to know," Kit said, furrowing her forehead, attentive.

Nina scrunched her lips meditatively, "Okay. It's like this. The F word is initials. Like your name: Karson Pryce Broker. The initials are K.P.B.—"

"Yeah," Kit said.

"The F word is the same way. F.U.C.K. means 'For Unlawful Carnal Knowledge.'"

"I don't get it," Kit said.

"It's about . . . sex."

Kit shook her head.

"Okay. Sex is a way of talking about making babies. Remember our talk about how Daddy and I made you?"

Kit's face contorted, recalling the description of Dad's testicles being full of swimmy things that swam out his penis into Mom's vagina, hunting for this egg. She had looked at her father funny for a month after that.

"Mom, that's gross."

Nina nodded. "And so is the F word for someone your age."

"I'm going to change the subject," Kit said.

"Fine," Nina said.

"Can we play the game?" Kit asks.

Nina smiled. "Okay."

Days when Mom was feeling better, like now, she'd let Kit play dress-up on her, like she was a special doll. Something she would never have done last year in Italy. Kit would parade the clothes she'd selected. But first she'd comb Mom's hair.

"I like it you're letting your hair grow," Kit said, gently drawing the comb through her mother's hair, ratting out the snags.

Broker stood at the foot of the stairs and listened to the muted girl talk drifting down from Kit's bedroom on a mist of hot water and body lotion. He smiled and sagged a little with relief, hearing the normal chatter. More and more there were these tiny healing moments, cutting back the bleak days.

He went back into the kitchen, where steam from the boiling kettle of pasta water had fogged the windows. When his girls came down for dinner, he saw that Kit had talked Nina into an artifact of her student days at the University of Michigan, this ancient flowing green *jabala* with threadbare gold embroidery. She had applied lipstick, dots of rouge, and streaked eyeshadow. Nina's red hair, for years shorn mob-cap short, had grown to an ambiguous length two inches off her shoulders. Kit had pinned it with barrettes at odd angles. A single crude braid dangled from the left side of her forehead.

Nina managed a wry smile and rolled her eyes. Kit led her by the hand, pleased with her efforts.

Broker encouraged, smiled back. "All right, looking good. Kit, go wash your hands." He placed a salad bowl on the set table, returned to the stove, thrust a ladle into the churning kettle, plucked a strand of pasta, took it in his fingers, and tossed it against the maple cabinet next to the stove, where it stuck in a curlicue.

Done.

"Al dente, bravo," Kit said in approval, emerging from the half bath off the kitchen. Her expression changed, remembering something. She dashed from the room.

As Broker drained the noodles in the sink, he heard Kit running up the stairs. Nina moved in beside him, began to grate the Parmesan. Their elbows touched.

"You look like a harlot in that getup," he said quietly.

For the first time in a long time, she sideswiped him with her hip.

"Hey," he muttered, his voice close to faltering at the warm pressure of Nina's flank nudging him.

She lowered her painted eyelids, pursed her painted lips. "Stay on task, Broker. You have to discipline your feral child, remember . . . punching that kid . . ."

"Right." With a slight lump in his throat, he continued through the efficient stations of his kitchen *kata*, cleaning as he went, doling out the noodles and then the thick sauce, sprinkling on the cheese, pouring milk for Kit, water for Nina and himself. Placing the bottle of dressing next to the salad bowl.

Then he faced his wife across the table, over the relentless, perfectly executed meal he had prepared.

"Dad?" Kit's voice lanced the moment, needling thin with alarm.

"What?" Broker turned.

"I can't find Bunny." Kit came into the kitchen, her forehead a washboard of wrinkles. "She's not in my bed."

Broker and Nina exchanged glances. The stuffed animal was a

fixture at the dinner table. "Maybe she's in the truck," Nina said.

Broker nodded. Sometimes she took the stuffed animal to and from school, left it in the backseat. "Go check the truck. It should be open. And while you're out there, bring Ditech back inside."

Kit's mood immediately rebounded. She darted out the door into the garage and called, "Hey, Ditech, where are you, you naughty kitty—"

Broker turned to Nina and raised his hands in a shrug. In less than a minute Kit was back, face bright with cold, her forehead still creased with concern.

"No Bunny. And Dad, there's something wrong with the truck."

Now Broker's forehead was stamped with wrinkles. What?

"The tire's flat," Kit said. "And I can't find Ditech. She's *gone.*" Kit's accusing tone brought Broker to his feet.

"Naw, she's just hiding—"

"No, she isn't. I don't hear her bell. C'mere, look," Kit demanded.

Broker followed Kit into the garage. She extended her arm, finger pointing.

Then he saw what she was pointing at as he felt the blast of cold air. The back door to the garage was open, filled with a sudden frenzy of snow.

"You left the door open," Kit said. "There's critters out there, and she's just a little kitty."

"Get inside, it's cold out here," Broker said.

"*Right,* Dad." Arms folded, Kit stalked back into the house and began to cry.

Broker went through the open door. More alert now, he stood on the cold back deck, letting his eyes adjust to the gathering dark. Then he scanned the edge of the forest that abutted the backyard. His fingers moved to the key on the thong around his neck.

He was absolutely certain the door had been closed.

But not locked.

◆　◆　◆

After confirming the flat, he went back inside and told Nina, "Those tires are practically brand-new." He reached for his coat, flipped on the yard light. As he went through the garage, searching for the cat, he thought back over the day, trying to fix on a road event. At the school, maybe? Distracted, had he run up on the curb? That could bust the seams on a radial.

No cat.

He stood in the drive and stared at the Toyota's swayback posture. The left rear tire mashed flat. Focusing. If he climbed the curb this morning, it would have been the right front . . .

He shivered in a gust of wind. The shiver moved deeper, under his skin; he was merely annoyed, innate suspicion a deeper shift and stir. He looked up at the black rumpled clouds, suffused with early moonlight. Shivered again. He'd need his gloves.

Back in the kitchen, he took the time to address Kit, who sat glumly picking at her food. "Don't worry, we'll find Old Bun." Then he added one of his mom's lines from his own childhood. "Nothing gets lost in the house."

"What about kitty?" Kit demanded.

"I'll put some food in a bowl on the back deck." To Nina he just threw a workmanlike shrug. "Gotta change a flat. Might as well get it out of the way. You guys go on with dinner. I'll just be a few minutes."

Nina raised her hand as if trying to snag an elusive thought from midair. Then she said, "Take out the garbage, pickup in the morning."

He nodded. "Good catch." A positive sign. She was making ordinary connections. But he had his own connections going. As he went out the door, instinct directed his hand toward the heavy-duty flashlight hanging on a lanyard under the shelf where they kept the gloves and hats.

Because . . .

He just didn't remember hitting anything that could take out a big honking new snow tire. So before he unloaded the jack and wrenches, he walked carefully around the truck, inspecting the tracks in the mashed snow. He recognized the cleat marks of his Eccos, Kit's Sorels. Nothing out of place there. He removed the full-size spare from the undercarriage.

As he pried off the hubcap and loosened the lugs, it continued working on him. He fiddled in the snowpack, making sure it was secure where he set the jack, levered up the jack handle. As the truck heaved up, the obvious racheted up in his mind. He was staring right at it. Stenciled in white type on the side of the rolling garbage bin next to the garage. *Klumpe Sanitation.*

The only thing he'd hit today, in a manner of speaking, was Klumpe.

Efficiently Broker changed the tire, lowered the truck, stowed his tools, and then minutely inspected the pancaked flat with his flashlight. If there was a puncture, it was out of sight, buried deep between the new tread. He tossed the flat in the truck bed, dusted off his work gloves, turned up his collar. Getting colder, the snow starting to squeak under his boots.

Slowly he wheeled the tall garbage bin down the long drive and positioned it, handles back. He scanned up and down the muzzy white ribbon of road. The ridge of snow the plow had thrown up was undisturbed, no sign of a vehicle having stopped on the shoulder near his house.

Okay. Broker fingered the tinfoil pouch of rough-wrapped cigars from his pocket, removed one of the stogies, took out his lighter, and lit up. Slow walk back up the drive.

The usual cautions. Don't assume. Probably nothing. Still . . . Klumpe came across as a rube who might strike out. Nutty wife egging him on.

So take a look around, walk the perimeter. Broker retrieved the flashlight and walked a circuit of the house, keeping an eye out for the cat. A few minutes later the flashlight beam picked up a wet yellow-green glare, out of place against the snow. Next to the unused doghouse behind the garage.

Broker stooped and inspected the frozen gob of meat resting in a pool of unfrozen liquid in a brown bowl. He could see the red residue of tomato soup still clinging to the bowl's rim.

Same bowl he'd served Kit lunch in today. Before they went out skiing . . . when Nina was sleeping upstairs . . .

Broker immediately switched off the flashlight, a deeper reserve of energy kicking in. He strained his eyes, tracking the tree line, adjusting to the dark.

Had someone been in the house?

Chapter Eleven

When he arrived back at his truck, Gator stowed his skis in the back, got in, started it up, and cranked the heater all the way over. He blew on his chilled fingers, stroked the warmth on his right side, where the kitty nestled in his pocket. Lit a Camel.

While he waited for the heater to kick in, curious, he removed the folder from under his jacket. Flipped it open.

Hmmm . . .

Suddenly he didn't need the heater to warm up.

Gator, who considered himself as an entrepreneur, had done time for transporting cocaine, which he saw as a purely economic gamble. A way to make a lot of money fast to finance his own shop. He'd accepted prison as a penalty for flawed planning. He'd never used coke or anything stronger than the occasional social beer. He believed that stuff about genetic predispositions; given his old man, he eventually gave up even the beer and drew the line at caffeine and nicotine. So he'd never really felt a drug rush.

Maybe this hot trickle fanning out inside his chest was how it feels coming on . . .

'Cause, no shit! The folder was full of old search warrants.

Fingers trembling, he squinted to make out a handwritten memo. Right there on the top, stapled to the front page. His lips moved, reading the personalized heading: "From the Desk of Dennis Lurrie, Chief of Narcotics Division, Minnesota Bureau of Criminal Apprehension . . ."

Then, oh boy . . .

To Special Fucking Agent Phillip Broker.

Thanks again for the inside work, Phil. I know you won't get credit, but we couldn't have pulled this off without you. It's an argument against your critics, who think you've been out there too long in the cold.

Gator held his breath. This must be how it feels to be in a spotlight, onstage. He paused to stroke the kitten squirming in his pocket.

Lucky black kitty.

He started to read. The deepening cold was forgotten as he struggled through the clumsy cop legalese.

DISTRICT COURT

STATE OF MINNESOTA, COUNTY OF WASHINGTON
STATE OF MINNESOTA)
)SS.
COUNTY OF WASHINGTON)

APPLICATION FOR SEARCH WARRANT
AND SUPPORTING AFFIDAVIT

Sergeant Harry Cantrell, being first duly sworn upon oath, hereby makes application to this Court for a warrant to search the premises. . . .

Boring, the way they write this stuff. God . . .

Since 1994, law enforcement officers, including BCA investigators, investigators of the Washington County Sheriff's Office Narcotics Division and the East Metropolitan Area Narcotics Task Force have been involved in an investigation of alleged large-scale drug dealing by John Joseph Turrie, aka "Jojo," and several other persons . . .

Holy shit!

JOHN JOSEPH TURRIE, AKA "JOJO!"

The type jumped off the page.

Quivering, his lips moved as he skipped back and forth, rereading the name, the date, the address. February 1995. Little over eight years ago.

Everybody in the joint knew about that bust in Bayport. The night Danny Turrie's kid, Jojo, got shot to little pieces by the cops. Resisting arrest, they said. But, Danny T. Holy shit, man; his biker gang ran all the drugs in the joint. Had a regular empire on the streets . . .

He went back to the top of the document and read it again in the gloomy light. Speed-reading now. Racing over the printed pages . . .

> . . . *A single-family dwelling located at 18230 Fenwick Avenue, City of Bayport, Washington County . . .*

Pages and pages that detailed buys, repeated mention of an undercover operator . . . all the meticulous constructed ratfuckery the narcs gloried in. Gator dropped the Camel butt that had burned down and scorched his fingers, lit another. Continued to wade through the tortured blocks of type until he came to the last paragraph:

> *WHEREFORE, Affiant requests a search warrant be issued commanding Sergeant Harry Cantrell and other officers, including an undercover BCA officer under his direction and control peace officers, of the State of Minnesota, to enter without announcement of authority and purpose between the hours of 7:00 A.M. and 8:00 P.M. to search the hereinbefore described premises motor vehicle person for the above described property and things and to seize said property and things and keep said property and things in custody until the same can be dealt with according to law.*

Gator read the last entries on the page. This Cantrell guy's signature sworn before a judge of the District Court on this 20th day of February, 1995.

Officers under his control and direction . . . including an undercover officer . . .

Looked at the memo on the front again.

Fingers shaking, he took out his cell phone. No service. Had to get closer to the town tower. He put the truck in gear and drove a few miles down the road until his phone display picked up extended area. Thumbed the number in St. Paul. Hit send. Watched the display connect . . .

Shit. Wait. Think.

There were rules. Getting ahead of himself, like the dummies in the joint. He ended the call, dropped the cell in his lap, and continued to the north end of town until he came to the Last Chance Amoco station and general store. He pulled up to a pump, started the gas, set the automatic feed clip, and walked to the phone booth at the edge of the parking apron.

Dropped in six quarters and punched in the St. Paul number.

Got the machine. Sheryl Mott's voice, sounding very officious, like she was a high-powered executive secretary in some corporation instead of a waitress at Ciatti's in St. Paul.

"I can't take your call at the moment. Please leave a message."

He pictured Sheryl's apartment off Grand Avenue in St. Paul. Like the cosmetics aisle at Target tipped over. He'd been unable to get it together in her space. Went in her bathroom one morning and couldn't find the sink, it was so covered with cosmetics and shampoo bottles. But, on the other hand, when she road-tripped . . .

So, grinning, he left the message: "Hiya, Sheryl, this is Joe at Rapid Oil Change. You're overdue on your three-thousand-mile service. Probably need your fluids checked, too." Then he left a made-up number and ended the call. She'd like the humor. Wouldn't like it if he came off all hyped up.

He went back to his truck, reseated the nozzle in the pump, and went in to pay. Remembering the kitty in his pocket, he grabbed a gallon of whole milk and a sack of Chef's Blend Cat food. After paying for the gas and items, he walked back out to his truck. A black Ford Ranger had pulled in behind him to gas up, and he nodded at Teedo Dove, the hulking Indian dude who stood watching the numbers tick off on the pump. Teedo gave him back one of those great stone-face barest of nods. Ugly fucker looked like one of those Easter Island statues. Worked for Harry Griffin, on his stone crew. Small world.

Then he climbed back in his truck. Heading back up 12 toward his farm, he imagined Sheryl swinging her butt between the tables, balancing a tray on her shoulder.

Man, he needed another set of eyes to look over his find, to vet it. And what Sheryl had going for her, among other things, was a steel-trap mind.

Oh, boy.

Cassie, you got no idea what you and Jimmy just stumbled your foolish asses into. Danny Turrie was one of the Great Monk Crooks, but he'd never get out of Stillwater because he killed two North Side Minneapolis dealers. His deepest desires were twofold: One, naturally, to get out of jail. And that would never happen. The other thing he craved, and would pay a lot for, was the name of the unknown snitch who set up his kid and got him killed.

Bouncing in his seat, reaching down frequently to caress the magic kitty, he drove back to the farm and parked next to the shop. First, he jogged to the house, went straight for the kitchen cupboard, got two bowls, and took them back to the office in the front of the shop. He placed the bowls on the floor, filled one with kitty chow, and poured some milk in the other. Then, carefully, he removed the skittish kitten from his jacket pocket, checked between its hind legs. She. He placed her next to the bowl.

"Go on, Magic, pig out."

The cat ran and hid under the desk. Be patient. She'd be back. He stripped off his jacket, retrieved the fax sheets, put them on his desk, and circled Broker's name and Visa number. Then he tucked them into the manila folder with the warrants and put the file in his desk drawer.

Had to calm down.

So he resorted to ritual. He poured the dregs from the Mister Coffee into a cup, selected a yellow number-two pencil off his desk blotter, and walked to the alcove off the office. It had originally been a bathroom. Gator had removed the door and put in a cot along the wall. Just the toilet and the cot.

His thinking place.

He sat on the floor next to the commode and snapped the pencil in half. Then, slowly, he peeled away the wood pulp with his thumbnail and eased out two lengths of graphite. Wrapped the ends in toilet paper.

He fingered a Camel from his chest pocket, then carefully inserted the pencil lead pieces into the wall outlet and crossed them. When they sparked and the paper ignited, he bent, placing the cigarette to the flame, puffing, until he had a light. Then he sat back and savored the cigarette. Smoke had never tasted so good. Or old reheated coffee. He could almost hear the night murmurs of the joint.

By the time he finished the cigarette, the kitty had edged out from under the desk and dipped her whiskers in the milk.

See. Like a sign.

Gator refilled the cat's bowl, brought the milk carton back into the house, and put it in the refrigerator. Then he took a hot shower, changed into fresh clothes, and heated a fast Hungry Man dinner in the microwave. After he bolted the food, he paced.

Calm down, wait for Sheryl to call.

He glanced out the window, across the yard at the lights in his shop, the spotlight illuminating the tractor in the front. Lot of hard work went into putting that operation together—even if it was a front for something more ambitious.

You gotta keep your eye on the overall plan. Go off half cocked, and you're just like those institutionalized fools on a revolving door. Wait for Sheryl to call. The way it worked, that meant another drive to the phone booth; this time the one in town, outside Perry's grocery.

They communicated strictly by pay phones. She'd call at six. He had some time, so he made a cup of instant coffee and slit the cellophane on a fresh pack of Camels. When the coffee was ready, he sat down at the kitchen table and worked on a difficult corner of the puzzle.

He was good at waiting.

Three end-to-end Camels later, he pulled on his coat, went out, got back in his truck, and drove back toward town. At 5:55 P.M. he was standing in the booth at Perry's IGA on Main Street. He always called her from the Amoco; she always called back at this phone at the grocery store.

The phone rang. Gator snatched it off the hook.

"You called," Sheryl said.

"I got something big for you," Gator said.

"Don't flatter yourself."

"No, I mean I found something big-time serious. It could affect everything. But I need help figuring it out."

"So, tell me."

"Uh-uh, too complicated. You gotta see it. Can you be here tonight?"

"Aw, bullshit," Sheryl said.

Gator heard the stretch in her voice. Reluctant. After the strain they'd been through two weeks ago. "C'mon, Sherylll—"

"Okay, but tonight's out. I was at work all day. I'll leave in the morning." She sounded final.

"See you then," he said and hung up. Back in the truck, driving, thinking; there were words for this expansive feeling. Found money. Luck. Fucking destiny. Whatever.

Nothing to do now but wait for her.

So go home, kick back. Which is what he did. He debated whether to bring the cat into the house. Nah, let her get used to the shop. So he went into the house, tossed a bag of popcorn into the microwave, and set the timer. As the corn started to crack, he went into the living room, thumbed the TV remote, and slipped a *Sopranos* DVD into the machine. While the teaser to the show ran on the screen, he retrieved his popcorn, dumped it in a bowl, and opened a cold can of Mountain Dew. He came back into the room, sat down in the recliner. Put up his feet.

First, the edgy theme music. Tony lighting his big cigar, working down the toll road out of New York City, heading for Jersey. The second season, still had the World Trade Center towers in the New York skyline.

Pleased with himself, he addressed the image on the televison. "Thing is, Tony, you were born with a silver coke spoon in your mouth 'cause your dad was a made guy. Me, I'm a self-made man."

Gator settled back and grinned.

It could work. If the right pieces fell in place. Yes it could. Special Agent Broker. Uh-huh. *Man, I got a feeling you're gonna make a big difference in my life.*

When the phone rang, he dived for it, thinking it was Sheryl, breaking the rules, changing her mind, coming up tonight.

"Gator, it's Cassie . . ."

Oh shit.

"You said you were going to bring me something."

Chapter Twelve

Nina, holding it together, coached Kit through supper. When Broker came back into the house, she was ushering Kit from the kitchen, heading for the stairs, getting ready for bed. For once, Broker was almost thankful for clinical depression; Nina struggled with the most fundamental tasks, like sleep. Getting dressed. Exhausted, focused inward, she missed nuance, mood.

Once she would have spotted the change in the way he moved and nailed him the moment he came through the door. *What's up, Broker? You're all jagged.*

Kit's fast eyes picked up on his edge but channeled it into an extension of her current personal drama. "Ditech?" she asked.

"I'm still looking, honey," Broker said.

"We had a talk," Nina said, her voice thready, as if unraveling with the effort. Then she signaled Kit with a raise of her eyebrows.

Kit balked, pursing her lips, then recited, "If Teddy Klumpe bothers me again, I should use my words and get help from a teacher. No hitting."

"And?" Nina prompted.

"—and tomorrow after school I have to vacuum all the rugs in the house."

"Good," Broker said. "We'll go over it again in the morning. Now, it's time for bed."

Kit huffed, folded her arms across her chest, and marched off toward the stairs. He turned to Nina, lowered his voice. "Maybe you should bunk with her tonight, until I find the kitty."

"There's wolves in the woods," Kit called out. "They'll eat her."

"The wolves don't come down this far," Broker said, and immediately regretted it.

"That's a lie, Dad; you showed me the tracks."

"I'll go out with a bowl of food and shake it. I'll find her. And the elusive rabbit."

"I heard that," Kit sang out, a room away. "She ain't an eloosof rabbit. She's a toy. She's not *real,* Dad."

"Sorry," Broker said. The kid had eyes like a hawk, ears like a bat. "Mom's gonna sleep with you."

Kit did not respond. Dejected, she trudged up the stairs. Nina shrugged, turned, and followed Kit.

First Broker scouted every room on the ground floor, looking for a sign that someone had been in the house. The new Dell computer was undisturbed on the small porch off the kitchen. Living room TV and DVD player still in place. Griffin's old stereo system was still stacked on a wall shelf.

It was a revealing walk-through. He had not, until this crisis, really appreciated how stark their living space was. Three stacks of boxes lined a living room wall where they'd been placed in January, when they moved in. The living room was strewn with the weights Nina used to rehab her shoulder. Triage dictated Broker's housekeeping efforts. Kit was not a TV kid, so, except for Nina's weights, not much went on in the living room. Broker concentrated on the kitchen, the only room in the house that needed to function every day.

His personal pile of boxes filled a corner by the desk. Books mostly, mementos, a few old piles of dusty paperwork stuffed among novels he hadn't read in years. A yearbook from Grand Marais High, circa 1970, poked from the top box. Boxes that had followed him, from closet to closet, for decades. Except now they were in plain view.

He raised the desk blotter. Bill statements verifying the automatic withdrawals on the Hong Kong Visa. A few letters. Nothing seemed disturbed. Then he spotted the letter from John E. at

Washington County, the note and remainder of a pay voucher. Shook his head. Once he'd never have kept anything around that hinted at his past in law enforcement. He reached out his left hand and raised the letter, let it drop, feeling the lingering ache as he extended his fingers. The ragged scar was still slick red where he'd taken a .38 slug through the fleshy pad of his left palm. Last July, disarming a crazy woman in Stillwater. On the Saint Vigilante Thing.

The day after he got shot, he'd followed Nina into the North Dakota Thing.

The North Dakota Thing had played out on a real bad day at the Prairie Island Nuclear Power Plant.

Now here they were in Glacier Falls, eight months later, still trying to fit the pieces back together.

Broker turned away from the gloom that linked these thoughts. Continued his inspection.

If someone had come to rob, they were out of luck. He kept very little cash on hand. Used plastic for their groceries and expenses. The question of rent hadn't really come up with his friend Griffin. Griffin took care of the utilities. They'd settle up later.

Think. Sometimes Kit played with the kitten outside and put food in a bowl on the back porch. Maybe that's how . . .

Immediately he walked through the kitchen and opened the patio door. And there, just outside the door, he saw the orange pellets of Kitty Chow sprinkled on the snow. Back inside, he stared at the phone on the kitchen wall, an old rotary Bakelite model that Kit regarded with awe. A cordless set was plugged into the wall on the counter near the stove.

Call the sheriff's office and say what? Speculate that Klumpe knifed his tire and tried to poison a dog Broker didn't own? How would that sound to a rural sheriff? Like some wimpy overreaction.

He turned away from the phone and walked into the living room. This was the kind of community where a certain amount of solving one's own problems was the norm.

Which brought him in front of a red-and-black-patterned

Hmong quilt hung on a portion of the wall. Nina had picked up the quilt in a Hanoi street market, back in '96. Broker tacked the hems to dowels top and bottom and rigged a cord-and-pulley system so the quilt could be raised.

The purpose was functional, not decorative. He raised it now, tied it off on the hook on the wall, and stared at two stout oak cabinet doors three feet long. Griffin had crafted this locker with stout hasps that Broker kept fastened with a thick Yale lock. He carried the key to the lock on a leather thong around his neck.

The lock and hasps were untouched.

But he withdrew the key and opened the lock, slipped it from the hasps, and opened the sturdy doors. A faint scent of solvent and gun oil seeped from the cabinet.

The interior was taller than the dimensions of the doors suggested and held a built-in gun rack and some shelves, two drawers across the bottom. The rack held a .12-gauge pump shotgun, the heavy-barreled .257 Roberts that Broker favored for whitetail hunting, and an AR-15 semiautomatic assault rifle. A green canvas case lay on a shelf and contained Nina's Colt model 1911 .45-caliber semiautomatic pistol. Four cleaning kits, one for each weapon, were stacked on the shelves. The drawers held empty magazines for the assault rifle, clips for the pistol, and several boxes of ammunition.

His hand briefly touched the black plastic stock of the assault rifle. He selected the shotgun and a box of .00 buck. Then he closed the cabinet, replaced the lock, snapped it shut. Lowered the hanging. Then he set the shotgun against the wall and paused at the foot of the stairs, listening to Nina's voice, reading to Kit.

The bunny would turn up. Always did. Christ, man, settle down. The bowl could have been on the back deck, and the tire could be a slow leak. A defect. The antifreeze in the bowl was real enough. A thrown elbow. Petty payback for his morning. Okay. He could play that game if it came to that.

But he had to find the cat. Kit was right; there were things in the woods that would scarf her up.

So he climbed the stairs, entered the bedroom, and kissed his daughter good night, Nina on the cheek. He reassured Kit that cats always land on their feet. It really wasn't that cold. The kitty would come home to eat. And Old Bun would turn up, like she always did.

After he had helped deliver the necessary clichés, he left them curled up with an American Girl Doll book. He came back down the stairs, put a bowl of cat food on the back deck, rattled it a few times, went inside. As he retrieved the shotgun, he stopped and solidly faced the fact he hadn't kissed his wife on the lips for months. Nor had she offered those lips to be kissed.

Broker pulled on his boots, coat, a felt hat, and gloves. He stepped into the garage and pushed four shells into the shotgun, racked the slide, and set the safe. His gut told him that the door didn't open by itself. The snow had stopped. Four fresh inches made a clean slate of the back deck. Switching on his flashlight, he walked out into the yard. Looking up, he saw that the lights in Kit's bedroom had been turned off. A fitful northwest wind grumbled across the lake. Iron waves muttered on the shore.

Okay. So walk the property. Shotgun slung over his shoulder, flashlight in one hand, he shook the stainless-steel bowl of cat food. The rattle disappeared on divots of wind. As did his voice, mouthing words he never thought he'd ever be saying:

"Here, kitty, kitty . . ."

Chapter Thirteen

Gator went and got what he needed and then found himself making the drive across the Barrens for the fifth time that day. Getting dark now, night creeping down like a black garage door.

He felt lucky; if he'd lived a different kind of life, he might say blessed. This Broker guy, the cop, had fallen into his hand like a gift, he thought as he watched the familiar jack pine and muskeg filling in with ink. He could afford to be magnanimous with Jimmy and Cassie. And besides, giving Cassie her piece of cheese to nibble on would bolster her incentive to keep Jimmy on task. He was shaky, but he'd hang in. Just had to keep them focused on the money . . .

Coming up on the crossroads. Hmmmm?

What's that? Alert behind the wheel, squinting in the twilight. Headlights knifed about a mile through the gloom. On the right side off the road . . . looked like they were over near the old Tindall place.

Gator shut off his headlights and turned off on Z going west, in the direction of the lights. There was just enough reflection off the snow to drive by. Soon he determined that the lights had indeed turned in at the Tindall place. About three hundred yards from the house, he pulled to the shoulder and turned off the engine. Several flashlights dipped and swung, outlining the windows of the old house.

Gator slouched back behind the wheel, reached for his smokes; decided to wait and watch. File it away for future reference.

There were five deserted farmhouses on Z alone. Another dozen sprinkled through the Barrens. Several times a week he would do a drive-by. Sometimes kids from town partied in the houses. And sometimes outsiders slipped in for less convivial reasons. Gator made a point to run them off. He kept the Barrens free of intruders. It was his buffer zone.

Sometimes outsiders coming in could be tough-guy wannabes, so Gator took more than a flashlight along on these nocturnal forays. Technically, as a felon, he had lost his right to own firearms. But Keith had sat down with Gator's parole officer and the game warden and worked out an accommodation. As long as Gator continued to sniff out meth operations in the remote north end of the county, where Keith didn't have the manpower to patrol, he could carry a gun north of Z to hunt in the big woods.

Tonight, he'd left his pistol back at the shop. Hell, being in such a good mood, Gator didn't feel like stomping in and wrecking somebody's party.

He started the truck, made a U-turn, headed back to 12. Half an hour later he was coming down Lakeside Road on the west side of the lake, thinking as he drove how he could spin this playground tiff with Teddy into something useful. Seeing's how Keith had already been on the scene . . .

He was good at plans. Hell, he figured out most movie plots in the first half hour.

Plus he could give Jimmy some responsibility. Jack him up.

Jimmy Klumpe. Gator shook his head, leaned back in his seat, and ran through Jimmy's story. Like the regulars at Skeet's Bar observed after a few beers: Jimmy Klumpe had won the Moose Lottery.

———

Jimmy's money dilemma started when his mom and dad were driving home from the little casino near Thief River Falls, three years ago January. Icy roads and a ground fog were a contributing factor, Keith Nygard wrote in his report. They rounded a turn, possibly too fast. Old Tom was known to have a heavy foot and also was an authority on everything, including how fast to drive on slick back roads. What it turned out he wasn't so smart about was the bull moose that trotted right through a barbed-wire fence and into the path of his old Bonneville. They died instantly, Ed Durning, the medical examiner, said. In an explosion of air bags, trailing barbed wire, entrails, and moose shit, Keith Nygard said. Took two hours with the jaws of life for the Fire and Rescue boys from Thief River Falls to free the antlers that had pinned the bodies in the front seat.

Jimmy, an only child, turned out to be the beneficiary on their life insurance policies, and found himself in possession of a million bucks. Up till then, Jimmy's life had been all downhill since he was homecoming king to Cassie's queen senior year. He always drank a little too much and stayed tangled in family apron strings, marking time as a driver at his dad's garbage company. Now he had inherited his dad's house on the lake and Klumpe Sanitation, which consisted of three trucks, a garage, the dump, and the county contract.

Nine years ago Cassie had married Jimmy. Which Gator thought was a dumb idea, knocked up or not. Marrying a garbage truck driver who likely as not ended Friday night facedown on Skeet's bar. Five months later Teddy was born. Gator did admit that Cassie had cleaned up her act and was working as a receptionist at True North Realty in town. She was positioned to watch the lakefront boom start to take off.

They made their fresh start about the time Gator started his bit in Stillwater. They sold their rambler in town and moved into the vacant Klumpe family house on Big Glacier. After an initial spending spree—a new bathroom, a Jeep Cherokee, a snowmobile, a sixteen-foot Lund—Cassie settled on a plan. The lakefront on Big Glacier was sewn up, but Little Glacier, to the north, was still open.

Gator, hearing of the insurance windfall, suddenly transformed himself into an attentive letter writer and devoted brother—"Really, Cassie, you owe me something for that thing I did on your behalf a certain October in high school." Cassie coughed up a modest investment so Gator could turn the garage on the old farm into a tractor restoration shop when he got out of prison.

Jimmy and Cassie got ahead of the real estate market and spent their windfall on three thousand feet of lakefront on Little Glacier, planning to divide it into ten lots. They hired an architect, settled on a set of plans, and went to the bank for a construction loan. They secured the loan and broke ground on a model lake home. Once the first house sold, they'd roll over the profit and build another until they had built on all ten lots.

Gator, the model prisoner, did his time and returned to Glacier County with a business plan to rehabilitate his criminal ass. He had a supportive parole officer, a new set of tools, an air compressor, and sixteen hot antique tractors sitting in the junkyard behind his shop.

Then came the fatal day that Cassie agreed to watch the neighbor's three-and-a-half-year-old daughter, Marci. Except she had an appointment at the spa in Bemidji to get a body wrap and her legs waxed. So she called their freaky cousin, Sandy, to watch Marci while she drove to Bemidji to soak in seaweed . . .

Dumb.

But the way Gator had worked it out was . . . well . . . nothing short of fucking brilliant.

For him, at least.

Gator wheeled up the drive of the dark house hooded with gables where old Tom Klumpe never used to give the kids candy on Halloween; where, in fact, Gator and Keith, twelve years old, had set a bag of cow pies on fire on Tom's doormat one Halloween and rung the bell.

He parked the truck and trudged up the porch steps, heard the loud beat of voice-over aerobic music. Anticipating the bittersweet headache he'd have by the time he left, he rang the bell.

The music stopped, and a moment later Cassie opened the door. She still looked great on the outside, but her eyes gave away the inside; two empty blue holes screaming to be filled. She was barefoot, wearing these little red gym shorts that rode up, revealing the start of her rear end. Her white tube top was damp and clingy with sweat. She had her hair heaped in a wild pony spray, fastening by a silver headband. Seeing the tallowy perspiration on her throat and arms still could halt his breath.

"You must have the heat turned way up," he said.

"What?" she said.

"That outfit."

"I was doing an exercise tape. C'mon in," she said, staring at his left hand. The way his fingers curled, holding something. Noting her attention, he withdrew the hand, put it behind his back. "Hey, don't tease me, now," she pouted, moving into his path, grabbing for his hand. They bumped torsos, then the sibling roughhouse got stuck hot at the hips. She reached around, trying to catch his hand.

"Hey, not so needy," Gator danced to the side, grinning, leaning back, loving the unbridled covetousness surging in her eyes. "You're starting to like this stuff way too much, probably should taper you off . . ."

"Gimme," Cassie demanded, flinging both arms around him, grasping.

"Said you just wanted to lose some weight. Looks to me like you lost it," Gator now held his hand straight in the air, making her go up on tiptoes. "Okay, you can have it if you promise me you'll stop—"

"Christsake, Gator, stop playing games."

"Promise me."

"Okay, I promise," she said, heaving her eyes.

Gator let the folded square of Reynold's Wrap drop from his palm. It glittered between them and landed on the floor. She immediately stooped and snatched it up, and as she started back up, he placed a heavy hand on her shoulder, holding her face level with his belt buckle.

Then he removed his hand and stepped back. Serious now. "Don't go smoking this stuff, you understand," he said.

"Not me," she said, making the packet disappear in the waistband of her shorts.

"So how's Teddy doing?" Gator said, staring at her throat, feeling his temples start to throb.

"He's okay, upstairs finishing his homework."

"Jimmy?"

"In the basement, watching an old Vikes-Packer game on Teevo."

"Get him," Gator said with muted authority, not taking off his coat. "You both should hear this."

Cassie padded off across the barnlike living room with the old brown leather chairs and couch she hated and called down the stairwell, "Jimmy, Gator's here." Then she hurried toward the kitchen, where Gator heard the door to the downstairs bathroom close.

While he waited, Gator looked over the living room, then the dining room with its lace curtains, framed duck stamps, and club-footed oak table. No wonder she was half nuts, living in this museum with Jimmy, doing her Buns of Steel tapes.

She kept it clean, though. Wasn't at all like Mom in that regard, except that she married a drunk.

Jimmy came up the stairs with a tall water glass of Jack Daniel's. His eyes were a medium blur at 8:00 P.M. Little dots of crumbly yellow junk food were smeared on his T-shirt. Popcorn maybe. When Cassie walked back into the dining room, she was much improved.

"Sit down," Gator said, indicating the dining room table with a toss of his right hand.

They sat.

"I had a look at your Broker guy," Gator said.

"And?" Cassie said. "Was I right?"

"You got no idea how right," Gator said, grinning, unable to suppress his pleasure.

Jimmy and Cassie exchanged looks. "So, what?" Cassie said.

"I got in his house and looked around. Saw some stuff. I think he was a cop down in the cities," Gator said.

"Jesus," Jimmy muttered and stared glumly into his glass. "You think he knows?"

"Not sure what he'd doing here. But I got an idea how to find out," Gator said. "The thing with Teddy, where you want that to go?"

"We want an apology, right," Jimmy said, glancing at Cassie, who nodded her agreement. "But a cop, jeez, I dunno . . ."

"Okay, here's the deal. I got a job for you." Gator leveled his eyes on Jimmy like he was a trusted lieutenant. "Jimmy, I need you to mess with him a little, just kid stuff."

"Like what kind of stuff?" Jimmy said, sitting up straighter. Cassie, her color up, her eyes now full and steamy, watched the play between the two men. Real curious.

"In the morning your guys pick up on Twelve, right?" Gator said.

"Yeah."

"So, you take the route, get there early when he's taking the kid to school, and do that trick with the mechanical claw so you tip over his garbage, fling it along the ditch. So he sees you. Do it so it looks like he put it out wrong."

"I can do that," Jimmy said.

"Just some little crap to drive the guy nuts, but not so he can prove anything. If he comes at you again, it'll give Keith something to do. You know how he loves to play Mr. In-Between."

Jimmy nodded. "Shoulda been a Lutheran minister, like his dad."

"Yeah," Gator said. "Plus, Keith's having a bad winter, since he had to put out that ordinance keeping trucks and sleds off the lake 'cause it didn't completely freeze over."

"Might cost him the election," Jimmy nodded.

"Yeah," Gator said, "needs something to do, so maybe if it gets going back and forth between you and Broker, Keith'll check him out, and it'll get back to us who he is. Worth a try."

"Uh-huh. So just little stuff," Jimmy said, more confident now.

"Yeah, but he'll be pissed. He might come at you. Hell, we want him to. Can you handle that?"

"Sure, Gator." Jimmy squared his thick shoulders. "Woulda nailed his ass today except I slipped on the ice."

"I hear you. So, tomorrow morning," Gator said.

"Piece of cake. People always leave the containers out back-asswards so they flip off the claw," Jimmy said.

"Good." Gator smiled, pleased with the way he set it in motion, giving orders sort of low-key. Like a good boss should. To underscore the point, he slapped Jimmy on the shoulder, comradelike. "Can't really tell you all of it, but I got a feeling we're getting close, huh."

"I'm for that," Jimmy said.

"Okay. I gotta go," Gator said. Cassie walked him to the door.

"You know what you're doing," she said happily. Not a question, eyes merry with the meth she'd eaten. This raspberry flush spreading up from the top of her tube top, creeping up to her collarbones, the smooth shoulders . . .

"Just don't smoke it, go easy," he cautioned, pulling his eyes away. Going out the door.

He sat in the truck waiting on the heater for a few minutes, watching the lights in the house. Maybe they wouldn't bicker about money tonight. Maybe Cassie would take his big ass to bed, shut her eyes, and pretend he was somebody else. Satisfied, he put the truck in gear and started down the drive. Musing.

Some crew he had. His desperate cash-strapped lush of a brother-in-law and his not quite reformed nympho meth-addled sister. Plus Sheryl, his biker groupie turned waitress.

Thing was, his plan was so good, not even this bunch of screw-ups could mess it up.

He had to believe that.

Half an hour later he came up on the crossroads and took the turn on Z, turned off his lights again, and coasted up to the empty farmhouse. This time he got out and walked close enough to hear rap music banging on the faint breeze. Lights swirling in the windows. Must have a battery CD player. Little rave going in there; good, keep it up. He turned and walked back to his truck. One of these days, he'd be back.

Chapter Fourteen

Broker started in the garage. No tiny paw prints led from the garage back door; a dusting of new snow where Kit had shoveled was unmarked. Then he got lucky. Kit had not been super-conscientious about her cleaning along the edge of the deck. He set down the bowl of cat food and studied the pattern of imprints filled in with fresh snow, spaced like footsteps next to the rail.

Way to go, Kit. Okay.

Broker exhaled, went down a level.

Someone had been here, had slipped over the rail.

It took a few minutes peering over the flashlight, but Broker saw enough to get a gut check on how the night visitor had entered and exited the yard. Came in serpentine, stepping in existing tracks. No new cleat marks, only the pattern of Kit's Sorels and Broker's Eccos along with the prints of their ski boots. But even filling in with fresh snow, Broker could see that those prints were mashed out where the intruder had stepped, widened.

Like the newer tracks off the deck.

Uh-huh. So you tied cloth on your boots to mask your tracks.

It took another ten minutes to follow the tracks through the edge of the woods. They led to the connecting path to the state ski trail. Where they vanished.

More stooping, more studying impressions in the snow. The path appeared undisturbed since their afternoon ski run. Just the wide-angled splay of Kit's skis next to Broker's parallel tracks.

But the parallel tracks were cleaner, the snow firmed by pressure.

Broker thought back to all the skiers on the trail this afternoon. *Okay, so you're smart. You came in on skis, stayed in the tracks I made earlier today.* Stepped out of the bindings, slipped some kind of wrap on his boots. Went in, came out, took off the wrap, and stepped back into the skis. Turned the skis around without disturbing the tracks. Not some casual vandal. *You put effort and planning into this.*

He straightened up, turned off the flashlight, and shook out his senses. He smelled the faint camphor of pine and frozen resin. Felt the invisible wall of cold up close. Almost silent now. Just the wind shifting through the pine needles; here and there dry dead branches rattled. Hazy moonlight sifted down through the tall old red and white pines and traced northern European shadows on the snow, bent and twisted together like stained-glass patterns. Could see where the Gothic cathedrals got their start, in among trees like this.

The trail beckoned, a curving band of open white.

At home in the woods, aren't you. Confident.

Broker had made a life of high-wire work, shifting his balancing act between caution and impulse. Going with his gut. With mood. At the moment he was still mainly curious; so he walked slowly up the trail.

Each step brought him closer to a bad feeling, so he instinctively tempered his curiosity with caution. Somebody this tricky could still be out here. He slipped off the trail into the trees. Focused now, ignoring the raw cold.

Took three slow, silent steps, stopped, and listened. Then repeated the pattern. An Australian sergeant had taught the still-hunting routine to Broker and Griffin at the MACV-SOG Recondo school in Da Nang. "Takes forever," a young Broker had protested.

The Aussie had cut them with the bemused utter contempt he reserved for regular American troops. "The object, mate, is to get to the other side of the fuckin' woods alive."

Broker had come home alive and trusted the method. It took him ten minutes to cover the two hundred yards to the end of

Griffin's land. He came to the yellow No Hunting sign posted on the property line where the connecting trail T-boned into the broader ski trail.

He stopped dead still, his alertness total and jagged, like a snapped tuning fork. Faint but definite, he heard a tinkle on the wind. Broker stood unmoving. There it was again.

He experienced a flush of almost preadolescent excitement. He could picture the smile on Kit's face. When Daddy found the kitty.

Okay. Don't blow it. Gotta spot her.

Slowly, straining his eyes in the haze of moonlight, he scrutinized the surrounding trees, stopping at the center of the T formed by the trail intersection.

This slender vertical shadow.

Out of place. Stark against the snow. A dark lump at the top.

Now impulse rushed to the surface, but he reined in the dark intuition that propelled him forward. It was Broker's nature to go quiet now, to keep his anger cold and controlled, to save it up. He stepped from the cover of the trees.

So this is how it is.

He removed his glove and reached out his right hand. Old Bun leaking stuffing. Impaled on one of Kit's ski poles, the handle driven deep into the snow.

Tenderly he patted the stuffed animal, then froze again when the movement caused Ditech's collar, carefully buckled around the bunny's neck, to jingle.

His experience dictated that he back off a space, take inventory. He was a little awed at the bile that rose in his throat. He'd stalked and collared men for the state of Minnesota. And he'd killed enemy soldiers in combat—that was a certain type of work.

He'd descended to the bottom of the adrenaline fear tank and made all the stations coming up. Never felt quite like this . . .

Klumpe. Coming at my kid.

So this was hatred. Nothing clean about it. Just visceral dirty rage. A hunk of rotten meat stuck in his throat.

At my kid.

Training and experience fell away. Fucker had been in the house, had taken Kit's stuffed animal from her bed. He back-tracked through the day. *When we were on the ski trail. Could have been in the house when Nina was asleep. When I left the cat in the garage. He could have been there, hiding. Snatched her, went over the deck rail . . .*

Ambush alert now, he half crouched, shotgun at port arms, and listened carefully.

Slowly he rotated his head and scanned the surrounding dark-ness. Listened again. Nothing but the soft wind rubbing the dry branches together, the heave and murmur of the pines. After another ten minutes of listening, he decided he was out here all alone. He removed a tinfoil pouch of cigars from his pocket, selected one of the rough wraps, took out his lighter, and lit the cigar. Then he squatted, Vietnamese peasant fashion, by the side of the trail, smoked, and thought about it as it began to snow again.

Jimmy Klumpe's face, this morning in the cab of the garbage truck, on the sidewalk in front of the school yesterday morning—his nutty wife yelling from the truck. Striking back against him and Kit. Had to be.

Broker shifted his weight, drew on the cigar, and studied the pole stuck carefully in the snow. At the exact intersection of two trails.

Like a signal. A warning. Back off.

Because my kid hit their kid . . .

He flicked the coal from the cigar, shredded the rolled leaves, and tossed them aside.The snow sailed down like forgetfulness, blurring the edges of the tracks in the woods, filling them in. He took one more look at the vertical ski pole. Leave it undisturbed for now. Make sure Kit didn't come here. He turned and started back to the house. Had to think this through. Maybe call Griffin. Bring him out to see this.

But not tonight.

Broker came around the garage and saw Nina sitting on the back steps before she saw him. He quickly rerouted around the garage, went in the front door, entered the kitchen, went into the living room, and tucked the shotgun in the couch cushions, out of sight. Then he retraced his steps back around the garage and approached her. It was a giant step, her coming outside at night. She was layered in fleece, boots, and a parka. Smoking. Holding a cup of coffee. She had removed the tangled braids from her hair.

"I saw your light in the woods. Any luck?" she asked.

He shook his head. "If the cat isn't back by morning, then it doesn't look good." He nodded up toward the bedroom. "How's she doing?"

"Whatever else we did, we didn't make a neurotic kid. Nothing gets between her and her sleep." Nina shifted, making room for him on the deck cushion she was sitting on. He sat next to her. She produced a steaming thermal cup from her lap and passed it.

The fresh hot coffee would keep him up. He only took a sip. He needed to sleep. See it fresh in the morning. He handed the cup back. Instinctively, they scooted closer together to keep warm. They watched the snow stream down. Every dizzy snowflake could have been a thought unsaid between them, building into a slow storm of unspoken words. She took out her American Spirits, cupped her hand, and thumbed her lighter. She inhaled, exhaled. He put his arm around her.

The snow came faster, no longer serene. Like confusion.

Finally Broker asked, "Where is it?"

Nina looked up to him with calm eyes. "In the woods. It stays mainly in the woods now."

They'd evolved a code to simplify the overwrought discussion; back in December, they'd talked it to death, and all the talk had just worn them out. So they settled on *it*. The depression. Winston Churchill's black dog.

Progress. Two months ago, when he'd asked where *it* was, she'd answer, walking on live grenades, "In the house."

He tightened his arm around her shoulders, and stared into the woods where'd he'd just been. Once she'd had strong shoulders and they would be strong again. But right now they didn't need the extra weight.

Broker pulled his eyes away from everything that could be pacing back and forth in the woods tonight and said, "C'mon, let's go inside."

She cocked her head, and he saw a flicker of her old smile; tough, smart, wry. "Nah, I'll sit awhile, finish my smoke."

His forehead bunched in concern, but also a ray of hope. "You sure?"

"Yeah, I'm sure. Take off."

He rose to his feet. "You'll stay right here on the porch, right?"

Nina shrugged, then turned back to her meditation on the woods. Going into the kitchen and shutting the door behind him, Broker glanced back, at her hunched hooded figure sitting alone on the deck.

First time in three months she'd stayed outside the house alone at night.

Nina Pryce tried to stare down the snow. It kept coming at her eyes, like pinwheeling hooks of panic. Pulling at her. Only a fragile connection with the solidity of the deck under her butt kept her from launching weightless into the swirling night.

One step removed from the snare of deep space . . .

She dragged on the Spirit, exhaled, and wished she'd taken a bullet on her last assignment, with Delta Team Northern Route. She'd come back from a bullet before. Instead she'd dropped her guard for a moment and had lost two buddies, the use of her right arm . . .

And her mind.

Now, after eight months of unrestricted sick leave, she faced the dark woods without illusions.

When she was a little girl, she had sat on her grandfather's lap and listened while he tried to explain living through the Great Depression. How he had once stood in an unemployment line in Chicago, rubbing his last two dirty copper pennies together in his pocket.

I hear you, Grandpa.

All the energy she could muster came from the friction of rubbing her last two pennies together. Broker and Kit. Last two pennies.

Nina suffered alone, without God. She'd operated in some of the great shitholes of the world and came away an unambiguous Hobbesian; man was a devious tool-making animal who was kept in line mainly through fear of his own violent death.

She had been part of a thin green line that made that fear palpable to Iraqis, Serbs, Filipino guerrillas, and Al Qaeda operatives.

Even in the depths of clinical depression, her mind was practical. It was all about energy. As a serious athlete in her youth, she understood that competition was psychologically anchored, mind over matter. Her body had been the testing ground in which she learned to function through pain. In the Army she'd upped the ante and performed through fear and even dread. When it got rough, she'd always relied on an unmovable part of herself to brace on. She had always taken her mind for granted. She'd absolutely believed that her willpower would still be kicking an hour after she was dead.

But then, a week before last Christmas, the source of her will, her mind itself, had failed. At the first sign of panic, she reached down deep to brace and fight back. To her immense surprise, the solid baseline gave way, and she catapulted off into an internal void. With nowhere to plant the fulcrum of her will, there was no way to direct her energy. She lost gravity. She lost up and down.

Worst time of her life.

Worse than the confused sandstorm fight in the dunes during Desert Storm, when she became the first woman in the history of the U.S. Army to be awarded the Combat Infantry Badge. Worse even than the death struggle with George Khari last July, when she wrecked her shoulder.

Finally, she was feeling a little traction. Maybe it was finally getting out of her own head long enough to see Broker struggling alone, nursing her, trying to take care of Kit. Something.

She'd earned the Distinguished Service Cross, the Silver Star, two Bronze Stars, and three Purple Hearts. And on this chilly evening she was making the scariest night jump of her life by merely sitting alone and facing the dark.

She puffed on the cigarette. The soldier's friend. As long as you had a smoke, you were never alone. Civilians pulled mere smoke into their lungs. Soldiers sucked in their fear. She clutched her cigarette, managed a tiny grin at how she'd wound up more of a fraidy-cat than she'd been as a five-year-old sitting on her grandpa's knee.

Christ. At five, I wasn't afraid of the dark.

Chapter Fifteen

Four-thirty in the morning. Broker and Kit were sound asleep, Kit in her bed, Broker curled on the living room couch. The TV was silent. Nina had tightly shut the kitchen door and now sat, elbow on the kitchen table, arm wrestling with a fifteen-pound barbell. By the light of the solitary lamp next to the indestructible snake plant, she studied the weight in her right hand, removed the cigarette from her lips, put it in the ashtray on the table. Took a deep breath. Then, methodically, she raised the compact hunk of iron. At between fifteen and twenty degrees of arc, she made a face. Not quite pain, more frustration.

Sonofabitch.

The warning light popped on the fifth repetition. A huge drag of fatigue. Then she raised the weight over her head, and the shoulder failed between 80 and 120 degrees; the classic painful arc.

She pictured the architecture of her rotator cuff; in her case, a train wreck where the coracoacromial ligament mashed into the acromion. The wear and tear of the life she'd lived had reduced the cushioning bursa to a blown-out tire. Useless.

What the doctors called a type 2 impingement; irreversibly damaged tissue.

She'd faked it for years out of denial, ignoring pain. She eeked out a few more years with concealed cortisone injections, gobbling anti-inflammatory drugs. On leave, when Kit was born, she'd slipped into a hospital in Duluth, Minnesota, for outpatient orthoscopic decompression surgery to trim back the ligament and bone. The tattoo on her shoulder concealed the scars, like it hid the cortisone needle marks. Didn't even tell Broker. That bought a few more years.

To prepare for her last Army PT test, she'd gone out on the street to score Oxycontin to blur the pain . . .

Christ. If it binds like this at fifteen, how'll I ever get to twenty-five . . .

Head snapping around, alert.

Something . . .

A tremble at the corner of her eye. And a low moaning sound that she couldn't place. Then, looking out the windows, she saw a faint wrinkle tug at the darkness. She dropped the weight, got to her feet, and switched off the single light. As her eyes adjusted to the darkness, the ragged black fringe of tree line across the lake sharpened and—moved? No. The motion was above the trees, in the sky.

Squinting, she made out the tall pliant silver-green towers, an electric Stonehenge swaying in a tapestry of constellations.

She was drawn to the eerie light. Anything that pushed back the darkness.

She pulled on her jacket, opened the patio door, and stepped out on the back deck. The sheer visual power of the northern lights commanded her to tilt up her head, and she almost forgot herself as the icy wind sucked the heat from her lungs in a frosty plume.

So cold she could feel the water snap. Little arrowheads of windowpane stuck in the crannies of the granite boulders along the shore.

Then the wind, honed on a million pine needles, ripped open an acoustic tunnel in the night, and straight down that tunnel raced the baying of the wolves who owned that creepy forest up north. Eyes pinned on the sky, ears ringing with the howls, she had an impression of an utterly hostile beauty.

In which she had no permanent place.

Time and isolation for a cure. Up in Glacier County. Right as usual, Broker, honey.

Wolves. The sky dripping icy midnight fire. The thrill of atavistic fear and dumb wonder almost spooked her out of the heavy inertia.

She shivered.

Christ, she wondered as she hugged herself. Which was colder, the thing that wouldn't stop turning in her mind, or the frigid wind? But even the pull of the dancing sky lights and the howling wolves could not slow her own personal flickering images . . .

. . . the pictures that played over and over in her head.

So she darted back into the kitchen and turned on all the lights. Then the TV. Poured a cup of coffee and lit another Spirit.

Broker had called it exactly. She was stuck in those three seconds, eight months ago. What Broker did not comprehend was that she was doing it to herself.

Northern Route had been a pure seat-of-the-pants operation. A batch of misfits willing to go off the reservation. They'd exceeded their orders on an unsanctioned high-stakes gamble to stop what they thought was a tactical nuke coming into the country. Intel suggested that Al Qaeda was using an American smuggling operation to bring it in across the North Dakota border.

They picked Nina because she'd played a few undercover games for Seal Team Six in Bosnia-Herzegovina. A novelty. The guys in special ops called them "Swallows," the extreme military gals attached to them, like Nina and Jane Singer, in lurid appreciation of how far they might have to go to get close to a target.

What the hell. At the time her marriage was on the rocks; she and Broker were separated. So she rolled the dice. Even used Kit in the play, and drew in Broker for added backup.

Her job was to get close to North Dakota bar owner Ace Shuster, who turned out to be a likable, handsome drunk with a chivalrous streak. Nina had spent several nights in Shuster's bed. But he had slept on the couch.

She had been totally unprepared to be courted.

And when they descended on him and his load of contraband, it turned out to be Cuban cigars.

The maverick operation was called off. Homeland Security was pissed. The Joint Special Ops Command at Bragg was furious at the spectacle of a Blackhawk helicopter and elements of a Delta troop being diverted into the North Dakota wheat fields. It looked like a career ender. •

These facts affected her mood that next morning when she impulsively decided to drop by the bar and say something to Ace. Her second lapse of judgment was leaving her personal weapon behind.

Because when she and Janey walked into the bar, the real bad guys in the smuggling operation were waiting.

In the end it all came down to that moment in the Missile Park bar.

She played it over and over, like a tape on a loop. And she had the remote in her hand. Just wouldn't stop thumbing the controls. Hit play: there's Joe Reed coming through the back door, holding the pistol in a two-handed grip. She watched herself yell, reaching for her pistol. Saw her hand coming up empty. Janey swinging around, bringing up her nine. Ace Shuster in motion. Janey taking the first bullet in her chest. Stop. Rewind. Play the stunned expression on Janey's youthful face. Reed efficiently shooting Janey a second and third time as she went down. Then Reed swung the gun on Nina. She played this part a thousand times. Never did get to see Ace's face.

When he put his body in front of the fourth and fifth shots.

And saved her life.

Then that asshole, Dale—Ace's loony brother—stabbed her with the syringe of ketamine.

Stop. Rewind. Play. Janey's stunned expression again. The protest in her eyes. Hey! Wait a sec, this is way more tomboy shit than I bargained for . . .

Janey gone.

Ace gone.

The tape played endlessly, the same several seconds over and over. Because that was Nina's role that day. To watch.

A witness to the death of Janey and Ace and by implication Colonel Wood—Holly—and the people who died at Prairie Island.

And every day since, she watched the creases of worry etch deeper in Broker's face when he looked at her, at Kit. As he contemplated the radioactivity that might have slipped into his blood and bones spawning tiny milky scurries of cancer and leukemia . . .

So she fixated day and night on editing the tape. Make a new tape titled "If Only" . . .

Rewind. Stop. Play Nina shouting, reaching for her pistol. If only . . .

She got up, eased open the door, padded into the living room, and stood over the couch where Broker lay sleeping. His face was obscure in the darkness but she knew his face; the way, even under all the strain, it relaxed into an unlined boyish reverie when he slept.

———

The first time she ever saw him, she was younger than Kit. Thirteen years separated them. Her dad had squired Broker through the bad fight in Quang Tri City. Brought him back, with his war twin, Griffin, to run the Ranger course at Benning. The two of them appeared in the cramped backyard of the tiny house where the Army billeted Major Ray Pryce and his family. The summer of '73.

Even at seven, Nina understood you sorted men by what they wore on their chests. Dad said there were two kinds of soldiers: the kind that fight, and the other kind. Broker and Griffin were identically lean and blooded in spitshined jump boots, new Ranger tabs, CIB and jump wings over the two rows of ribbons above the left blouse pocket of their summer khakis. Even the individual ribbons were the same: Silver Star, Bronze Star, and Purple Heart on top.

Her mom had called her to the kitchen and sent her back into the yard, carefully clutching three frosted bottles of Lone Star beer.

She sat in her dad's lap, long used to the smell of beer and cigar, while he harangued against the Army, the war. The stupidity of taking the 101st off jump status, putting them in helicopters.

She remembered every word he said. "See these two boys, Kit. They're American Praetorians. That's what the airborne and the marines divisions are, the volunteer backbone. This special operations crap we're stuck in just goes on missions—hell, airborne and marine divisions win wars . . ."

But not that war, Daddy.

She remembered his words because they were some of the last words she ever heard from his mouth. Two days later he took his two boys back to Vietnam. He left before dawn, coming into her room and kissing her gently on the forehead, whispering so as not to wake her, "I love you, Kit. I'll always love you." Softly his blunt fingers caressed her chest. "Remember, you have a Pryce heart in your chest. Don't quit, honey; don't cry."

She had fought her way up through sleep and reached out her arms.

"Daddy?"

But he was gone. And this time he didn't come back. Not even his body.

Nina bent over her sleeping husband and wanted to reassure him; she knew he feared the consequences of being exposed to radiation at Prairie Island. Feared that cancer was simmering in his blood, his bones. *You won't get cancer, Broker. You're not the type.* Her mother had died of breast cancer. But her mother had given in. Five years after her husband was taken off the missing list and presumed dead, she compromised and married a creep. She gave up.

Nina believed that Broker would never get cancer because he didn't know how to give up.

She backed out of the living room and pulled the door shut behind her. What Broker didn't understand was that the greatest fear and sense of loss she suffered was not for her dead comrades.

Of course she grieved. With her arm in a sling, she attended three funerals. Janey's in North Carolina. Ace Shuster's in Langdon, and Holly's—closed, mostly empty casket—in a military chapel in Arizona. They found about as much of Holly as they did of some 9/11 victims. Some tissue that fit in a DNA-coded envelope.

The point was, *her arm in that fucking sling.* She had lost the use of her right arm, and after eight months of rehab, it wasn't coming back. In the fight with George Khari last July, she had saved her life but destroyed her shoulder. She suspected that the doctors at Bragg had studied her MRIs, knew the problem, and were just giving her time to come to terms with it.

Patronizing her.

She backed away from the thought. Better to keep playing the tape over and over, backing it up, splicing into the seconds, trying to make it come out right. Because that was the real her going into that gunfight. Major Nina Pryce. D-Girl Nina Pryce.

Broker called it her Joan of Arc fantasy. Her uphill fight against the Army patriarchy. She'd soldiered through all the dumb jokes, sent two would-be military rapists staggering away clutching their genitals—*you wanted me to touch it, asshole, you didn't say how* . . . She'd made up her mind: I *will* be the first woman general to fight a brigade in combat. Gone now, all that headstrong bravado.

But if she gave up the drama of that moment, she had to face herself as she was right now: a woman, another mom, closer now to forty than to thirty, with a bum shoulder . . .

Depression was just a waiting room where she paced in a circle until her name was called. She'd go into the doctor's office. The doctor would run her through a simple set of range-of-motion exercises, note that she couldn't remotely bend her elbow and reach up behind her back. Would write on a piece of paper: "Unfit for duty."

Nina shook her head, unwilling to look her demons in the eye: her pride, her arrogance, her willingness to let Broker and Kit follow in the wake of her career like baggage . . .

Shit.

She had always been an unusually gifted tactician. So she knew exactly what she had to do. Just hit the fast-forward button. Accept her life in real time. The way it was now.

Uh-uh. Can't deal with that yet.

So she hit rewind. Then she hit play and watched that last moment: Nina, always getting the jump, ahead of the situation, a kinesthetic fucking intellectual calling the play, going for her gun. There was still that split second before her hand came up empty.

When she was still somebody . . .

Chapter Sixteen

Broker awoke, alert and rested after seven hours on the couch. He reached into the back of the couch cushions, retrieved the shotgun, and unloaded it. He listening carefully for Nina, who was in the kitchen and had been since 4:00 P.M., after a few fitful hours of sleep. He quickly raised the wall quilt, opened the locker with the key around his neck, and replaced the gun and shells. Locked it up and lowered the quilt.

Then he took a quick shower and checked himself in the bathroom as he shaved. Last night's events still glowed in his eyes. Calling for revenge.

But you won't do anything dumb. You'll call Harry, talk it through. Not go rip Klumpe's fat throat out. Agreed? Agreed.

Okay. Because of the readmission conference, he woke Kit at eight, an hour later than usual for a school morning, bringing her a short glass of orange juice and a Sesame Street multivitamin, which he placed on the shelf next to her bed. Then he raised the blinds on her small room's one window. No help there, just gray overcast. Nina would have another bad day. He turned back to the bed, grabbed Kit's toes under the covers, and wiggled them.

"C'mon, get up. Daylight in the swamp."

Kit emerged from a tangle of covers and quilts, stretched, flexed her hand, and studied the stiff scab forming on her skinned knuckles. After she drank the glass of juice Broker held out to her and took her vitamin, she stared straight ahead, blinking the sleep from her eyes. Aware that Broker was watching her especially closely this morning, she said in a stoic voice: "You didn't find Bunny, did you?"

"Not yet." He pictured the toy standing lonely vigil out on the ski trail.

"Did Ditech come home?"

Broker shook his head.

Kit wrinkled her forehead. "She's dead, isn't she? She got in the woods, and some critter ate her."

"We don't know that, not for sure," Broker said. The bunny and the cat. Sounded like a kid's book. Maybe the first real lies he'd ever told his daughter. Two small utilitarian lies.

Kit studied her father. "Where do we go when we die?"

Broker came back glib. "Us, or cats?"

"I mean, when I die, will I get to see Ditech again?"

Blindsided by eight-year-old early-morning judo, Broker gestured vaguely, slow on the uptake. Too slow.

Kit spoke first. "Dooley says, if you believe in God and you're saved, you go to heaven, and it's a perfect place where you have the best times of your life all at once. How come he knows that, and you don't?"

Broker proceeded gently in this terrain. "Dooley doesn't *know* that, honey; he *believes* that."

Kit scooted closer under the covers. "Uh-uh. Dooley is sure. You don't know because you don't believe."

"Well, I believe things that I can prove," Broker said carefully.

"Like?"

Broker looked around, saw a smooth, slightly oblong Lake Superior cobblestone on the dresser. The size of a goose egg. His mother, Irene, had painted it red with white dots and a green sprig, like a strawberry. He reached over, picked it up, and told Kit, "Like . . . hold out your hand."

Kit raised her palm. Broker placed the stone in her hand.

"Now toss it up. Not too high. Just up."

She flipped it up. It rose about a foot and a half and fell back to the comforter.

"Again," Broker said. "Do it four more times."

The stone went up and down five times. Kit picked it up and looked at it. "So?"

"There are physical laws. Everything in the world obeys them. What goes up comes down."

"So?"

Broker tried to say it a different way. "Well, some people, maybe like Dooley, have faith that the stone will keep going up someday. That it won't come down."

"Maybe you got to throw it harder," Kit said.

"No, it's always going to fall back to earth."

Kit knit her brow, plucked up the stone, and deposited it in Broker's hand. "Maybe God isn't a rock. What if God's a bird? A bird won't come down when you throw it in the air."

Before he could respond, Kit let him off the hook by vaulting off the bed and asked, "What's for breakfast?"

Broker blinked several times, not sure he entirely followed what had just happened. "Oatmeal. Now hubba-hubba. You get dressed, and don't forget to comb your hair."

Broker went down the stairs and into the kitchen, which since 4:00 P.M. had been an insomniac zone of nicotine, coffee, and the War in the Box. *"Tanks from the 3rd ID have been pushing up this road all night taking small-arms fire . . ."* Nina stood by the stove making an attempt to blow her cigarette smoke up into the powerful vent fan, watching the drag race to Baghdad.

Broker cleared the debris from her night watch off the counter, scrapped the remains of a sandwich into the garbage—good, at least she was eating.

Her sleep patterns were erratic. Sunny days she had a limited amount of energy and did her exercises. Cloudy days she was a zombie, slept in the afternoon, and walked the kitchen all night, watching cable TV.

He adjusted to her pattern. If she was in the bedroom, he slept on the couch. If she took the couch, he took the bed upstairs. Nights she slept with Kit, he had a choice. Sleeping in the same bed just did not work.

He stacked the plates and glasses and cups in the sink, wiped down the counter, and launched into his routine. Nina moved off as he measured Quaker Oats and milk into a pan and set them on the stove. From the corner of his eye, he checked her fast.

She stared at the dishes stacked in the sink like they were ancient ruins; not quite sure where to start deciphering the puzzle of their archaeology. She'd lost the ground she'd gained last night "Broker, I . . ." The thought lost its trajectory and burned up midway across the space between them. Efficiently, not losing a beat, he put two slices of bread in the toaster. He turned to Nina and asked, "Bad night?"

"Couldn't sleep." Her eyes darted out the windows and fixed on the overcast sky with a look of palpable dread.

He nodded and said nothing as she walked past him, left the kitchen, and went up the stairs. She'd take a shower, try to sleep.

"One eight hundred sandals . . ." Fast glance at the TV. The tanks had disappeared. A happy couple in bathing suits sprinted joyfully into an emerald surf. Broker took a jar of peanut butter and a plastic honey container from the cupboard. *"At Sandals we can please all of the people all of the time . . ."*

He checked the oatmeal, stirred it a few times, then walked to the front of the house and shouted up the stairs, "Five minutes." Then he returned to the kitchen, selected a pear from a bowl on the island, washed it, and sliced it. The toast popped. He checked the oats, turned off the burner, took a wooden tray from the top of the refrigerator, put a bowl on it, shoveled in the oats, sprinkled cinnamon, brown sugar, a pat of butter. Grabbed the remote, turned off the damn televison.

Okay.

Peanut butter and honey on the toast. Milk. He assembled the breakfast on the tray and took it to the living room just as Kit came down the stairs, pulling a comb through the snags in her hair. Best for her to take it in here, away from the lingering cigarette smoke. Broker left Kit with the tray, spooning oatmeal with one hand, pulling the comb through her hair with the other.

"I thought we're going to school late because of the meeting with the principal," Kit said.

"We are, but I gotta drop off the flat tire at the garage."

He stepped into his boots, pulled on a coat, went outside, started the Tundra, cranked up the heater, left it idling. As he walked back to the house, he stopped and scanned the misty gray tree line. The black trunks hanging like roots from the gray fog reminded him of what his dad, a veteran of the Bulge, called Hitler weather.

Then he caught the brown mass of the garbage truck parked up the road, just sitting there in its own cloud of exhaust. To get a better look, he walked down the drive.

The truck started up, then slowed and stopped in a squeal of brakes next to the garbage bin he'd wheeled down to the road last night. A hydraulic whine. The jointed mechanical arm with the pincer arched over the top of the truck descended and fastened on the bin. Then halfway up, the rack jerked and shook the bin sideways, and the cover swung open.

"Hey!" Broker yelled, breaking into a jog as a week's garbage spewed out along the snow-covered ditch. Then the rack released the bin, and it crashed down on its side.

Gears ground as the truck accelerated, but not fast enough to deny Broker a clear glimpse of Jimmy Klumpe's profile, eyes fixed straight ahead, in the foggy windows as the truck pulled away.

Penny-ante bullshit. This time Broker coldly controlled his anger and spent the next couple minutes swearing under his breath as he collected the soggy garbage barehanded and shoved it back in the bin. Then he walked up the drive, got in the truck, drove down, got out, lowered the tailgate, hoisted the heavy bin into the bed next to the flat tire. His conversation with the reasonable man in the bathroom mirror was nowhere in sight.

Well, two can play this silly game.

Broker stopped in town at Luchta's Garage and told Kit not to unfasten her seat belt. Stay put. Then he got out, lifted the tire from the truck bed, and carried it in through the service door. A wiry older man in blue overalls regarded him over a short-stemmed pipe.

"Got a flat, some kind of puncture," Broker said.

The old guy jerked his pipe at a Dodge Ram dually up on the rack. "Can't get to it till afternoon." Then he jabbed the pipe at the wall. "Set it down there."

Broker left the tire and followed the guy into the small office, where the guy scrawled something unreadable on a numbered tagged, handed it to Broker.

The guy studied him. "You're the new guy out at the Hamre place Harry Griffin bought and fixed up."

"Yeah," Broker said.

"Uh-huh, that's Harry's truck I got up on the lift. Tell him I'm still waiting on the part," the old guy said, continuing his inspection. "Be ready this afternoon."

Coming up on the school, Broker turned and eyed Kit in the back seat. "So you just sit up straight and say 'Yes ma'am' and we'll get through this . . . okay?"

She stared straight ahead as they pulled into the school parking lot. Like an echo of yesterday morning, the playground was filled with kids who, undeterred by the gloomy sky, romped in the snow.

Broker half expected the garbage truck to be parked at the curb. Klumpe in the office, waiting for him. Be cool. Save it up. Don't give him the satisfaction.

No garbage truck and no brown Ford F-150. Okay. Doing his best to look humble, Broker ushered Kit into the school. They went in the office and sat in two of the three chairs that faced the receptionist's counter.

They were five minutes early for the meeting. No sign of the other family. The receptionist nodded, noting their arrival, got up from her chair, knocked on the principal's office, stuck in her head, said something, then returned to her chair.

Broker watched Kit, who had fixed her eyes on the second hand sweeping around the clock on the wall. When the minute hand nudged onto the 12, Mrs. Helseth emerged from her office and summoned them with an open hand, not unkindly: "Mr. Broker, Kit."

They entered the office and took the chairs in front of the desk. Kit sat up straight and stared at the principal. Broker was satisfied that her face was alert and not defiant.

The principal stood behind her desk for twenty seconds, silently observing. Then she said, "Kit, have you had time to think about what happened yesterday?"

"Yes, ma'am. If I get picked on again, I should use words. And, ah, no hitting."

"Good. And that's not a bad idea even if you don't get picked on."

"Yes, ma'am," Kit said.

"Fine. Now we're going to make two changes, one temporary, one permanent. For the rest of the week you'll be staying in during recess. And you'll be moved to a new home base so you and Teddy are in different classes."

"Yes, ma'am."

"That's all, Kit. You can go into the office, and Ms. Hatch will help you get settled in. Your dad and I are going to talk a little more."

Kit looked at Broker, who nodded. She stood up, shouldered her book bag. Helseth walked her into the office, conferred with the receptionist briefly, then came back in and closed the door. This time she sat down in the chair next to Broker, the one Kit had been in.

"We'll forgo the usual mediation process in this case, after the scene between Jimmy Klumpe and yourself," she said, staring down at the floor. "Frankly, I don't think it would make any progress. We'll take some extra precautions to minimize flash points between Teddy and Kit." She inhaled and said, "It's probably better to find an informal way to smooth things down outside the school. Between the families." She raised her eyes and looked directly at Broker to see if he got the point.

"I'm not sure . . ."

"Keith, Sheriff Nygard, he's good at this sort of thing. Maybe you should talk to him."

"Mrs. Helseth, I'm missing some information here. What's so special about this case?" Broker said directly.

"Talk to Keith. That's my best advice."

"Okay, I'll sure think about it." Then Broker thanked Trudi Helseth, shook her hand, and left the office. In the hall he encountered Susan Hatch standing by the front door. She was wearing her coat.

"Kit's settled in to her new home base. I'll keep an eye on her," Susan said.

"Thanks," Broker said. She didn't leave, just stood waiting, so he held the door open for her. They stepped out into the cold. She turned up her collar, cocked her head to the side, and asked, "How did the readmission conference go?"

"Not what I expected. Is this what you call a special-needs situation?"

Susan pursed her lips. "Let's walk."

They walked around the side of the building down the shoveled walk and stopped by the Dumpsters, big brown bins with the white cursive type; "Klumpe Sanitation" coming at Broker like another poke in the eye. An aroma of fried food drifted from the school cafeteria and hovered over the more gamy smell above the bins.

Susan turned, squinted seriously, and said, "I saw you and Jimmy Klumpe yesterday, out front."

"And?"

"And I don't know who you are or where you've been, but I'd be real careful rubbing up against our local soap opera if I were you. I'd watch out for Jimmy Klumpe—he's capable of doing something really dumb."

"He already has," Broker said softly.

"There you are. You're in Minnesota Appalachia, Mr. Broker; these people are into clan feuds like the Hatfields and McCoys, except here it's Bodines and Klumpes. You can go from two kids in a fistfight to the emergency room real fast. And this town hasn't got an emergency room."

"Why are you telling me this?"

"People talk. They decided you're a question mark. Like,

nobody has seen your wife. Kit is an island. People say you don't fit."

"I just got here."

"Yeah? Talk to Harry Griffin about that."

Broker raised his eyebrows. "You know Harry?"

Susan rolled her eyes. "Gets so a single woman will do just about anything up here for some decent conversation. Yes, I know Detroit Harry." She lowered her eyes and raised them in a certain way.

The bold remark, along with her knowing and saying Griffin's street name, created instant intimacy. Broker looked her up and down and couldn't help grinning, "And?"

"Harry's been up here ten years, and people say he doesn't fit either."

Now it was Broker who narrowed his eyes.

Susan shrugged, "Look, you're up north. The men up here are prone to drinking too much and fighting." She smiled painfully. "I know you didn't ask, but here's my two cents anyway—you and Harry are getting too old to fight. You just don't know it yet." Susan blew on her bare hands and plunged them into her coat pockets. "Tell Harry to be careful. You too."

Susan Hatch walked back toward the school's front door and left Broker standing by the Dumpster, inhaling the greasy odor wafting out from the lunch-room grill through the exhaust fan.

The smell reminded him he had one more stop to make.

Klumpe Sanitation housed its trucks and maintained an office in a big Morton building behind a cyclone fence on a lot a mile west of town. The gate was open. Driving up, Broker saw no trucks, no lights in the office windows that straddled one corner of the garage. No sign of anyone, in fact.

Slightly disappointed that he didn't have an audience, he pulled into the parking apron, then backed up until his tailgate was almost flush with the office door. He got out, climbed into the truck bed, lifted the heavy bin, and upended it, dumping the trash dead center on the welcome mat.

Chapter Seventeen

At 11:00 A.M. Gator paced on the front porch in his Carhartt parka, hunched against the drizzly mist, sipping a fresh cup of coffee. He was a few drags into a new Camel when he saw the gray Pontiac GT's low beams poke through the gloom, sweep across the Fordster on display next to his sign, and swerve into the drive.

Sheryl.

Just like she was supposed to, she drove the car into the open sliding door on the lower level of the barn, so it was out of sight. The locals, stir-crazy with cabin fever, noticed a new car in the neighborhood. Would drive clear into town and tell everybody at Lyme's Café, "Hey, I seen this strange Pontiac going out Twelve, near the big woods . . ."

Sheryl came out and struggled, hauling the wide wooden door shut. She turned toward the house.

Sheryl Marie Mott.

They had met in the visitors' room at Stillwater. He'd agreed to make a pickup for Danny T.'s organization, to pay his tax to stay in population. So they put her on his list. She walked up to the table in the visitors' room like some improved hippie dream in a beige pantsuit. Leaned over the table and planted this open-mouth kissed on him, expertly ramming a tiny balloon full of cocaine down his throat with her tongue. Then she patted his cheek and whispered, "Hey, you're kinda cute; now swallow, don't spit."

One look, and he knew he had to see her again. Kinda cracked her up when he asked for her phone number, like it was a blind date.

Gator had read this story in the joint, and he figured her secret was like in the story; some Dorian Gray deal with the devil that enabled her to keep all the debauchery of her life compacted inside so she looked so damn good on the outside. Couldn't even begin to guess her age. Older than him.

Sheryl had deep indigo eyes, flared cheeks, and long black hair down past her shoulders; the kind of dusky looker who coulda played a blue-eyed Indian princess in 1950s Hollywood, alongside Sal Mineo.

An East Side St. Paul street kid, somewhere around seventeen years old she'd discovered she liked really bad white guys who rode fat-boy Harleys even more than real bad black guys.

Biker chick. Rode with the Outlaw Motorcycle Gang, the OMG.

Central to the hard-core OMG ethos was the injunction, You must know the difference between good and evil and choose the evil. She traded in her patched jeans and tie-dye for greasy leather and denim. She'd done it in the dirt, pulling the shaggy biker trains at bonfires in the woods with the predatory relish of an MBA trying to make the cut on Donald Trump's *Apprentice*. In two years flat she went from anybody's groupie to briefly becoming a fixture on the back of Danny Turrie's chopper.

Always thinking. Mind-Fuck Mott. The story was, she'd moved Danny out of weed, and almost convinced him to sidestep the urban crack drama with its well-armed gangbangers. Got him into the suburbs, into coke. Then Danny shot those two North Side jigs and went away forever. Gang bangs were one thing; gangbangers and real bullets were another.

Sheryl split the cities, moved to Seattle during the great meth awakening, and shacked up with a guy who owned a perfume company. She took some chemistry course at a community college, learned her way around chemicals, dabbled in designer drugs, learned to cook meth, and socked her money into a lot on the beach in Belize.

Then her Seattle boyfriend had a weak moment and couldn't resist buying List I chemicals in bulk from a firm going out of business. Except the firm was a DEA cover operation, and Sheryl beat the battering ram coming through the door by half an hour. With just the money in her purse and a credit card, she took a cab to the airport and arrived back in Minnesota with thirty-four bucks.

When Gator met Sheryl she was marginally connected, but out of the loop. Burned, paranoid; she cooked a few batches of meth for the OMG, didn't like the flaky level of the operation, and wound up muling dope into Stillwater Prison to help make her car payments.

Gator heard the stories about her in the joint. When he got out, living in a halfway house, taking a tractor mechanics course at Dunwoody Institute that he could have taught better than the pencil-neck instructor, he asked her out for coffee.

He had this idea, see, that he'd been refining for a year behind bars . . .

Waiting tables, barely paying the freight on her apartment and the GT, Sheryl was ready. They started out in a Starbucks and conducted the second round in her bed, where his performance had lagged considerably.

This was before she understood Gator never really could get it going in a bed.

Gator grinned. Sheryl in high-heeled boots taking little bird steps through a foot of soggy snow. The biker-girl duds were long gone. Now she was more into business casual—designer jeans, the Donna Karan sweater picked up at Goodwill, the fancy hip-length leather car coat, a joke in this weather.

"What the hell is this?" she protested, kicking the snow off her footwear, coming up the steps. "It's the end of March."

"Your memory is impaired by global warming. This is old Minnesota normal. How you doing, Sheryl?"

She walked up to him, shrugged her shoulders, and went up on tiptoe. "Here I am. What's so urgent?"

He shied away from her upturned face. "Not yet."

She furrowed her brow, studied him. "Aw shit, aren't we done with that routine yet?"

"Let's go inside," Gator said firmly.

Sheryl followed him, shaking her head. "I forgot, isolated up here you didn't get the word how when the apes climbed down from the trees they invented these things called beds . . ."

Gator ignored her, knowing how much she really dug the weirdness of it. He walked through the kitchen, down the hall into the bathroom, and turned on the shower.

"Aw, jeez, what you got better be good." She grimaced. "I was up at six, been on the road for almost five hours driving straight drinking coffee. Man, first thing, I gotta pee." She wiggled out of her coat, unzipped the boots and kicked them off, and headed for the bathroom. When she returned, she drew herself up, knit her brows, and pointed a finger. "No gas, understood."

Gator nodded. "Agreed. No gas."

"Good. I can do weird. I draw the line at fucking crazy."

"C'mon, humor me," Gator chided, his voice wide, stuck in his throat. Maneuvering her back into the bathroom.

"Been missing it, huh?" She slithered out of the sweater, elbows out, hands back in that contortionist trick chicks do, unclipping her bra. Then she peeled off the jeans and panties. "I don't suppose you got a shower cap?"

Gator didn't hear. He was staring at her. Sheryl and her tattoo. Not like the twisty flowery bullshit the girls these days get, curled around their waists and back. Uh-uh. This was from the old days when tats were the exclusive domain of crooks and GIs. This pair of red Harley wings spread out two inches below her navel. Hip to hip. Framed just so in her bikini bottom tan marks. Gator didn't trust his voice. He pointed at the shower.

"Okay, okay." She reached her hand past the curtain and tested the water, adjusted the handle, and stepped into the tub.

Gator let it build for about a minute, then threw back the curtain. She stood face to the nozzle, drawing her hands through the dark glistening stream of hair. He reached out and clamped his hand on her wrist, pulled her.

"Hey." She stumbled over the side of the tub, banging her shin. She collided into him, slick, shadowed, her ribs tiger-streaked with tan fading from the beach in Belize. He spun her and forced her forward over the sink, his left hand straight-arming her, pressing on her neck. His right hand fumbled with the buttons of his jeans.

She always resisted, at first; like now, rearing at his rough grip on her neck, swinging her head around, dark eyes flashing, the long wet hair swinging round like black whips. "Christ's sake, Gator; can't we work this out a little?"

"Shut up, face forward. Stand."

Pouting, she turned back to the sink and muttered, "Too damn old to get fucked flatfooted . . ." Then she broke out of her brooding stance, hips warming up in a slow canter. ". . . then again, maybe I'm *not* . . ."

"Shush," he said hoarsely.

"There . . . you . . . go . . ."

He finally got his angles working and hit the rhythm. Unsteady on his feet now, jeans around his knees, he leaned forward, forcing her head down with both hands so all he saw in the mirror was the top of her dark hair and the water beaded up glistening on her back, jiggling where her smooth ass . . .

Oh, yeah.

Shower running, little chain hanging down from the lightbulb got to dancing as she grabbed the sides of the sink with both hands to brace against the thrust of his hips.

"Ain't you slippery." He groaned.

He watched the muscles in her arms and back tense, corded, popping sweat; her voice a throaty chant: "One a . . . these days . . . gonna . . . tear . . . this sink clear outa THE WALL!!!"

When her cherries lined up, she just paid and paid—*ca-ching-ca-ching*—the coin coming in a hard hot rush handled endlessly, loaded by the sackful . . .

Gator just holding on now; ears plugged with blood, other parts of him getting away, runny with his sweat, her sweat. Panting, staggering back, he watched the cannibal gene seep down the inner curve of her thigh. Only way it worked for him. Worked really good. Here in this damn moldy room with the floor joists rotting out under the crummy linoleum. Sheryl, thinking he had potential, patiently went along. All year they'd been starting like this, here in the bathroom.

Breathing not quite returned to normal, Sheryl rolled to the side and sat heavily on the toilet seat; hair tangled, arms down straight between her knees like a spent runner.

"So much for foreplay," she said, getting her breath.

Gator grinned, wiping off, doing up his jeans.

The real sex happened out in the shop, where everything was clean and in its place.

Where they talked about the plan. And where he would reveal his find.

Chapter Eighteen

Broker drove back home, parked the truck, climbed up into the bed, and kicked the garbage bin off his tailgate. Standing there in the sour wind, he gauged the anger pulsing in his throat, hot in his chest.

Usually his anger was fast surface burn, like spit hissing on a griddle. This was inside, and he couldn't get it out. It just kept circuiting on this loop. His eyes traveled back into the woods, where he'd left Kit's toy stuck on the pole. Sagging, he got down, closed the tailgate, and straightened up the bin, positioning it where it belonged.

Should call Griffin. He knows these people.

But Griffin had a tendency to go from insult to breaking bones in seconds flat; once he got involved, it might be impossible to hold him in check. Have to think about that.

He went inside, and after confirming that Nina was sleeping upstairs, he resolved to work it off. Clean the house. Stow the clutter. Wipe down the surfaces. If not a solution, at least a distraction. First he moved all the unpacked boxes into the garage and arranged them neatly along one wall. Then he attacked the downstairs bathroom, where he got stuck for a moment staring at the cat litter box as Kit's words from this morning washed back in a wave.

When I die, will I get to see Ditech again?

Like dying was a reasonable price to pay to be reunited with a cat? Did he think like that when he was eight? He stood, holding a scrub pad and Comet cleanser, peering at the lathered washbasin, trying to remember. The main thing he recalled was his mother yelling at him about wearing a hat and unthawing his fingers and toes after playing hockey until after dark in subfreezing weather.

He shook it off, removed the cat box, and put it in the garage. When he finished in the bathroom, he went into the living room and stacked Nina's weights in a tidy row. Then he brought a basket of laundry from upstairs and loaded the washer.

As he stuffed in towels and washcloths, he speculated how Mrs. Helseth's admonition to contact the sheriff would now be complicated by his ad hoc garbage dump at Klumpe's office. Then he considered how he had not advised Nina about his engagement in low-intensity yokel warfare. How he had enlisted Kit as an accomplice in keeping mom out of the loop.

He revisited his talk with Susan Hatch, who had weighed in with more advice. Both Helseth and Hatch were suggesting he needed filling in on Cassie and Jimmy's "local soap opera."

That he was getting his foot into . . .

Twenty minutes later he left the bathroom in perfect sparkling order.

As he opened the hall closet and took out the Kenmore canister, he caught himself again and looked upstairs. Vacuuming would wake her. Take a break.

There was still coffee in the thermos on the kitchen island, so he poured some into a travel cup, put on his coat and boots, and went out on the back deck, where he sat down on the steps and lit a cigar.

Didn't work. He found himself staring at his footprints in the snow, leading into the trees. Where he'd been out walking around last night with a loaded shotgun.

Okay. Klumpe was here. But he could have found the bunny in the truck when he knifed the tire.

If he knifed the tire.

There was even a chance Broker had not entirely closed the garage door and the cat had escaped on her own. But someone—Klumpe—had definitely removed the cat's collar and strapped it on the toy and rammed it on the pole at the trail intersection.

Kit was still missing her cat.

With considerable effort, Broker tried to step back from the spiral of anger and evaluate motive. *You humiliated Klumpe in front of his wife and kid.* No need to slap the choke hold on him like that. The sheriff was getting out of his car. *All you had to do was back up.*

He'd always taken his ability to function under pressure for granted . . .

Broker sipped his coffee, puffed on the cigar, and watched the smoke dissipate in the wind. Kinda like Nina, always taking her iron will for granted.

Okay. So maybe it was time to back off. Reach out.

Broker actually grimaced at the idea of calling Griffin and asking for personal help. Help with Nina was one thing. But help for him personally . . . Jesus . . .

Up till now Griffin had provided a place to stay and the bare bones of a cover story. That done, he stayed at a respectful distance. How much did he know? Broker assumed Griffin gossiped with J. T. Merryweather and Harry Cantrell. They all used to come up here to hunt. He was one of the few "civilians" those two allowed into their confidence.

Face it. The problem with reaching out to Griffin—besides his tendency to overreact—was that he was a Vesuvius of advice waiting to erupt. He had almost thirty years saved up, twenty-five years of it stone cold sober. And Griffin tended to be blunt.

And even being longtime friends, they had some issues.

Broker finished his cigar and came back into the kitchen. He was still pondering making the call when Nina wandered in, doing her bathrobe shuffle but, Broker observed, with a little more swing than usual. She stopped, cocked her head to the side, and said, "Broker, you feeling all right? You don't look so hot."

"Yeah, sure," he said, backing up a step. Not used to her making and maintaining direct eye contact. Not used to seeing the hint of color in her cheeks. "Just cleaning the place up."

She nodded, "Uh-huh. How'd it go with the principal this morning?"

"Ah, they're moving her to a different home base, away from the kid she hit. No recess for a week. They'll keep an eye out," he said, thinking, first eye contact, now she's tracking and making conversation. Christ, she *is* coming back. Not used to being scrutinized by her green eyes, he had to remind himself that Nina coming back was a good thing.

Then she poured a cup of coffee and took up her position at the stove, flipped on the overhead fan, and lit a cigarette. Broker was actually relieved when she pointed the TV remote like an escapist wand. The set popped on, dropping an electronic curtain over the room and hopefully cloaking his agitation.

For once he didn't mind.

Usually the cable shows reminded him of undercover work that had taken him into endless barrooms where it was always 11:00 P.M. The time when the smart people had long departed and only the drunks remained, yelling their pet peeves at each other. Chris Matthews brayed on one stool, Bill O'Reilly on another. Sean Hannity off beating his meat in the john. CNN had less volume and droned in a thorazine monotone. PBS was different, a station that delivered its monotone with footnotes.

C-SPAN was okay, free of commercial breaks, it came at you in agonizing real time like a dogged AA group crusading to get the nation to go on the wagon of sober politics.

Broker retreated to the washer and dryer in the bathroom and reached in to haul towels from the washer, except the goddamn towels were tangled like wet pythons around the washer stalk, resisting him. Suddenly he yanked at them, jarring the machine. He stopped and stared at his hands. Close to shaking. The flash point idling hair-trigger . . .

Primed and ready, just a surge away.

Deep breath, center down. Slowly, he disentangled the twisted towels from the washer column. Looked up through the doorway, snuck a look at Nina, thinking how she'd always favored colors that complemented her hair and complexion; shades of green and amber. Harvest colors. Now she grabbed whatever came to hand first in the drawer or laundry basket. At this moment, under the green terry-cloth robe, she wore a gray T-shirt, a pair of red sweatpants. Purple sweat socks.

Kit was just beginning to be aware of her appearance and how to dress. She would avert her eyes from her mother's outlandish costumes. Come to him with tops and bottoms, ask him if they matched . . .

Broker blinked, caught in mid-spiral; Nina was looking back at him. No, *watching* him.

Deliberately now, under the gaze of her increasingly alert eyes, he transferred the towels into the dryer, sorted another load into the washer, measured soap, set the control, started the water. When he went back to the kitchen, she continued to check him from the corner of her eye as she paced and chain-smoked and watched the Abrams tanks and the Bradleys rolling up the Euphrates River valley.

"So, what do you think?" she asked in a level voice, gesturing at the televised war just as some particularly sharp audio threw a rattle of shots into the kitchen. This distinctive whoosh, then an explosion.

"The AKs and RPGs sound the same," Broker said, turning away. "I gotta go in town, pick up the flat, do some shopping before I get Kit," he said over his shoulder, accelerating in an uninterrupted motion toward the door, stepping into his boots, grabbing his hat, gloves, carrying his coat, which he put on in the garage.

He didn't have to check his wristwatch. He knew it was just after noon. Three hours till school let out.

As he wheeled down the driveway and onto 12, he decided he needed some drive time away from the house. He'd been living too close to her.

And her ghosts.

Janey, Holly, and Ace Shuster. The casualties from Northern Route. He repeated the names in his mind like a diagram of her condition. She blamed herself for Janey most, and then Ace.

Holly had disappeared, vaporized from the face of the earth in the explosion at Prairie Island. Broker had been two hundred yards away . . .

He shook his head, focused on the road. Ghosts were mind games, just mental artifacts. Invisible.

Like radiation.

Broker had come to view Nina's depression as an asylum where all the ghosts got out. Thing about ghosts. You had to keep them locked up.

Broker stabbed his right boot sole down, heavy on the gas. Maybe not the best time to call Griffin.

Chapter Nineteen

Gator was jangled on too much morning coffee, and now rubber-kneed from the bout at the sink, but when they entered the shop, he immediately started another pot. As the Mr. Coffee gurgled and dripped, he paced and watched Sheryl drift over to the cot in the alcove, tuck her knees under her, and start combing out her hair.

No afterglow booze. No drugs. He and Sheryl agreed. The first rule of the Great Monk Crooks was, they never used. Like Danny T. said in the joint: "You use, you lose the count."

"So?" Sheryl asked, drawing the comb through her long hair, staring quizzically at the black kitten that emerged from a folded blanket under the desk and arched up against Gator's shin.

"Jojo," Gator said, picking up the cat, stroking it.

Sheryl's eyes clicked around. "You mean . . . Danny T.'s Jimmy Jo?"

"Yep." Gator gently put the kitten down, poured a cup of coffee, and handed it to Sheryl. She set down the comb, took the cup in both hands, blew on it to cool it.

"The bust in Bayport, what? Eight, nine years ago, she said. "I hear it still cuts Danny like a knife."

Casually Gator opened his desk drawer and took out the sheets of paper. "No one ever figured out who snitched on Jimmy Jo. Gave him to the narcs."

Sheryl nodded. "Eats at Danny. Gave him ulcers, losing his only kid like that."

"Wasn't a snitch. Was an undercover cop." He tapped the paper.

Sheryl narrowed her eyes, taking the papers; she drew up her knees cross-legged, got comfortable. "This is a search warrant," she said as she flipped up the blue memo stapled to the top page, raised her eyebrows.

"Read," he said.

She put on her serious thinking face and carefully read the warrant. Then she scanned it again. He reached in the desk again and tossed her the Washington County letter, the Visa statement.

"Connect the dots. I don't trust myself," Gator said.

Sheryl took her time reading, turning the pages, going back and forth, sipping her coffee, the student in her engaged. Times like this, he was grateful she was onboard. His deep bench. She glanced up, her eyes luminous, impressed.

"This guy, Broker," she said slowly.

"I figure he was an undercover they didn't want to show in court."

"Maybe." They locked eyes. "How'd you get this? Where?"

Gator smiled, "Never mind how. I got it from a house, yesterday afternoon. Where he's staying."

Sheryl's eyes popped. "Up here?"

"Yep."

"A state narc is up here?" Showing lots of whites, her eyes darted around the shop. "Shit, man . . ."

"Relax. If something was up, I'da heard from Keith. In fact, I'm working on that, to make sure," Gator said.

Sheryl wrinkled her nose. She didn't entirely approve of the way he played footsie with his childhood buddy, the sheriff.

Gator hurried to reassure her. "Way it looks, I don't think he's on the job anymore. Just living with his crazy old lady and his kid."

Sheryl uncrossed her legs, got off the cot, and paced the narrow office. "Let me get this straight. You just *stumbled* on this?"

Gator shrugged. "If I told you how, you wouldn't believe it. Doesn't matter. What's it mean?"

As Sheryl pondered her response, the black kitten reappeared from under the desk and glided to a bowl of water, then poked its head into a second bowl of cat food.

"I think Danny T. had a contract out on whoever snitched Jojo," she said slowly. "It never went anywhere."

"So," Gator tossed up his hands in a gesture of great abundance, "let's renegotiate the contract."

Sheryl inclined her head so her hair fell in this dark cascade, and their eyes batted the idea back and forth. She frowned. "You mean . . . ?"

"Make an approach, propose trading this ratfuck narc for . . ."

"A reliable supplier of precursor," Sheryl said.

Gator took her hands in his, pulled her up from the cot, and twirled her in a celebratory circle. Sheryl went along for a moment, then her face went beetle-browed with concentration. She released Gator's hands.

"Easier said than done, making an approach. When I tried putting out feelers to Danny's guys, they treated me like a retread throwaway bitch. They're still pissed at me 'cause I walked away from cooking for them. Shit, Gator, they wanted to know if I'd do prison visits again."

"But this is different," Gator said. "It's got a personal angle, like a favor to the great man. We start out humble. Give them the guy like a gift. Don't go to street guys. Go right to the top, Danny's lawyer . . ."

An authentic ripple of disgust distorted her face. She clamped her arms across her chest. "*You* go see Dickie Werk, *you* blow him."

"C'mon, this is *different*," Gator insisted. Then he took her hand and walked her through the shop, past the disassembled tractor and the partitioned area where he kept his paints, paint gun, two protective suits with state-of-the-art rebreather masks. They entered the paint room. Hooks dangled from the ceiling on which he hung tractor parts. It was an almost hallucinatory space, swirled with layers of spray from the paint gun—red, orange, green, yellow. Empty now, kept scrupulously clean. Just a long workbench, a wide elaborate fume hood, and a color photo taped to the wall; a view of Sheryl's sand beach lot in Belize. Gator believed in visualizing goals.

"We're all set up—we got an industrial-rated exhaust system, the glassware, the mantles, the generator," he said. "Got the perfect location, a pig tank full of anhydrous in the barn . . . and I got pickup, delivery, and disposal all figured out."

"Figured out in theory," Sheryl said tartly, bringing him back to earth. "Or have you forgotten what a mess it was two weeks ago, just cooking two pounds? All thumbs, the country kids . . . you getting stuck in the woods with a truck full of precursor and chemicals you ripped off . . ." She raised her finger and wagged it. "You got it figured out on paper, honey; not in real life."

"Okay, two weeks ago was hairy; but we needed operating cash. I owe my brother-in-law, remember . . ."

"Your brother-in-law the lush, your buddy the sheriff"—she rolled her eyes, then clamped her arms across her chest—"fucking wolves howling all night." Again the wagging finger. "No way I'm going back to those West Side Mexican creeps; I don't need the exposure. To lay off that shit we took a fifty percent cut in price"—her eyes flashed—"and me digging around in the water tank of some crummy nightclub toilet for the bread . . . there was vomit on the floor, in the woman's john." Sheryl finished up fierce and indignant.

"You're absolutely right." Gator made calming motions with his hands. "That's why we need a reliable organization that can assemble the chemicals in volume, discreetly. Dead drops."

"Gator, I don't even know if OMG has a network in Canada to bring stuff down. They're still a bunch of fucking bikers, man."

"Work with me, here, will ya?" Gator pleaded. "Not like we're in hurry; this year's shot. If it happens, it'll be next winter. We got time. Long-term, remember?"

Sheryl's tantrum passed. She unfolded her arms and paced the room. "Okay, maybe it could work." She pirouetted and raised the stern finger for a third time. "You're forgetting something," she said, still beetly, still thinking. "If this guy checks out and they go for it, they're going to kill him. We can get indicted as coconspirators in murder one. This won't be like the last time. Your buddy, the sheriff, is going to have to investigate an ex-cop with a bullet in the back of his head. Says in the paperwork he worked for BCA. They'll bring in the state investigators. And they're pretty good."

Gator made a quashing gesture with his hands. "I thought of that. We'll make it part of the deal. He dies in a house fire. They put a plastic sack over his head or do him with a small caliber in the ear, huh—that ain't gonna show if he's burned up. Bad connection on the propane. Gas rises to the pilot light in the furnace. Boom. Happens all the time in old houses up here."

Sheryl enlarged her eyes. "*Another* house fire, Gator? You just had one last year . . . And for starters, you don't dictate to these guys . . ."

"Aw, c'mon, maybe they'll do it somewhere else, huh? Let's take a shot. Take the papers to the lawyer. He can talk to Danny on the phone, and no one's listening; they turn the tape off, right, when he's talking to his lawyer?"

Sheryl chewed the inside of her cheek, angling her head back and forth, weighing it. "So go in humble, serve them up this guy, then later we angle for an audition," she said.

"There you go, think positive," Gator said.

"They'd have a whole year to put it together. And they'll want to check out the operation, send out an appraiser, like a bank doing a mortgage."

"Hey, we're ready."

"No more little jobs. No more sweating middlemen. All we do is cook and get paid. The big batch," Sheryl said.

"Biggest batch ever cooked east of California. Right here," Gator said.

"With the right support system, we could cook ten pounds a heat . . ."

Gator shook his head. "Hell, with our setup we could do twenty pounds of ninety-nine-percent pure glass. Easy." He couldn't help laughing, picturing it as he shuffled toward her in a stilted Frankenstein stagger, jerking his arms. "Our stuff hits the street, it's gonna look like *Night of the Living Dead* out there, all the dumb doomed tweakers lurching around the countryside."

His comic routine finally brought laughter to her eyes. Why she liked him; he had a sense of humor.

"Okay, okay, cut the clowning. This is serious," she said. "One heat a week, at twenty-five K a pound. But then there's overhead and Danny's cut. Still, shit, man . . ." She walked across the paint room and touched the beach photo taped to the wall. Then she turned to him. "There's a lot of ifs; if they can deliver in volume and on time, if they don't screw up washing the money, if you can get a new set of ID . . ." Finally his enthusiasm swept her up and she grinned. "Shit, Gator, in two months we could get free. Disappear."

"Say good-bye to winter," Gator said.

"Belize."

"Placencia, here we come. Build on that property. I could work on boat engines. Two-cycle diesel, not that different from tractors. Go straight, live on fish and coconuts." He put his arm around her and walked her back into the mechanics bay. Then he gently pressed her forward against the disassembled bare metal of the old tractor, nuzzled her ear, inhaling the great hair. "Lean over, baby; grab some Minneapolis Moline."

"I guess this is what they call progress, huh," Sheryl sighed as she unbuttoned her jeans.

Chapter Twenty

When Broker picked Kit up at school, their conversation consisted of three words.

"Kitty?" Kit asked.

"No kitty," Broker said. After a glum drive home, they walked into the house, and it was immediately apparent that Nina's morning rally had continued into the afternoon. She still wore the odd outfit, minus the robe, but she'd combed and gathered her hair in a ponytail. The weights were strewn around the living room in a circle that suggested she had been working out. More than circumstantial was the tone of her voice when she saw her daughter:

"Young lady, you are vacuuming all the rugs, remember . . ."

Broker left them debating over the sound of the vacuum cleaner—Kit trying to make a case that all five rugs were too many demerits to work off.

Broker went into the backyard, making a vague reference to the woodpile. He walked far enough into the woods to verify that the ski pole and bunny were still in place.

All afternoon he'd driven the roads, his thoughts accelerating. He'd lost something. A cushion between his skin and everything else in the world. More and more he felt pressed right up against days full of sharp edges. It was a new sensation for him. Life hurt.

Wasn't hard to figure out why.

If she really was thawing out . . . then the truce that had existed between them as he nursed her would also melt away. They'd be right back where they were before Northern Route tricked weird—facing the unresolved issue in their marriage.

Would she go back into the Army?

Would he revert to dangling military spouse? Would Kit again become a bouncing ball between Nina's duty stations overseas and Broker playing stay-at-home mom?

Suddenly he was in a trip-wire region of resentments that had suspended, hang fire, during her bout of depression. When would they get aired? For starters, she had used Kit as part of her undercover ploy to penetrate the smuggling ring in North Dakota.

So damn consumed by her goddamn mission, she put our daughter in the potential line of fire.

The feud with Jimmy Klumpe was forgotten as he tipped into the pit of grievances he had been saving up.

But.

One day does not spell recovery. Go slow. She was still balanced on the lip of her own pit. So Broker stuffed the clamor back in his head. He carried an armload of oak into the kitchen, built a fire in the Franklin stove, and went through the motions of creating his perfect family hour.

He boiled water for noodles, reheated spaghetti sauce, tossed a salad. Kit came into the kitchen, arms clamped across her chest, dagger-eyed. "Mom is getting mean," she said.

"No, Mom is getting better. You set the table."

He followed her as she placed the plates. Then made sure she got the fork on the left, knife and spoon on the right.

Then he served the food and announced, "Mangia." One of Kit's favorite imports from her time in Tuscany.

They took their seats.

Kit, eyes down, stared into her spaghetti. The vertical intensity lines made deep dents in her brow.

Nina raised her fork, chewed dutifully, and made an attempt to keep the new normal rolling. "This is good. I'm impressed."

Broker shrugged.

She continued. "You know, I think Irene is right . . ."

He looked up at the mention of his mother. "About what?" he said, not used to ordinary conversation with her.

"Well," she said, "Irene has this theory your stifled creativity gets expressed in odd ways; like in the kitchen, and in the role-playing of undercover work."

They studied each other in a perfectly routine way for two people who had been married for eight years, who had a child, who knew where all the hot buttons were.

Broker averted his eyes, turned to Kit. "So how's your food?"

Kit let her fork drop, sat back in her chair, folded her arms tight, and planted her chin on her chest.

"Kit, I asked you a question."

"If the wolves didn't eat her, she's gonna freeze to death." Not looking up.

"Not now. There's other stuff we have to talk about, like what happened today at school. How's the new homeroom?" Broker asked, a bit testy.

Kit raised her eyes in full glower. "She's the only friend I got to play with. You won't let me bring anybody over."

"C'mon, honey, you know it's just for a little while." Broker was speaking gently to Kit, but his eyes moved to Nina's face, concerned the subject would rub her wrong.

"You always say that. But it's not a little while," Kit said. Her eyes flashed up, shot an accusing look at Nina, ducked down again.

Nina's fork trembled in her fingers. Broker reacted. His hand a blur, he snapped the fork in midair before it fell into the plate.

Broker's sudden movement made his daughter snap alert, wary. Seeing her uncertainty, he slowly set the fork back on the table where it belonged on the left side of Nina's plate. Then he placed his hands, palms down, on either side of his plate and spoke slowly. "Look, we've been over this. Mom needs to get better, okay . . ."

Kit slowly bobbed her head and said, "Right. So when kids ask me over to play, I have to make excuses why I can't because you don't want to meet the parents or have them over here and then the kids don't ask me anymore and I wind up playing alone on the playground. Dad! They think I'm weird."

Nina said in a calm voice. "She's right, Broker. No surprise they're starting to pick on her. We should have left her with your folks."

Broker shook his head and said firmly, "No, she's been *left* with people half her life."

Kit grimaced. "It's not my fault that Auntie Jane and those people died," she cried, tearing up. "Why do I have to get punished for it?"

Broker and Nina locked eyes; unspoken between them the charge they had robbed their daughter of innocence. Abruptly Nina pushed her chair back from the table. "This isn't working. We should have left her with your parents," she restated in a taut, hard voice.

Broker put out his hands in a pacifying gesture. He was losing control of the situation. "Okay. Nina, calm down. We'll start over."

That's when the phone rang.

Broker stared at the Bakelite relic on the wall. When he didn't move to answer it, Nina got up, picked up the receiver.

"Hello." Pause, then, "Not bad, how's yourself." Her eyes turned to Broker. "It's Griffin."

Broker heaved up from his chair, took the receiver, put it to his ear.

"I figured *you'd* be calling *me*. Looks like you got a little situation going," Harry Griffin said, his voice coming to a point.

Good old blunt direct Harry. "Oh, yeah," Broker said ambiguously.

"You met Keith Nygard, right?"

"We met," Broker said.

"Well, being the sheriff, he don't exactly need an invite. But he stopped in to see me. He's here right now, he's got some questions for you. Figured he'd put me in the picture. He's low-key, likes to keep it friendly. He ain't in uniform. Tell Nina it's about the crew. Ah, put on your coat and boots. You might be taking a ride."

Broker picked up the cordless phone from the counter, hung up the rotary, and walked into the living room. When he was out of earshot, he asked, "What'd you tell him? About me?"

"Not a whole lot. That you were a cop; but he'd pretty much figured that out. Up to you how much more you tell him. But he ain't dumb. Relax, this dustup with Jimmy Klumpe is nothing major, humor him. We'll be over in half an hour," Griffin said, ending the call.

Broker walked back in the kitchen and hung up the phone. Saw Nina and Kit watching him. They didn't get many phone calls. "Griffin's coming over with a friend. Wants to talk," he said, sitting down at the table.

He felt Nina's eyes map his body language. *Christ, she is coming back.* All the deadly green range-finding optics swimming into focus.

Broker shrugged and sat back down at the table. "Something about the stone crew."

"Uh-huh," Nina said.

"Yeah. Wants to look over the woodpile. Maybe take a drive, check out a job."

"In the dark?" Nina wondered.

"You know Griffin—when he gets an idea in his head, he never quits." Broker let the thought hang. Then he turned to Kit and said, "C'mon. Eat your dinner." He picked up his fork and looked down at his own plate, where the spaghetti lay twisted in a meaty red coil like a belly wound.

The sheriff. Great.

Chapter Twenty-one

The first time Broker laid eyes on Harry Griffin was thirty-two years ago—this surreal red figure from a Fellini movie that emerged from the soaking white morning mist next to a sandbar in the Trieu Phong River. Griffin had been walking point with a squad of Popular Forces, moving between night positions. A roving ambush. He collided with a VC point man on a muddy trail, and they exchanged fire point-blank in the fog. The Viet Cong's AK rounds ripped through the red smoke grenades that had been hanging off the side of Griffin's radio, and the smoke seeped out and completely coated him in the thick chemical pigment; his hair, his teeth, his skin, and his gear.

They met because of a bomb.

Buck sergeant Griffin, the radio man on the local district advisory team, had killed the lead VC. The rest scattered. He also killed two water buffalo on the trail behind the VC point. The animals made an unreal racket going down, but not so loud that Griffin didn't hear the screeching metal ricochet. The Viet Cong had been moving four buffalo across the river. The two dead animals and the two survivors were lashed together with a bamboo yoke on which they were transporting an unexploded 2,000-pound bomb.

"Well, I'll be dipped in red shit," Griffin had said to brand-new Second Lieutenant Phil Broker, who had choppered in from Hue City with Major Ray Pryce and a gaggle of brass to inspect the find.

They met again, a short while later, in the cauldron battle for Quang Tri City. They stayed together until the end, in '75.

◆　◆　◆

Broker, with a flashlight in his pocket, stood in the driveway smoking a cigar as Harry Griffin eased up the drive in his runaround vehicle, a '99 Jeep Sport. His work truck was still on the hoist at Luchta's. Griffin parked next to the Tundra and got out. He was in his late fifties now, and as he approached, Broker saw how the harsh yard light really dug into the creases and hollows under his gaunt cheekbones. After way more Peter Pan years than a guy should have, Detroit Harry was finally starting to look his age.

Griffin was alone. He walked up to Broker, followed him through the garage to the back deck, and glanced at the video flicker in the kitchen windows.

"Why do I get the feeling she ain't watching *Survivor?*" Griffin said.

"The War in the Box," Broker said.

"She feels left out, huh?" Griffin asked.

Broker shook his head. Not so much an answer as a weary dismissal of the subject. He did notice, even in the dark, that Griffin was watching him closely.

"You're no fun," Griffin said, "don't want to talk about the war—everybody's talking about the war; how cool it is. Reporters gushing all over themselves, getting to ride on tanks . . ." He paused, nodded toward the TV flicker. "How's she doing? I was surprised she answered the phone. She sounded more like her old self."

Broker nodded. "She coming out of it." Looked back through the garage. "Where's the local copper?"

Griffin shrugged. "A few minutes behind me."

"What's he know?"

"I been living up here ten years, so he knows me, some of what I did in the Army. He's called me a couple times, to help out in a pinch." Griffin shrugged. "Knows we were on the same team in the old days."

"Great, what else did you tell him?"

"Hey, numb-nuts, you were the one whipped a Kansas City lateral restraint on Jimmy Klumpe yesterday. Keith says you did it perfect, like it was pure reflex. Says he learned the technique in Skills and never has been able to get it right."

Broker turned and looked at the bluish flicker of the TV in the kitchen. "Does he—"

Griffin shook his head. "No. Nothing about her."

Broker changed the subject, poking Griffin not quite playfully on the shoulder. "Talked to Susan Hatch at the school today, huh? Actually, *she* talked to *me*. She got right down to cases, asking questions about Kit. And me. Let it slip she knew you in the biblical sense. What have *you* been telling *her*, like in bed?"

The question hung unanswered in the falling snow as a pair of headlights swept across the tree line to the side of the yard. Broker and Griffin walked back through the garage into the driveway. Keith Nygard drove a gray Ford Ranger, not his Sheriff's Department cruiser. He parked it next to Griffin's Jeep, got out in jeans, a Filsen parka, and bulky La Crosse boots. He walked over to the two older men.

"He's okay," Griffin said, watching the sheriff approach. "Young but okay."

Broker nodded and said by way of greeting, "Sheriff."

"Jimmy Klumpe called the office today and lodged a complaint; says somebody dumped a can full of garbage at his office door. His driver, coming back from a route saw a green Tundra leaving the yard." Nygard said. His wire-rim glasses gleamed in the yard light, the lenses slightly fogged.

"That why you're here?" Broker asked.

"You tell me." Nygard's voice was low, almost quiet. His hard cop stare, however, was unmistakable in the bad light. Broker matched him, stare for stare.

"Guys," Griffin chided.

Broker relented, dropped his eyes. "Okay. This morning Klumpe was driving the truck that collected my canister. He picked it up with the hydraulic auto reach arm, then dumped it deliberately in the ditch and drove away. Took his time so's I got a good look at his face. I guess I overreacted, considering all the strange shit that's been going on."

"Define strange shit?" Nygard asked.

"This way," Broker said, starting to walk. They fell in step through the snow in the backyard. Stopped at the side of the garage by the doghouse. Broker shined his flashlight on the bowl of meatball antifreeze. "That showed up last night," Broker said. "Right after I found a brand-new tire flat on my truck. Had it repaired—old man Luchta said it was a puncture."

"You have a dog?" Nygard asked.

Broker shook his head and motioned to the two other men to follow him. As they left the radius of the yard light, Broker pointed the way up the connecting trail.

When they came to the ski pole where the trails T-boned, Broker stopped and switched on the light. Griffin and Nygard continued forward, stood looking at the stuffed bunny for a full minute. Slowly Griffin took out a pack of cigarettes and an old Zippo lighter. He lit the cigarette, put the lighter back in his pocket, then turned to Broker.

"Bloody nose to crucified bunny. He escalated on you," he said.

"Every morning Kit makes her bed and puts that bunny in the same exact place on her pillow. Last night after the tire and the antifreeze happened, the toy was missing. I'm thinking somebody was in my house yesterday when Kit and I where out on the ski trail. Maybe he was watching the house, waiting until we left . . ."

"What about your wife? Was she home?" Nygard asked.

"She wasn't feeling good and was taking a nap when we left," Broker said.

Nygard waited for Broker to continue. When he didn't, Griffin steered off Nina, asking Nygard, "Jimmy?"

Nygard nodded. "He's dumb enough to do something like this, 'specially if Cassie was egging him on."

"There's more," Broker said, extended his hand, finger pointing. "Check the collar around the bunny's neck. Our kitten disappeared last night. Nina and Kit think the cat got out because I left the garage door open."

"*Was* the door open?" Nygard asked.

"No," Broker said. Then he bit his lip, thought. "I don't think it was."

"You positive someone came in your house?" Nygard asked.

Broker exhaled. Saw where Nygard was going. "Not for sure. The toy could have been in the truck, the truck wasn't locked. The bowl with the antifreeze could have been on the deck with cat food in it."

"Okay," Nygard said carefully, "without getting too far into exactly who you are—'cause it ain't really my business—" He stared at Broker for several seconds. "What I want to head off here is you and Jimmy going back and forth with this feud until you bump into each other at the gas station and somebody winds up in an ambulance."

"I just want to be left alone," Broker said.

"Don't take this wrong," Nygard said, "but to stop this fight that's brewing here, somebody gotta step up and be the adult." The comment, coming from the younger man, struck Broker as quietly bristling with hair-shirt Scandinavian piety.

"Sheriff—" Broker started to protest.

Griffin interrupted, "Hear him out, Broker." Broker relented, raised his hands, gloved palms open, let them fall.

"Okay, then," Nygard said. "Griffin and I are thinking you and me should take a drive, fill you in on some background about Jimmy Klumpe and Cassie Bodine. Might help you manage this situation better."

Broker nodded. "Uh-huh. This teacher at the school cautioned me about 'rubbing up against the local soap opera.' Is this what you're getting at?"

"I guess," Nygard said. Then he turned and walked back up the trail.

Broker looked at Griffin. "You two are in cahoots."

"Yep," Griffin said. He plucked the bunny off the ski pole and thrust it in his parka pocket. "Somebody's got to sew this up so

Kit don't notice. That wouldn't be you or Nina." He pulled the pole from the snow and handed it to Broker. They walked back toward the house. Nygard went through the garage and got in his truck, started the engine.

"So what's Nygard know about me?" Broker asked, placing the ski pole with its twin in the garage.

"Ask him," Griffin said,

"You think he can smooth over all this bullshit?"

"Yep."

"Hey, Griffin, somebody broke into my house—"

"You assume."

"Bullshit. This guy had a plan. He took my kid's toy, then he took the cat. Shit, man; there's tracks leading off the deck into the woods, doubled back." Broker flung his arm toward the trail behind them. "I spent an hour working out his pattern. He came in on skis, through the woods. Yesterday afternoon there was all kinds of folks coming down that trail on skis."

"On skis, huh? You sure?" Griffin stopped, thought a moment, then turned deliberately. "Maybe you're a little stressed right now and not thinking too clearly. In the scheme of things, this really where you want to make a stand? Defend your homestead, put down roots, plant a garden?" He puffed on his smoke, looked away. "Ain't why you're here. Hell, man. I can get you another cat. You go on with Nygard. I'll hang back, keep an eye on the house."

Broker ducked into the kitchen, kissed Kit good night, and told Nina he was going into town with Harry. She protested mildly when he took her fresh carafe of coffee and three travel mugs. He left her heating water for another pot and staring at *Hardball* on the TV screen, where Chris Matthews was talking twenty times faster than General Wesley Clark about the invasion of Iraq.

Griffin took his cup of coffee and parked his Jeep down the road. Broker got in Nygard's Ranger and doled out coffee as Nygard drove up 12, away from town, continued north, and shifted the Ranger into four-wheel drive as they went beyond where the snowplow had stopped. They followed a single set of tire tracks dwindling in a foot of snow. Soon it was pitch black, no yard lights, just a light snow sparkling in the high beams. Nygard slowed as a doe and two fawns meandered across the road.

"Jack Pine Barrens, big fire in here, oh, twenty years ago," Nygard said, waving his hand at the darkness. "Hardly anybody lives up here anymore." After another three minutes, Nygard addressed the silence in the Ranger. "Okay. The way you put Jimmy on his ass got my attention. So I called Griffin, and then I called this copper in St. —"

"Who?" Broker asked.

"Jack Grieve, sergeant in narcotics. We met when I went through the academy. We keep in touch. He comes up summers to fish. Stays with me."

"I know Jack," Broker said. "Good no-bullshit cop."

"Asked him if he knew of a Phil Broker," Nygard continued. "'Why do you ask?' Jack says. Got him staying in my county, I says." Nygard turned and looked directly at Broker for emphasis. "'Won't get anything direct from me about Broker,' Jack says. Fair enough. How 'bout indirect, I says. 'But that would be gossip,' Jack says." Nygard paused to sip his coffee. Waited.

Broker accepted Nygard's workmanlike preamble. "So we're off the record," he said.

Nygard grunted affirmatively. "Hell, man; we're driving into the Washichu. Pretty soon we'll be clear off *everything*."

"You mind if I smoke?" Broker asked, pulling out his cigars.

"Crack the window," Nygard said. He probed his pocket and withdrew a toothpick, which he held in his fingers like a cigarette before putting it between his lips.

Broker dialed down the window several inches, lit the rough wrap, and waited.

Now Nygard was direct. "Basically Jack said you were always more an adventurer than a cop. Paid your dues in St. Paul, made sergeant fast, and developed a real taste for undercover work. Then you worked a deal with BCA. And here Jack says something happened. A supervisor made a mistake; let you take the bit in your teeth, go too deep, and stay there. You got out eight years ago. Married this heavy-duty lady in the Army. Rumor is, every once in a while, you do things that don't get written down. For the feds. Got this little resort up on Lake Superior. But Jack says that ain't really where you get your money."

"That it?" Broker said, staring ahead, rolling the cigar across his mouth.

"Yeah, except Jack said to give you a lot of room. Said the rumors put you and your wife smack in the middle of whatever really happened at the Prairie Island Nuclear Plant last July. 'Nuff said."

Now the darkness crowded in closer to the road. The spindly jack-pine muskeg gave way to thicker pines and ghostly stands of birch. They drove through a tunnel of overhanging branches.

Broker stared into the darkness. "Years ago we'd come up here and hunt. Bunch of young cops. When Griffin first bought the old place on the lake. Great place for whitetails, nobody else around. Hardly any shots on opener except us. But . . ." His voice trailed off.

"Spooky," Nygard said.

"Yeah."

Nygard rolled his toothpick across his lips. "A few Indians come here around this time of year, tap the paper birches. And not many of them . . ."

Abruptly he pointed into the high beams. "There, on the right. See him?"

Broker caught a fleeting impression of the large gray wolf before it danced back into the trees.

"There's two packs in here now; got the woods divided up. Maybe thirty animals." He settled back. "Any rate, Indians got a story about these woods. Two early settlers thought they found gold nuggets in a stream and set to fighting and eventually shot each other. Turned out to be fool's gold. A Sioux hunting party found the dying men. According to the story, even both gut-shot, they were still struggling over a bag of rocks. The Sioux considered it so strange that men would kill for stones they named the place Washichu, which became their terms for whites."

Broker nodded. "Means something like 'unnatural,' doesn't it?"

"Exactly," Nygard said. "Got so only one family lived up here, the Bodines. Cassie's family lived on a farm deeper in. Her cousins lived on another farmstead right up here. Where we're headed." He slowed as the forest on the passenger side thinned into an overgrown field. He turned into a drifted-over road. When the snow breasted his front bumper, he stopped, backed up and put the Ranger in neutral, set the emergency brake, and left the high beams on. He glanced at Broker. "Hope those are good boots. We gotta walk."

They got out, and Nygard switched on a heavy-duty flashlight.

Plodding through knee-deep drifts, they outdistanced the headlights, and up ahead, the swinging motion of Nygard's torch illuminated the carcasses of old cars, cast-off debris of all kinds. Then they came upon piles of fresh wreckage; scorched wood siding, shingles, a blackened, half-burned mattress and bedsprings clotted with snow.

The light hit a snarl of yellow tape flapping in the night, and webbed orange plastic emergency fence strung on a perimeter of engineer stakes.

Thirty feet ahead, a sign blocked the road: "Hazardous Waste Site. Keep Out. Minnesota Pollution Control Agency."

Chapter Twenty-two

"Smell it?" Nygard asked.

Broker sniffed the air and caught a lingering reek of cold smoke-soaked solvents. Not even the new snow could cover it.

"Acetone, freon, methanol, xylene, anhydrous, hydrochloric acid, and sulphuric. Residues still pooled in the basement. The warm weather we had before the snow got it to stinking again," Nygard said.

A house had been here, an old four-square two-story farmhouse. Snow blanketed the wreckage, but Broker could discern the signature pattern of a gas explosion; walls blown out and collapsed in a mangle of burned timbers and shingle into the cratered basement. More debris ringed the site than even an explosion could scatter—several generations of cast-off auto parts, tractor parts, cannibalized snowmobiles, a rusted kid's playground set tipped on its side.

"No sense in getting too close to it," Nygard said. "PCA came out and put up the fence and the sign. That was a year ago. We ain't exactly first on their list up here. They did some spot tests on the water table." Nygard toed a clump of snow, let the flashlight play over a scatter of scorched Sudafed blister packs. "Fuckin' meth lab blew up."

"Read about this, but never seen it; after my time," Broker said, shaking his head. "When I was on the street, the bikers brought speed overland from L.A. in the crank cases of their Harleys. Nothing blew up."

"You're showing your age," Nygard said. "That was kid's stuff compared to the stuff they cook in these labs. It's ninety-five, a hundred percent pure. Smoking crack gets you high for twenty, thirty minutes; smoke this stuff, and the boost can last twelve hours. And it's cheap. A high school dropout with a recipe off the Internet can go out, spend a hundred bucks on ingredients at the drugstore and hardware store, siphon off some anhydrous ammonia from a nurse tank in some farmer's field, and cook a batch worth two thousand dollars in twenty minutes."

"How many were in here when—"

"Four," Nygard said. "Four dead. All of them Bodines. Cassie's cousins. Five, if you count Marci Sweitz. She was three and a half—"

Nygard's voice clipped short saying that last part. He abruptly turned and trudged back up the road. Broker followed him, stepping in the sockets of their inbound footprints. They got in the warm truck. Broker opened the thermos and poured the last of the coffee. Then he reached for another cigar, to chase the smell of the ruin. He lit it and said, "Tell me."

Nygard bit through his toothpick, discarded it, produced another, chewed on it. "Hell, you see how it is up here. I got one full-time deputy for the whole county in the off season. We pretty much patrol the south end—the town, the highway, the big lake. Couple times things got tense, I've asked Harry to come along as a special deputy. He can be a pretty handy fella. But I guess you know that." Nygard turned his face, but Broker couldn't read his eyes in the dark. "Anyway . . . the goddamned Bodines . . ."

"There's a kind of family you run into, being a cop," Broker speculated. "Kind of folks who put a big dent in your budget."

"I hear you. If you got out the arrest records going back forty years, you'd find the name Bodine on twenty percent of them. Real—"

"Assholes," Broker said, finished his thought.

"Amen. Always were involved in smuggling, going back to Prohibition. Never robbed here, though. Know what? In the old days, when there was more of them, they'd go up through the woods into Manitoba on actual raids, rip off whole farms. They come out of Canada originally, French Canuck, some métis thrown in; story is, they came from voyageur stock. Bunch of powerful stumpy little fuckers." Nygard shook his head. "Twenty years ago we'd have Canadian Mounties down here poking around, joint operations.

"Well, by the time I got the job, it calmed down to this bunch living out here in a trash house, we called it. Played at farming, cutting pulp wood, ran a few cows. Didn't have a lot of contact, they had the school board convinced they were home-schoolers. Like I said, people don't really come up this way much. Cassie and her brother tried to break the mold, sort of, after their folks basically killed themselves."

"Suicide?" Broker said.

"Suicide by alcohol. Drunks. Cassie and her brother, Morg, would come to my house when the drinking got too bad. My dad took care of them. One night, after a real ugly scene, they said they weren't going back, so the sheriff went out next morning and found Irv and Mellie Bodine dead. Been drinking, passed out, had turned on the oven, forgot to light the pilot. I guess . . ." He faced forward and watched the road. "They lived at my house till they finished high school.

"Her brother, Morg, went into the Navy. Always was an ace mechanic. No problem him finding a job when he got out. But he wanted the money faster and got caught up in a cocaine scam. Spent a year in Stillwater. He's back now. Keeps to himself. Got a tractor restoration shop set up on the old farm. Does pretty good with it. He's the only person who lives up there now. Him and the wolves."

Nygard sighed. "Then Cassie had to marry Jimmy, got pregnant. Probably married him 'cause he was homecoming king senior year." He turned to Broker. "She was the queen. Was town bad girl for a while, then straightened up, got a job at the real estate office about the time the lakefront took off. So she married Jimmy, and he's going nowhere, driving a garbage truck for his dad. And drinking too much."

Nygard cleared his throat. "Three years ago Jimmy's folks

got killed taking an icy turn too quick. Hit a freakin' moose. All of a sudden Jimmy's got the garbage company and has all this insurance money. Cassie's got her ear on the real estate market . . . then this meth house business blew up.

"See, Cassie, she's gotta go into Bemidji a couple times a month and get her legs waxed at the Spa, whatever. But she'd agreed to watch the neighbor's toddler. So she called her cousin, Sandy, over to babysit the kid. Her boy, Teddy, was in school." Nygard shook his head. "I didn't really know what to look for then when it came to meth use. Now I do." He grimaced and tapped a fingernail against his teeth. "Sandy was twenty going on fifty, way too skinny, and her teeth were gray, turning black, rotting out. Joke around town was how she was giving too many blow jobs to the regulars in back of Skeet's Bar."

Nygard turned in his seat. "We were starting to see meth show up, but I figured it was the Mexicans; the work crews putting the new houses up on the lake. Hell, I busted two of them actually selling it. I was sure it was Mexicans bringing it up from the Cities."

"If they were putting out volume in that house, where were they unloading it?" Broker said.

"Over on the Red Lake Rez, mostly, that's how we put it together." Nygard flopped back in his seat, stared straight ahead at the snow gently boiling in his headlights, and continued talking.

"Sandy took her babysitting seriously, up to a point, I guess; because when she drove to the trash house to score some meth from her brothers, she left little Marci out in the yard by the swing set." Nygard smiled briefly. "Didn't want to take that cute little kid into a filthy place like that, huh? Problem was, there was this big burn pile of cook waste next to the swings, and Marci got playing with it and apparently chewed on some coffee filters they'd used to strain that shit. Among other things.

"When Cassie came home from Bemidji, there was an ambulance in the driveway. The EMTs were up in a bedroom working on Marci. She was hemorrhaging, blood all over the floor. Pulmonary edema. Raced her to Bemidji."

"Did you question the cousin?" Broker asked.

"Couldn't find her. She had made the 911 call, then ran once the EMTs arrived, before my deputy got in the house. All hell broke loose, the Sweitzes went ballistic. Medical examiner was searching the house like crazy, trying to find the poison."

Nygard paused, sipped his coffee, kept staring at the snow. "Then 911 got this tip; that they were cooking meth at the Bodines', and how Sandy had been out there with Marci. How Marci had been seen by the swing set playing in the trash. How there were six kids in that house, and how somebody should get them out.

"Got a court order, no questions asked, and went out there. The adults spotted us coming and split into the woods. Left the kids. Went in there, and I had never seen anything like that. Knee-deep garbage, backed-up toilets, a crop of maggots all over a two-week-old dead dog, human feces. And all this makeshift paraphernalia: Pyrex dishes, hot plates, gas cans with tubes running out of them, battery casings, Mason jars full of gunk. Ether. One room was stacked with empty Heet and Drano containers. Paint thinner cans. Stuff was all mixed in with leftovers and cans of spoiled food. My first meth lab. I couldn't make sense of it, and we had to get those kids to town, to have them examined.

"I called Beltrami County to get some advice, the State Health. Was waiting on some Beltrami cops and firemen who had the training, who had protective suits. That's when the call came in."

Nygard grimaced, swallowed the last of his coffee, and said, "The way we reconstructed it, we figured the Bodines musta snuck back in after we left, to collect their stash. And got careless with fire, somehow ignited all that volatile mess. Got trapped in the building about ten that night when it burned. Marci died the next day in the hospital, respiratory failure."

Broker continued to listen patiently, seeing an obvious payback scenario. He pictured a posse of citizens marching on the house like the peasant mob in *Frankenstein*, tying the Bodines to stakes and setting the fire. Questions occurred about the emergency response, the fire department, whether the fire marshal suspected arson. The autopsy results? But this wasn't a give-and-take conversation, so he kept them to himself. Instead he asked, "What about the babysitter, Sandy?"

Nygard inclined his head down the road in the direction of the pyre of wreckage. "One of the four."

After a moment, Broker hunched his shoulders and shivered slightly, even though the heater was going full blast; his street nightmares were confined to the time when he was single, before he had a child. He didn't ask, but Nygard probably had kids. "So what you're saying is—Cassie and her husband have local sympathy when they go a little crazy paranoid and overprotective about their own kid."

"Wouldn't call it sympathy, exactly. Small town's cruel. More like audience participation. Watching to see what's next." Nygard put the Ranger in gear and carefully backed out onto the road. They drove in silence until they exited the thickest part of the woods.

"Not a good place to break down," Broker finally said.

"You got that. Next place to gas up is sixty miles, South Junction, Manitoba."

When they came out into the jack-pine barrens, Nygard said, "Next stop is closer to town. See, there's a second act."

"How do you mean?" Broker said.

Nygard gestured out the window. "The next couple miles is all swamp, empties into Little Glacier two miles north of the big lake." He lapsed into quiet for a while, then slowed and pulled over next to a barely visible turnoff snaking off into the swamp. "When Pollution Control showed up to do water tests, they talked to the older Bodine children. Kids told them their parents had been dumping the cook waste in the swamp at the end of this trail for years." Nygard pointed off the road, to the right. As they continued down the road, the snow tapered off.

"You see, Jimmy had sunk his windfall into buying half the lakefront on Little Glacier. Divided it into lots and started building a model lake house. Bank got so excited they connived with the county board, rerouted some of the Homeland Security money to put up another cell-phone tower."

More silence ate up the road. Broker looked out the window into the pitch-dark, lonelier now, more empty without the snow falling. Just the spindly black trees. They came to the end of the open barrens, and Nygard turned right down a hilly road. A few minutes later they drove out from the tree cover and stopped overlooking an expanse of faintly shining water hemmed by granite bluffs.

"Pretty," Broker said. Then his eyes adjusted, and he saw the blond wink of a naked lumber frame.

"Jimmy's model house. Construction stopped when the pollution folks found the water table full of junk that leached out of the meth dump up in the swamp. Bank called in his construction loan. He bet everything he had on this development. Now he has to come up with the money to clean it up before he continues construction."

Nygard craned his neck toward the south. "And people are pissed he hasn't cleaned it up. Whole town's scared shitless the crap will travel over to the big lake. Kill the summer trade. Any rate, Jimmy lost his boat, his sled, and one of his garbage trucks. Had to lay off half his help. Now he drives routes twelve hours, six days a week to cover the county. They're still holding on to Jimmy's dad's house on the lake. Don't know how they're making their other payments. The Sweitz family retained a lawyer, trying to sue over their daughter's death." Nygard laughed without humor. "People call this place the Skeleton House. Kind of a local monument to Cassie Bodine's vanity and overreaching. But any rate, there it is. What you stepped into." Nygard looked away, deliberately leaving it there without editorializing.

He turned around and headed back for the main road. "Getting late, let's get you home."

Broker and Griffin stood in the driveway and watched Nygard's taillights fade off around a turn in the road.

"Story from hell, huh," Griffin said. "So what do you wanna do?"

Broker heaved his shoulders. "Guy's got enough problems. Hell, I'll let it go if he will." The fact was, Broker felt a tremendous sense of relief. The stops on Nygard's night tour had moved him off his tight loop of anger. Gave him some perspective.

"Okay, but you may have to toss Klumpe a softball, some little gesture. You handle that? I can talk to him," Griffin said.

"Whatever. Let me know." Broker cuffed Griffin on the shoulder. "Say. Maybe I'll drop by the lodge and help out tomorrow. Nina's feeling better, and I'm the one who's starting to go nuts. I need to get out of the house, man. Work up a sweat. Shoot the shit."

"Cabin fever, I can dig it," Harry said.

"Yeah, whatever," Broker said.

"Great, see you in the morning," Griffin said. Despite Broker's swing into elevated banter, he watched him closely in the harsh yard light. "Now go home to your crazy but very sexy wife," he said, waving good night, walking to his Jeep.

Chapter Twenty-three

Harry Griffin drove toward his house nearer to town, on the south end of the lake, something Broker said sticking in his mind. He just couldn't see Jimmy coming in stealthy through the woods on skis. Jimmy was strictly a tub-of-guts, snowmobile kind of guy.

Have to think about that. Then he turned his attention to Broker. Edgy, sure, but above all, a measured control freak. Throwing that choke hold on Jimmy in a schoolyard in front of the sheriff? That was looking like a loose cannon. Very un-Broker-like.

Harry knew that Broker believed in walling off his ghosts and personal monsters in a system of compartments. Well, it looked like the locks on his control method were starting to go.

In Harry's estimation, Broker had been running damn near thirty years of rope. And now he had reached the end of his tether. In fact, Broker's life had come to resemble a proof of the old Chinese adage: be careful what you wish for. You might get it. He had wanted to reunite his splintered family ever since Nina returned to active duty after Kit was born. Now he had. And look what it was doing to him.

The quiet snow-cloaked woods slid by, his asylum and buffer to a world spinning out of control. Being in proximity to Broker the last three months had started to pry at Harry's own system of controls. The life choices he'd made.

He had walked away from the madness. Broker and Nina were still out there trying to fix it.

And Broker had that judgmental cop streak; never actually

came out and said it, but sometimes Griffin got the feeling Broker thought he had turned tail and run.

Griffin swung into his driveway, drove past the pole barn that housed a rock splitter and the long attached shed with bins for fieldstone and masonry sand. Coming up on the house, he smiled and shook his head when he saw Susan Hatch's tan Honda CRV parked at his back door.

Susan, his on-again, off-again girlfriend. Broker said she'd taken him aside at school this morning. Damn. The woman was more curious than a cat. Her ex-husband had taken their daughter to visit his parents in Bemidji, where he now lived. Susan had the night off.

He went inside, removed his boots and parka on the mud porch, and entered the main living area; one long vaulted room with a kitchen at one end and a massive stone fireplace at the other. A stairway led to another level below, built into the bluff overlooking the lake.

Susan rose from a chair by the hearth to greet him. She'd built up the fire, burned some incense, and made herself comfortable, stripping out of her school clothes and pulling on the shiny threadbare black silk kimono he'd picked up in Bangkok a long time ago. He could almost feel her earnest energy throb across the room; big brown eyes wide open, ears alert for new information.

Susan glided through the firelight playing off the pine paneling with a swish of silk on bare skin. Her eyes and the way she moved always said it the same way: *Old wolf like you is never gonna get another chance like this* . . .

She capitalized on her lean, angular physicality, a type Griffin had always found irresistible; what she lacked in padding she made up for in extra-fast-fire nerve clusters packed close to the surface. She had discovered that Harry Griffin, tight-lipped, rugged to a fault in all the other areas of his life, had a pillow-talk Achilles' heel.

"How'd it go?" she asked, casually shaking out the snare of her curiosity.

Susan knew a little about the Brokers, the new folks in town and therefore a focus of gossip. She knew Broker and Harry had been in Vietnam together for a long time. She knew Broker had been a cop. But she knew virtually nothing about the mysterious "Mrs. Broker." Now, like all the women at the school, she was anxious to hear more.

Griffin shrugged. "We'll get it fixed. Keith's doing his peacemaker number, filling in the background on Jimmy. Why he's a hair-trigger mess. Took Broker out and showed him the Bodine house, explained about Cassie and the Sweitz kid. The fire. The pollution mess. The skeleton house."

"Did Keith tell him Gator Bodine burned the place? With the town's blessing?" Susan asked.

"C'mon, that's hearsay. Nobody knows for sure; all the flammable crap they had in there, anything could have set it off," Griffin said, mouthing the official line.

Susan wrinkled her nose. "Right," she said. "Ruled an accident. No real autopsy. Not what Jeff Tindall said . . ."

Jeff owned the hardware store and was a volunteer fireman.

Susan continued. "Jeff says the people in that house got real confused because they crammed themselves into this tiny, centrally located bathroom. Stoutest room in the house. Good plan for a tornado. Not so good for an exploding meth lab. Jeff found them stuck together"—she wrinkled her pert nose—"layered, kinda like lasagna."

Griffin made an effort to ward her off with his eyes, like he always did, for starters.

"Everyone believes it was Gator, avenging that little girl. He always hated his cousins, going way back. Maybe he saw it as sticking up for his wronged sister, like he always does—"

"Small-town gossip," Griffin said.

Susan didn't even pause. "He went over there, saw what happened, called Keith to get the children out and went back that night and killed his own kin," she said, moving in close. "You know that, like Keith knows it. Everybody knows they have a deal. Since Marci Sweitz died, Keith keeps Gator out there, stalking down anybody cooking that stuff. In return he lets a felon have guns and hunt in the woods. You know that just like you know a lot of things about your pal Broker and his wife—don'tcha."

She eased up and nuzzled his throat, following the angle of his chin with lips and tongue, bit his earlobe, and then moved on to his mouth.

Harry pulled back. "C'mon. I been sitting in the Jeep chain-smoking and pounding down coffee for two hours. I gotta brush my teeth—"

"Or," she whispered, pressing against him and tilting her face up, bold, "you could dip your face in something sweet . . ."

For Susan, sex was merely prelude to the talk that followed. Griffin had come to think of these long talks as the job interview for the open position of long-haul partner and stand-in father figure to Susan's daughter. Trust was an important part of the negotiation.

And trust was achieved through the sharing of personal information.

Griffin sat naked on the rug in front of the hearth. Susan reclined in front of him, firelight tracing the curve of her hips and good legs. Legs crossed, he worked with a needle, thread, and some stuffing from an old life jacket. Squinting, he methodically ran the needle in and out, repairing the blue-and-white bunny. Good with his hands. At fifty-eight, he could lay stone all day, come home, go belly to belly with a woman twenty years younger, and still thread a needle.

"You know," she said in a dreamy voice, "you and Broker are kinda the same size from a distance. Anybody ever have trouble telling you apart in the dark?"

Griffin ignored her. He recalled a TAC sergeant in Ranger school who used to call them "Heckel and Jeckle," but damned if he was going to tell her.

"So you gonna tell me what you're doing?" she asked with one of his Luckies hanging from the corner of her mouth.

"Nope." It amazed Griffin, how she could stretch out naked on the rug and smoke just one cigarette. He fluffed the toy, inspected the restored proportions, and decided Kit would never know her bunny had been disemboweled by a ski pole. He set the bunny aside.

"Code of the West? Post-Vietnam Lost Boys Sacred Oath?" Susan arched an eyebrow. "Just what is your pact with Phil Broker?" She leaned forward and trailed her fingers over the thick blight of withered scar tissue that wrapped the muscle above his left knee. "Does it have something to do with this?"

He removed her hand, reached over, plucked the smoke from her lips, and took a drag. Gave it back. "What's the point?" he asked.

Susan studied the burning cigarette between her fingers, looked up. "Maybe I can help."

Griffin grumbled but did not break eye contact. Encouraged, Susan continued. "I've been watching Kit Broker at school. She plays alone. She's way too self-contained for an eight-year-old. She's learned how to distance. Knows how to deflect any questions about her family, her past. It's like she's being . . . coached. That's masking behavior . . . stuff you might see in kids with abuse at home, or criminal activity."

Griffin uncrossed his legs, recrossed them, reached for his own cigarette, lit it. Stared at her.

"What's Kit got at home?" Susan asked. "What's the big deal? You tell people he works on your crew, but he really doesn't. He hardly ever shows up. You're providing sanctuary. Why?"

Griffin stared at the fire and thought about it. After Nina had her head-on collision with depression, Broker had called in some chits. He'd just been up for deer hunting and knew the house on the lake was unoccupied for the winter. It was the perfect remote retreat for Nina to tough it out . . .

He engaged the concern in Susan's eyes. True. They had not considered Kit as a factor. Figured she'd go along as obedient baggage. Now Susan was raising flags. He turned from the fire and faced her.

"You're asking a lot," he said.

Susan shrugged her bare shoulders. "What I see is the kid. Especially after she punched out Teddy Klumpe. She's way too tough for eight. That could come from carrying too much weight. Like she's wearing armor. Somebody should say something to the parents. Is trying to stop a kid from getting damaged asking a lot?"

"Broker and his buddies do have a code," Griffin said. "The main part of it has to do with loyalty."

"Okay," Susan said. "That's for them, cops. Ex-cops. Whatever. Not you. Or is this because you were Army buddies back in the day?"

"Jesus, you don't give up," Griffin said.

Susan grinned and poked his flat stomach with her finger. "Nope." She scooted closer, rested her elbows on his knees. "C'mon. Who are they?"

"I thought you were concerned with Kit."

"Sure, and I'm thinking, my Amy's the same age. We could get them together for a play date, for starters. That way I could meet her mom, get it going back and forth," Susan said.

"They didn't come up here for play dates and coffee with the moms. Pretty much the opposite," Griffin said. His voice sharpened and Susan saw the fast warning shadow pocket his face.

Sensing she'd hit a boundary, she sat back, folded her arms across her modest breasts, and gave back a little challenging edge of her own. "You're overdramatizing, as usual."

"Listen, Susan; they're not going to be here long enough for Kit to get damaged," Griffin said.

"You sure about that? He's your friend. You should help him."

True. Which got Griffin thinking . . .

Susan waited patiently. She'd been North Woods raised on the big lake and was a seasoned angler. She knew when she felt a nibble, knew the proper time to play out a little more line.

Except Griffin was now thinking about the other thing; how no way Jimmy could come into the place on skis. So somebody else could be in this. Somebody who played real rough. Finally he said, "Look, it's complicated . . ."

Susan took a last drag on her one cigarette, twisted, and flipped it into the fireplace. When she turned back, she took her time, letting the firelight play over the very serviceable curves of the only intelligent eligible woman in Glacier Falls who would take a chance on a silvertip loner like Harry Griffin.

Griffin started over, speaking carefully. "It's like this with Broker and his wife. You know how when there's a crisis—say a building catches fire—everybody runs. Except there's two people who go back into the fire to take care of the casualties . . ."

Susan sat up straight. She had never felt his eyes range in on her quite this way, like hard iron sights. She nodded her head slightly.

"Well," Griffin continued, "it's good we have people like that around when all hell breaks loose. But maybe it's not such a good idea if they get married to each other and have a kid."

Deliberately, Griffin stood up and stared at her, to let it sink in. She knew him as an intense guy; and now she'd hit a new wall in him. Macho guy loyalty. Whatever. She sobered a bit, seeing the warning frown in his eyes. Shucks, so much for afterglow. And he was standing in a certain way, this quiet power stancing, cautioning her away from the subject. Then he turned and walked from the main room toward the bathroom. A moment later, Susan heard the shower start to run.

Susan hugged herself in front of the fire. She looked down and saw a faint tickle of goose bumps rise on her forearms. It was the first time he'd revealed a part of himself that actually worried her.

Chapter Twenty-four

The alarm went off, and Sheryl Mott got up in her efficiency apartment on Lincoln Avenue in St. Paul. Five-fuckin'-thirty in the morning. Still dark out—and this is after doing a six-hundred-mile round trip yesterday, missing work . . . she gingerly touched the rash on her cheeks from Gator's Brillo-pad four-o'clock shadow.

Mission Impossible theme music was playing in her head. *Your assignment, if you choose to accept it . . .*

Her assignment today was Dickie Werk, Werky for short.

Richard M. Werk maintained an office in the Ramsey Building, a liver-colored brownstone near Mears Park in downtown St. Paul. He employed a secretary, two legal clerks, and an "investigator." Simon Hanky, the investigator, was a vetted OMG soldier whose main job was to keep an eye on Werky and clean up messes. Sheryl had some history with Hanky, and he was one scary fella.

Werky rented space to three young, eager, world-saver attorneys who rallied to the defense of disadvantaged inner-city youth who had difficulty finding gainful employment in a tough economy . . . and were forced to support themselves by robbing and selling dope. And stabbing and shooting people.

Sheryl rolled her eyes, shook her head, planted her feet on the chilly hardwood floor, and pushed up off the bed.

Werky was the kind of overly self-dramatizing guy who never outgrew snarfing his first line of cocaine in law school, blowing his brains out listening to Warren Zevon's *Lawyers Guns and Money* at max volume. He ate too much, sweated too much, talked too much and had this absolute, and potentially fatal, fascination with rubbing up against hard-core criminals.

She had heard him blab at a party once; comparing himself to Robert Duvall playing Tom Hagen in *The Godfather*. How he only had one client. Wink, wink.

But pulsing in all that corpulent narcissism was a brilliant legal mind totally devoted to getting Danny T.'s convictions over-turned. So the gang indulged Werky's affectations. So far.

Sheryl sighed and headed for the bathroom. A few minutes later she was worried she had a mild kidney infection. Goddamn Gator wouldn't use condoms. Made her stand around after so he could see his jizz . . .

Back on task. Werky.

How to proceed. After Seattle had exploded in her face, Sheryl didn't indulge nobody anymore.

She didn't trust Werky's office help or his do-good office mates.

She didn't trust the office phones.

Neither did Werky. He handled his One Client's real business affairs exclusively by cell phone in his car. Had a whole stash of cells. Use them one time and toss them. So she'd have to catch him in his car.

She took a shower, washed and blow-dried her hair, put on minimal makeup, a long denim skirt, a mock turtleneck, and a long leather coat that reached down past the tops of her tall leather boots.

No sense in giving Werky ideas by showing skin.

She tucked Gator's stolen paperwork into her purse, went down to the street, and started the Pontiac. Then she stopped at the Grand and Dale drugstore, bought a pack of Merit filters. Two blocks down, she picked up a tall cardboard cup of Starbucks with a couple shots of espresso. Then she joined the steel-and-glass bumper-to-bumper escalator of commuters going down Grand Hill into St. Paul. She inched through the business district and turned into the parking garage next to the Ramsey Building. Drove to the contract parking level in the basement. Some things don't change. Werky still had a parking stall with his name on it.

The stall was empty.

She parked one floor up in hourly, took the stairs down, and walked a figure eight in the crowd of sleepy-eyed nine-to-fivers getting out of their cars and marching into the skyways. She kept a sharp watch on the parking stall.

Two Merits later: bingo. The shiny black Escalade wheeled in on a plush squeal of Michelin radials. Sheryl took a deep breath. The OMG gang had matured around dope from street thugs into serious big-time crooks. Trick was to be nimble, like a fly zipping through a sticky spiderweb. Get in and out fast. And not get wrapped up and eaten. She walked up to the tinted driver's-side window and tapped.

The window zipped down an inch. An eye appeared in a thick puddle of a glasses lens.

"Yeah?" said the eye.

She watched the eye cross-reference a databank of faces, names, levels of trust and threat, and quickly reach a decision:

"How you doin', Sheryl?"

"Hiya, Werky."

"What's up?"

"Need you to look at something."

The eye fluttered, amused. "Like your tattoo? You still got it?"

Mastering an impulse to puke all over his fancy wax job, Sheryl said, "You gonna make me stand out here in the cold?"

The door locks snapped open. Sheryl walked around the front of the SUV, opened the passenger-side door, and slid into the deep leather bucket seat.

Same old Werky, piled up like Jabba the Hutt's pinstriped baby brother. He licked his gummy lips and said, "You're looking well, Sheryl. Threadbare but righteous. Sorta like the Little Match Girl."

Sheryl resolved to keep her cool. She had once known a Las

Vegas hooker who swore that men were all just physical extensions of their dicks. Werky fit the pattern; short, sixty pounds over-weight, and lopsided with a head too small for the rest of him.

She removed the sheaf of papers Gator had lifted from Broker's house from her purse and handed them to him.

Seeing the documents, Werky's demeanor changed. Focusing fast, he flipped through the pages, his voice concentrating in a meditative "Hmmm." Sheryl sipped the remains of her coffee and waited. Another, longer "Hmmmm" followed by an impressed: "No shit." Now Werky had tilted his thick glasses down his nose, looking over them as he scanned the warrant, the memo, the Visa statement, and the Washington County pay voucher. "The missing puzzle piece. Perhaps," he said slowly. When he looked up at her, his eyes darted fast and alert. "Where'd you get this?"

Sheryl gave him a brief, ambiguous smile.

"So," he said.

"So?" she said.

"You want something," Werky said, waffling the papers in his hand. "In exchange."

Sheryl pursed her lips and said, "Consider it a gift. For now, just make Danny aware of what's in those papers. I know it nags him, the way Jojo checked out. You can talk to Danny, right? So no one's listening in."

"I can do that." Werky cocked his head.

"Just tell him I said hello. And, ah, maybe, after you make that call, we could talk again," Sheryl said.

"I see," Werky said slowly, watching her as he heaved in his seat, reached in the back, and pushed open a square leather briefcase the size of a small Duluth pack, started to insert the papers. "May I?"

Sheryl shrugged, "Sure, they're yours."

"Good," Werky said. He tucked the papers out of sight and removed a yellow legal pad, picked up a pen from the dash, and handed pen and pad to her. "Give me a number where you can be reached day or night."

Sheryl jotted down her cell, handed back the pen and pad, and started to open the door.

Werky laid his porcine hand on her arm, friendly. "Nice seeing you again, Sheryl," he said, no games, level and businesslike.

"Yeah, me too," she said.

Werky maintained the pressure on her arm. "Welcome back," he said.

"Yeah," Sheryl said, trying to maintain her unassuming expression and stuff her building anticipation. *Shit, they might actually go for this.*

Werky released her arm; she opened the door and got out. As she closed it, she saw him reaching for the car phone. She headed for the stairs. Three minutes later she was strapped into her seat belt and pulling the Pontiac out of the parking garage.

Chapter Twenty-five

Nina lay in bed watching the stucco ceiling slowly emerge from darkness; a hieroglyphic of veined cracks and blots of water that had taken months to master and finally read:

"Crazy," Nina whispered to the half-light in the shuttered bedroom.

Just a word, two syllables, two sounds. That is, until it finally wears you down like a sweaty high school boyfriend who just won't stop insisting: "If you really love me, you'll . . ."

At some point you give in.

She had not made love to her husband in over a year. Crazy was the Thing that shared her bed, and now she knew it more intimately than Broker's body. Its smell, its familiar stir, the urgent touch of the incessant demands it made in the night.

The last word she said at night. The first word she said every morning.

But this morning something was different, as, beyond the ajar bedroom door, the sounds and smells of morning filled the house and meandered up the stairs. She heard Broker enter Kit's room, pull the window blinds. Heard him say in an upbeat voice, "Not a cloud in the sky. It's gonna be sunny today." Then to Kit, "C'mon, get up. Feet on the deck."

Less distinct was Kit's grumbling as she stirred in the warm covers. Nina pictured her rotating her hips, planting her feet on the floor, rubbing her eyes, and staring at her father as he left the room and went down the stairs.

Kit dressed, made her bed, descended the stairs. Breakfast; a muted clatter, far away. Nina continued to lie on her back, arms across her chest, motionless as a medieval statue on top of a tomb.

Then she moved her arms, stretched, and enjoyed the movement. The inertia trembled around her, crumbling. She dry-washed her arms, her chest, ran her fingers over her face, touched her hair. Pushed off the invisible detritus. In the faint light creeping at the edges of the drawn window shades, she saw the first glow of a Monarch dawn.

Broker entered the room wearing his busted-out work clothes. He cocked his head, seeing her sitting up in bed. He'd always been a man who approached you slow and quiet, reserved. Today he was too upbeat. A little jagged.

"Sun's out. You got the house to yourself. I'm going to hang with Griffin today, do a little work," he said.

Then Kit vaulted up on the bed and kissed her on the cheek. "Bye, Mom."

She waved vaguely, thoroughly enjoying the tactile glide of her skin through the musty air. Then she flopped back in the covers as Broker and Kit left the room. Again she studied the ceiling stains and cracks. Now they hovered; Delphic, potent.

What had changed?

The answer came as she heard them leave the house. She remembered . . . all of yesterday. Normally, in real-time sequence; not sliced in random wedges. The ceiling had not changed. It was the way she looked at it.

For the first time in months her first thoughts were not of herself, but of Broker. Depression seemed to turn on a simple inside/outside trick. The more you climbed out of your own head, the more you broke its hold. So Broker. After he dropped Kit off at school, he'd go help Griffin at Glacier Lodge. Which was good. He'd been cooped up in the house all winter, and now he was starting to screw up, like leaving the garage open. Losing the cat. His explosion of nerves yesterday morning—raging at the towels in the washer . . . Then Griffin dropping in after supper. What was that about? She heard the door shut. The truck start up. She was alone.

As she swung her feet off the bed, she felt the sheets and covers; they were dry. Cool to the touch. No longer sweat-fouled. She pulled on her robe, put on her slippers, and walked down the stairs and into the kitchen.

Coming into the room, she paused, eyes downcast out of habit, and braced for her first look at the sky out the windows at the far end of the kitchen.

Fear of clouds that would steal the light.

Nina Pryce—B.A. in liberal arts, master's in business administration, University of Michigan; Phi Beta Kappa; eligible for Mensa, too cool to accept—had come to exist on the superstitious level of an Egyptian peasant from the Middle Kingdom; paying homage to the sun.

This morning she felt a blush of warmth eke in from the east and caress her face. Galvanized by the sunrise, she continued into the room. Broker had cleared away the debris of the previous night, loaded the dishwasher, straightened up the clutter, and wiped all the surfaces clean. A fresh carafe of coffee sat on the counter. She poured a cup, sheltering it close to her chest, and stood huddled in her robe. She faced east, staring out through the patio door, over the deck, the shoreline, and the broad gray expanse of Glacier Lake.

The platinum flare of late-winter sun burned through the mist, revealing a layered dawn of burnished seashell pink and purple. She smiled, sipped the coffee, and watched the eastern tree line ignite into a happy morning sunrise that hurled bright skipping stones across the lake. Then long shadows jumped out from the cluster of paper birches in the yard. There were mornings she'd recoiled from the birches, seeing skeletal fingers in the crooked white trunks with their black markings. The shadows reaching for the house . . .

Today they were just trees, and she was able to remember an

afternoon when Griffin had stopped over with Teedo, the Indian guy who worked with him. Teedo had explained to Kit how the birches got their markings. Nanboujou, the Ojibwa trickster, had angered the thunderbirds who were pursuing him through the forest. He'd ducked into a hollow birch trunk. The thunderbirds, unable to stop, had smacked into the trunk, leaving for all time their skid marks . . .

A normal thought.

Just trees. The shadows they cast stopped midway up the yard.

Nina set down her coffee cup and walked through the entire first level of the house, opening the shades and drapes, drenching the rooms with light. Stronger now, she refilled her cup and threw open the patio door, stepped onto the deck, and felt the pale sunlight on her face. The nip of the cold air.

She went back in hungry. A bowl of Total, a banana. Toast and peanut butter. Fuel. For the weights in the living room.

After breakfast, a tremble of doubt as the force of habit set in. A lingering whisper of the Crazy. A time of pacing on the deck, opening a fresh pack of cigarettes, brewing a second pot of coffee, waiting for the sunlight to slowly exorcize the darkness from the house. As the sun arced overhead, the shadows fleeing to the west would stall, retract, and began to shrink down and finally disappear. When the house was cleansed of darkness, she could finally begin her day.

Not today.

She poured the coffee into the sink, extinquished the cigarette, and went into the living room to confront the second challenge of the day.

The weights.

The dumbbells lined up on the broad seat of the bay window in the living room; nine pairs of them—five pounds to fifty.

The numbing two-pound repetitions of the physical therapy had been completed. She raised her right arm, no longer anticipating the tug as it approached shoulder level. Rotated her elbow left and right. No tug. No pain. Okay. The soft tissue had healed. To a point. She drew her shoulder blades together, aligning the bones in her shoulder and her back like the tumblers on a combination. Almost audible clicks as she slowly elevated the arm over her shoulder. She paused there, evaluating the slight hitch. Lowered her arm. Encouraged, she picked up the ten-pound weight. Lifted it smoothly.

She put down the ten and grasped the fifteen. Brought it up in a biceps curl. Then she raised her elbow and lifted her whole arm and felt the warning catch in the complicated architecture of her right shoulder. Just like yesterday. The impinged shoulder accepted ten, but protested and quit at fifteen.

She inhaled and started up again. Sweat popped on her forehead. A strand of hair fell across her eyes. She huffed a breath, blew the hair away, and lifted the weight, got to shoulder level, and hit the solid lock of the blown-out bursa.

Trembling, she lowered the weight. For a month she'd been telling herself: tomorrow, just keep gobbling down the Tylenol. Placate the inflamed bursitis. It'll start mending tomorrow. Knit back together, then the strength would come . . .

She let the weights fall to the carpet, turned, walked into the kitchen, out the door, and sat on the deck.

Stop kidding yourself. It was time to face the truth.

Chapter Twenty-six

Harry Griffin woke up feeling the warm impression Susan had left in his bed. She'd left early, in a hurry, driving to Bemidji. But her words were fresh in his mind, how he should help his friend.

He unsheathed the notion slowly over breakfast, as he filled his work thermos with coffee, made a sandwich. Sort of laid it out on the table, looked at it. There was another layer to this thing. The skiing part kept coming back, didn't track. Not for Jimmy.

Susan had invoked the subject of Gator Bodine. Another local mystery man, living alone in his spooky woods with his treasure trove of antique tractors. Only came into town to get his groceries, or dicker over machine parts at Shulty's Implements.

And to ski the trails around the big lake.

He pictured Gator, hard packed with his grease-monkey muscles. Convict pensive. Spiky hair and perpetual two-day beard like a sweaty wire brush. Sporting his famous tattoo. They had never actually spoken, only nodded from a distance at the Last Chance Amoco or Perry's grocery. Like two big dogs, maybe. Knew of each other by reputation, respected each other's territory.

Bound to collide eventually.

So instead of driving straight to the job site, he took a run through town, out to Jimmy's garage. Coming up on Klumpe Sanitation, he saw Jimmy's brown Ford parked in front. Saw Jimmy through the open garage door, washing down one of his trucks in a billow of steam.

Okay, let's do a little community outreach.

He parked next to the Ford and walked in through the open door.

Jimmy, hosing down his best Labrie garbage truck, wearing high rubber boots, watched the red Jeep wheel into the yard. Knew it was Griffin. Knew every car and truck in town. Now what's he want? He turned off the hose and waited for Griffin to approach through the cloud of steam rising off the wet concrete.

They didn't particularly care for each other.

Like Keith, Griffin was one of the men in town Jimmy couldn't intimidate. In fact, Griffin could be downright scary. Jimmy'd been in Skeet's couple years back; the November night a group of drunk hunters, up from the cities, jumped Keith's deputy, Howie Anderson, brained him out with a cue ball. Keith showed up a few minutes later with Griffin in tow for backup. The drunks unloaded a volley of pool balls, and Jimmy recalled in pins-and-needles detail how Griffin had flashed fast-forward into the drunk-footed crowd. How he had snapped off a pool cue in a corner pocket, butt-stroked two guys to the floor in blinding succession, and then jammed the jagged end of the stick up against this big dude's throat.

Jimmy clearly remembered the little beads of blood on the guy's neck, Griffin looking unhappy it was ending, taunting in a voice that had given Jimmy the shivers, "What's the spirit of the bayonet, motherfucker."

Happened so fast.

No way Jimmy wanted Harry Griffin speeding up into his life. Not now, especially with the dicey arrangement he and Cassie had going with Gator. Uh-uh.

"Morning, Griffin," he said in a neutral tone.

"Let's skip the chitchat. You don't like me, I don't like you. But me and Keith had a talk with Phil Broker last night . . ."

"Yeah?"

"There's been some petty shit going back and forth. Nothing that can be exactly pinned on anybody. Is that a fair assessment?"

"Fucker dumped his garbage in front of my office. That's what I know, 'cause Halley, my driver, saw him leaving. So I called Keith. And his sneaky kid sucker-punched Teddy," Jimmy said slowly, belligerently. Adding a scowl.

Oh-oh, the scowl was a mistake.

Because Griffin stepped in close and stabbed his right hand, stiff fingers tight together, into Jimmy's chest. Hard, so it hurt. Jimmy's hands started to come up defensively but stopped when he saw the merry anticipation in Griffin's eyes, like he'd enjoy seeing Jimmy bleed at eight in the morning. Jimmy backed up. Griffin grinned, a sort of wild, mindless face, like an animal who smells fear. Damn.

"What about you?," Griffin said slowly. "You been doing a little cross-country on the trails back of my place where Broker's staying, huh? Sneaking around puncturing his tires?" The hand hovered, ready to strike again.

"Not me," Jimmy said sincerely.

"Don't bullshit me, Jimmy—"

"No bullshit. I ain't been on skinny skis since high school," Jimmy said.

"I thought so," Griffin said slowly, watching Jimmy's eyes. When he moved his hand, Jimmy winced, but Griffin only softly rubbed the spot on Jimmy's chest where he'd poked him.

"I got no quarrel with you," Jimmy said, indignant. "What do you want, coming in here like this?"

"Keith wants to nip it. Make it stop between you and Broker. So what do you need?"

"No kidding?"

"Hey, Jimmy, I'm losing daylight here. What will get us over this hump?"

Jimmy thought about it. "He's gotta apologize to me and Teddy in front of people. At the school. How's that?"

"I'll talk to him, see what I can do," Griffin said. "If he meets you halfway, in front of people, you'll shake on it, okay?"

Jimmy narrowed his eyes. "And he buys Teddy a new shirt to replace the one that got blood on it."

Griffin held up his hands. "That's fair. I'll get back to you." He turned and started walking back to his Jeep. Then he turned and said, "You ain't been on skis since high school, is that a fact?"

Jimmy rolled his eyes. It was getting complicated. He shook his head, like a man trying to comprehend an absurd question. As Griffin drove away, Jimmy went immediately to the phone on the wall and called Gator.

"Griffin was just here throwing his weight around."

Huh? In five seconds flat. Throwing his weight around, how? "What do you *mean*?" Gator said, going from zero to max exasperation. Fucking dummy. He had his cell phone wedged awkwardly between his shoulder and his ear as he jockeyed the clutch plate on the Moline. Actually hoping it was Sheryl who was calling.

"He was pushing at me. Accused me of messing with Broker's truck, giving him a flat tire. I didn't do that," Jimmy huffed. He was careful to leave out the ski part. The obvious part, because everybody knew he didn't cross-country. Whereas everybody knew Gator had a wall full of ribbons.

"Anything else?" Gator said.

"Ah, yeah," Jimmy said, spanning the sins of omission with a hint of relief. "He says him and Keith will get Broker to apologize to me and Teddy. He caved."

Moron, Gator thought, as he watched the black kitten wolf down the Chef's Blend through the open office door. He said, "That's great, Jimmy. So you got what you wanted."

"Ah, what about Griffin? Coming around. I don't really want to mess with him, you know."

"Aw, he's probably just sticking up for his buddy. Nothing to it. We'll just let Keith do his thing, like I said."

"So everything's all right?"

"Yeah, Jimmy. Everything's cool," Gator said. When he hung up, he didn't share his brother-in-law's sense of relief. Griffin showing up as a wild card was far from cool. They'd never crossed paths, and Gator hoped to keep it that way.

Distracted, staring at the clock on the wall, then at the phone on his desk; he didn't think Griffin was anything to worry about. Yet. It'd blow over, the petty feud part. But the other thing . . .

He wiped off his hands on a rag and walked into the office. Chided himself. Stop watching the phone. Too early for Sheryl to check in. And she didn't deal in maybes. She'd wait until she had something definite.

When he reached down to stroke the kitten, she darted away under the desk.

"You'll come around," he said. "Because I feed you and give you shelter. You need me." Just like Jimmy and Cassie came around. He turned back to the tractor in his bay. It took time. Like the Moline. Be months before he could make it whole.

Gator held that the combustion engine resembled the human body; used fuel like food, used air just like lungs.

Then he paused and considered the plan he'd set in motion against Phil Broker's life. Well, there was one fundamental difference between people and machines: once they turned Broker off, no way he was going to start up again.

Chapter Twenty-seven

Broker dropped Kit off at school, drove back through town, and turned north on Lakeside Road, which served as the frontage road for the west side of the lake. After about a mile, he wheeled toward the lake at the Glacier Lodge sign. A thick stand of balsam and spruce masked the empty parking lot in front of the gabled lodgepole pine building set on a rocky point. Didn't see Griffin's Jeep, just Teedo's black Ford.

Broker parked and walked around to the lakeside, where the carpenters had put up a shelter, two-by-sixes and two-by-fours supporting a tent of black insulated tarps. Inside this tent, warmed by a propane heater, Griffin and Teedo had been laying a flagstone porch and patio—winter work, the lodge owner's late February inspiration. He wanted the patio ready for fishing opener in May. Pallets stacked with Montana flagstone and sacks of mortar surrounded the tent. A Bobcat. The locker where Griffin kept his tools.

Teedo Dove, Griffin's apprentice, was feeding pieces of familiar split oak into a fire he'd started in a length of steel culvert. That oak was Broker's main contribution to the crew he was supposed to work on. Put all the days he'd actually handled the stone in a string, and it wouldn't stretch two weeks for the whole winter. A mound of masonry sand heaped over the culvert with a half fifty-five-gallon drum of water heating on the top. A gasoline-powered cement mixer and wheelbarrow was positioned alongside. Teedo, at twenty-seven, stood six-two and went around 250. A Red Lake Ojibwa, he was soft-spoken, bearlike, light on his feet, and a quiet drinker. Hounded by Griffin, he sporadically attended the local AA meeting. He originally blamed his drinking on his decision nine years ago not to take the full-ride scholarship he'd been offered, playing right tackle at Bemidji State. Griffin's simple advice on alcoholism was typically blunt: "Don't put it in your mouth."

He'd taken Teedo on as a reclamation project. Griffin was big on stuff like that. Interventions. Rescues. He'd been resocialized by Alcoholics Anonymous. Up to a point. Sometimes Broker glimpsed edges of the old Griffin, the brilliant but erratic risk taker in Vietnam. Broker had looked on their war as a job with really shitty working conditions. Griffin was more the dark romantic, in Broker's opinion; a man who had been more than a little in love with death.

"Morning, Teedo," he said. "Where's the boss?"

"Ain't here," Teedo said with blank Zen presence. "Feed the fire. I'll set up some stone. Then we'll mix some mud." He disappeared into the tent to arrange the stone.

After tossing more wood on the fire, Broker unscrewed the cup from his thermos and poured some coffee. He looked out over the lake, felt the warm sun on his face, saw it sparkle on the calm water. The temperature was thirty degrees and rising. If this kept up, they wouldn't need the fire to warm the sand and water. They could peel back the tarps and work in the morning light.

The sunlight dissolved the harsh cold out of his crystallized breath. Panes of thin ice glistened, about to melt in the puddles. He could almost smell a softness in the air—sap rising—hear the tentative bird calls. A faint hush of green buds trembled in the branches of the aspen and birches.

Buoyed by the caress of the sun, he thought, Damn. It was just possible, that, like Persephone emerging from the underworld, he and Nina and Kit had survived their black winter.

Teedo plugged his radio into an outlet in the porch siding and filled the tent with a wail and groan of country music, punctuated with news of the war. Broker mixed mortar, shoveled it into the barrow, and wheeled it out of the sunlight into the limbo of naked lightbulbs strung in the tent. Teedo troweled the mortar down and leveled the patio flags.

Broker was mixing the second batch of mud when Griffin arrived and waved Broker over to his Jeep, then handed him the new improved bunny and the cat's collar. Broker stuffed the collar in his pocket and, after inspecting the subtle repair job, said, "Thanks. I'll tell her I found it jammed under the seat." He put the stuffed toy in the Tundra, came back.

"I stopped off to visit with Jimmy Klumpe this morning," Griffin said.

"You been busy," Broker said carefully.

"Here's the deal. You gotta come up with a face-saving gesture, something he will accept as an apology."

Broker shrugged, "No sweat, sure. After what I saw and heard last night—"

"And he wants you to replace the shirt Teddy got bloody."

"Jesus, you got me running the gauntlet," Broker made a mock show of protest.

Griffin laughed. "Do you good. An exercise in making amends. Practice some humility. C'mon. Time to work."

As the morning continued warm, they fell into a rhythm. Griffin sliced the flagstone sheets into irregular slabs with his heavy diamond-blade saw. Broker loaded the wheelbarrow, ferried the pieces into the tent, and arranged them in a pattern on the concrete patio footing. Teedo followed Broker, adjusting the spacing, leveling, and mudding them in place.

As Broker loaded the raw stone, he watched Griffin work. Years ago he'd speculated Griffin would watch *Jeremiah Johnson* one too many times, give up entirely on people, and migrate north clear through Manitoba into the territories.

Griffin reminded Broker of a story from his youth about a hermit who'd lived in the canoe country north of Ely, who resisted being relocated when the government created the Boundary Waters canoe area. When it became clear that the law would come in and forcibly move him, the guy had forted up on an island with a crate of dynamite, sat down, and lit the fuse.

Rather than return to civilization.

Griffin preferred to work alone. Or in Teedo's large, quiet shadow, which was the next thing to being alone. And Broker wasn't sure if the repetitious lifting and placing of the heavy stone was a meditation or a form of solitary penance. One morning, returning for a second consecutive day, he noticed that Griffin had torn apart a mosaic of stone Broker had laid out on the concrete base and then rearranged it to his own satisfaction. The gesture was consistent with a theory Broker had about his friend; that Griffin constantly tore himself down and reshaped his image.

Because he couldn't accept who he really was.

It was a persistent point of tension between them, going all the way back to the old days when they first operated together in Vietnam. More than any man he knew, Broker believed Griffin should have stayed in the Army. Not a particularly kind observation. But a true one.

Half past eleven. Break time; they retrieved their lunch bags and thermoses, sat in a corner of the tent, ate sandwiches, and poured coffee. Then the jive games began.

Griffin squinted through the smoke from the Lucky in his lips at Teedo. "You notice how Broker kinda creaks when he moves, like's got sand in his crank case? Hey, Broker, when's the last time you got laid, anyway?"

Broker fired back without missing a beat. "I don't know about you transplants from Detroit, but up on the North Shore, where I grew up, a guy only gets allotted about five hundred million erections. What can I say—when they're gone, they gone."

Undeterred, Griffin winked at Teedo. "He ain't seen all the ads on TV; Viagra, Cialis . . ."

"That's 'cause they ain't aimed at him; they're for old farts like you who can barely eat a little pussy between naps," Teedo said.

Broker grinned and held up a Ziploc bag full of raw cut broccoli, cauliflower, and carrots.

Teedo passed, wrinkling his nose.

Griffin grinned. "He don't eat vegetables, among other things."

Teedo grunted. "We got a word for people who eat too many vegetables."

"Yeah, what's that?" Griffin needled.

"Bad hunter," Teedo said with flawless timing.

Broker felt the muscles of his face loosen in a genuine grin. Not to be outdone, Griffin appraised Teedo and said with great formality, "What I heard is you Indian guys don't go in for oral sex."

Teedo's round face revealed nothing. "My daddy always said that Ojibwa can eat beaver and stretch it too."

Griffin hung his head, laughing, unable to top that. After a pause, he turned to Broker. "Speaking of pussy, you ever find the cat?"

"No kitty; one way or the other, she's gone," Broker said. "Kit's pretty bummed—the cat was all she had to play with."

"Want me to find another?"

Broker ground his teeth lightly. "Might be best to get one back in Stillwater."

"Oh?" Griffin raised his eyebrows. "You got something to tell me?"

Broker shrugged. "Things are looking better. Let's wait and see . . ."

Hearing that, Griffin studied Broker for a moment and added, "Uh-huh." Then he signaled that the break was over. "Enough grabass, we got work to do."

The early afternoon passed quickly, and Broker felt himself loosening up, enjoying the work tugging at his muscles. The tease and dig of easy male company was an antidote to the estrogen bends, he decided; he'd been too far down in that house with Nina and Kit. When he prepared to leave to pick Kit up from school, Griffin caught up to him at his truck.

"You know," Griffin said, "I was thinking about what you said—the cat being Kit's only playmate . . ."

"Yeah?"

"You met Susan, right, at school?"

"Yeaahh . . ." Broker drew it out, watching the wheels turning in Griffin's eyes.

"So I was thinking. Susan's got this daughter, Amy, same age as Kit. Maybe we could line them up so Kit's got somebody to hang with . . . might make it go easier."

Broker worried his lower lip between his teeth, his eyes weighing the idea. "I'll think about it."

"If we get the kids together, could be a good idea for Susan and Nina to maybe talk . . ."

"This one of your half-assed interventions?" Broker smiled when he said it, amiable.

"Can't hurt," Griffin said.

Broker turned and headed for his truck. "We on for tomorrow morning in the torture chamber?" Once a week Broker joined Griffin in his basement weight room, where they went through a lifting routine.

"Sure."

"We'll talk about it then, along with how much politically correct crow I gotta eat to make the peace with that asshole Klumpe," Broker said, getting in his truck.

Teedo walked over to Griffin. They stood watching Broker drive off.

"You heard what's been going on?" Griffin asked.

Teedo nodded. "Heard the gang talking it up at Skeet's. How Broker put Jimmy Klumpe on the ground. Started when Broker's kid knocked Teddy Klumpe on his butt at school. Then yesterday Broker dumped his garbage at Jimmy's garage, right on the welcome mat."

"There's more. Two days ago, after the scene at school, somebody came in on skis through the woods, punctured a tire on his truck, tried to poison his dog"—Griffin paused—"maybe got in the house . . ."

"Country payback. Except he ain't got a dog," Teedo said.

"Yeah. But they took some stuff, a kid's toy, maybe the cat. Weird, huh? Can you picture a klutz like Jimmy going in on skis?" Griffin picked up two empty gas cans, started to put them in the open lift door of his Jeep.

"Don't sound like Jimmy. Day before last, huh?"

"Yeah."

"Day before last, I gassed up at the Amoco and the truck in front of me was that old beat-up Chevy Gator Bodine drives."

Hearing Gator's name, Griffin stopped in mid-motion, loading a gas can in the back of his Jeep. He turned, giving Teedo his full attention. "What time was this?" he asked.

"Ah, midafternoon. We quit early, remember. And I stopped before I went to Skeet's for a couple beers. Thing was"—Teedo paused for emphasis—"there was cross-country skis and poles in the truck box. With snow on them. And when Gator come out of the station carrying a bag, he was wearing those ski boots. And winter camos, like for bow hunting."

"Gator, huh?"

"Yeah. He's a demon for skinny skis." Teedo turned toward his truck, climbed in, started the engine, zipped down the window, leaned out. "Griffin, you're getting that look in your eye. Like when you first hauled me to an AA meeting."

Griffin shrugged.

Teedo paused to let Griffin appreciate the serious shadow that came into his quiet eyes. "I'd be real careful around Gator. He ain't true."

"C'mon, Teedo, what?" Griffin straightened up, prodded by the fast lick of danger in Teedo's expression.

Teedo gnawed his lip, looked away, and spoke into the distance. "Take a minute to think. You want to go into it, I'll be at Skeet's. You can buy me a beer, huh." Then he zipped up the window, covering the bare hint of an ironic grin, and drove away.

Alone behind the lodge, Griffin lit a cigarette and poured the last of the coffee out of his thermos, thinking about what Teedo had seen at the Amoco.

Gator. It tracked. Cassie's kid gets thumped. Gator always fought his sister's battles. And if the story about the meth house fire was true, he had a propensity to go insane deep into vengeance.

He ain't true? What was Teedo getting at?

Chapter Twenty-eight

It was game time.

Nina sat on the back steps, smoking the one last cigarette allowed to the condemned. Except, in this case, to face the firing squad, she had to take *off* the blindfold. For the first time since the veil of darkness had cloaked ordinary life, she didn't avert her eyes. She looked at her sorry ass directly, like a tactical problem.

Among her talents was an unique ability to get inside an opponent's time, his intent and tactics. Disrupting them. Observe. Orient. Decide. Act. Boyd's celebrated OODA Loop. This reflex, which they now taught at the service schools, was hardwired in her synapses. It had made her military reputation.

Instinctively she understood how to defeat the depression. It required a simple trick of personal jujitsu.

All she had to do was face in the right direction, meet head-on the thing she dreaded more than her own death . . .

Admitting weakness. Admitting defeat.

She had been here before.

That summer in 1988, the Olympic swim trials were held at the Lee and Joe Jamail Texas Swimming Center, University of Texas at Austin.

One of the fastest pools in the world.

Nina Pryce had finished her sophomore year in Ann Arbor. She had medaled in three events in the NCAA nationals, forcing herself through a grueling season, living on Darvoset to block the persistent bursitis in her shoulder.

Mind over matter. Make the cut. Next stop Seoul, Korea.

She knew the shoulder was a time bomb, and she kept it from her coaches. Hell, they'd done a lot to create the problem—an absence of moderation in the weight room, when they threw the girls at free weights with the football team. A dedicated Title Nine Hari Kari, she held nothing back. Probably the bench press did the damage. Along with too much weight on the fly machine.

Seeded second in the 200 butterfly. Her best event.

Only the top two would go.

She ignored her coach's advice to go out smooth, stay with the pack for two laps, and make her move on the third lap. Then bring it home hard. Once she got up on the starting blocks and took her mark, she only knew one way forward—get out in front from the buzzer and stay there.

The humid air is charged, drenched with chlorine. The tiled walls rock with applause from the sweating bodies in the stands. In the pool, the quiet blue world of racing water churns with silent screaming muscles. Bursting hearts. Leading the pack, going into the wall on the third lap, she felt the shoulder start to freeze. Ignore it.

Don't quit, don't cry.

Make the turn. Now. Bring. It. Home. In mid-lap the shoulder locked. She thrashed on, lame on one flipper. Finished third. Missed a seat on the Olympic plane by four hundredths of a second. Pride. Vanity. That last obstinate twenty-five meters did more to wreck her than all the previous wear and tear.

Who she was.

It took a year with trainers to rebuild the inflamed muscles and ligaments around the shoulder. At a sobering meeting, the sports doctor stoically told her she had the shoulder of a thirty-five-year-old woman.

You keep pushing like this, it'll only get weaker, not stronger.

Stubborn, she took her middle-aged shoulder back to swimming after rehab and was still fast enough to make the final heat. But she was never able to coax that extra surge from the shoulder—the surge it took to win. She never medaled again. Just outside lanes. After she graduated, she'd put the Olympic dreams away and joined the Army. There were other medals.

Not even Broker knew how far she'd stretched the rules. He thought the skull-and-crossbones tattoo on her right shoulder was bravado going into Desert Storm. The tat disguised the needle marks from years of black-market cortisone injections, as she trail-blazed through the Army.

Jump school. Ranger school. HALO. SCUBA.

Desert Storm. Bosnia three times. Classified stuff in the Philippines. Undercover games in Italy, chasing the elusive Russian suitcase.

A triumph of will, steroids, and prescription-strength Tylenol.

After 9/11 she was invited into a clandestine Delta subset that eventually took the field as Northern Route. Before deploying, she discreetly met with an Italian physician in Lucca and wheedled a prescription for narcotics to control the pain.

Now she had the shoulder of a fifty-year-old woman. No cushion left. She bowed to the needles one last time.

Nina Pryce took a deep last drag on her cigarette and flipped it into the snow. Made a face. Kit would lecture her about littering. What would she say if she found out her mother, the steroid junkie, had been living a lie?

She didn't shy away from a nauseous wave of remorse, guilt, and shame. It was time to accept it, all her petty selfishness. Christ, she still had her arms and legs and fingers and toes. Men and some women were being blown to pieces in Iraq this very minute. Maybe people she knew.

After the nausea came the wringer of self-pity. Broken wing. You're never gonna fly again, girl; not like you used to. Never gonna get it back. Never rope out of a Blackhawk again in full gear. The fucking men always watched her for the slightest sign of weakness. They'd never let her back on the teams with a bum shoulder. Hell, she wouldn't let herself back . . . They'd give her a desk for pasture. Training cadre maybe.

Forget that.

After self-pity, the bile of resentment. She whipped her head around, throwing a rueful glance at this rented house Broker had brought her to. Good for housework, maybe. He'd like that. Down deep she sensed he'd always wanted her to fail. Like all of them.

Finally the emotional binge dissipated. She stood up and dusted herself off.

No, he was different. He'd exhausted himself caring for her. More than father, husband, lover, and friend. Her buddy.

By midafternoon the sun had passed overhead and had started to decline in the west. The darkness, which had been driven into the woods, now regrouped, emerged from hiding, and started to creep out from the tree line, to counterattack over the ground it had lost during the day.

Watching the clock, Nina showered, washed her hair, and drew it back in a clean ponytail. Then she dug in a drawer and found the clean, carefully folded sweat suit. ARMY in crisp black type across the front. Absolutely focused, she pulled it on, tied her running shoes, and went outside.

She approached the somber western woods.

Egged on by the lowering sun, a ragged phalanx of shadows now extended from the trees and lengthened across the snowy lot. Pointed toward the house.

She lit a cigarette, paced, then walked right up to the farthest extension of the shadows and placed her foot inches from the tip.

Waited as it slowly, relentlessly crept toward her.

The shadows would cross the yard, mob the house, and penetrate the walls. They would fill the air, bleeding black, and finally find their way into her flesh and drain their darkness into her blood.

Not today.

"Fuck you," she told the shadows.

Okay, she'd come halfway back. Now for the rest. Get real, Pryce. Listen to your body. Her body told her she had turned into the thing she feared most in her life.

She was weak.

She saw it in her daughter's eyes. In Broker's. A mix of pity and shallow empathy. Nina had raised Kit to be strong and compassionate toward the weak—to an extent. But the fact was, as Nina had now discovered, that the strong, even as they vow to protect the weak, do not understand them.

Nina took a deep breath and said aloud, "It's over."

She opened her arms and walked forward, and as she embraced the shadows, she felt the last weights sloughing away. Unencumbered, she tilted up her face and felt the fading sunlight sink into her like an invigorating current. Lightly, she walked into the deep snow and the close-packed trees, breathed in the cold dark air. She turned, came out into the deep black hedge of shadows, and twirled; then, arms spread behind her, she ran in circles. Like Kit might do, enjoying the sheer kinetic thrill of motion.

No more medals. Just outside lanes.

Her soldier days were over.

It was time to come home.

Chapter Twenty-nine

Broker sat in his truck in front of the school, showing no expression as Kit moped out to the truck, sagging under her book bag. Then she climbed in the backseat and squealed when she saw her bunny propped up in the corner, its stubby arms arranged around a taboo Snickers bar and a plastic bottle of Gatorade.

"Dad! Where was she!"

"Way under the front seat. I told you, nothing gets lost in the house."

"She was in the *truck*, Dad; not in the *house*," Kit announced.

"Well, I was close," Broker said.

Kit sat back, hugging her battered toy as the fleet of yellow school buses receded behind them and they headed out of town on County 12. The afternoon punched up clean and sharp under a blue sky. The welcome sun hung in the west and stamped crisp black shadows on the softening snow cover.

Broker slouched back, one hand draped over the wheel, actually feeling pretty good. For a change. Nearing the lake, they drove past the busy Mexican carpenters who were now putting down the underlayment on the roof of the new house—Keith Nygard's original meth bust. Until that meth lab blew up in his face. Probably the biggest thing ever happened up here. And he had, what, one full-time deputy . . .

Thinking how Nygard had mentioned taking Griffin along to help out. Didn't know if he approved of that. Once Griffin got started, he only had one forward gear . . .

Broker glanced around. Great scenery, superb fishing, and

not a lot of backup. Broker didn't hold with most city cops who rolled their eyes at their rural counterparts, making cracks about Andy of Mayberry operating mostly solo out in the boonies.

Hell, he'd spent seven years undercover operating without a net— The train of thought switched abruptly. Suddenly he was remembering the old continuing fight with Nina; his angry sarcasm at her uphill gender war with the military. Xena the Warrior Princess syndrome. A Joan of Arc complex. She countering, pointing out that his undercover police role was *his* flight from reality, called him a frustrated actor . . .

Got that from his mother.

Christ. That's what had been missing these last months.

The fights.

They'd be apart for most of the year while she ran around saving the goddamn world, and when they finally did get together for a birthday or Thanksgiving or Christmas, the brawl started. Kit at five, six, seven—standing with her hands over her ears.

The arguments could start about almost any topic, but it always came down to, essentially, who was in charge of their marriage; like it was a fucking unit in the Army, and she, being a fucking major, outranked him.

It had taken unipolar depression to shut her up.

Now she was getting better, which meant they'd inevitably start fighting about something. Preoccupied with years of pyrotechnic flashbacks, driving on automatic, he wheeled around the last turn on the road, coming up on the long stretch about a half mile from the house . . .

"Dad!" Kit shouted, lurching forward so hard she hit the tension on the seat belt.

Broker instinctively toed the brake, jerked alert, scanned the road, the surrounding trees.

He caught a jerk of movement at the far end of the road, breaking in and out of the deep lattice of shadows.

"Deer?" he said.

"Runs like a deer," Kit said.

Broker squinted, put up his hand to shield the glare of the

sun. He couldn't compete with his daughter's 20/10 vision. Then. Well, no shit. It *was* her, back at it, loping along. But not like a deer—more like a predator chasing a deer, more like a cougar.

"Dad, stop, *please*." Kit flung off her seat belt and yanked the door handle. Broker braked the truck, but Kit had already leaped out as the tires stopped rolling and hit the slushy snow in a dead run. She opened up her stride, racing up the road.

Broker followed slowly, idling along the shoulder, and stopped by the mailbox. He could see Nina clearly now, red ponytail bouncing as she ran steadily, a little off her old gait. He could see the gray sweat suit, could read the hard-edged prophetic black type on her chest. Christ. Her lungs must be a trash fire. Three months of nicotine burn. She'd be a mess of cramped sore muscles in the morning.

He turned off the truck, got out, and waited, watching Kit bound, closing the distance, and then jump to hug her mother around the neck. Broker noted how Nina stooped to lift her, using her left arm. The right arm hanging back, guarded.

After the brief hug-fest they continued up the road, running now side by side. Snatches of girlish laughter carried on eddies of breeze, bounced off the trees, ringing in and out of patches of light and shadow.

Broker felt the stranglehold of the last three months release and fall away, like dropping a heavy ruck and gear at the end of a long forced trek. *We did it.*

Knock on wood.

But there it is. She was moving more like her old self. When he jogged to meet them, his feet were light, almost dancing.

"Wipe off that grin. You'll cramp your face," Nina panted as she stopped and leaned forward, bracing her hands on her knees. No mistaking the flush of healthy sweat on her freckled cheeks and forehead, the gaunt energy steady in her eyes. Broker wrapped her in his arms, and as she buried her forehead in his chest, Kit hurled herself between them, joining the huddle. Then she tugged on Nina's arm.

"C'mon, Mom; race you to the house."

Nina rolled her eyes and set off after Kit, who was sprinting up the driveway. Broker got back in the truck and drove up to the house, collected Kit's backpack and the errant bunny, and went inside.

"Take off your boots," Nina admonished as he came in through the door from the garage. Broker grimaced and kicked off his boots, seeing the spotless maple floor, smelling the lingering scent of Murphy's Oil Soap. Nina had been busy this afternoon. The kitchen was more than spruced up, it was squared away like a barracks before an inspection. No cigarette smoke. No TV. Even the exhausted snake plant seemed to stand taller.

Nina leaned against the counter, drinking a glass of water. Straight ahead in action, she was forever indirect about intimacy. It always snuck up on them. But the signals were there in the way she stood now, head tilted a little to the side, eyes slightly lowered.

It always surprised him, the way the silent shadow of desire appeared, not unlike seeing a ten-point buck slip through the trees opening morning. Felt the movement quicken in his chest.

He smiled. Going on fifty, and he could still feel the excitement brand-new.

He put his arm around her, and she leaned into his chest. No kiss yet. Or even words. Too many ragged edges needed to be knitted together. He had a lot of questions. But they could wait.

"How about we get cleaned up and all go out to eat," he said.

"You know," Nina said, fingering the binder from her sweaty hair, "let's hold off till tomorrow. I'd kinda like to get out the phone book, see if this burg's got a beauty shop—"

"Beauty shop?" Like a foreign language coming out of her mouth.

"Yeah, you know; get this rat's nest fixed up," she said, tossing her hair, combing her fingers through the tangles. Then she put out her hand and placed it, open palm, on his chest, feeling the slow steady chug of his heart through his shirt. She raised her eyes and said, "You should smile more, Broker; does wonders for your face."

Her eyes were wise, deep, and deadly. Athena climbing back on her pedestal. Whatever. Or as Griffin put it, his crazy sexy wife . . .

. . . was back in play.

Chapter Thirty

Griffin wheeled into the parking lot of Skeet's Bar and parked his Jeep next to Teedo's truck. Two drinking establishments in town stayed open in the off season; the Anglers, where you could take a family out to eat and which Keith and his deputy did not keep an eye on, and Skeet's, a strictly beer and bar whiskey hangout, where they patrolled on Friday and Saturday nights.

Griffin walked through the front door. Just a long room, bar on the right, tables on the left, pool table, two booths, and the johns in the back. Five guys sat at the bar, watching boxing on the satellite TV hookup.

Teedo leaned over the pool table, shooting a solitary game of eight ball.

Griffin ordered a ginger ale, asked Willie Skeets what Teedo was drinking. Willie opened a bottle of Linnies. Griffin paid for the drinks and took the bottles back to the rear of the bar, set them on a table. Took off his coat. Teedo, intent on lining up a shot, did not look up.

Griffin selected a cue, acknowledging with a nod that the shattered cue from that night years back, when he helped Keith break up a fight, was still gathering dust at the end of the rack; it had become part of the local lore. He flipped a quarter on the table. Teedo pocketed the balls, inserted the coin, and started racking. Still not saying a word, Teedo broke.

Stripes. He sunk three balls and missed. Griffin lined up on the cue ball, eased back the stick. Teedo's square hand closed over the white cue. They locked eyes.

"So you gonna buy me a beer?" Teedo said with a trickster glint in his brown eyes.

Griffin reached back, picked up the Linnies, and placed the bottle on the green felt with an emphatic thump. Teedo picked up the bottle and nodded at the rear booth. They put their cues back in the wall rack and sat down.

"Thought you might come. Wasn't sure you'd buy the beer," Teedo said.

"So you gonna tell me what you meant about Gator not being 'true'?" Griffin said.

"You ever been out to his place?" Teedo asked.

"Drove by it a few times, during deer season."

"So think about it—he's out there all alone now, huh?"

"Yeah"—Griffin narrowed his eyes—"since his cousins got burned out."

Teedo tipped the bottle to his lips. "Kind of convenient. Them not being around. Kind of people who snoop, steal stuff. Could pry into your business, big-time."

"C'mon. What are you getting at?"

"Kinda storybook, don't you think?" Teedo said. "The way everybody gives Gator plenty of room, since the meth house burned? Made him into a local hero, their avenging angel, for Marci Sweitz. It's an open secret Gator's snitching for Keith. They busted those Mexicans. Fact is, in the last year, Gator's run all the nickel-dime meth dealers out of the county, especially anybody setting up shop in those empty houses north of Z."

Griffin nodded—it was common knowledge. "The way people tell the story, Gator's trying for a fresh start up here." Hearing the words come from his mouth in the context of this conversation, they sounded too good to be true.

"Yeah, right, he's fuckin' Robin Hood. Or maybe"—again, the sly smile—"he's knocking off the competition, huh?" Teedo said it quietly, raising his eyebrows slightly, conjuring a depth of hard-knocks insight into the backwoods drug scene. He'd done six months in Beltrami County for selling grass couple years back before he cleaned up his act. Knew the players.

Griffin leaned back, mulling over it. "Teedo, you got a suspicious mind."

"No," Teedo said, "I got a cousin, Jerry, who brews that poison. Remember that cold snap last month, hit twenty below?"

Griffin nodded.

"Yeah, well, Jerry figured nobody'd be out in that weather, so he snuck into one of those old houses to cook. And Gator shows up, knocks him around, and chases him off at gunpoint. Jerry didn't run far—he pulled off into the trees to watch what Gator would do. See, Jerry didn't have a shopping bag from Fleet Farm and a few cans of solvent. He had a whole truckload of supplies, two big boxes of pseudoephedrine he smuggled in from Canada. Jerry was looking to cook a couple pounds of that shit.

"So Jerry waits, freezing his ass, for the sheriff to show up. No sheriff. Instead, Gator loads all the chemicals and stuff in *his* truck and drives it north on Twelve, toward his place." Teedo leaned forward and pointed his beer bottle at Griffin. "One of the ways you catch meth heads, is you follow them when they run their trapline, picking up supplies, huh? But if you're fucking Robin Hood, you just steal from the meth heads and give to yourself."

"So—no exposure." Griffin thought about it.

"Plus, he's got what amounts to police protection. Way Jerry tells it, Gator brings Keith in on the little fish, but if he finds a big stash, he keeps it for himself."

"So, say something. Anonymous tip, 911," Griffin said.

"Oh, right," Teedo shook his head. "Uh-uh, not me, man, word'd get out. I believe those stories about Gator. He *kills* people and gets away with it, going way back. Some people even think the way his folks died was no accident."

Teedo drank a few swallows of beer in silence, smacked his lips. "But I did go out there to Gator's and take a look."

"Hey," Griffin said, "you're the one blowing smoke about staying clear."

Teedo lifted a hand. "I had an excuse. This time of year, I go back in the woods near his farm. 'Bout two hundred yards in from one of the fields, there's this grove of birches. Put in some test taps. Been so warm, I figured the sap might be early. Not as good as sugar maples, but you can still make syrup. Not bad if you cook it twice."

"For Christ's sake, Teedo . . ."

Teedo took another pull on his beer, stretching it out. "You know how to find Camp's Last Stand?"

Griffin nodded. "Turn off Twelve east on County Z. Go in on the old logging road." It was a local landmark set back in the woods.

"Two miles past the crossroads. Clock it on your odometer, 'cause it's grown over, hard to find. When you get to the stand, take the trail that forks to the left, that'll bring you up to the grove, you'll see some tin buckets I put out."

"Yeah?" Griffin hearing Teedo give him directions . . . *like he's sure I'm going out there . . .*

"You'll be a couple hundred yards from his house. That's where I was two weeks ago when I smelled it."

"Smelled what?" Griffin asked.

"A smell like a big litter box full of cat piss and shit. This real stink. I went in closer and heard the generator running . . ."

"Generator?"

"Yeah, he's got a big-ass generator going in the shop. Now why do you suppose that is? He's got enough four-forty to run all his tools coming in on the line. Had the fans running in the paint shop. So I went in closer, along this windbreak of pines that goes from the woods, stops about fifty yards from the shop." Teedo leaned forward on his elbows, taking his voice even lower. "You know how Gator is supposed to be out there all alone?"

"Yeah?"

"Not that day. Jimmy Klumpe was there, bigger'n shit, sitting in his garbage truck, had Gator's trash container up on the lift. Top open. Just sitting there, engine running . . .

"Then this person comes out of the shop. Got this paint suit and breather mask on. When they took off the hood, saw it was a woman. Thought it was his sister, Cassie, at first. She had this black hair, same build."

"Really?" Griffin said, "I heard Cassie never goes out there, hasn't been back since their folks—"

Teedo shrugged. "Wasn't Cassie, though. 'Cause little while later Gator and her brought these black heavy-duty garbage bags out from the shop and loaded them in the Dumpster. Jimmy hoists her up and drives off. But he goes north, not back toward the town dump. Goes into the woods. And Gator, he starts up his Bobcat and moves all these boxes and big plastic drums from the shop into the garage part of his barn. Then him and the woman went into the farmhouse . . .

"Wind was right, could hear them in there. Windows musta been open. Was the bathroom, 'cause the shower was running." Teedo flashed a grin. "Heard the kinda noise you ain't suppose to make with your sister."

"So you think he's cooking dope out there?"

"Cooking dope?" Teedo laughed. "Man, when's the last time you were on the streets?" He raised his beer. Before he got it to his lips, Griffin clamped his hand over the bottle top and looked Teedo directly in the eyes.

"Why you telling me this?"

Teedo shrugged. "I don't know. Maybe because you're the only person around who's crazy enough not to be afraid of the guy." Then he set the bottle down and reached for his wallet. "Hey, and I got this." Teedo took his wallet from his hip pocket and withdrew a salmon-colored slip of paper. An old Powerball lottery ticket. He handed it to Griffin. "That woman? She drives a silver Pontiac GT. Never seen that car in town. Had it hidden in the barn. Look on the back."

Griffin turned it over; three letters and three numerals printed in ballpoint. Set it on the table.

"License plate on the Pontiac," Teedo said.

Griffin narrowed his eyes, waiting.

Teedo shrugged. "You know people, those guys who come up from the cities to hunt sometimes, Broker's pals. They're cops, right."

"So? Keith Nygard's a cop."

Teedo shook his head and said cryptically, "Him and Gator's high school buddies. When the meth house blew up and all Gator's cousins burned, Keith, he looked the other way."

Teedo finished his beer, set the bottle aside, leaned forward, and lowered his voice. "So. Jimmy was there, using his truck for something Gator's up to. Just saying—if Broker was my friend, and he's messing with Jimmy, the person who comes back at him might not be Jimmy. Might be someone who needs Jimmy. In which case it might not be about kids fighting on the playground."

Griffin exhaled, picked up the slip of paper, and turned it slowly, weighing it. He looked up at Teedo. "You willing to go back out to Gator's farm?"

"Nope. Ain't my fight. No disrespect, but fuck a bunch of white guys. It would be interesting, though, to find out if the lady driving that Pontiac has a record, huh?" Teedo gave Griffin the barest smile as he stood up and put on his coat.

Griffin said, "Anything else you can tell me?"

Teedo shrugged. "Every Saturday morning, nine A.M., Gator comes in town and eats bacon and eggs at Lyme's Café."

After Teedo left, Griffin sat for several minutes studying the number on the slip of paper. Okay. This was something Keith should know about. He went out, got in his Jeep, drove into town, and pulled into a diagonal parking slot in front of the old two-story redbrick county courthouse. The snow on the barrel of the Civil War four-pounder cannon on the lawn had melted during the warm day. Since sunset, the temperature drop had formed a long fringe of icicles.

Griffin stared at the icicles, organizing his thoughts. The sheriff's office occupied one side of the lower floor. He could see Howie Anderson, Keith's chief—and only—deputy during the winter, standing in the well-lighted window, leaning over, talking to Ginny Borck sitting at the dispatcher's desk.

He knew they had a new computer and radio setup purchased with Homeland Security money; primarily to monitor Border Patrol and Highway Patrol advisories. Be easy to run a license plate check.

Then he considered Teedo's cryptic snapshot of Keith being Gator Bodine's high school pal, how they'd teamed up, since the Marci Sweitz episode, to rid the county of meth. Remembered Susan's remark about the cursory medical examiner's report after the trash house fire. Accidental death. No arson investigation. The cursory autopsies.

Griffin looked up and down the empty street; not much going on except the slush starting to set up and freeze. Everything seemingly hunky-dory—except that, just below the surface, the pollution cooking under Jimmy Klumpe's property on Little Glacier might leak over into the big lake.

And kill the summer trade that supported the town.

Could that kind of hovering phantom cause a solid family man like Keith Nygard—wife, three kids, second-term sheriff, deacon in his dad's Lutheran church—go into the drug business as a hedge against the future?

Nah— he could see Keith getting blindsided, but the guy was just too rock-ribbed Lutheran to go over the line. It was time to slow down and think this through. All he had was Teedo's hearsay story and a number scrawled on a lottery ticket. Walk in there with a bunch of bar talk, and he'd sound like an excited citizen who'd been watching too many detective shows.

He needed a little more specific information before he approached Keith. One thing he could do was reach out to J. T. Merryweather, see if he'd run a check on the license number. His mind made up, Griffin backed out of the parking space in front of the courthouse and drove slowly out of town, slowing as he went past the lighted windows of Lyme's Café.

A few minutes later Griffin stood in his kitchen, phone in hand, tracing a number in his phone book with his finger.

Teedo's slip of paper lay on the open page. Without hesitation he tapped in J. T. Merryweather's number, down on his ostrich farm in Lake Elmo.

Denise Merryweather answered the phone, her voice tightening when she placed Griffin in the part of her husband's life that involved Phil Broker. "Is it important?" Her tone was cool. "We're eating supper."

"It's important."

A moment later, J. T., St. Paul PD captain of homicide when he retired, came on the connection. "Griffin. What's up? This about Broker and Nina? How's she doing?"

"Actually, Nina's coming out of it. Broker? He's stressed to the max, but he won't admit it."

"Figures," J. T. said.

Griffin picked up the piece of paper with the number on it and said, "J. T., I need a favor . . ."

Chapter Thirty-one

Sheryl spent the rest of the morning and early afternoon smoking, watching daytime TV. And watching the phone. She imagined Gator pacing in his shop, watching *his* phone. No sense talking about what they didn't know. Especially since it would involve signaling on his pager with a phony number, which would send him on a half-hour drive to the pay phone at the grocery store. So she didn't make the call. Finally, at one-thirty in the afternoon, her phone rang.

"Country Buffet, in Woodbury, that mall off Valley Creek Road and 494, you know it?" said a calm voice without introduction. She knew the restaurant . . .

. . . and the voice.

"It's a dump," she said.

"Correct, dress according. Wear a Vikings sweatshirt. Say in an hour. Two-thirty."

Jesus. It was moving fast. "I'll be there." The call ended. Sheryl was impressed. That was fast. Which meant Werky's "investigator," Simon Hanky, was on the job. Simon wound up going by his first initial. There was a word in poetry, *onimana* something. Like when a words sound like the thing it describes. That was him to a T.

Drop the Y.

S. Hanky. Then drop the Y.

Shank did some time for manslaughter after Werky pleaded him down from second degree for killing his ex-wife's boyfriend. In the joint, Danny's organization was impressed by his icy focus and recruited him after he decimated a bunch of Mexicans in the showers.

He had matured in prison and never killed in hot blood again. Now he only operated with methodical planning. Some people were into beginnings, and some people like to stretch out the middle. Shank was an expert on endings.

He killed people.

This corkscrew sensation squirmed through Sheryl's chest. Old tapes. She had been around a lot of dangerous men in her life, and most of them had made her nervous, mainly because they were unpredictable and had poor impulse control. Shank had zero impulses, barely a pulse.

Wow.

Shit, man, something must have clicked for them to trot out the Shank.

At two-thirty sharp, Sheryl, face washed clean of makeup, hair gathered in a ponytail, stood at the check-in line at the Country Buffet chewing Juicy Fruit. She wore a pair of faded Levi's, a brand-new, itchy purple Minnesota Vikings sweatshirt, scuffed tennies, and a cheap Wal-Mart wind jacket. Some Spanish was being spoken in the line, several gangs of Mexican laborers coming in for all-you-can-eat—a grotesque gallery of obese flesh fighting a losing battle against gravity. On top of which, excessive meat was apparently difficult to wash; the place smelled like an elephant house. Should hose them down, she was thinking when she heard the familiar voice behind her, in a loud whisper: "Hey, Sheryl Mott, long time no see."

She turned and saw Shank, icy smooth, standing behind her. Sinewy, six feet tall; he had white-blond polar bear hair and eyebrows and startlingly pale blue eyes. They'd been an item briefly, when she returned from Seattle, just before she quit cooking for Danny's crew and took up her waitress career.

The smooth pigment of his face avoided the sun and reminded her of the texture of mushrooms under cellophane in the produce section. He wore busted-out denim work duds and beat-up steel-toed boots to fit in with the crowd. Looked skinnier than the last time she saw him.

"Shank. You lose some weight?"

He heaved his shoulders, said, "I feel like a real heel—I shoulda called. You see, right after the last time we were together I tested HIV-positive . . ."

Sheryl clasped his horn-hard hand, noting the manicured nails set like jewels among the callus. "You're shitting me, right?"

"Yeah," he grinned. "It's the South Beach diet."

She cast her eyes around, sniffed. "You sure know how to show a girl a good time."

"Let's say I'm comfortable around real fat people. They eat like gamblers play slot machines. Totally oblivious to what's around them."

Sheryl gave him an appreciative nod. She liked what she saw so far. They were treating her decent for a change.

Shank paid admission, and they followed a tired-looking waitress who seated them at a booth, brought them glasses for their beverages, and said in a tone both cryptic and bored, "You can *start* now."

"You hungry?" Shank asked after the waitress left them alone.

Sheryl rolled her eyes in mild revulsion at the shuffling feeding frenzy and shook her head. "Coffee black," she said.

Shank got them two cups of coffee, resumed his seat across the table, and spread his hands in a respectful preamble. "First, Werky says Danny says hello."

"Yeah, okay." Sheryl took a deep breath, let it out.

"And he says to treat you right. You're the birthday girl. 'Cause, guess what—so far your end checks out. There was a dude name Broker who hung out on the fringe of things. Seems he was more into running guns around than dope. Though there is a story about him bringing in a semi flatbed from North Dakota; piled with hay bales on the outside, bales of weed on the inside. He fixed things, had a bunch of tools in a truck and some landscape equipment. You been out to Danny's place in Lakeland?"

"Yeah, before the feds took it away for taxes."

"So, remember the backyard, all the terracing, rocks and shit?"

"Overlooking the river?"

"Yeah, well, Danny told Werky this fuck, Broker, did all that. And one of the guys recalled he put in Jojo's sound system in Bayport."

"Bingo," Sheryl said.

"Meets our probable-cause threshold," he said. "I don't suppose you have a picture?"

"'Fraid not." Sheryl thinking, *Christ, I just became an accessory to murder one.*

"No problem." He leaned forward, agreeable. "So what's it take to locate this ratfuck? You know where he is, correct?"

"Uh-huh. Him, his wife, his kid."

"And to give them up you want . . . ?"

"Let's just say, down the line, I got this little project you guys might be interested in . . ."

"Uh-huh. You know, your name came up a couple weeks ago. Billy Palmer saw you in Arelia's on University. Said you were talking around selling some shit?"

Sheryl sniffed, looked away, "Billy wasn't interested, treated me like some meth whore."

"So, what? You sold to another culture, huh? Mexicans probably, the brothers aren't really into meth . . ."

"Do I have to answer that?"

"Nah, it's cool," Shank said.

"Heck, you know me." She wiggled her hips in a taut rumba. "Wanna rattle my pots and pans."

"I thought you gave it up."

Sheryl leaned across the table. "Look, the reason I been laying off the scene is there's too many meth suicide bombers out there burning down houses and littering the countryside with toxic waste. Agreed?"

Shank folded his arms across his chest, listened.

Sheryl carefully arranged her coffee cup, a spoon, and the napkin on the table. Tidying up before she began to speak. Then she said, "I'm not asking for anything for this narc. He's a gift, understand?"

"Uh-huh. Right. Continue," Shank said.

Sheryl's face clouded with concentration. "Let's just say I've spent the last year assembling state-of-the-art gear, the perfect partner, the perfect location, and the perfect operation."

"Perfect," Shank said judiciously, giving her his best North Pole stare.

"Absolutely fucking perfect," Sheryl insisted, meeting the stare.

"Okay, go on . . ."

"Thank you. My problem is logistics and distribution. I need someone who can provide precursor and chemicals in large volume and deliver it in a discreet and timely fashion. If I can get that—with my setup—I can cook twenty pounds a heat—"

Shank made a face. "Twenty pounds, bullshit."

Sheryl's eyes didn't waver. "Twenty pounds. No mess. Pfizer couldn't do it cleaner. That's twenty pounds of ninety-nine-per-cent-pure crystal four times a month for two months."

Shank rubbed his chin, squinted at her. "How're you going to have all that smelly chemical crap coming and going without drawing attention?"

"We're way out in the sticks, right? So we have a huge tank of anhydrous parked in a barn, and"—Sheryl paused for effect—"we got the local garbageman."

"Huh?"

"Here's how it could work. Somebody with the resources—maybe you guys—phonies up the supplies to look like trash and trucks it to the local garbage dump, after hours. We can work out some bullshit contract to make it look cool. Our guy loads it in his truck and delivers it when he runs his normal route. We cook, then the garbageman disposes of the waste back in the woods, then brings the product back to the dump. You pick up when you deliver the next load of supplies." Sheryl savored the way Shank's cool eyes appreciated her, like he'd just spotted a plump seal on an ice flow.

"No shit," he said, steepling his fingers, sounding impressed. "A super lab."

Encouraged, Sheryl's voice raced ahead, "Yeah, and we take our time. We're thinking next January and February. See, we need winter—"

Shank had sat patiently. Now he leaned abruptly across the table and silenced her speech with a medium harsh look. "No disrespect, Sheryl; but *let's nail this Broker guy first.*"

"Absolutely," Sheryl agreed, sitting up straight, grinding her teeth together. "How about we meet again tomorrow."

Shank studied her for several long seconds, and Sheryl got this feeling she was like the chick in the stage show, strapped to a rotating wheel while the magician threw knives at her. Except these were icicles.

She continued carefully, "That'll give me time to contact my partner. He's the one who got the line on Broker. You're gonna have to talk to him."

"Sure, makes sense," Shank said slowly. "Give us time to tidy up some details, think over your project. This, ah, place you got your lab; it's way out in the sticks, right? Real remote . . ."

"Yeah, you're gonna hear wolves," Sheryl said.

"No shit." Shank grinned spontaneously. "I never seen a wolf, except at the Como Zoo; they run along the chain-link fence . . ."

"Yeah," Sheryl said, nodding, blindsided by his disarming easy smile. "I been there."

"Okay. Cool. So your partner lives there . . . and there's wolves." He looked off, thinking. "Where'd you meet this guy?"

Sheryl heaved her shoulders. "When I got back from Seattle, I was bringing balloons into the joint. You guys put me on his list."

Shank narrowed his eyes. "One of our members?"

"Nah, he was just, you know, paying his rent, so your guys wouldn't jack him around. He was in Education, right. Practically lived in the Vo Tech Shop. He didn't want to get stuck in seg. Did a year for transporting coke with intent to sell."

"I need a name, Sheryl. We know you. But we won't do business on this scale with strangers, you understand," Shank said frankly.

On this scale. It was gonna happen. "Okay, it's Morgun Bodine. Spelled with a *u*, gee-you-en."

"Anything about him we'd remember?"

"He's got this alligator tattoo on his left forearm. Goes by Gator."

"So it's up north." Shank gnawed his lower lip, running it in his mind. "So maybe he bumped into Broker near where he lives?" He raised his eyebrows.

Sheryl pursed her lips, balked.

Shank lifted his palms in comic exasperation, "C'mon, Sheryl, let's put this motherfucker on the fast track. You got a lot riding on this. Whatta ya say?"

Sheryl's palms started to sweat. She rubbed them together in a nervous reflex, then put them in her lap. It was rushing the plan. But they were so close. And she didn't want to piss Shank off, not now. She brought her hands back up and placed them on the table and said, "North of Glacier Falls, near the border. And yeah, that's where he is."

"Where Broker is?"

"Yeah."

"Good girl," Shank said emphatically, reaching over and squeezing her right hand. "Okay, I'll talk to some folks. But I'll need a day. Tomorrow's kind of tight. How about we . . . have breakfast Monday morning? Where should I pick you up?"

Instinct kicked in; Sheryl didn't want to tell him where she lived. "Ah, I'll be on the corner of Grand and Dale, in front of the drugstore."

Shank stood up. "Monday. Eight A.M.; you handle that?"

"Sure, what're you driving?"

It took Shank a moment to answer, like he had to think about it. "Gray Nissan Maxima; got all the bells and whistles," he said. Then he gave her a thumbs-up, "You done good, Sheryl." As he turned to leave, he grinned again. "Wolves, huh?"

"Lot of wolves," Sheryl said, again catching some of his infectious smile.

"Sounds like my kind of place," Shank said, then he padded off through the milling herd of grazing food zombies and vanished out the door.

◆ ◆ ◆

Sheryl drew the moment out. Reached down and raised the coffee cup, enjoying the slight tremble in her fingers. Then she left the booth and put a medium swing in her walk going into the women's restroom, where she jockeyed around with the lumbering herd animals to get some face time at the mirror. She removed the binder, shook out the ponytail, and leisurely combed her hair. Then she applied lipstick and a touch of eyeshadow. Walked out of that bathroom stepping like a Thoroughbred.

Two minutes later she stood in the parking lot next to her car, removing the Wal-Mart jacket, bundling it, and tossing it under the swayback rusted-out Honda Civic parked next to her. She thumbed the remote, opened the door, and pulled out her good leather coat, put it on. Then she got in, turned the key, and just sat in the Pontiac for a while, waiting on the heater, running her hand over the leather seat. Gonna miss this car, she thought. Took a deep breath, exhaled, and punched in Gator's pager number in her cell. When the voice mail came on, she punched in seven sixes, so he'd know it was her.

Now give him half an hour to get to the phone booth at the store.

Longest thirty minutes of her life.

She sat and smoked and listened to people on Minnesota Public Radio talking about the dumb goddamn war. Then she took a roll of quarters, went back into the Country Buffet, and made the call on the pay phone.

He answered immediately, his voice shaking with excitement. Or maybe it was cold.

"They remember Broker being around at the time Jojo got killed. I think we're eighty percent go. I just met the guy who's gonna do it. You ever hear of the Shank when you were inside?" Sheryl said.

"Before my time. I thought he was just a story," Gator said.

"No story. He's real, I had coffee with him thirty minutes ago.

He says if it happens, it's going to happen fast. So start getting ready."

"How soon?" Gator said.

"Dunno. I got another meeting to talk details Monday morning. If it's on, how do you want to handle it?"

"Have him call me at the shop. He'll say he's interested in the restored 1919 Fordson I got sitting in front. Maybe he wants to get it for his dad or something. I'll give him directions."

"All right." Sheryl paused for three heartbeats, wondering if she really could peel off the life she'd lived like the cheap Wal-Mart jacket and throw it away. Then she just said it. "Love you, babe."

"Yeah," Gator said.

"Later," Sheryl said.

She ended the call, got back in the Pontiac, and put it in gear. Two minutes later, accelerating down the 494 ramp, she marveled. *Shit, man, haven't said that to a guy and really meant it since . . . high school.*

Chapter Thirty-two

After supper, Kit sat at the desk on the insulated office porch, practicing her cursive penmanship on a ruled worksheet. The porch was an add-on to the original house, so she could see into the kitchen through two windows set in the wall. Mom and Dad were doing the dishes, bumping into each other, slow like, way more than usual. In fact they were laughing.

Since she and Dad had come home from school and seen Mom running on the road, a different mood had been building between her parents. Kit got the part of about being happy that Mom was getting more like her old self, but there were parts to it she couldn't figure out; like whatever they were seeing when they looked at each other was invisible to her, a grown-up mystery.

She did have a basic idea about the difference between good things and bad things, and she decided that, whatever it was, it was a good thing. She turned back to the worksheet and drew a loopy G.

As Broker and Nina removed the dishes from the washer and stacked them in the cupboard, they played billiard with their eyes; soft cushion rail shots, indirect. Not an urge, not yet a desire, more like a discreet question that hovered over them. Physical contact? Whattaya think?

Broker thinking, Probably be the time to fill her in on the local soap opera that had been percolating offstage. He made a start.

"You know, when Kit had that fight at school?"

"Yeah?"

"Well, the kid's dad got a little aggressive in front of the school and, ah, I kinda dropped him," Broker said.

Nina grimaced with mock severity, "What? You hit him?"

"No, no," Broker was quick to add, making frantic erasing motions with his hands. "I just sort of threw a choke hold on him."

"Uh-huh. Just a choke hold. And Kit? She knew about this?"

Broker folded his arms tightly across his chest, and as he talked, his right hand jerked out and back, punctuating his explanation. "We thought it best not to bother you with it. And, well, he came back at me. The tire on the truck? That was probably him. And Kit's bunny was probably in the truck because it wound up planted on a ski pole"—he pointed his jerking hand out toward the woods—"out by the ski trail. Griffin took it home the last night, stitched it up." He took a breath, exhaled. "Had Ditech's collar buckled around the neck. So he probably got the cat too."

"Jesus, Broker. He came on the property?"

"It's cool. When Griffin came over, he brought the sheriff—"

"The *sheriff*, what the—"

"Ah, oh yeah, I left something out. The kid's dad is the garbageman; he was driving the truck yesterday morning, and he flung our garbage in the ditch while I was watching. So I collected it, took it to his garage, and dumped it in front of his office. Ah, that's why the sheriff came out."

Nina grinned. "Christ, Broker; we came up here to keep a low profile. And you started a war?" She shook her head.

"Me? He started it, asshole came at me—"

"Well, I guess this explains you being more snaky than usual."

Broker unfolded his arms and went back to making the brisk scrubbing motion with his hands. "No sweat. It's all taken care of. The sheriff is affecting a rapprochement. I'll meet him halfway, maybe replace the kid's shirt that got bloody, like that. Griffin went and talked to the guy . . ."

Nina actually laughed, and it was good to see her bubble with spontaneous humor. "Harry? Oh, great, and he's so good at quiet diplomacy. He'll just cut the guy's throat, along with his wife and kid, kill the pets, burn the house, and spray the land with dioxin so nothing ever grows there again."

They were both laughing now. Infectious giggles. Months of pressure surfacing and popping like cold bubbles.

Kit wrenched open the porch door, deep glower creases in her brow. Clearly, she felt left out. "Keep it down, you guys," she announced. "I'm trying to *study*."

"She right," Nina said. "Get a hold of yourself." She rinsed a dish in the sink and handed it to Broker, who obediently put it in the washer.

Despite her show of annoyance, Kit went fast into sleep, tucked in happy with her risen bunny. Broker and Nina stepped carefully down the stairs. As they walked into the kitchen, their eyes met once, then glanced away. It was mutual.

The laughing jag at the sink had exhausted the requirement to talk. And the loud drifting silence dwarfed mere language. Broker thinking how the vectors of their lives had flashed in tangents, fiercely independent; now they had been united during this crisis. The big dangling question: Now what?

The wrong word might betray a lurch of hope or fear, precipitate an avalanche. Tip her back into the darkness.

For months they'd moved in a clumsy deliberate weighted dance around each other, two deep-sea divers in old hard suits. They'd bump surfaces, but their skin remained remote, not really touching, covered by layers of protection. Air hoses trailing, getting tangled.

And that was also in the signal of their eyes. Careful now, kicking off the deep-sea weights. Could be danger in ascending too fast.

So they treaded forward, side by side, through the tactile silence. They were coming up from a great depth. Still braced for the riptides, undertows, and threats . . .

. . . that had coiled and thrashed in the close shadow of madness.

Griffin had built a plywood platform in one corner of the office off the kitchen that supported a queen-size futon. The bed was covered with a lush green-and-orange quilt of vaguely Polynesian design. Bolsters and pillows to match. The colors were an exception to the stern North Vietnamese blacks, browns, and grays that Griffin favored. A souvenir perhaps, left behind from some forgotten amorous interlude. The bed beckoned now, a shallow protected place. They rambled there.

Still no words.

Nothing needy or hungry. Slow moves with no wasted motion. Nina striped off her clothes efficiently—the precocious birthday girl unwrapping a present. Chaste almost, until you saw the grinning skull-and-crossbones tattoo on her right shoulder. And the scars.

Two pairs of jeans mingled on the floor, socks, underwear; his shirt, her blouse. Chilly on the porch. Goose bumps. An almost adolescent scramble to get under the sheets and quilt.

Christ. How long? More than a year.

Since he'd strayed with Jolene Sommer.

Their first kiss was tentative, gentle. Cautiously, they found each other with a slow innate mastery of all things physical. They did it almost weightless, hummingbirds guarded on a bed of eggshells. She was especially wary, having lost control and not sure she had regained it.

Broker was making love with a woman who matched him scar for scar. His fingertips grazed the slick braille on her hips, her butt, her shoulder, her legs. And the one he couldn't claim; the cesarean below her navel. Her birth canal had been scarred by fragments of the Kalashnikov round that had clipped her hip. After Kit's difficult birth, the doctor told them they would be taking chances having another child.

Still no words. A final perfect fit of hope and fear. They took courage for granted, were less honest about being stubborn.

What was she thinking behind her green eyes? Probably what he was thinking: What happens now that we're getting through this crisis?

Will we go back to who we were before?

Will we be changed?

Slowly she fingered the pack of cigarettes and lighter from her jeans, put one in her mouth, and lit it. Then she held it to his lips. He puffed but did not inhale, watched the smoke curl up to the tongue-and-groove ceiling. He remembered the Vietnamese connection. ARVN soldiers jotting on slips of paper, then burning them in the predawn. An airstrip at Phu Bai, Broker watching, waiting for the helicopters that would take them in. Smoke was the prayer language of the dead.

No words.

Chapter Thirty-three

Harry Griffin passed a fitful night that was not altogether unpleasant. Sometimes, like now, when he'd get excited, this auxiliary energy kicked in. He woke up, ready; electric in the dark. And it seemed as if all twenty-five years of his sobriety surrounded him like a thick magnifying lens. Images from his past life jumped up huge, in aching detail.

Four-thirty A.M. He got out of bed, went into the kitchen, and heated water, ground coffee, put a filter in the Chemex coffeemaker.

Waiting for the water to boil, he went into the living room and sat on a cushion in front of the fireplace. He folded his legs in a half lotus, shut his eyes, and tried the TM trick: let his runaway thoughts stream away like rising bubbles. Tried to calm down.

Didn't work. He startled when the teakettle shrieked, boiling over. So much for the tricks. He got up, poured the water into the ground coffee, and slit the cellophane on a fresh pack of Luckies. Since he couldn't get his night horse back in the barn, he settled down to ride it out with coffee and cigarettes.

Sitting at a stool at his kitchen snack bar, he held out his right hand, thick-veined, bone prominent, absolutely steady. Vividly he remembered the last person he'd killed. Ten years ago, when he got talked into that last-minute hunting trip in Maston County . . .

———

Coming in on a dead run toward the shots and screams, seeing Chris Deucette, sixteen, working the bolt, ejecting the spent car-

tridge, then aiming the deer rifle at his stepdad, Bud Maston. Maston lying in the snow, already bleeding. Supposedly Harry's buddy . . .

Felt again the smooth reflex swing, his own 3006 coming up. Safety clicking off . . .

Snap shot, peep sight, eighty yards.

Easy.

The Maston County prosecutor didn't even convene a grand jury. Called it self-defense.

The Viet Cong and North Vietnamese he'd slain were just numbers on a time card. A job. Didn't bother him. None of them did, not even that whole family in Truc Ki, the night that stealth had required he use the knife. Broker had puked and walked away, struggling to believe there were still rules even down in the bottom sewer of guerrilla war.

Nothing he could remember bothered him.

Griffin curled his fingers into a fist.

It was the one he couldn't remember . . .

That night, after the war; blacked-out drunk, walking the Cass Corridor in Detroit, maybe a lingering scent of sweat and perfume from a stripper at the Willis Show Bar. Or maybe the hooker in Anderson's Gardens down the street. Had his .38 jammed in his waistband because he sure as hell found it there in the morning with four rounds fired . . . trouble easy to find . . . all the jive punks on the street, flipping gang signs, pulling up their fucking shirts, showing off their 9-millimeters . . .

It was that single image of a zombie homicidal clown that haunted him; a mindless drunk composed of reflexes staggering around in the night. Reason he'd called Broker in Minnesota, got in his old cherry '57 Chevy, and driven to the frozen North. Reason he'd sobered up with Broker's help. Got to keep that jokester locked up . . .

Griffin squashed out his cigarette in the full ashtray and watched the sun rise thin over the lake. Okay. Be honest. Maybe the last one did get to him, the kid. There'd been a woman in St. Paul he thought he might marry, even start a family. Maybe Broker was right. He'd run away. After that scene in the woods, he'd quit his newspaper job and migrated up here. Do some honest work with his hands where there were fewer people.

Fewer people to hurt.

But there were exceptions. And possibly Gator Bodine was one them.

Quarter past nine Saturday morning Gator was dipping his toast in an egg yolk at Lyme's Café, looking at a picture on the front page of *USA Today*—soldiers in chocolate-chip camo riding a tank all covered with red dust.

He looked up and saw Harry Griffin come through the door and walk straight to the booth where he was sitting. Stood there looking down with that shrink leather face, looking a little shaky with a wild aspect. Hadn't shaved.

"We never been properly introduced, you and me," Griffin said.

Gator tucked the toast in his mouth, chewed, then dusted the crumbs off his thick fingers. "That what this is, getting introduced?" he said, keeping his voice neutral, sizing Griffin up close. A real bad boy in his time, people said, but now he was starting to show his age. Still had this solitary yard-bull intensity to him, like a very few guys in the joint who stood their ground alone. With no group affiliation. The way you fought that kind of guy was, you caught him asleep with a club.

Griffin sat down in the opposite seat, casually leaned his elbows on the table, and said, "This is about proxies—you with me so far?"

"Like stand ins?" Gator nodded, working at keeping his face calm.

"Yeah, like for instance, if Jimmy Klumpe got into something he couldn't handle and someone was to stand in for him. Say sneak into a guy's house, steal stuff, and knife his truck tire. Chickenshit stuff like that."

"You lost me," Gator said, not real comfortable with the cold disquiet in Griffin's ash-colored eyes. Sure had a lot of leftover balls for an AARP fart.

"Okay, let's get you found," Griffin said. "The house where Broker's staying, that somebody was snooping in—it's my fucking house. Anybody comes around, like in through the woods on skis, they're gonna find me standing in." Griffin paused. "What goes around, comes around."

"Yeah, I recall reading that saying in a book about the sixties. And I think maybe you're reaching a little, connecting the dots. What I heard," Gator said carefully, "is they made up. No reason for anybody to do anything on it. Like dumping garbage."

"Yeah?"

"Yeah."

"Just so we understand each other," Griffin said.

"Hey, you're a badass old man, and I was brought up to respect my elders, what can I say," Gator said with a straight face.

"You're on notice; we'll leave it there for now," Griffin said, standing up. "Oh, yeah, and nice meeting you."

"My pleasure," Gator said in an icy fuck-you tone.

As Griffin turned to leave, he paused, raised his finger and pointed. "And, Gator?"

"Now what?"

Griffin smiled. "You got egg on your chin."

Driving home from his weekly sit-down breakfast, Gator briefly entertained the notion of shutting Griffin off like an antique tractor. Then he calmed down and went over the story about Griffin beating up that bunch of drunks in Skeet's with a pool cue. But that was three, four years ago. And he only *heard* it, he didn't *see* it. So he decided the intelligent thing to do was let Griffin have his little senior moment, raffling wolf tickets, showing solidarity with his friend. Maybe drop a hint to Keith that Griffin was getting cranky with him. Off-his-meds kind of thing.

Had more important business to think about.

◆ ◆ ◆

Griffin drove back to his cabin fast, drifting the Jeep around the turns with an almost adolescent glee. The whole aggravated knot of insult and age and punk-ass youth and past and present unraveled when you yanked one cord:

Okay. Now it's personal. And he started it.

Don't go off completely half-cocked. Wait for J. T.'s call.

And Teedo had given him directions how to come in on Gator's place through the woods.

So go take a look for himself.

The notion toyed with him with a palpable prod of danger. Felt like this sleeping figure was waking up in his chest, unfolding its limbs, putting him on like a suit of clothes. Susan Hatch would counsel he was too old . . .

"No, I ain't," Harry Griffin said aloud. Hell, he'd always been at his best alone, on his own. Mindful that Broker was coming over in an hour, he decided to keep this one to himself. And if it turned out that Teedo's story was true, he could tell Broker about it later.

Run away, my ass.

Chapter Thirty-four

J. T. Merryweather woke up before the alarm on Saturday morning, and as his feet searched for his slippers on the chilly floor, his first thought was about Phil Broker.

Griffin didn't specify in so many words, but J. T. was thinking this had to do with Broker being up north.

Moving quiet, so he didn't wake his wife and daughter, he selected clothes from the closet and dresser in the dark. Then he padded downstairs, plugged in the coffee, and showered in the first-floor half bath.

After he dressed and breakfasted on a quick bowl of cereal, he retrieved Griffin's license number request and made some phone calls, taking notes. Not entirely satisfied with what they told him on the phone, he decided to take it a step further.

J. T. stepped out on his front porch and studied the hazy dawn that cloaked his fields, the paddocks, and the fences in mist. He'd made it up to homicide captain in St. Paul before he took the early retirement and put his savings into 160 acres in Lake Elmo and tried raising ostriches.

The specialty meat was slow to catch on in a fast-food culture, so now he was trimmed down to breeding stock and covering his bets with beef. Never regretted farming. Not one bit. He started his town car, a Crown Vic he got at a police auction—interceptor package, good Eagle tires—and headed out his driveway into the fog.

His weather-wary eyes scanned the muddy fields to either side of the road; first the early rain, then the frost, now clogged with wet snow. Like his own land. How soggy would the spring be, how soon could he get in with a tractor?

He drove south and west on back roads until he hit State 95, which he took until it T-boned into 61. He turned south, and soon he was driving across the bridge over Mississippi at Hastings. He continued through town and turned left on Highway 361, following the red-and-blue toucan on the sign for the Treasure Island Casino that pointed the way with lifted wing.

J. T. thinking. Broker had been one of the least likely cops he'd ever partnered with. Harry Cantrell was the other. Now he was on his way to find Cantrell. Saturday morning was Cantrell's Treasure Island day.

He made the last turn and headed down the road toward the casino. Off to the right he saw the twin gray domes of the Excel Prairie Island nuclear reactors hover in the steam clouds over the scratchy bare trees.The sight of those reactors reminded him that he and most of the people in the state owed Broker a debt of thanks.

Last July there had been an explosion at the plant.

A construction accident, they said.

Nine people had died. Dozens were injured. The official story descended from Washington and walled off the incident like a solid steel trap; no way in or out. So far the press was unable to dent the official story that a fuel tanker had ruptured, flooding a ditch with gasoline, that a spark ignited a truck full of oxygen and acetylene. The explosion had rocked the plant and cracked the spent-fuel pool. But no significant radiation had been released, the governor had insisted. The state quietly provided doses of potassium iodide for thousands of citizens in a ten-mile radius as a precaution against possible low levels of radiation poisoning. Now a lot of people who'd taken the iodide were looking at their kids closely every morning at the breakfast table.

Broker had been in the blast area when the explosion occurred, with a Delta colonel. They had diverted an explosive device away, from the cooling pool. It had been a near thing. Broker survived. The colonel did not. Nina had been thirty miles away fighting for her life against George Khari, who'd infiltrated the explosives into the plant.

Khari had links to Al Qaeda. Nina killed him, tearing her right shoulder to shreds in the fight.

J. T. took his pipe from the pocket of his Carhartt jacket and nibbled at the stem. You think you know a guy, how much he can take—all his life Broker had loved the shadows. Saw Gary Cooper in *High Noon* when he was a kid, took his cues, and never looked back. Married a woman who was his fierce mirror image.

J. T. shook his head.

After Prairie Island, Broker and Nina shrugged it off. Just another op. But people who knew them, people like J. T., observed that they were different.

They should have seen God in the inferno of that day.

Just too damn dumb and proud and stubborn—both of them—to admit the damage they'd taken below the waterline. It hit Nina first.

J. T.'s eyes drifted to the northern sky, socked in with brooding gray clouds. They were up north now, hiding out in a backwoods retreat. Healing up, playing house, pretending they were all right . . .

Griffin was looking out for them. J. T. shook his head again. Jesus, Griffin, the reformed angel of death, playing nanny, hovering over them. Except something had happened, and now Griffin needed a favor.

So, to do this right he'd take another old partner along on this day's work.

J. T. shook his head one last time.

Cantrell. Cleaned up now, after Broker hauled him kicking and screaming into treatment. He'd retired from Washington County after he sobered up. A pure, unreconstructed redneck son of a bitch. Cantrell didn't answer his phone. Made himself hard to find. You had to track him down and get him face-to-face.

So here was J. T. driving to a fucking casino, which he considered a monument to stupidity, on a dreary late March morning.

He parked in the mostly vacant lot and went into the pink

pleasure palace. As a favor to his wife he was trying to give up smoking his pipe, and now the cloud of cigarette smoke fluttered against his nose like the smudged wings of tiny tempting devils.

Seniors mostly. Old guys with wars on their hats. One of them shuffled by, with a silhouette of a World War II destroyer on his baseball cap; dragging his oxygen tank, transparent tubes running to his nose.

J. T. checked the blackjack tables. Cantrell was primarily a blackjack addict. No Cantrell. Then he walked into the high stakes slots alcove. Cantrell knew you couldn't beat the slots. But he believed you could surprise the slots. Sneak up on them at random moments.

Cantrell believed you could get lucky.

J. T. spotted him slouched in jeans, a black T-shirt, and a leather jacket on a high-backed chair like a flesh-and-blood extension grafted onto the machine. Tapping the spin button, recirculating the energy between himself and the slot.

Cantrell didn't age. In his late fifties, Minnesota by way of New Orleans PD, his face was still Elvis smooth and ruddy, his sleek dark hair still combed in a fifties duck-ass hairdo. To J. T., who considered himself a mature black man, the rebel twinkle in Cantrell's eyes. had always raised the worst abiding ghosts of Dixie.

"You lost, J. T.?" Cantrell asked casually without moving his eyes off the rolling sevens on the machine screen. Always had great peripheral vision.

"You don't answer your phone," J. T. said. "We got a mandatory formation."

Cantrell nudged the spin button again. Scattered sevens. Not lining up. "We do?"

"Griffin called me last night. He needs a favor."

Cantrell turned in his chair and squinted through the smoke coming off the Pall Mall straight in his lips. "And?"

"I got a feeling it involves our buddy, the unsung hero."

"Broker, really?" Cantrell removed the cigarette from his lips. "I thought he was bulletproof. So whattaya got?"

"A name. Some chick. We got to check her out."

Cantrell shook off his casual slouch, straightened up his back. "Let's go."

A few minutes later they were breathing the cold fresh air in front of J. T.'s truck. Cantrell looked in the direction of the two gray nuclear reactors poking above the trees. "Fuckin' Broker," he said. "You know, I ran into Debbie Hall last week."

J. T. grunted. Debbie was now a lieutenant in St. Paul homicide. Years back, when she'd been a profane fireball, she and Broker'd had this explosive street romance.

"She confessed she'd made a pass at him, couple years ago when he and Nina were separated. She put it out there, and know what he said? He said, 'If I wanna play games, I'll go to a fuckin' casino.'" Cantrell shook his head.

J. T. handed Cantrell a sheet of fax paper. A one-paragraph criminal history on Sheryl Mott from the St. Paul gang task force. "Griffin had a license number. I ran a DL, talked to Tommy in the gang task force," J. T. said.

"Known affiliation with OMG. Suspected of transporting narcotics into Stillwater Prison . . . no charge . . ." Cantrell looked up. "Not much here. You talk to Dave at Corrections about the prison stuff?"

J. T. gave him a slow smile and shook his head. "I thought maybe . . . Rodney."

Cantrell shrugged. "Hell, you don't need me to talk to a piece-of-shit snitch like Rodney."

"Wrong. I always . . . sort of scared Rodney. He's poop-his-pants terrified of you."

"Yeah." A rakish grin spread across Cantrell's face. "Good ol' Rodney," he said with slow glee.

Cantrell followed J. T. back through Hastings, then up 95 to Stillwater, where he left his Outback sedan in the Cub parking lot. He got in J. T.'s car, and they drove a few blocks and pulled into the parking lot at the River Valley Athletic Club.

"Why here?" Cantrell asked.

"His scumbag body is a temple, remember," J. T. said. "He works out here every Saturday morning, according to Lymon at Washington County. Check this: Lymon says Rodney is trying to go straight, they got him working full-time in a health food store—"

"You can sell a lot of dope in cute little bottles in health food stores," Cantrell said.

"Whatever. Okay. We wait. He's still driving that red Trans-Am."

As they waited, Cantrell watched the midmorning female traffic alight from their SUVs and saunter into the club.

"Where do they get these chicks, man? Lookit that blonde— she's got Spandex skin; she's got makeup looks airbrushed on—"

J. T. nibbled the end of his pipe and said, "I hear they got this Stepford Wife production line pops them out at this new McMansion development a little ways west of town."

Cantrell marveled, "Sounds about right; whatever happened to old-fashioned nasty pussy? I mean, they're so *clean*."

J. T. did not respond. Cantrell grumbled, took out a Pall Mall, studied it, then placed it behind his ear. "He was always lucky, Broker was."

No response.

"Debbie said she talked to a guy who talked to a guy at ATF," Cantrell said.

"Uh-huh."

"'Bout the Prairie Island thing."

This time J. T. looked up. "Yeah?"

"Said they found lots of this residue, like clay silicates or something. Wasn't the usual shit they find when you blow off a lot of plastique . . ."

"And?"

"Just a stupid wild-ass guess, but the guy thought maybe those terrorists got short weight on their explosives. Somebody sold them a bunch of play dough mixed in with the Semtex. Guy said that's why the shock wave didn't stove in that cooling pool."

"Bingo." J. T. pointed his pipe at a red Trans Am that wheeled into the lot and parked six stalls away. The shaggy driver bounded out of the car in a silky blue wind suit and hefted his gym bag, looking like a young buffalo wearing lifter's gloves.

"Rodney all right," Cantrell said, sitting up. "What's his last name again?"

"Rodney Jarue," J. T. said. "Let's give him a few minutes to settle in."

They entered the club lobby and were immediately challenged by the lean, tanned redhead wearing horn-rims behind the reception counter. "Excuse me, but are you members?"

She kept her smile in place, but furrowed her brow ever so slightly. A big black guy traveling with a stringy well-preserved Elvis clone didn't fit her normal Saturday-morning walk-in client pattern.

"I'll make this easy," J. T. said amiably, opening his coat so she could see the gold detective shield on his belt. He left out the part about taking the badge off a decorations wall mount in his den.

"You guys are *cops*," she said, biting the inside of her cheek, lowering her voice, casting her eyes around like she was relieved they were alone in the lobby.

"Hey"—Cantrell scowled indignantly—"it's just a job. Take it easy."

Still wary but a bit more agreeable, she asked, "Is something wrong, Officer?"

"Nah," Cantrell said, coming closer, leaning over the counter, staring at her blouse, which was very tight and had this string tie dealy that accentuated her bodice. "Say, I used to play racquetball here . . ."

"Things have changed. The new manager tore out two of the courts, put in a nursery," the woman said. Then her eyes clicked on J. T.

"Look. We just want to talk to one of your members, kinda quiet like." He dropped his voice a register, oozing sympathy. "You know, don't want to bother him at work . . . in front of people . . ."

Her eyes darted back and forth between them.

Cantrell said, "Just be a few minutes." They were already

heading for the stairs in the right corner of the lobby. "Weights still upstairs?" Cantrell called to her as they started up the stairs.

"What's she doing?" J. T. asked.

"Not sure. Possibly debating whether to reach for the phone."

They jogged up the stairs, peered through the glass door to the right, where an aerobics class was in progress on a highly polished gym floor. To their left a long room with two rows of cardio machines stretched the length of the building, facing three wall-mounted TVs. Halfway down the machine room the club opened into another area with lots of stainless steel showing, half fixed weight stations, the other half free weights. Floor-to-ceiling mirrors lined one wall. They headed into the weight room.

"There he is, on the bench press," J. T. said.

"Perfect," Cantrell said.

Maybe a dozen people were scattered among the shiny equipment, four guys, the rest women.

"I love it," Cantrell said, "the way they flex and sneak looks at themselves."

Rodney had removed his jacket and lay on his back on the bench wearing a loose armless T-shirt with an "A.S.I.A. Security" logo on the chest. He was adjusting his grip on a bar that rested in the lift rack over his head. Two forty-five-pound plates were on each end of the bar, held in place by steel squeeze clips. He was just finishing up a few deep clarifying breaths, getting ready to lift the bar off the rack, when he looked up.

"Oh, bullshit," Rodney said as his eyes scanned J. T. and then came to settle on Cantrell.

"Rodney? What's this?" Cantrell said, bending down and pinching Rodney's right biceps, where a band of subtle scarring and healing skin circled his arm. "Didn't you used to have this barbed-wire tattoo?" He glanced over at J. T. "You know what? I think our boy is cleaning up his act."

"I don't have to say shit to you," Rodney said. "You ain't on the job anymore. I know my rights." He focused his eyes upward, then powered the bar off the rack and slowly lifted it. Locked his elbows. Exhaled.

Cantrell shrugged, then reached over, deftly pressed the handles of the squeeze clamp, slid it off the bar. J. T. immediately did the same with the one on his side.

"Hey, don't fuck around," Rodney said.

Cantrell then reached over, grabbed a thirty-five-pound plate off a peg on a nearby machine, held it up. J. T. nodded, found a similar weight on his side. They quickly slapped the weights on either end of the bar behind the twin forty-fives.

Rodney grunted, his arms trembling slightly as he started to lower the bar back toward the rack. J. T. moved behind the bench and put his fingers lightly on the bar, nudged it away from the rack.

"Jesus," Rodney muttered. Arms wobbling slightly, his elbows caving in, he shoved the bar back up to full extension.

"Sheryl Mott. Used to hang around with OMG, tell us about her," Cantrell said.

Rodney grimaced. Dots of sweat squirted up across his broad forehead. Strips of muscle jumped under the flushed skin of his shoulders. "Fuck you," he hissed between clenched teeth.

"Again," Cantrell said. He quickly plucked two more thirty-fives from nearby pegs, raised his leg, straddled Rodney's torso, and slapped the weights on the bar, one side, then the other. J. T. maintained the subtle stand-off pressure on the bar. Cantrell looked down at Rodney, who was now making this deep grinding tectonic noise in his chest. "Sheryl Mott," he repeated.

"Guys," Rodney gasped. "You ain't been around. I *am* trying to go straight. Talk to Lymon at Wash Co. for Christ's sake . . ." His bulging brown eyes blinked away the gush of sweat, darted at the nervous gallery starting to assemble around them. Then he whispered, "C'mon, cut me some slack. I'm trying to get a job here, personal trainer . . ." His arms were shaking now, deep tremors running down into his pecs.

"C'mon, Rodney," Cantrell said impatiently. He was mashing the handles of the squeeze clip in one hand, reached up with other, selected the Pall Mall from behind his ear, and put it in is lips.

"You can't smoke in here," an indignant female voice said. Cantrell turned his head, saw a perfectly coiffed woman, maybe forty-five, cute little halter, Spandex shorts, bare midriff clean and smooth like it'd been run off a lathe. She glared at him through a sheet of meticulously applied makeup.

Cantrell took a Zippo from his pocket, popped it, lit the Pall Mall.

"Eekkk," squeaked the woman, backpedaling like a mouse in *Cinderella*.

Cantrell turned back to Rodney, blew a stream of smoke in his face. "We're waiting."

"OMG's bad folks, too bad for me," Rodney panted. The pressure had traveled down his arms into his chest, up his red corded throat into his bulging eyes. Sweat streamed down his swollen arms as they struggled to hold off the inexorable weight pressing down.

Frustrated, Cantrell was now mashing the squeeze clip in his right hand. Inspired, he twisted, pressed the handles together, opening the spring circle, and thrust the clip into Rodney's writhing crotch, probing the cod of bunched blue material for something to clamp down on.

"Okay, okay," Rodney moaned. "What I hear . . . she's the perfect chick. She loves to fuck and cook. Fuck bikers . . . and . . . cook . . . meth. Learned her business in some big lab in Washington state. All I know, honest."

"See," J. T. said, releasing the pressure on the bar. "That was easy."

"Spot, *SPOT!*" Rodney hollered in a desperate hoarse voice as the bar shivered, descending on his spasming arms.

Shouldering through the gaggle of wide-eyed people rushing to Rodney's aid, Cantrell said, "Not to worry, it's the new Afghan extreme lifting—"

"The near-death school," J. T. said.

Cantrell pointed out an alternate route of egress through the gym. Trailing a contrail of his cigarette smoke amid the aghast aerobics class, they beat it down another flight of stairs and out an exit door on the first level, next to the pool.

Chapter Thirty-five

An hour after he returned from his face-off with Gator Bodine, Griffin heard tires crunch through the windowpane in the puddles of his driveway. He walked out on his deck and saw the green Toyota Tundra pull up. Hello? Broker got out from the passenger side wearing cross trainers and an old blue sweat suit under his jacket. Nina lowered the driver's-side window and leaned out. Kit waved from the backseat.

"Hey, Harry? You ever been to Dawn's Salon on Main Street?" Nina said.

Broker held up his hands in mock despair. "I was getting used to her hair longer. Now she's gonna cut it all off."

Harry walked up to the truck and studied Nina's face. "Going to the beauty parlor, huh?"

"Me too," Kit said.

Nina nodded. "It's time. Her cowlicks have turned into a briar patch the last two months."

There was an ease in the talk Griffin hadn't seen with these people since they appeared at the rental house in January. Nina said good-bye, put the truck in gear, and steered the Toyota back down the drive. Griffin walked Broker under the deck, into the lower level of his house. "When did she come out of it?" he asked.

"Yesterday, boom, just like that."

"So?"

"If she stays steady, we'll probably be heading back to the Cities in a week," Broker said. "No sense hanging around. Kit needs to get back with her friends and activities."

Their different styles collided awkwardly in the silent interval. Griffin was grinning, waiting for Broker to say more. But he'd known Broker for thirty years and had learned that the man kept his emotions carefully embedded between his mind and his muscles. More like the steady instincts of an elusive wild animal.

Broker had assessed a problem, laid out a plan, and soldiered through. His expression was not so much relief as a confirmation of the correctness of his decision.

"So," Griffin said, "you ready to grab something heavy and pick it up?"

Broker looked at his old friend, unshaved, fairly vibrating with the caffeine shakes. Probably had one of his bad nights. But he did grin, this fond, indulgent exasperation. His thick eyebrows beetled as his eyes scanned the room where they stood. The walls were a gallery that marked the stations of Griffin's errant life. Griffin had spiraled out of the Army and become an underground cartoonist. After he sobered up, he briefly became a newspaper artist.

Several of his old drawings had been enlarged and framed: a gaunt haunted depiction of Christ could have been a comical self-portrait. The Cartoon Christ trudged under his crown of thorns and a huge picket sign that bore the caption: "Don't Trust Anyone Over 30 Who Hasn't Been Crucified."

Another, a favorite of the old East Metro Drug Task Force, showed two hippie dopers looking up from lighting their weed as a ten-foot-tall tit smashed through the door. One of them said, "Cool it, man, it's a bust."

A talented, conflicted man who had loved and hated their war, Griffin had always rebelled against his true nature. Broker wasn't fooled; he had seen Griffin in the field.

He'd assessed instantly what Griffin spent his life denying.

Harry Griffin was a natural killer. Broker had always approached this perception with caution. Acknowledging the fact that looking too closely at Griffin was like peering into a mirror . . .

He shook his head and turned his attention to Griffin's latest

Peter Pan fixation. The barbell on the floor, a leg press, an over-head draw-down lift, triceps pulls, a set of fly cables, and the crunch chair.

After Korean karate, yoga, and Transcendental Meditation, Griffin, looking sixty dead in the eye, had discovered high-intensity weight lifting.

So Broker tossed off his coat and actually laughed. "Christ, remember the time you tried to teach me to stand on my head?"

Griffin snorted and pointed to the barbell on the floor. It was fitted with two forty-fives and a twenty-five on each end. "Classic deads," he said. "You first."

Broker rotated his shoulders, loosened up, took the lift straps off the floor, inserted his wrists, looped the straps around the bar, snugged them up, and stooped.

"Remember, keep your shoulder blades tight and your butt back. Push down with your feet," Griffin said.

"Yeah, yeah." Broker took a breath, held it, and lifted the bar slowly. Ten-second count going up and then back down. By his third slow repetition, Broker was sweating and panting for breath.

"One more," Griffin admonished with glee as he slapped half a ton of iron on the leg press, getting the next station in the torture ready.

Less than half an hour later they were through the five stations. Broker was covered with sweat and out of breath. Griffin, barely breathing hard, the eternal contradiction, lit a Lucky Strike. "Half an hour a week, it's the cat's ass, huh?" Griffin winked.

Shaky on his feet, Broker followed Griffin upstairs, where they poured coffee and took their cups out on the deck. The morning was mild, with a tickle of greening in the air.

Broker sipped his coffee, squinted out over the lake. "Think it's finally going to be spring?"

Griffin shook his head. "Looked at the Weather Channel this morning. We might have another clipper on the way. Big rumpus kicking around in Manitoba." He shrugged. "But you could be on your way south before it hits."

"Maybe," Broker said.

"You pulled it off."

"She pulled it off. I just held her coat," Broker said.

Griffin decided it was time to pop the big question. "So now what? She going back into that good old spooky shit?"

Broker studied Griffin's face as he said that, always the lilt of the road not taken in his voice. "It's all changed, Griffin; you wouldn't recognize special ops anymore. The people are different, the gear, the thinking. Hell, they even have a different map of the world."

"Yeah," Griffin said wistfully, slouching back, drawing his neck into his shoulders as a gust of cool breeze blew over them. "I saw that snappy consultant guy, Barnett, give his briefing on C-SPAN. There's the globally connected core. In the middle you got Africa, the Middle East, Southeast Asia; all the ragheads in the nonintegrated gap."

"Face it, man. We're dinosaurs," Broker said.

Griffin held up his cup in a toast. "To the old neighborhood, where we grew up," he said as they clicked rims. "Northern Quang Tri Province." He settled back. "Guess the only thing I got to look forward to now is whether I'm going to wind up a geezer, a codger, or a coot."

"Buck up. We got in our licks."

"Yep. Killed our Communists." Griffin grinned. "And George W's and Dick Cheney's too." He studied the bottom of his coffee cup for a moment, then looked up frankly. "You never really told me. One month Nina's an MP captain in Bosnia; the next she's mobbed up with Delta Force. How'd that go down?"

Broker listened to the wind toy in the trees like a palpable sigh of desire. Decided he owed Griffin that much. "She embodies a concept," he said finally.

"Say again?"

"She took a course on tactical decision-making at Bragg before she deployed to Bosnia. The Boyd thing. The OODA Loop."

Griffin nodded. "I read the book. Not sure you can teach that. You got it or you don't."

"Well, she aced out all the guys in the course. One of them was a Delta colonel who was into thinking outside the box—" Broker's voice stuck briefly. "Holly, Colonel Holland Wood," he said.

"There was a Delta colonel with you at Prairie Island," Griffin said directly.

"The same." He paused, closed his eyes briefly, and continued. "Any rate. He ran into her in Bosnia, remembered her, and invited her in for an interview. I only know snatches. After 9/11 she disappeared into the black side. Thing that still pisses me off is, she took Kit with her last time out. Used our kid to set up her cover in that North Dakota thing."

"Kit," Griffin said simply. "You want her to turn out like you, or Nina? She's headed in that direction, you know. Unless you guys change."

Broker listened to the soft breeze rise and fall, drawing silky through the pines.

"Think about it all the time," he said.

Griffin backed off. Figured it was as close as Broker would get to answering the question about what Nina would do next.

Broker's prediction turned out to be inaccurate. When Nina and Kit left Dawn's Salon, Nina's reddish amber hair was cleaned up but styled longer than it had been since her undergraduate days. Kit sported a matching cut; the snarl of her cowlick bangs resolved under Mom's watchful eye. Nina tossed her new do and looked up and down Main Street.

"We're going out tonight, so let's splurge a little, maybe get new outfits," she said. Her eyes prowled the storefronts. Stopped on a funky hand-painted sign across the street, next to the red-brick courthouse: "Big Lake Threads." "There," she said. She took Kit's hand, and they started across the street.

The door jingled when they entered, and Nina scanned a display of hats, gloves, and scarfs that tended more toward fashion than the practical; accessories for women who didn't worry about getting cold. So it was a boutique that catered to the high-end summer crowd. Probably kept open as a labor of love through the winter. The lady sitting behind the counter looked up, smiled, then went back to reading her book. The store was empty except for one other shopper, a slim, striking woman with long black hair who stood among the racks, holding a blouse at arm's length, staring at it with a tangible longing.

"Mom," Kit said urgently, tugging at Nina's hand. "Let's go."

Nina tracked Kit's sudden alarm, found its source when she saw a stout little boy peek around the dark-haired woman.

"That's Teddy Klumpe, you know; the boy at school," Kit whispered.

Their tense conversation was mirrored down the aisle between the woman and her son. Nina saw surprise on the woman's face and instinctively decided to move before her dazed expression focused into something harder. With Kit in tow, she walked up the aisle and extended her hand.

"Mrs. Klumpe, I'm Kit's mother—"

The woman drew herself up, wary. "It's not Klumpe, it's Bodine, Cassie Bodine."

"Well, I'm Nina Pryce. I didn't take my husband's name either. Although I did give him the option of taking mine." Her hand was still outstretched.

Nina's casual remark was just enough to skew the building tension.

Cassie's face was pinched gorgeous, with nervous blue eyes. She transferred the blouse to her left hand and cautiously shook Nina's hand.

"My husband tells me we owe you something," Nina said, searching her memory for just what it was that Broker had said they owed by way of a peace offering.

Cassie swept her arm behind her and hauled Teddy out in plain view. Kit and Teddy looked up at their mothers for clues, then both stared at the floor.

"Actually," Cassie said, her hand touching her throat and then her hair in a jumpy reflex. "Actually, Teddy . . . this is Teddy," she said, dropping her hand, patting the boy briefly on the head.

"Hello, Teddy," Nina said easily. "You got some shoulders on you, boy. I'll bet you play—"

"Hockey," Teddy said, his eyes shifting sideways.

"Hockey," Nina repeated. Then she patiently looked back at Cassie.

Cassie said, "Well, it was his shirt, it got—"

"Blood on it," Nina said, nodding, extemporizing. "Probably ruined it."

"Well, yes, it did."

"Ms. Bodine," Nina said carefully, "we've had quite a talk with Kit about playing too rough, and we'd appreciate it if you let us replace Teddy's shirt." She glanced down the store. "I don't suppose they have anything suitable here?"

Suddenly animated, Teddy tugged at Cassie's sleeve. "Mom, they got those X-Men in the back."

"There is a small kid's section, but it's on the pricey side," Cassie said. Grinding her teeth, that jerky eye movement again.

"X-Men's cool; right, Kit?" Nina flashed a warning to Kit, who was struggling to contain the mortification creeping up her neck and reddening her cheeks. "Let's take a look."

They followed Cassie and Teddy to the rack of specialty T-shirts. He selected a black one, boys' extra-large.

Nina said, offhand, "Maybe you should get the red one—if you get skinned up playing hockey, won't show as much."

Cassie blinked, not sure if there was a discreet stinger in the remark. Teddy stuck with the black. They walked back up to the sales counter, and Nina explained to the clerk that she was starting a tab. The clerk removed the price tag, set it aside, then folded the shirt and put it in a bag.

Nina shook hands with Cassie a second time, saying earnestly, "We're real sorry about what happened. Let's hope things work out for the best."

Cassie shrugged, eyes and facial muscles flitting. Not entirely certain what had happened here. "We'll see . . . how it goes," she said. And they left it at that.

As Cassie and her son walked from the store, Kit elbowed her mother, "Mom, I am so *embarrassed*. He's a bully, and *his mom is mean*. She was yelling for his dad to hurt my dad in front of the school . . ."

"Calm down. You'll learn that sometimes you catch more flies with honey than vinegar."

"I don't know what that means," Kit said.

"It's a cliché. Sometimes when you deal with dumb people, it helps to say dumb things. That's a cliché." Nina brightened, turned Kit by the shoulders, and pointed her into the store. "Now, let's buy some frivolous stuff."

"I don't know what that means either."

"Fun. It means fun," Nina said.

Chapter Thirty-six

Nina and Kit returned to Griffin's house with their new hairdos and the backseat of the Tundra stuffed with shopping bags. They collected Broker and bumped away down the rutted driveway.

Griffin showered, shaved, then started pacing his house, smoked one cigarette, then another; made another pot of coffee. Antsy. The thing was building up momentum. He reined himself in. *Wait on J. T.'s call. If the check comes up empty, forget it.* But just in case, he laid out his pack, unfolded a county map, and studied the solid green bulge where the Washichu State Forest dipped into Glacier County. Traced County 12 where it entered the green and petered out into a secondary gravel road . . .

Where Gator lived.

He threw on his jacket and went back out on the deck with the cordless phone, to enjoy the soft afternoon. As he drank his fresh coffee, he smoked and watched the clouds slowly drift together over the northwest horizon. Like the gathering clouds, pieces of a plan scudded in his mind. Simple, organic: a variation on a poetic justice theme that Gator Bodine himself had scripted.

Okay. Don't go jumping to conclusions . . .

Finally, the phone rang.

Griffin picked it up, thumbed the power button. "Hello."

"Harry, it's J. T.; I got a read on the license plate and talked to some people. You, ah, gonna tell me what this is about? Like, does it involve our friend?"

"Not directly. Fact is, they were all three just here, looking like

Ozzie and Harriet; you ask me, they're getting close to packing up and coming home."

"Yeah?" J. T. said, waiting.

Griffin opted to be straight with J. T., up to a point. "Look, you been up here, the sheriff is spread kind of thin."

"Uh-huh. And you help out, is that it. The Community Watch." More waiting.

"Okay. I think we got a guy way back in the woods cooking meth. I come up with a license on a silver-gray Pontiac. This mystery lady visits him—"

"Bingo," J. T. said, his voice on surer ground. "Sheryl Marie Mott. Caucasian female, thirty-six, goes five feet eight, one-thirty pounds, dark hair, blue eyes. Drives a 2001 Pontiac Grand Am GT. And Harry—watch the cowboy shit. She's associated with the OMG motorcycle gang, some real bad-news bikers."

"She got a record?"

"Nothing that resulted in convictions. She was looked at a few years back on suspicion of smuggling dope into the prison. Nothing that would stick. And dig this. Under identifying marks on her sheet, it says 'red Harley wings tattooed under her belly button hip to hip.'"

Griffin chuckled, "Talk about getting your red wings, huh?"

"There it is. And to answer your question, to quote my unimpeachable source; she's the perfect chick, strictly likes to fuck and cook. Cook meth, that is."

"Thanks, J. T. Now when I talk to Sheriff Nygard I got a little more to go on than just my overactive imagination."

"I can make some more calls—BCA's got a flying meth squad could help out the sheriff—"

"I'll let him know."

After a pause, J. T. asked, "So they're all right, huh?"

"Hey, when I saw her an hour ago she just came from getting her hair done."

"I guess. Question is, what's she gonna do next? She goes back in the Army . . . ," J. T. said.

"It'll kill Broker, she does that," Griffin said.

"He won't admit it, though; dumb fuck. Maybe nothing changes. Okay, look, Harry; you watch your ass, hear?"

"Lima Charley. Thanks again."

Griffin switched off the phone, stood up, and stretched. Looking around, he thought, Not a bad day for a walk in the woods. But first he went in the house and sat at his desk computer, connected to the Net, and Googled "meth labs." Got some book titles, clicked to Amazon.

Christ, lookit all this shit: *Advanced Techniques of Clandestine Psychedelic & Amphetamine Manufacture,* by Uncle Fester. *The Construction and Operation of Clandestine Drug Laboratories; Second Edition, Revised & Expanded,* by Jack B. Nimble.

After almost two hours clicking his way through the sites, he thought he had a basic fix on the kind of equipment to look for. Okay. Let's do it.

He pulled on silk-weight long underwear, a fleece sweater, tan wind pants, and a pair of wool socks. Then he laced on his Rockies. In the bedroom, he reached behind the books on the first shelf of the bedside table and withdrew a folded chamois cloth, unwrapped it, and removed the classic 1911 Colt .45 semiautomatic and two magazines, one loaded with seven rounds, the other empty to rest the spring. He inserted the magazine, racking the slide, and set the safe. Then he felt behind the socks in his top dresser drawer, took out a box of ammo and a shoulder holster, loaded the second magazine, slipped it in the leather carrier on the holster, and shoved in the pistol.

No big thing. Most of the locals carried a sidearm when they ventured into the big woods. They didn't believe the tree-hugger propaganda about wolves never attacking humans.

After he'd strapped on the pistol, he pulled on a bulky fleece sweater and a lightweight Gore-Tex windbreaker and emptied the coffeepot into a thermos. He put the thermos in his pack with a plastic bottle of water, two energy bars, and a pair of binoculars. The pack already contained a first-aid kit, a compass, and a small but powerful halogen flashlight.

His mind at this point was still relatively empty. Whatever he found would dictate taking it to the next level.

His gear assembled, he went out, started up his Jeep, and drove north though the Barrens. When he came to the intersection where County Z crossed 12, he turned right, following Teedo's directions. Checking the tenths clicking off on his odometer, he watched the tree line along the left side of the untracked road, alert for the overgrown logging trail. About two miles. One-point-nine . . . There.

He slowed, shifted into four-wheel low, and turned left through an opening in the trees. Branches batted the windshield, snagged at the fenders. Fifty yards in, the wheels started to spin, so he stopped. The snow was deceptive, the ground beneath it thawed and wet. He unfolded the county map again.

Getting out, shouldering his pack, he oriented to the map and visualized the vector of the trail cutting across the acute angle formed by 12 and County X. Maybe three miles to Gator's farm. He folded the map, tucked it in his parka and started to walk.

Soon the tall pagodas of red and white pine boughs blocked the sky, and he moved in limbo light, hemmed in by balsam and black spruce. Since the sun didn't penetrate in here, the snow still clung to branches, not soft and fluffy but thawed and refrozen into thick chains that weighted down the boughs.

Sweating now, he unzipped his parka, removed his hat and gloves. The silence played tricks with his ears, sometimes buzzing, sometimes ringing. Nothing moved, no birds, no squirrels; just the hushed tramp of his boots in the snow.

Then, when it seemed the dense tangle of trees would never end, the trail opened ahead and dipped. The sky returned, and he picked his way down the granite shoulder of a wide ravine. Coming up the other side, he saw the four-foot-tall cairn of small boulders that marked Camp's Last Stand.

He stopped, removed his pack, took out the thermos, unscrewed the cup, and poured coffee. Then he lit a Lucky, and as his sweat evaporated, he revisited the story of local legend Waldo Camp. Desk clerk in the Granite Falls Post Office, Camp had trudged out here all alone on deer opener in 1973 to hunt this wide ravine. He had constructed such a perfectly camouflaged blind up on a granite shelf that they didn't find him for three days after he went missing. The temperature had been mild on opening day when The Big One crushed his heart. A much younger Ed Durning, doctor at the town clinic and acting medical examiner for the county, made this deduction when they found Camp sitting on a stump, slouched against a pile of deadfall. His trousers and long underwear were tangled down around his boots. To a man, the search party swore that Camp had never looked so good; eyes locked wide open, and this beatific grin frozen on his parted lips.

Underscore the frozen. A serious cold snap had moved in, and Camp was slumped, petrified, in a sitting position, left hand holding his .243 perfectly erect, and his right hand clamped around his limp frosty pecker.

His family took it in stride and put Waldo's other claim to fame on his tombstone: "Sold a joke to *Reader's Digest,* June, 1969."

Griffin finished his coffee, stowed the thermos, and hiked up the ravine. Just like Teedo said, the trail forked. Griffin took the left path, and soon the canopy and thickets of spruce closed in, plunging him in dim silence broken only by the rush of a stream coursing through the granite boulders.

Then, up ahead, the skeletal white trunks of the paper birches shimmered in the gloom. Walking closer, he saw the dull twinkle of three tin buckets hooked to the trees.

Close now. Just a few hundred yards.

Moving more cautiously now, he caught glimpses of a clearing to his left. He left the trail and worked his way to the edge of the tree line. A collapsed snowbound barbed-wire fence bounded an overgrown pasture. Must've run cows in here once. Crops were hit-and-miss, just alfalfa in the open spaces; go down ten inches, and you hit the solid bedrock of the Canadian Shield.

Griffin settled in, took out his binoculars, sat on his pack, and studied the layout of the farm. Slow memories of watching other houses in other climates informed his patient scrutiny.

Gator's red Chevy truck was parked in front of the house. As the sun settled on the western tree line, the lights were more pronounced in windows of the square cement-block shop. No lights on in the decayed story-and-a-half house or the barn. Then. Boop. The display light came on, highlighting the restored red antique tractor set next to Gator's sign.

Griffin ran the binocs over the tractor graveyard that spilled off the back of the shop. Made a note. Gator was smart. Don't underestimate him. Like Rumpelstiltskin, he had figured out a way to spin that rusty old iron into gold.

No sign of a dog. Looking down the field, toward the road, he saw the windbreak of pines. Set in orderly rows, the trees extended from the woods to within fifty yards of the shop.

In the fading light he tried to examine the ground between the pines and the shop. Looked worked over, hints of shadows forming in tire ruts. Get a little colder, it might harden enough to let him go in without worrying about making tracks.

Then he popped alert. He had movement. Gator coming out of his shop. Just pulled the door shut, didn't look like he was locking it. Then he walked toward the house, carrying something in the crook of his arm.

It got better. Five minutes later Gator reappeared, got in his truck, started it up, and rumbled around the horseshoe driveway in front of his shop. As he turned toward the road, his headlights swept across the field, and Griffin watched them travel across the brush where he sat, touching his face.

Up in a crouch now.

As the taillights faded down the road, he started toward the pine windbreak, moving sure and steady.

Damn. Like going in on a raid.

Chapter Thirty-seven

Driving back from the pay phone at Perry's, bouncing in his seat. Man, it was happening. Sheryl had talked to a big-time hitter. The Shank. Get ready, she said.

Okay.

So first thing—he had to start arranging his alibi. Just in case. He'd need some trading material. Wanted to be sitting back talking in the sheriff's office, handing some meth trade over to Keith, if Broker got hit up here. Be good if he had more than just some lights moving around the old houses on Z in the dark. What he needed was something tangible, like some names Keith could go slap the cuffs on.

Driving into town, he'd seen those lights again at the Tindall place. Now was the time to make a check. So go trolling. Work his pattern.

As he slowed for the crossroads and turned west on Z, he was curious, strictly from a professional point of view, what Shank would use on Broker. Would he take the wife and the daughter, too? Wondered if the guy would be willing to compare notes with an amateur. Always wondered what he was like. A young guy? Older? And how much did he get paid for a job like this?

Then the saw the flicker of light in the windows of the Tindall place. He switched off his headlights 300 yards from the house, then cut the motor and rolled up to the driveway. Yep. Somebody in there with a flashlight. He reached under the seat, withdrew the Ruger .22 pistol, his own flashlight, and a two-foot length of one-inch pipe wrapped in electrical tape.

So who we got? Go see.

He eased open the truck door, left it ajar, and stuck the pistol in the back of his waistband under his coat. Then he hefted the pipe and padded up the drive. A rusted-out '89 Chevy Nova was parked in front of the house. Car he'd seen in town. Some kid driving. Miracle he got the piece of shit up the drive in the snow.

Silent on the snow, he eased up to the porch, starting to remove the pistol from under his coat. He could make out a single figure moving in the strobe of the light beam. Uh-huh. This was no beer party. One guy, looked like he was searching for something on the baseboards of the musty living room. Flimsy plastic bags, some containers, tubing, and what looked like a hot plate appeared in a flash of beam near the guy's feet.

Gator slid the pistol back under his coat and gripped the pipe. The beat-up Nova was a clue; this was strictly *Beavis and Butthead* hour. He went through the open door fast, switching on his light, holding it up at arm's length in his left hand, angled down like cops do.

"Hi there," Gator said. Closing the distance fast. The person froze in his light. Neither getting ready to fight or run. Stone froze. Like he thought: a kid, maybe eighteen, nineteen. A kid as rusted out at the car he drove. Gator immediately saw there was no threat in him. Definitely starting to get the look: circles under his bugged-out eyes, pinched face, unkempt hair, dirty jeans and jacket. Dumb shit, wearing tennis shoes in the snow. Gator even noticed his filthy fingernails. "Drop the light, get your hands up," Gator yelled, grinning in the dark as he tried his best to sound like every pumped-up, control-crazy cop he'd ever met.

The kid's flashlight clattered to the floor, illuminating a corner of peeling wallpaper, backlighting him. "Who's there?" he blurted. His voice sounded like he looked—skinny and desperate.

"I'll ask the questions. Now slowly lift your coat and turn around." Gator put the light in his eyes.

The kid did as he was told. "I didn't do anything . . . ," he whined.

"Shut up," Gator ordered. "Empty your pockets. Real slow. Drop everything on the floor."

Car keys, a wallet, some crumpled bills, change. A pipe for smoking meth wrapped in a red bandanna. Gator noted that the pipe and the scarf were the only items that came out of the pockets that appeared tidy and well cared for. Reluctantly the kid let a folding buck knife fall.

"Kick the knife toward me." The knife skittered across the floor. "Now turn around, approach the wall, and get on your knees."

"You gotta identify yourself," the kid said uncertainly as he turned around. "Can't just—"

Gator took a step forward and swung the pipe, slamming it in a short, powerful arc into the back of the kid's right thigh just above the inner knee.

"Ow, shit." He crumpled to his knees.

"Belly up against the wall, motherfucker!"

"Okay, okay, goddamn—" The kid scooted on his knees and hugged the wallpaper, digging his fingers into it. He was gasping, no, sobbing.

What a pussy. "Now, put your arms straight back, palms up. Do it!"

"Am I under arrest?" He extended his arms, hands shaking.

Gator tested an old chair, decided it would hold his weight, and sat down. "Name?"

"If you're a cop, you gotta identify yourself, don't you?"

"I don't see any cops. You see any cops?" Gator said amiably. "Just you and me. Nobody else for miles."

"Oh, shit. It's you." The kid's voice began to shake. He cast a furtive look over his shoulder, trying to make out the dark shape behind the bright multiple halogen bulbs.

"Turn around. Keep your hands straight back. Now, what's your name?"

After a long moment the kid said, "Terry Nelson."

"Any relation to Cal Nelson?"

"My dad."

"Cal was a year ahead of me in school. He still work for the power company?"

"Yeah."

"He know you're into this shit?" Gator aimed a kick at a can of paint thinner, sent it crashing across the floor into the wall.

"Aw shit; it *is* you," Terry said hopelessly.

"I asked you a question."

"My dad and me ain't talked much lately." From trembling lips, Terry's voice sounded lost, confused. Like a child's.

Gator let him build up his shakes for almost a minute, then he said, "Okay, kid, since I knew your old man I'm gonna give you a break. So turn around and sit down." He'd been through this routine with local kids four or five times in the last year. He really enjoyed this part; first he'd jack 'em up, then let them down a notch on the hook. He extended the pack of Camel Reds. "You want a cigarette?" Uncle Gator.

Terry took a cigarette from the pack with shaking fingers, leaned forward, and accepted a light. He puffed and huddled, drawing up his knees, wrapping his arms around them.

"You got a problem, Terry," Gator said.

"I wasn't gonna sell it. I just needed a little for—"

"I mean the hot plate, dummy. You're not thinking too clearly, are you? What the hell were you planning to plug it in to? Power's been off here for years. Shit, your dad probably shut down the line."

Terry puffed nervously, his face twitching in the circle of halogen light. "Last time I was here, I thought . . ." His voice ended in a tic of nerves that distorted his face.

"When's the last time you got high?" Gator asked.

Terry's shrug collapsed into a shuddering spasm. "Don't know. Couple days. Over in Thief River."

"Tell me about the last time you were here. You weren't alone, were you? And you didn't use a hot plate."

"I don't feel so good," Terry muttered.

"We'll get to that. Now who were you here with?"

"You gonna let me go?"

"Depends. One way you can walk outa here. Another way, we call Keith Nygard."

At the mention of the sheriff, Terry attempted to concentrate. When he furrowed his brow, it looked like he was herding a scurry of tiny mice under the skin of his cheeks and mouth, struggling to get them corralled in his twitchy eyes. "We had a camp stove, I guess."

"Who's we?"

"Aw shit, man."

Gator held up his cell phone. "Works real good, now they built the towers for the summer folks. Got Keith's number right here in my phone book. All I gotta do is poke my finger. Gimme some names, Terry."

"They're my friends," Terry sniveled.

"Pissant little tweaker like you got no friends. All you got is that pipe. Now take your time and think. While you're thinking ponder about Keith's jail. Not much to it. I hear it's kinda grim." Pause. "I'm waiting."

"Danny Halstad and Frank Reed," Terry said glumly.

"They local?"

"Danny's a senior. Frank graduated last year."

"Guess you guys didn't get the word, huh? This Danny—he bringing shit into the school?"

"No way. Everybody knows about the people you—" Terry panted, dry swallowing, then gulped, "who burned up."

"What about outsiders, say from Beltrami or Red Lake, coming in to these old houses on Z, cooking?"

Terry violently shook his head.

"Stand up," Gator ordered. Terry scrambled to his feet, bent over, rubbing the back of his leg where Gator had laid the pipe. Gator put the light in his face. "Push up your lips so I can see your teeth and gums."

"Huh?"

"Do it."

Apprehensively, Terry manipulated his lips, revealing a grimace of teeth.

"Don't look too bad, you ain't that far gone. You could rehab your ass. You ever think of that?"

"Ah, sure. All the time." Terry bobbed his head in a comic attempt to placate the dark forceful presence behind the flashlight.

Lying little shit. "Good. But first let's get something straight." Gator sidestepped, stooped, and snatched up the can of paint thinner he'd kicked. He put the flashlight under his arm, twisted the cap, then splashed some of the liquid on Terry's chest. "I'm gonna keep this can and put your name on it. I catch you stinking up my woods cooking meth, you're gonna drink this whole half gallon."

The stark reek of mineral spirits underscored Gator's words as he capped the container and lowered it to the floor.

"I won't come back, honest to God," Terry stammered as a glimmer of hope quivered in his dilated pupils.

"Right. Look, Terry. I'm going to give you some advice. If I was you, I'd get in that Nova and drive straight to Bemidji. You know that big Target store north of town?"

"Yeah. In the mall. I been there."

"To the Sudafed aisle, smerfing for precursor, huh?"

"Drive to the Target store," Terry said solemnly, like he could see it shimmering in the darkness.

"You go in and walk to the back where they keep the electronics. Where they got the big color TVs. Find one of those new flat screen plasma jobs. Easy to carry. If they got it chained down, go to hardware and pocket some bolt cutters . . ."

Gator lowered the flashlight so the beam tiled up, revealing the shadowed planes of his face, making it into a stern disembodied mask.

". . . check the price tag. You want one that costs over $500. That'll put you in felony theft. You grab that set and run for it through the back doors, into the warehouse."

"Shit, I'll never make it."

"That's the whole point. It's a classic cry for help. Hell, they'll do a drug screen and stick you in county for six months. Beltrami's a Holiday Inn compared to Nygard's dungeon. They got programs, counseling. Get a dentist to check out your teeth. Could turn your life around."

Then Gator grabbed Terry's arm and shoved him toward the floor. Terry panicked at the touch, the downward movement. "Please . . ."

"Pick up your shit," Gator said, not hiding the disgust at this kid's callowness. "Go on."

Terry scrambled on the floor, grabbing at items. His hand hovered near the pipe. Gator's mashed the heel of his work boot down, crushing it. "How much money you got?" he asked.

Terry stood up and held out the crumpled bills. Four singles, some change. Gator palmed his wallet, selected a twenty, and handed it to Terry.

"What's this?"

"Gas money. Get some McDonald's. A malt."

"Ah, thanks," Terry mumbled, staring at the bill.

Gator took Terry by the arm and walked him to the sway-backed porch. "One last thing."

"Sure, anything," Terry said, antsy, seeing his car just thirty feet away.

"Say, 'Who was that masked man,'" Gator said,

"What?" Terry's voice cracked wide open with fear, sensing some freaky trick coming just as he was about to get free.

"C'mon. It's just words. Say it."

Terry swallowed, took a breath, and said, apprehensively, "Who was that masked man."

Gator smiled. "Good. Now get the fuck out of here." He shoved him hard and sent him sprawling off the porch into the snow. "Run, you little shit. Run for your life," he taunted as he put the light on him.

Terry scuttled on all fours, gamboling through the snow. Got to his feet, surged for the car, hurled open the door, and jumped behind the wheel.

Gator watched the kid fishtail the Nova, hell-bent with a twenty in his hot hand, heading for the nearest dealer who'd sell him a chunk of ice. But probably not in Glacier County. The kid would get high and embellish the story. Tell 'em to keep clear of those spooky woods where nobody lived but crazy cousin-killer Gator Bodine. And the wolves.

And that's just how Gator wanted it.

He went back in the house, shone the light at the cook ingredients strewn on the floor. *Leave it. Give Keith the names. Plan it so they're sitting in his office, talking, when Broker goes down.*

That'd work.

Chapter Thirty-eight

Griffin studied the squat gray building just fifty yards away, checked the road, then, seeing no headlights, left cover and jogged leisurely toward the shop. He had no preconceived plan; it all depended on what he found. Freeform. The thing would dictate its own course.

He went right to the front door, twisted the knob, and went in; knelt, unlaced his boots, stepped out of them, and did a fast walk-through in his socks. The square cement-block building was divided roughly into three rooms. In front, the office took up a partitioned corner and contained a desk and shelves with this open alcove at one end with a bunk and an exposed toilet.

The office door opened into a machine shop area with a steel lathe, milling machine, metal saw, grinders, and a drill press.

The second room was the garage. A disassembled rust orange tractor was raised up on blocks and bottle jacks. A tall tool caddy on casters was positioned next to the tractor; lots of drawers, with a workbench on top. Looking around, he saw a wire-feed Mig welder, welding tanks, an air compressor, and a big Onan diesel generator. Gaskets hung on the wall next to a Halon fire extinguisher. Lots of wood blocks, a few jack stands. What you'd expect to find in a mechanic's shop.

Griffin briefly inspected the partitioned storeroom between the garage and the paint room. It contained a paint gun, two protective suits with breather masks connected to filter packs, and buckets of paint. Last, he walked through the paint room. The walls and floor and ceiling were rainbow-mottled with spray from the paint gun, as was the sink and a long worktable with a wide elaborate fume hood that he assumed led up to the blower exhaust fan on the roof.

He walked up to a small color snapshot taped over the workbench: palm trees, a sand beach, sea blue water, and surf that looked like ocean. He shrugged and walked back through the shop into the office, taking his time now. He noticed two things. There was a pile of rags under the desk and two bowls; one with a residue of milk, the other with cat chow.

And on the desk, a blue-green pamphlet caught his eye, lying on top of a pile of tractor magazines. *Tropics View* under a red logo. He opened it and thumbed through. It was a brochure for a puddle-jumper airline that catered to Belize, on the east coast of Mexico.

He put down the brochure. Nothing in the shop struck him out of the ordinary; the paint room *could* be dual use. Okay. Teedo said that he'd seen Gator moving boxes and drums with his Bobcat, to the barn.

Griffin put his boots back on and walked to the barn.

The hayloft was vacant, so Griffin went to the lower level and pulled open the tall, stout sliding doors. The basement floor was walled in two broad stalls; the one on the right was obviously used as a parking garage for Gator's truck and was empty except for a battery charger and plastic gallons of wiper fluid and antifreeze.

The other stall looked more promising. He searched inside the door jam, found an electrical box, and flipped the switch. A chain of four overhead bulbs came on, illuminating a long interior space. A working tractor with a snow bucket and the Bobcat were parked alongside a huge white oblong tank on wheels. "Anhydrous" printed in blue on the side. Stacks of yellow bags; rock salt. A bank of chest-high feed bins made of heavy three-quarter-inch ply lined the entire length of the partition to the right.

The long basement abutted cattle pens and a lean-to that was open to the fenced pasture. He saw half a dozen heavy green plastic fifty-five-gallon drums arranged in the corner of one of the pens. Inspecting the drums, he found them empty and clean-smelling, like they'd been scrubbed with disinfectant.

Griffin was running out of places for Gator to hide things. Briefly he considered digging through the tangled tractor grave-yard in back of the shop. Then his eyes settled on the row of ply-wood bins. He walked over and lifted one of the lids. Immediately he stepped back, making a face at the stench. It was heaped with blackened smutty feed corn, garnished with a jumbo decomposing rat sprawled next to green poison pellets. He went down the line, opening the lids. Five in all; another corn, a bar-ley, two oats, all of them years gone to mildew and rot. A remnant of the hobby farm that had been here.

Griffin thought about it.

The rest of the place was so shipshape. Why would he have these bins full of rotten feed? Decided to give the bins a closer look. He rapped his knuckle on the side panel; a solid thump. Moved his hand down a foot. This time when he struck the wood with his fist, he got a hollow-sounding bounce.

Well, well.

After fiddling with the plywood, he determined that the bins had been constructed with lift-out front panels; the wood screws that appeared to pin them in place had been trimmed back, didn't go through. Cosmetic.

Grunting with the effort, he forced the tightly fit panel up and revealed a compartment beneath the false feed tray. It contained a tall cardboard box. He removed the box, opened the flaps. Three round-bottomed glass flasks and a long twin-tubed glass apparatus were carefully packed in wadded newspaper. Tubing, stoppers, and clamps were tucked in crevices between the flasks.

Gator's little home chemistry set. Okay.

Griffin stood up and looked down the row of bins. He didn't have time to open all five bins. After carefully repacking the box, he put it back in the compartment and forced the panel in place. Then he went to the last bin and swiftly wedged open the front panel. This compartment contained a stash of over-the-counter chemicals, just like he'd read about in his Internet search. Stacked gallon cans of camping fuel, toluene, and paint thinner. A tightly packed box of lithium batteries, cans of Red Devil lye drain opener. A row of red Iso Heet plastic bottles. And a bottle of ether.

Talk about fire in the hole.

Griffin surveyed the basement. Now the yellow bags of rock salt piled along the wall behind the anhydrous tank didn't look so innocent.

Looking up at the series of overhead lightbulbs, he suddenly smiled. The old cartoonist in him suddenly frolicked in the image. *Pop!* Caption of the old lightbulb coming on in a thought bubble. It looked to Griffin like Gator's tidy work ethic had broken down here in the old barn. Because all the volatile chemicals hidden in the bins posed one serious fire hazard. Yes, they did. So.

Maybe just skip a step, leave Keith out of it. Besides, Keith probably wouldn't really appreciate the concept of Gator's karma working itself out, so to speak. It had the added elegance of poetic justice. Seeing's how Gator made his Robin Hood reputation blowing up a meth lab.

Well, turnabout is fair play, motherfucker.

Griffin vaulted up on the bin and unscrewed the lightbulb over the last bin, tossing it in his palms, hot potato, until it cooled; then he inspected it. Like he thought, a lightweight commercial bulb. He screwed it back in, jumped down, and hurried to the door and switched off the light. He needed a rough-service bulb with a more durable filament.

Then he slipped out the door and checked the road for headlights. Seeing none, he walked back into the pines and melted into the murky forest. Touchy going in the shadowy trees, jogging his way back along his tracks; but he immensely enjoyed every step of the trek back to his Jeep. Doubly enjoyed it because he knew he was coming back.

When it was really dark.

◆　◆　◆

An hour and forty-five minutes later, Griffin was back home in his own modest garage workshop, taking three items from a bag he'd just purchased at Tindall's hardware in town; a package of heavy-duty lightbulbs, a sixty-milliliter vet's syringe, and a can of starter fluid.

Griffin opened the bulbs, selected one, placed the metal-threaded nob in his bench vise, and carefully tightened the jaws until the nob was secure. Then he took an electric hand drill, inserted a one-eighth-inch bit, and bored a hole in the metal thread. He repeated the procedure with a second bulb. Two should be enough.

Then he looked around for something to carry the fluid in, that would be easily accessible to the long syringe needle. He settled on a soup-bowl-sized Tupperware container filled with woodscrews, dumped out the screws, poured in the fluid, and secured the lid with duct tape.

He tucked the bulbs, syringe, and fluid in his backpack. Then he went into the house, found his small head-mounted flashlight, and replaced the batteries. Going back outside, he paused to look at the patchy clouds drifting past the constellations. The fattening half-moon. Fifty percent illumination. What the hell, now he'd be able to see in the woods.

Thirty minutes later, the only thing moving on the back roads, Griffin arrived back at the logging road off Z, parked the Jeep, and set off trotting back along his fresh tracks.

Like he thought. Didn't need the light. The snow glimmered with faint moonlight, enough to see his tracks. As he moved, he thought about how this escapade had started because Kit Broker got in a fight at school. Messages were sent back and forth by the belligerent families. Now Griffin was adding his own anonymous little communiqué, and he was going to use a trick that Ray Pryce, the grandfather Kit had never known, taught him in Vietnam. The dormant artist in him loved the family symmetry.

Breathy with sweat, staying on his earlier tracks, Griffin approached the farm and stalked back along the pine windbreak. Gator's truck was parked in front of the barn, the chassis an oily yellow in the sodium vapor light on the barn. The farmhouse was blacked out except for the flicker of a TV in two of the first-floor windows.

Part of the fun, going in while Gator was there, awake.

Griffin crossed to the side of the barn, away from the yard light, and entered from the rear through the open shed and pens. Once inside, he pulled on the small headlamp and climbed onto the farthest bin from the front door. He took off his pack, and removed the bulbs, syringe, and plastic container of fluid. Then he reached up and unscrewed the lightbulb from the fixture, put it in the pack, and replaced it with one of the drilled bulbs. Snapped on the headlamp. Gingerly, working by the narrow light, he rotated the bulb just until the thread caught, leaving the hole exposed.

Now for the hard part. He untaped his container and drew a syringe full of fluid. The trick was to insert the needle in the hole and squeeze the fluid into the bottom of the bulb without disturbing the filament, then very carefully screw the bulb back into the socket so the liquid didn't slosh around, disabling the circuit.

Which he accomplished, holding his breath, with steady fingers. Then he repeated the operation, replacing and loading the next bulb. When he'd stowed his gear back and put the replaced bulbs in the pack, he switched off the headlamp and hopped to the concrete floor. He judged the danger close distance to the front door and the light switch. Should be enough cushion.

The next time that light was turned on, the bulbs would explode and spew liquid fire down on the plywood bins, hopefully igniting all the volatile crap in the area. He wanted to give Gator a scare and hopefully burn his stash, not kill the guy.

Satisfied, Griffin exited the rear of the barn and ran back to the pines. Twenty minutes into the woods, he slowed his pace and allowed himself a cupped cigarette.

Not quite like night work in the old days. In Vietnam, he would have waited until the lights were off in the house, crept in, and cut Gator's throat.

But close enough to elevate the pulse.

Chapter Thirty-nine

Saturday night. Nina wore a new green peasant blouse with flared sleeves. Kit had a smaller version of the same garment in burgundy. Broker cleaned up as best he could, left his work coat on the hook and dug a decent leather jacket from the closet, ran a comb through the shaggy hair curling over his collar.

Then he took the newly coiffed girls out on the town. Such as it was. The Angler's Inn was the only good restaurant that stayed open during the winter. It was located off the frontage road, near Glacier Lodge. The dining room was closed, but the bar side was open and served an abbreviated menu.

They entered the old eatery tentatively, like a family venturing into church after a long absence. Only two people sat at the bar; half the booths were filled. The TV was off. A ceiling of antique stippled tin stretched down the long room, etched gray with generations of nicotine, grease, and wood smoke from the open-hearth fireplace. Kit walked solemnly, hugging her bunny, inspecting the gallery of photos and taxidermy on the walls— musky, walleye, a wolf. A moose head projected over the bar like an incoming antlered spaceship.

Like a shrine to the departed twenthieth century, an old Wurlitzer jukebox pulsed and bubbled red and green in the back of the room. Kit had never seen one before, so Nina led her to the music box with a handful of quarters. Broker sat in a booth watching as Nina helped Kit load up songs. The waitress brought water and menus.

At a moment like this, he could be as sentimental as the next guy. He allowed himself a vacation from suspicion about the future; enjoying looking at his wife standing next to his daughter. Nina in the new green flowing blouse, one hand planted on her hip, filling out a pair of Levi's 501s like a north-country road-house dream.

The women returned, and they ordered food as the songs came on. Some Gary Puckett. Jay and the Americans. Deliberate flourishes echoing back to their tornadic courtship.

"Come a little bit closer" . . . like that.

Midway through grilled walleye and moose burgers, he put the idea in play with a casual remark: "You know, I could call Dooley, have him get a housekeeper in to clean up the Stillwater place."

Nina looked up from her plate, blew a strand of hair away from her eyes, nodded, and said, "Give me another couple days to be sure. But I'm for that."

Seeing her mom and dad grinning at each other, Kit bounced in her seat. "You mean?"

"That's right, Little Bit," Nina said. "We're going home."

As they gabbed about Kit's friends on North Third Street, and swimming and piano, Broker rode the happy thermals. Nina mentioned that she and Kit had bumped into Teddy Klumpe and his mother when they were shopping.

"How'd that go?" Broker asked, momentarily snapping out of his glide.

"It was icky," Kit said. "Mom was *so nice* to her."

Nina shrugged. "She's one uptight lady, so yeah, I made nice. Bought the kid a T-shirt to replace the one that got bloodied up—"

"When *he* started a fight, and *I* got suspended. It was *very icky*, Dad," Kit said emphatically.

Broker grinned as Nina and Kit went back and forth on the etiquette of the meeting. The waitress cleared their plates, and Broker asked for the dessert menu.

Nina was trying to explain to an eight-year-old the difference between necessary and unnecessary conflict. Kit scowled, furrowing her brow, looked to her dad for assistance.

Broker made a stab. "Remember our little talk about laws of human nature?"

Kit swelled her eyes. "Are we gonna throw more rocks in the air? Oh, boy."

Nina masked her laugh with her hand.

"Well," Broker said, "another basic law is there's two kinds of people—"

"Yeah," Kit said, "there's girls and there's fat creepy boys like Teddy—"

"Close. More like there's people who like themselves and people who don't like themselves. I don't think Teddy likes who he is. See, it's important to know the difference. Because the people who aren't comfortable in their skins make you miserable."

By way of response, Kit held up her bunny, holding its stubby arms over its ears. Broker turned to Nina and asked, "Whatta *you* think?"

"I think I'll have the German chocolate cake and ice cream," Nina said, suppressing a snicker.

"I give." Broker tossed up his arms. The waitress returned and he ordered German chocolate layer cake and ice cream all around.

A little later, as they drove back to the small house on the lake, he found himself sneaking looks at Nina and pondering his glib, simple cliché: What goes up must come down.

Broker built a fire in the Franklin stove, and they played two rounds of Sequence, a board game Kit liked, on the kitchen table. Kit won the first game.

"Don't pull your punches," Broker hectored Nina as he reshuffled the cards and they sorted the plastic chips.

"Hey, I didn't," Nina said, a little testy.

"Mom doesn't like to lose," Kit said.

Kit won the second game and yawned. Haircuts, shopping, dinner, talk of going home, dessert, and the fire had worn her out. They put her to bed and returned to the kitchen and the embers of the fire. Sat across the table from each other.

Nina took out a cigarette and instead of lighting it manipulated it in the fingers of her right hand, like a prop in a dexterity exercise. Finally she set the cigarette vertical on the table, balanced on its filter. Then she poked her finger and knocked it over. Looked up at him.

"You got something you want to say, say it."

Trying to keep the mellow mood going, he shook his head. "It can wait."

She studied him for a moment. "You're thinking, When is she going to call the doctor at Bragg, huh."

"I guess," Broker said. *There it is.*

"Pretty soon," she said with a sliver of the old steel in her voice. "And then we'll have a long-overdue talk. You and me." She grimaced ever so slightly, looked away, and picked up the cigarette, started out of reflex to put it in her lips.

Broker felt the tiny slippage in the air, the day starting to slide.

But then she snapped her wrist and darted the cigarette across the table into the glowing coals in the stove. "You know," she said, giving him that sidelong glance, "I wouldn't blush if you wanted to fool around again tonight. Unless Griffin snapped your dick string lifting those weights this morning . . ."

Chapter Forty

Because Gator generally didn't trust excitement, he compensated for his giddy Saturday and weird brush with Griffin by working all day on the Moline. Important to keep the shop running normally. Never tell when Mitch Schiebel, his parole officer, might stop by for a spot-check and cup of coffee. By sunset he'd finished replacing the clutch and flywheel.

He put away his tools and washed up. Sheryl had not left a message. And he was all right with that. She wouldn't talk to the gang until tomorrow morning. Why waste a drive to Perry's pay phone just to be anxious together?

Just after he turned the display light on his show tractor the phone rang. It was Cassie.

"Gator, you think you could *drop by* again?"

"Uh-uh, I'm through making house calls," he said in an idle voice as he watched the black kitty jump up on the office desk and stretch.

"C'mon, just one more time, honest," she said.

Gator reached out his hand and stroked the cat's glossy fur, feinted with his finger, sending the cat back on its haunches, paws up; then he darted in the finger, tickled it on the chest. "You want something, you're going to have to come get it," he said into the phone.

"I thought you didn't want me to come out there?"

Gator lifted the cat and let it pour from his hand, this smooth effortless motion. "Maybe I changed my mind," he said.

"I gotta think about *that*," Cassie said.

"You do that," Gator said. Then he ended the call. For a moment he had a fleeting sensation of what it might feel like to get everything you want.

He pushed up off his chair and, feeling more balanced after a day spent with his tools, took some coffee, put on his coat, went out through the paint room door, and walked through the old machines in back of the shop. Looking at the sky filling in with dark clouds, he made a mental note to check the Weather Channel; see exactly what was behind the front taking shape to the northwest.

As the light left the sky, an afterglow seemed to cling to the snow cover on the fields in back of the shop. The snow cover had melted then frozen again, forming a tough crust. Faintly, then louder, he heard a swelling chorus of howls. The pack was active. Wolves could run across the crusted snow in which the deer foundered. Made them easy targets.

From the accelerating howls, he assumed they had located such a deer; a straggler, injured or just weak.

People in town had come to associate him with the wolves, because he lived alone out here. Even attributing to him some of the animals' wildness.

He did see one comparison.

The meth they cooked would prowl along the margins of the population, selecting out the dumb, the naive, the weak. Like the wolves, it would devour the strays who, ensnared in their addiction, could no longer run.

Fact was, he would be providing a social service. In producing the drug, he would be culling out the weak and infirm. By killing them, he was improving the quality of the herd.

The wind gusted, and he turned up his collar and sipped the coffee. Hearing the howls and thinking of Sheryl negotiating with a killer brought to mind his own kills.

———

In addition to the tractors, his dad had left a locker containing a rifle, a shotgun, and three pistols. After his folks "died," he greased the weapons up with Cosmoline and wrapped them in oilcloth; a souvenir German Luger, two small .22-caliber pistols, a .12-gauge shotgun, and a 30–06 deer gun. Took them into the tractor grave yard and hid them in the chassis of an ancient Deere. They stayed there for years. As a kid he favored the Luger, but as it turned out, when he returned to the farm, the Ruger .22 proved more useful.

Homicide 101 on Cell Block D over bootleg cigarettes and contraband potato hooch. A .22 works just fine, but you gotta put the sucker right up against the poor fuck's head you're gonna kill. Or better, stick it in his ear and burn the body. That way, nobody's gonna know the body has a bullet in it 'cause the round won't exit the skull.

Like a TV show beamed in from a satellite on the dark side of the moon. Stuck way off the menu past the music channels, the auctions and the religious nuts. Always ran in the back of his mind. Way back.

He could watch it if he chose.

Not his mom and dad. That was more like fate. Predetermined—he had just provided an extra nudge. Like the wolves again, cleaning some slime out of the gene pool.

The rule certainly applied to his cousins, who were filthy people. Untidy in their morals and their housekeeping. Preying on their own kids. Fucking scum.

The day Marci Sweitz got poisoned, he saw a way to solve his biggest problem, them snooping around his shop. Not that much different from taking out the trash for Jimmy to pick up. Clean up the neighborhood. Shot them fast coming into the stinking house. Herded them into the bathroom to control them and popped them all carefully in the throat. Multiple times with the Ruger .22. Soft tissue bleeder wounds, taking care to avoid the bones. Soft-tissue wounds would burn away in the fire. Billie, Vern, Doug, and Sandy last of all. Disgusting little tramp kid poisoner, down on her knees, slobbering in the spoiled food and dog crap. Begging, had this baby pacifier in her mouth; all that Ecstasy and meth had given her fits of jaw-clenching and teeth-grinding and had proba-bly ruined her oral sex career.

"Calm down, Gator, please. Let me do you. You know how good I am."

She was actually frantically grabbing at his belt when he put the barrel to her throat.

Swallow this, bitch.

Then he opened the propane coupling on the hot water heater in the disgusting basement, turned on the hot water full blast in the kitchen and the bathroom. Half an hour later, standing on his porch, he watched the sky light up over the tree line.

The world could only improve when you stuffed all that walking garbage in a plastic bag.

The howls rose in their usual spooky intensity, toying with the short hairs on his neck. At this point the wolf logic hit the unre-solved contradiction of his life. His contribution to upping the mental hygiene had amounted to killing off Bodines, his own family.

That left Cassie. And him.

Got him thinking how there's wolves and there's wolves, like the alpha wolves who cull the pack.

He had watched Broker chopping wood in back of his house that first day. But he'd only seen him up close once. Fast but close, going past him on the ski trail. But he got a good look at the man's severe agate eyes under those shaggy eyebrows. Thinking back on it now, Broker looked sort of like a wolf.

To hear Sheryl tell it, this Shank fella was a real pro. Looks like they were going to find out.

Gator looked up at the dark wall of nimbostratus clouds com-ing in low—snow clouds. He shook off the chill, dumped his cof-fee, walked to the house, went inside, and shut the door tightly against the baying of the hunting pack. Dumb, thinking like this.

He jumped when the wall phone rang in the kitchen.

Approached it tentatively. Picked it up and heard Barnie Sheffeld's gritty voice. Barnie had the antique Case on display at his implement showroom in Bemidji.

"Thought you might want to know," Barney said. "Got a buyer for that Case. When it's all wrapped up, you be looking at eighteen thousand, how's that."

"Hey, Barnie, that's great," Gator said, grinning.

After a few more pleasantries they ended the call, and Gator paced the cramped kitchen. It was like a sign.

Like—after all the planning and hard work, he and Sheryl were going to succeed. He was dreaming barefoot, sand between his toes. Boat engines would be cleaner than country tractors. Surf and sun. No more skinning his knuckles in a freezing junkyard, looking for parts. He'd take his time. Put together his own boat. An island runner. Things to learn, navigation, charts . . .

Never seen the ocean. Just Lake Superior.

Damn. He cocked his head and imagined a gruff shadowy gremlin god for grease monkeys and dope-dealing jailbirds who rewarded hard work.

Imagined this crafty demon looking up from counting his money. Imagined him smiling.

Chapter Forty-one

At 8:03 on a sunny but brisk cloudless Monday morning Shank wheeled the gray Nissan Maxima to the curb in front of Grand and Dale Drugs, where Sheryl was standing in dress jeans, boots with two-inch heels, a slightly clingy blouse, and her good leather car coat. No hat, no gloves, no scarf. As she got in the passenger side, she missed the way he appraised her choice of clothing, like it might be a problem.

"Hey," she said, upbeat, scanning the leather interior. "Nice wheels."

Pulling smoothly into traffic, Shank pointed to an envelope on the dash. "Check it out," he said.

Sheryl picked it up, an old Fotomat envelope with a blurred date entered in ballpoint, "7/23/92." She opened the flap and pulled out a stack of four-by-six colored photographs. An almost starry moistness came to her eyes when she saw the top one; the old gang in better times, more hair showing, bare-chested, tank tops, tattoos taking the summer sun . . . maybe two dozen guys and their old ladies, clustered around a tall ponytailed already gray eminence. Danny Turrie, hands on hips in the middle, anchoring the crowd. They were arranged linking arms in a cluster. This smoky pile of dirt in the foreground. And there she was right in front, ten years younger, nut brown in cutoffs and a bikini top. Blissed-out grin on her face . . . musta been tripping . . .

"Jesus, this was—" She thought back.

"Uh-huh. Back in the day. The pig roast, on the bluff out at Danny's Lakeland place. Before my time," Shank said.

"Where'd you get these?"

"Spent all day yesterday tracking them down. Joey Chatters took them."

"I know Joey," Sheryl said.

"He ain't doing so good, type-two diabetes," Shank said.

"Jeez, next to Danny, that's—"

"Yep. Jojo, holding a bottle of Bacardi. Check out the dude in front, with the shovel. Take your time."

Sheryl sorted through the pictures. They diagrammed a process; the crowd watching the lean guy with the shovel, shirt off, glistening with sweat, tiger muscled. No tattoos. He was digging into the smoky coals, opening a hole in the pit, unearthing a long greasy bundle. He had shaggy dark hair, prominent cheekbones, and these heavy eyebrows that grew almost together in a line across his forehead.

"I sorta remember him, we called him . . ." Sheryl bit her lip, concentrating.

"Eyebrows, you called him Eyebrows back then," Shank said.

"Yeah," Sheryl said. "Eyebrows. He roasted the pig. Wasn't patched, sort of a—"

"Handyman, helped Danny out. Made himself useful," Shank said. He had turned off Dale onto westbound I-94, accelerated into the rush-hour traffic. "Remember, Saturday, I asked you if you had a picture?"

"No shit; that's *Broker.*" She looked up, her face conjuring with the information. "I never . . . I mean, Gator, he found the guy. I never put eyes on—"

"Up north," Shank said.

"Yeah," Sheryl said.

"I spent all Sunday talking to three people in those pictures, they all remember clearly the guy's name was Phil Broker."

"You been busy," Sheryl said.

Shank shrugged. "You got a job, sometimes you have to actually do it, huh. Ain't done yet. I need one more ID."

Sheryl thought about that as Shank expertly threaded the car through lanes of traffic on the 280 curve near the University of

Minnesota; the IDS tower up ahead, Minneapolis skyline catching the morning sun.

Seeing the question taking shape on her face, Shank gave her a sidelong glance and asked, "How do you usually drive to Glacier Falls?"

So it was happening fast, Sheryl thought. Important now to lean forward, into it. She answered crisply, "I take 94 to St. Cloud, then pick up 371 going north, then west on Highway 2. Gets a little tricky when we head north again past Bemidji."

Shank focused on her. "How, tricky?"

"We'll bypass Glacier Falls, work a jigsaw on back roads. Gator says, in the winter, the locals notice every new car. This Nissan will be like a neon sign. We gotta come in the back way, like that."

"Gotcha." Shank nodded and concentrated on working through a cluster of cars. When he passed then, he said, "Here's the deal. We do a photo spread for Gator just like the cops do. If he picks Broker out, we're in business." He removed his right hand from the wheel and gave her a thumbs-up.

Sheryl exhaled and leaned back in the seat. "I gotta call Gator. We got this system. I page him, he goes to a pay phone, then I call from a pay phone . . ."

Shank said, "We'll wait till we get free of the metro, then we'll stop. Gotta have breakfast anyway. And keep your eye out for an outfitters. I checked the weather; you're gonna need some boots, a sweater, gloves, stuff like that. We could hit some snow. I got stuff in the trunk but I don't think it'll fit you."

"Thanks," Sheryl said, "that's thoughtful of you."

Shank shrugged. "Hey, no biggie; I'll expense it."

They settled back for a few miles, Sheryl thinking about what he had in the trunk. Jesus. She'd see soon enough. Then Shank began to talk, casual, to pass the time.

"You know Joey, how he loves to talk? Well, he told me about that whole day of the pig roast. Broker shows up the day before. He's got a load of firewood in his truck, has the pig on ice from a butcher shop. He digs this pit, oh, four feet deep, and starts a fire . . ." He turned to her. "Joey says, Danny's coming out of the house, bringing him a beer, whatever he needs. See, Danny was always interested in learning new things. Like how to roast a pig."

"Yeah," Sheryl said. "Danny didn't miss much."

"Missed this fucker." Shank pursed his lips. "Can you imagine those fucking narcs, sitting in a bar, yukking it up about roasting a pig. Some of those assholes have these little pig studs they wear in their ears when they hang out. I seen that once." He shook his head, curling his upper lip in a ghastly smile, showing an elongated canine. Turned to her.

"Joey said when you roast a pig, you wrap it in burlap, then truss it up with barbed wire. Wet down the burlap, that seals in the flavor or something. Put it in the coals, put more coals on top. Put in a piece of corrugated tin to hold the heat, then fill the pit with dirt, let it cook for ten, twelve hours . . ."

Sheryl nodded her head along with his conversation, careful not to bring up the lab plan. Don't rush it. Let it develop. Be attentive, a good listener.

"Yeah, well," Shank said. "We're gonna have our own pig roast."

They had rounded the Minneapolis metro and were coming up on west 94; the roadside clutter starting to fade, the land unrolling brown and tired. Snow dusting the ditches and fields.

Sheryl removed her cell from her purse. "Should make my call," she said.

"Go ahead. We'll grab a Perkins in half an hour. Grease down. They'll have a pay phone."

Half an hour later, Gator stood stamping his boots in the phone booth outside Perry's Grocery, watching the Monday-morning shoppers wheel their carts into the parking lot. The wind had picked up ice-pick sharp, chipping flecks of stinging snow off the looming iceberg clouds.

The excitement was heavy and compact in his chest, purring like a motor. When the phone rang, he took a moment to compose his voice. "Yes?"

"Hi, hon, thought I'd give you a heads-up. Shank and I are on the road. We should roll into the farm about one this afternoon. We're driving a gray Nissan Maxima."

Listening to her saying this in a normal voice, like it was routine, riding up north with a killer. "That car's gonna stick out like a sore thumb up here," Gator said in a calm controlled voice. Behind his voice the motor in his chest was smoking. *Holy shit! It's on, it's happening.*

"We'll come in careful on County Z."

"Grab some local stations on the AM, we got some weather."

"Maybe you should get the garage door open," Sheryl said.

"Will do. Ah, anything else?" He wondered if Shank was monitoring her conversation, standing there.

"Let's just not get ahead of ourselves. Take it one step at a time, okay?"

"I hear you. I'll get ready."

Sheryl hung up the pay phone in the lobby of a Country Kitchen and waited while Shank paid for breakfast at the cashier's counter. When they got back in the car and pulled back on the road, Shank just asked, "Everything all right?"

Sheryl nodded. "Told him we'd be in around one in the afternoon. He said to check the local stations when we get up north. Could be a storm coming down."

"Good idea." Then, after a pause, "Not to pry, but what's he like, Gator? I asked around, and he kept a low profile in the joint. Just a few pickups in the visitors' room to keep our guys off his back."

Sheryl thought about it. "He's a real hard worker, crackerjack mechanic." Thought some more. "A compulsive planner."

"A mechanic would be, they know how things fit together," Shank said.

They settled in for the long middle of the drive. Sheryl thumbed through the photos again, mentioned how times had changed. People weren't hanging it out on the street in leathers, tooling around on fat boys, like they used to.

Traveling north on 371, coming up on Little Falls, they started talking about *The Sopranos* on HBO.

"I don't buy the bit about a boss going to a shrink," Shank said. "That's contrived. I think they do that to suck in a wider audience. None of them ever known a gangster, but lots of them go to shrinks."

"You got a point," Sheryl said. After a moment, she wondered out loud, "How do you think it's going to end?"

"The way I see it, there's two possibilities; you got a war brewing with Johnny Sack in New York, then you got the family angle cooking underneath."

"Yeah, Carmela and her thing with Furio. That ain't over. He'll be back, Furio will," Sheryl said seriously.

"True. Furio is a stand-up guy," Shank said.

"So Furio returns and has a showdown with Tony over Carmela," Sheryl said.

Shank smiled and wagged his finger at her. "No offense, but you're thinking like a woman. Making it all romantic—"

"Hey," Sheryl countered. "TV shows are like everything else. They're a business, and I bet most of the viewers are women."

"Granted, they could pussy out and do it that way," Shank said. "But I think, ah, what would be more true to life is Tony gets caught making this big choice between his family and the mob."

"How do you mean?" Sheryl said.

"Well, what's he going to do if push comes to shove? Sacrifice his family to save his business? Al Pacino would do that, right. He had Fredo killed in *Godfather II*. But Tony goes to a shrink, right? He's got guilt and panic attacks. No, I think the way to end it is, he has to turn into the thing he hates to save the thing he loves."

Sheryl considered it, cocking her head.

Shank continued. "So Tony makes a deal with the feds, rats out all his buddies, and goes into Witness Protection. There he is, living in a crummy track house in Utah, driving a garbage truck. Carmela is shopping at Wal-Mart. The End."

"Jesus, that's grim," Sheryl said.

"Yeah. I kinda like it," Shank said.

Sheryl took out her Merits and her lighter. "You mind?" she asked.

Shank shrugged, hit the window controls, zipped the front seat windows down an inch, and turned up the heater.

Sheryl lit the cigarette and blew a stream of smoke into the icy draft. After a minute or so she turned and caught Shank watching her.

"What?" she asked.

He shrugged affably, turned back to watching the road. "Shouldn't smoke those things," he said. "They're bad for your health."

Chapter Forty-two

Monday morning was another first. Nina drove Kit to school. Not just to drop her off, but to go in and talk to the principal about gathering Kit's records and transferring them back to the elementary school in Stillwater. Maybe sit in on some of her classes. Today would be Kit's last school day in Glacier Falls. Nina had set the tone at Sunday breakfast when she casually suggested that Broker should call Dooley.

He'd called Dooley and told him to get the duplex straightened up and turn up the heat; they be arriving Wednesday afternoon. That gave them Tuesday to finish packing and clean Griffin's place. He called Griffin, explained their plans, and they agreed to have supper Tuesday night at the Anglers to settle up and say good-bye.

Now it was almost one-thirty in the afternoon, and Nina hadn't returned yet. Broker stood in the garage studying the stack of boxes and suitcases that he, Nina, and Kit has assembled on Sunday. Seeing them, he remembered the tense days last January, the rushed packing. He raised his right hand to his throat, felt the key to the gun locker on the leather thong. The guns would be the last thing he'd load in the Tundra.

His cell rang. It was Griffin.

"You think I could get a little more work out of you, before you split?" Griffin said.

"What's up?"

"My truck's still in the shop. And my wood trailer's got a broken axle. Teedo's home with a sick kid, so I don't have his truck. I need a couple loads of oak carted over here at the lodge. Want to get it under a tarp before this big mother of a storm moves in."

"Sure," Broker said. "I'll get on it as soon as Nina gets the truck back."

"Look, I know you're packing. Just bring one load over. We can trade cars, and I'll come back for the second load."

"No problem, any way you want to do it," Broker said.

After he ended the call, Broker walked out into the driveway and looked at the storm clouds marshaling over the northwestern treetops. Persistent spitballs of frozen snow rattled on his parka. The mini sleet drew a faint veil over the road, and he saw Nina's high beams knife through it. He watched the Tundra pull up the drive. Walked out to meet her.

"How'd it go?" Broker said.

Nina gave him a droll smile and did a snappy little curtsy. "Am I a soccer mom from central casting or what?" She was wearing the cross-country ski outfit he'd given her for Christmas. "I talked to the principal, Helseth, and sat in on a reading and math class. Kit wanted me to stay for lunch and for her gym class. You know, she wanted to put me on front street. Like, 'See, I got a mom, too.' And the paperwork is all set. They'll ship it end of week. How's it going here?"

Broker explained Griffin's call, how he'd drive over to the lodge with a load of wood, then use Griffin's Jeep to pick up Kit.

"You might want to go in early to school. When I left, they were all watching the weather in the office. They might start the buses early if this thing rolls in before school lets out."

"Okay, I better get on it."

Nina nodded. "I'll sort through the upstairs bathroom, pack everything except essentials, then—" She perused the sky. "Maybe get in a run before we get dumped on."

They set off to their separate tasks. Nina went inside as Broker took off his good parka and pulled on the beat-up brown work-crew jacket. Then he started the Tundra and backed it up to the woodpile. Half an hour later, he had the bed full of oak, got in, and headed off for the lodge.

When Broker arrived at the lodge work site, he found Griffin upbeat, busy squaring away his gear as if he relished the prospect of working in the midst of a severe winter storm. They unloaded the wood, covered it with a tarp, and weighted the tarp down with hunks of flagstone.

"You planing to work tomorrow?" Broker asked.

"Nah, but if we really get a lot of snow, it'll take a day for the plows to clear the roads. Might as well get the wood in before it hits, so we can start on Wednesday," Griffin said.

They hunkered in the lee of the warming tent, drank coffee from Griffin's thermos, and watched the gauzy afternoon light slowly filling in with billows of white. Start to pick away details on the lake.

"Nina still on track?" Griffin asked.

"Life is good," Broker said. "She went to school this morning with Kit. Stayed through lunch."

"And the other thing?"

"Well, we're coming to that. She said we're going to have a long-overdue talk. But we ain't there yet. There's this doctor at Bragg she has to check in with. It'll happen then."

"Well, good luck." Griffin squinted at the rising wind. "You still planning to head back Wednesday? This could make a mess out of the roads."

"Why they made four-wheel drive." Broker shrugged and studied his friend, standing there in the identical jacket and black watch cap. "Remind me to give you this coat back," he said.

"Hey, keep it," Griffin said, his face ruddy, his gray eyes merry, more youthful and alive than usual, as he watched the whipping snow.

"You're in a good mood," Broker observed. "Your lady friend Hatch come over and whip some Class A maintenance on your relationship?"

Griffin grinned and quipped, "There's some things more exciting than mere sex."

"Oh, yeah?"

"Yeah. Like winter storms." Griffin smiled, then upended the dregs of his coffee and pounded Broker on the shoulder. "C'mon, I gotta do a few more things here. Keys are in the Jeep. See you over at the place in an hour or so."

Chapter Forty-three

Quarter to one, Gator pacing on the farmhouse porch, peering into the light sifting snow. Felt like he was onstage, coming up on a big job interview. He could feel the barometer dropping, pressure building like it was in his throat. They were auditioning for the big time. So take it one step at a time, Sheryl had said on the phone. Don't rush it. Presumably she meant stay focused on Shank's business with Broker. Don't expect anything. Play a support role. Just be competent and keep your mouth shut.

The garage door was pulled open. He had a fresh pot of coffee perking in the shop. He'd put the cat in the house to be out of the way. Maybe this guy was superstitious about black cats. Who knows.

Jesus. Hope they didn't run into trouble coming in on Z. Near as he could tell, the storm was still to the north and west, but the wind could whip up small whiteouts in the open spaces.

Then he saw the high beams cut through the wavy tissue-paper light. The Nissan Maxima glided through the snow like a low gray shark and turned off into the drive. Gator's hands moved in a silly tucking-in gesture, straightening his jacket. He took a deep breath, let it out, and walked toward the barn as the car slipped into the garage.

Sheryl got out of the passenger side and smiled. Gator saw she was wearing sensible new Sorel boots for a change. The guy behind the wheel got out, and Gator had a look at him. In the joint, Gator had roughly classified scary guys into two categories; there were the muscled-up brutes and then there were other guys who had this weird intimidating energy. Crazy waiting to happen. Shank struck him as a very controlled version of the second type.

He was lean and too white, like he had bleach in his veins, whitish hair and eyebrows, pale blue eyes. He moved smooth and deliberate, walking right up to Gator and extending a hand.

"It's Gator, right? I'm Shank, good to meet you." Cool dry hand. Didn't make a handshake into a show of strength. More like a probe. "Where can we talk?" Shank said.

"In the shop," Gator said.

Sheryl yanked a thumb toward the house. "I'm going in to use the john. Let you two get acquainted." She turned and walked toward the house.

Shank thumbed his remote, and the spacious trunk popped open. He hauled out a rugged gym bag, the kind with lots of zippered side pockets, shouldered the bag, and waited for Gator to lead the way.

Gator opened the door to the shop and stood aside to let Shank enter first. Shank went in and lowered his bag. "Mind if I have a look around?"

"Sure." Gator opened his right palm in a gesture of welcome. "You want some coffee?"

"Yeah, black is good." Shank removed his jacket and set it on the cot in the alcove, then walked through the door into the garage bay. He returned in a minute. Gator handed him a cup of coffee.

"What do you do here?" Shank asked.

"Restore antique tractors. Got three completes in the yard out back of the shop. Can cannibalize parts off another half dozen."

Shank sipped his coffee. "The one you have in there. How long to get it ready for sale?"

"That's a special one. My Prairie Gold 1938 Moline UDLX. C'mere for a sec." Gator led Shank into the garage and proudly pointed at the color centerfold on the wall.

Shank pointed to the sleek photo. "That's"—he pointed to the gray bifurcated jacked-up heap of junk—"*that*? No shit."

Gator shrugged. "Might take me another six months to get it exactly like the picture, all the authentic gauges and tinwork."

"How much they pay for something like that?" Shank said.

"It's like *rare*. Restored inside out? Mint condition; a hundred K."

"Christ, our guys go to jail, and they wind up taking computers apart. We should be getting into tractors." Shank laughed. Then he looked around and nodded. "This is a real squared-away shop you got here."

"Thank you."

"Yeah, well"—his voice dropped a decibel—"you figured out that I ain't here to buy tractors."

Gator wasn't sure whether to respond "yep" or "nope," so he just nodded.

"Okay," Shank said, looking Gator pointedly up and down. "We asked around, got the book on you when you were inside. You were a stand-up guy. When OMG leaned on you for some favors, you were practical." Shank paused, sipped his coffee, his pale eyes burning into Gator over the rim of the cup. "You ever meet Danny?"

"No. I spent most of the time in Education, was an assistant in the Vo Tech Shop."

"Yeah, I spent some time down in the basement doing slave labor for MinnCor; built those goddamn hay wagons, some docks for the DNR. So you never met him, huh?"

"Just saw him at a distance, in the chow hall."

Shank cut him with a hard look. "As far as you're concerned, Danny's watching you right now through my eyes. You with me?"

"Yeah, hell." Gator shrugged his shoulders. "Whatever it takes."

"You help me now, it'll pay off later. But right now, first things first." Shank crossed to the alcove, reached in his jacket, took out an envelope, and returned to the desk. He removed a stack of color photographs and spread them on the desk. "Your move," he said to Gator.

Gator studied the pictures. Bunch of bikers hamming it up for the camera, including a younger Danny Turrie and Sheryl showing lots of tanned skin and fucked-up eyes. His index finger smacked down on the lean guy with the shovel. "Broker," he said.

"You sure? The picture is pretty old," Shank said.

"That's him. I saw him close as you and me are standing, a couple days ago. That's him. Those eyebrows . . ."

"Okay. This kind of thing, you gotta be sure. So, where is he?"

"In a lake cabin near town, about twelve miles south."

"What's it like, the layout?"

"Secluded, thick woods. There's houses two hundred yards on either side, but hidden away. County Twelve runs right in front of the place, but people up here notice strange cars. This time of year, they'll come out and look just to see who's driving by. I'd go in through the woods, there's a ski trail. Be real quiet, with the snow." After a moment, he added, "Lake ain't iced over. I suppose you could go in by boat, except I don't have one."

Shank reached to the fax machine on the desk, peeled off a sheet of paper from the tray, took a pen from the desk blotter, and handed it to Gator. "Draw it—the lake, the road, the trail, and whatever you know about the house."

Gator stared at the sheet of blank paper like it was an entrance exam. Balked and said, "We should go in the house. I got a county map with the ski trail to scale."

Shank nodded, retrieved his coat, and picked up his bag. "Let's go."

A few minutes later they were in the farmhouse, standing around the kitchen table, on which Gator had spread out the county map over the half-done puzzle. Shank summoned Sheryl, who stood off to the side, sipping a cup of tea. "C'mon, you're part of this."

Swiftly, Gator marked significant reference points; an X marked his house, a second X located Broker's. He circled the trailhead turnoff of County 12, indicated the relevant portion of ski trail with arrows between the trailhead and Broker's cabin. Then Gator stepped back and stood next to Sheryl, waiting while Shank leaned forward on his locked arms, like a general pondering over a tactical problem. Just then the kitten made an appearance, hopping lightly up on a chair, then onto the table.

"Fuckin' cat," Gator muttered, coming forward.

Shank slid a hand under the kitten, expertly palming it over and cradling it belly up along his forearm. "It's okay. I like cats. Only animals I get along with." He gently eased the cat back on the chair and watched it jump to the floor and pad into the next room. Then he looked back to the map. "Cell phones work up here?" he asked.

"Yeah. They built a couple towers for the summer people," Gator said.

"Okay." Shank reached into his bag and took out three cell phones, handed one each to Gator and Sheryl, kept one for himself. "These are cold—we lifted them from people who are on vacation. Let's get our numbers straight."

They turned on the phones. The displays showed normal service. Gator snatched a piece of paper and pen off the counter and made a list—Shank's number, his number, Sheryl's number. Then he copied it three times, folded the sheet, tore it in thirds, and handed out the individual lists.

"Now," Shank said, "we do a dry run. Check the travel time going in on the trail, make sure the cell phones work. Make sure he's there. Then we go back for real. You with me?"

Gator chewed his lip, unable to disguise the pained expression on his face.

"What is it? C'mon," Shank asked.

"Well, the whole reason this happened, how I got the warrant is—Broker's kid had a fight at school with my brother-in-law Jimmy's kid. Then Broker and Jimmy got into it in front of the school. And the sheriff saw it. My sister asked me to kinda fuck with him, like payback. That's how I wound up in his house and found the warrant. So if something happens to Broker, one of the first people they'll look at is Jimmy and probably me."

"And?"

"Jimmy's no problem, he's on the road all day picking up routes. But maybe I should be someplace public, like be seen having dinner in town, you know."

Shank thought about it. "Makes sense. But you go in with

me on the trial run, make sure I can find my way in and out. Make sure Sheryl can find the house when I call her to come pick me up."

"Ah, if somebody sees your car—" Gator said.

"It ain't my car. It's like the phones. Stolen. It belongs to a Carlos Izquierdo, who lives in Excelsior. He's in Ireland selling Snap-On tools. We took his car from long-term parking at the Minneapolis–St. Paul airport. We got this gal who works at a travel agency, gives us leads on people who are out of town."

"Ah," Gator said.

"And I don't give a fuck if someone remembers *seeing* the car. I just don't want anybody *stopping* the car and seeing *me*. Because if this goes off on schedule, I'll be driving all night back to the Cities. Tomorrow morning when the sun comes up, that Nissan will be parked on University Avenue, in St. Paul, in front of the fuckin' State Bureau of Criminal Apprehension. With Broker smelling up the trunk." The smooth demeanor changed as Shank smiled, curling his upper lip, showing his prominent canine teeth. "Gonna shoot the fucker in the mouth. What we do with snitches."

"What about—" Sheryl started to say.

"You?" Shank interrupted. "I thought of that. You can stay here, or I can drop you in a town farther south, where you can rent some wheels. It ain't your job to drive back with me."

"That's cool, but what about, ah . . . the guy's got a wife and kid," Sheryl said.

Seeing the strangled expression on Gator's face when Sheryl said that, Shank raised a calming hand and said patiently, "This ain't the time to be sentimental, Sheryl. What about the wife and kid Jojo never had—you think of that?"

"You got a point," Sheryl said quickly.

"Any more questions?" Shank asked. "No? Then I got one." He reached in his bag, withdrew a stumpy dense SIG-Sauer nine, and cradled it in his palm. "Where do snitches get it?"

"In the mouth," Gator said, like he was reciting an oath.

"Good," Shank said. "Remember that, and we'll do just fine."

◆ ◆ ◆

As Gator changed into his long underwear and winter camos on the mud porch, Sheryl stood next to him, nervously smoking a Merit. "Probably shouldn't a said that about the wife and kid," she said.

"No shit. This guy's got his own ideas."

"I hear you," Sheryl said between puffs.

Gator sat on a stool and pulled on his boots. When he'd laced them, he stood up, picked his cell phone off the workbench, selected Cassie's number, and pushed send. When she answered, he said, "It's me. Yeah. Look, where's Jimmy today? Good, okay, he's got the long route south of town. Then he's back at the garage? How late? Is he there alone? Good. Johnny's with him, washing down the trucks. No, ah, maybe I'll drop by and see him at the garage, later tonight." Then his forehead bunched. "Yeah, right. We'll talk about that later, okay? Right now I'm busy. No. Not now. We'll talk tonight." He ended the call, shook his head.

"What?" Sheryl asked.

"Nothing. My fuckin' sister." He waved her off and went into the kitchen. Shank had changed into new Rocky boots, black Gore-Tex pants, a red parka, and red knit cap. Gator clicked his teeth together. "You know, we'll have light the next couple of hours. That red's gonna stand out against the snow cover big-time."

"You got a better idea?"

"Yeah." Gator went back on the mud porch and returned with a winter camo hunting smock. "Pull that over the parka." He tossed a black ski mask. "And this'll be handy, hide your face."

Shank slipped on the smock, bunched the mask on his head, and said, "Better?"

"Much," Gator said.

Shank handed Sheryl his car keys. "Get the car out. You're gonna be driving tonight."

When she'd left, Gator said, "I was wondering, should I bring something?"

"Like what?" Shank asked.

"Like a gun, you know—usually carry a pistol in the woods."

Shank grinned. "Wanna get your cherry busted, huh? Sure."

For the first time Gator felt a genuine flash of resentment at this smooth city fucker who had so much power over him, with his expensive pussy winter gear and stolen Jap car—going into the woods dressed like a Christmas tree to kill a guy. He opened the kitchen utility drawer and removed the Luger.

"Shit, is that a real one, like World War II German?" Shank asked, a gleam coming into his pale eyes.

"Yep, my dad brought it back from Europe," Gator said, stuffing the pistol into his fanny pack, thinking, *Fuckin' bikers all go for that Nazi shit like little kids.* "See these markings on the grip? That's SS."

"Like to look that over. But another time. Let's go," Shank said.

Chapter Forty-four

Sheryl Mott sat in the idling Nissan and watched Gator and Shank march off down the trail, past this sign of a stick figure on cross-country skis. Wearing those white-and-black patterned outfits. Kinda blending in with the scenery and blowing snow. So here she was. Sitting in a stolen vehicle. The guy walking alongside her boyfriend was a murderer on his way to work.

She looked again and they were gone, swallowed up in white.

Okay, they'd crept down the road to the green house with the tin roof and clocked it on the odometer—1.6 miles from the trail head. Hank made her write the number of the sign in the yard in ballpoint on her palm; the fire number, 629.

She cracked the windows, lit another Merit, and found herself thinking about the Las Vegas hooker's observation that guys resembled their dicks. Shank, as near as she could remember, was white and bony, peeking out of a nest of wispy albino hair. And Gator, well, he had this sturdy handle. Get a good grip on him, and she felt she could move the world a little.

At least move a hundred pounds of ice. Fidgety, she extended her finger to the steamed windshield and traced "C10 H15 N" in the moisture, the chemical formula for methamphetamine . . .

Suddenly, like somebody had tapped the mute on a big remote, the wind stopped, the snow disappeared, and it was so quiet and still, she dialed the window all the way down. Leaned her head out, strained her ears to hear. How could pure silence be so . . . loud?

First she thought it was a radio playing, but the way the sound corkscrewed right down to the roots of the tiny hairs on the back of her neck told her, uh uh, that was fucking *real*, man. That was wild animals howling out there in the woods.

Ice. Snow. Trees everywhere, and now wolves. This place could use a few Burger King signs. She shivered and hugged herself, turned up the heater. Think about something else. Belize . . .

Didn't work.

Shit, I hope we know what we're doing . . .

"What happened?" Shank looked around. One minute there was snow like a burst featherbed. Then nothing.

"Lull," Gator said. "Won't last long."

They trudged a few more steps, and Shank stopped again, head rotating around. "Hear that?"

"Yeah," Gator kept walking. "Deer must be moving."

"That ain't deer." Shank jogged to catch up.

Gator was starting to enjoy himself. The farther they got from a road, the more Shank, the heavy hitter, seemed to diminish in ferocity. Christ, they could see the lake through breaks in the trees. Houses.

"That ain't deer," Shank repeated.

"When a storm moves in, the deer do weird things. They can hunker down, or they can start moving. The deer move, the pack follows. Usually they stay farther north," Gator explained like a guide on a nature walk.

"Yeah, the wolves," Shank said. "Sheryl told me about that. They don't attack people, right?"

"I read about this wolf in India. Some kids killed her cubs, and she went into this village and took forty kids, right out of the houses. They found this big pile of bones in the den. I don't care what the tree huggers say. I wouldn't want to be lying out in the woods bleeding, know what I mean." Gator suddenly raised his hand. Stop. He pointed down the trail at a yellow No Trespassing sign. "We're there."

Shank checked his watch. "Not bad. Seventeen minutes." He reached in his smock and took out his cell phone.

"Wait, let's go in closer, so we can see the house," Gator said. More cautious now, they followed the narrow connecting trail through the trees. Gator raised his hand again. "Hear that?"

"Yeah." This clunky wood-on-metal sound.

"C'mon." Gator lowered his voice and made a downward pushing motion with his palm. Time to go quiet. They moved forward in a crouch. The trees opened more, and they saw the source of the noise. A hundred yards away, a man wearing a brown jacket and a black cap was piling wood in the back of a green Toyota Tundra next to a garage. The garage was attached to a cabin, the siding painted green. It had a rusted tin roof and a deck wrapped around the back.

They scurried a few steps closer and hunkered next to a thick patch of low spruce. Shank dug in his pocket, brought out a small pair of Zeiss binoculars, and eased the snow-laded boughs aside. Lensed the guy.

"No shit, lookit," he whispered. "It's *him*. Right fuckin' there." He passed the binocs to Gator, who had a look and confirmed, "Yep, that's him."

"Right fuckin' there, like low-hanging fruit," Shank whispered. "It'd be easy, just walk up, say we're lost or something. Whattaya say?"

Gator worried his lower lip between his lip. Not the plan. You hadda stick to the plan. "I ain't supposed to be here when it—"

"Oh, shit, shit!" Shank moved up out of his crouch. The guy was getting in the truck, starting it. "He's driving away. Sonofabitch."

"Get down, be quiet, somebody could be in the house. What's the time?" Gator said.

Shank pushed up his sleeve and checked his watch. "Almost two-thirty."

"They only got the one truck. School's out in an hour. Maybe earlier, with the storm moving in." Gator thought about it, said, "He turned toward town, so he's probably going to drop off that wood where he works, then pick up his kid."

"How long?" Shank said.

"An hour, little longer."

Then like a giant white mare rolling over above them, the wind squashed down on the trees and set them to rattling. The silence erupted into snowflakes.

Gator seized Shank's shoulder and pointed with his other hand. "Check it out."

A woman dressed in an oatmeal gray sweat suit appeared on the driveway beyond the house, walking toward the road. She tucked a red ponytail into her cap, paused to look up at the sky, then up and down the road. Then she pulled on gloves and started running. At the end of the drive, she turned right and ran down the road, in the same direction the truck had taken. Shank followed her with the binoculars.

"Bitch can run. She's really moving," he said, lowering the binocs. He turned to Gator. "Whattaya think?"

Gator looked up at the thickening snow. "This looks like the real thing. You up for hiking back to Sheryl, then coming back in while she takes me home?"

Shank glanced back toward the trail in the woods, then at the house.

Gator said, "You could go in the house, be waiting for them."

Shank shook his head. "Nah, too messy, people showing up piecemeal. I want them all together when I go in. But let's go have a look at the house, want an idea of the floor plan, the doors." He took out his cell, removed his glove, and made a call. When it connected, he said, "You hear me all right?"

"Yeah, it's starting to snow like hell, what's up?" Sheryl said.

"We're going to check around a few minutes here, then Gator's coming back to the car. You run him home and get right back. Call me the minute you get back."

"How much time are we talking?" Sheryl said.

"Nobody's home. We're all waiting. Maybe an hour and a half, tops."

"Okay," Sheryl said.

Shank ended the call, stood up, took out his pistol, and said, "Okay, this is it. Once you take off, I won't see you for a while.

Then in a month or so, we'll get together in the Cities and talk some business."

"I'm for that," Gator said.

"But first, let's go have a quick look before the bitch gets back." Gator rose to his feet and removed the Luger from his fanny pack. Then he pulled his ski mask down, covering his face. Shank grinned and did the same. Guns at the ready, they jogged toward the house.

Chapter Forty-five

Five minutes into her run, Nina was having doubts about being out in this weather. The wind doubled in velocity and tore through her cotton running suit and the flimsy silk-weight underlayer. The first tiny ice worms were forming in her eyebrow sweat. She could do ten miles in this stuff if she had to. Do it easily. But this was not a survival endurance test. She needed to unkink after cleaning the goddamn bathroom.

Then, as if she needed more convincing this was not a good idea, she slightly turned her right ankle on a rock under the snow. She slowed and tested her weight. Not that bad, not even a strain. But she'd make it worse if she continued.

I give. Time out. The new sensible Nina.

She turned, pulled up her hood, plunged her gloved hands under her jacket, and walked back down the road toward the house. A few minutes later she was rounding a slight rising turn, about two hundred yards to go, thinking about her running course in Stillwater, up Myrtle Hill, out toward Matomedi. This time next week she'd be running up that hill. By then she'd have had her talk with Broker . . .

A different kind of cold gripped her chest. A twinge of panic anticipating the conversation, telling him what he wanted to hear, after all these years. Admitting to the way she'd compromised her shoulder with the steroids. Jeez, thinking it was one thing. Actually doing it was—

She took a deep freezing breath and constructed a box around the panic, tucked it away. Suddenly the box flew open . . .

Holy shit!

A decade of conditioning and experience flung her off the road, rolling through the snow, scrambling in a fast low crawl to the cover of the trees.

Two of them. At the house?

As her mind protested the image, her reflexes pushed her forward, hugging the tree line; fifty, sixty yards to see better.

She rubbed her hand at the fine white squall, like she was trying to clear a windshield heaped with salt. Nothing out there now but the snow. House going in and out. Thought she saw one of them flattened against the side of the garage, like a lookout; the other testing the garage door. Black ski masks, winter camouflage tunics. She had 20/10 vision in both eyes. Those were pistols in their hands.

Gone now in the storm.

The image in her mind was absurd but compelling. She was staring at a blur of green cabin in northern Minnesota and she was seeing familiar spectral figures; Arkan's fuckin' Tigers, the Serb paramilitary she'd stalked in Bosnia and Kosovo . . . same camo, same masks . . .

Don't think. Gain position.

Need a weapon.

She pictured the gun cabinet in the living room behind the wall hanging. And the key to it on the thong around Broker's neck.

Running now along the ragged edge of the trees, instinctively knowing the blowing snow and the color of her clothes gave her cover. The two figures had vanished from the side of the house; around the back, maybe.

She paused at the edge of the trees. Not dressed for this, getting disoriented by the cold and wind. How far? Maybe eighty yards to the house. She'd locked the doors, had the keys in her pocket.

Do it.

She burst from cover and crossed the open space; her lung-burning sprint turned into a slip-and-slide, batting her hands at the stinging white. Shuddering, she piled into the angle formed where the garage and house met. The snow was a froth at her ankles; dry, fine, in furious motion. No tracks. Where are the tracks? Can't tell. They were *right here?* She whipped out the garage door key and opened the door. Slipped inside. Now a second key to get into the kitchen.

She froze when she heard the faint scrape on the back deck, then the rear garage door rattled. Were they testing the door? Or was it the wind?

But did I lock the patio door in the kitchen?

She looked around. Saw the ski poles stacked along the wall. Started to go for one of them. Mid-step, she changed her mind and grabbed the heavy splitting maul in her left hand. Twenty pounds of steel; didn't trust her right arm.

Very slowly she eased open the kitchen door and edged up to the side of the cabinets that blocked her from the end of the room and the patio door, thankful she had turned out the lights. The room was limbo-lit by the flurry moth light of the snow. Moving in fractions, she peeked around the end of the cabinet, thought she made out this grainy figure, pressed against the patio door's glass panel, peering into the darkened room. Looked like a German Luger in his hand.

Darted her head back.

A German Luger, c'mon. Are we spiraling out here or what? She blinked icy sweat to clear her eyes. Couldn't blink away the crazy swerve in her head. It occurred to her she could take one step forward and five steps back.

Warily, she peeked again. Nothing but the churning snow and dim twisting shadows, the trees tossing in the wind.

A line from one of the books: *"There are infrequent but documented cases where persons suffering from depression can hallucinate . . . see things that are not there . . ."*

Suddenly she couldn't move. *Stuck. I'm stuck.* Not her body. She slowly bent her knees and lowered her back down the side of the cabinet and squatted on the floor. She removed her cold wet gloves and pressed her icy palms on either side of her face.

. . . things that are not there . . .

Then where was she to see the things that are not there? *Jesus Christ, I got* Alice in Wonderland *in my head.*

Bullshit. *That's a guy out there with a gun trying to break into the house.*

She sat shaking, squeezing her head, arguing with herself. Just . . . gotta . . . slam the door on the widening crack of indecision; the whole black fucking pit of where she'd been.

Peeked again from the lower angle. The snow seemed thicker now; sticky, drifting on the deck. Nothing.

I see nothing.

Nothing with a Luger.

The patio door was solid soapsuds. The wind had accelerated to whiteout intensity. And this irrational voice raged in memory, shaking the Georgia pines; apoplectic southern white male, subset TAC sergeant, tested beyond all mortal patience: *This ain't the fuckin' women's studies program, Pryce; the only way you finish this course is DO YOUR JOB!'*

Right. Thank you.

Nina bounded to her feet, grabbed the maul, and dashed for the living room, tore the hanging off the wall.

Took a half second to orient. Use the strong left arm to lift and swing, steady with the weaker right. In a fierce chopping motion she brought the heavy steel wedge down on the Yale lock on the cabinet doors. The lock spun, bitten, but still held. She raised the maul again, brought it down. Better—it shattered right through the stout door panels. The third hack splintered the hasp completely. She dropped the maul and tore open the ragged door.

Her hand went first to the .45, jamming in the magazine, jacking the slide, setting the safe. She stuck it in her waistband. Grabbed at the rifles. Ammo. Boxes of rounds and magazines scattered on the floor. Broker's deer gun had an elastic bandolier around the stock with six rounds in it. She slung the rifle over her shoulder, moving now toward the kitchen, paused to tap a magazine for the AR-15 against the doorjamb, aligning the rounds, inserted it in the familiar black rifle, pulled the bolt, shot it home.

Now, let's try this again, you fuckers.

Sighting down the assault rifle, she quick-stepped, hugging the wall, into the kitchen, urban warfare room-clearing mode. Thumb on the selector switch, finger on the trigger.

The kitchen door creaked opened. *Shit, left it unlocked!* She spun, felt the cushion of sweat between her finger pad and the trigger compress . . .

"Nina?" Broker gasped, filling the doorway, face turned to wax, staring into the barrel of the rifle.

She snapped the muzzle off target, held it at the ready, poised, eyes darting to the patio door. "Get in, quick, they're out there, in back"—a hoarse iron whisper of command.

For another fraction of a second Broker stared at her. Kit stood behind him, eyes wide with incomprehension, not yet fear, holding her bunny and her school pack.

Seeing Kit's expression, a corner of her vision collapsed, and she started to sink.

When her eyes moved off Broker toward the patio door, he was on her in a blur, knocking the rifle barrel up and away with his right hand, coming on through and shoving her chest hard, stepping in and tearing the pistol from her waistband. Stripping the slung rifle off her shoulder. One swift complete movement. The rifles clattered to the floor, the .45 secure in his right hand, he wrapped her in a bear hug. She heard his voice; high, uncertain, scared: "Kit. Stay in the garage. Shut the door."

As the kitchen door swung shut, Nina pushed back at him. "Broker, man; I'm not kidding, two guys . . . she shouldn't—"

"Calm down." He was almost shouting.

"You calm down! Listen, goddammit!" Her eyes burned at him, but already the controlled fire was starting to sputter.

Broker dropped his arms, stepped back carefully, stuck the .45 into his belt and stooped quickly, snatching up the AR-15. Part of him was still reeling in shock, the other part, the street part, gauged her tense posture—the way she balanced on the balls of her feet, arms floating up. Personal overruled practical.

He grabbed her arm and pushed her into the living room. Saw the splintered cabinet. The maul.

"Aw, Jesus, Nina," he said, releasing her arm.

The way he said it caused more sinking.

As they panted, glaring at each other, his hands were busy, removing the magazine from the black rifle, clearing the action. The tidy lethal .223 round ejected with a brass twinkle and plinked to the floor. He popped the pin behind the trigger assembly, breaking it open, removing the bolt, stuck it in his back pocket. Locked the trigger housing back together, secured the pin. The loose operating handle rattled. His hands were shaking.

Practical again, he realized she was gathering herself, sizing him up. Heard Kit's fists banging on the kitchen door, her voice muffled, urgent, "Mom, Dad; *let me in.*"

"There's two of them," Nina said patiently. "In winter camo, ski masks, pistols; like Serbs . . . in the woods . . ." Saying that, seeing his face react; she knew it was a bad choice of words . . .

Sounded nuts.

Nina bit her lip. Sounded *crazy* . . . how it must look to him. The doubt bounced back fast, ringing her vision with blackness, closing in.

"Serbs in the woods," he repeated slowly. The words echoed in his mind—*Where is it? In the woods.* "Aw, Christ," he said. His face working now, thinking out loud, saying, "Too soon. Got ahead of ourselves . . ."

The boiling snow outside the living room windows bloomed with headlights. Their eyes snapped on the motion. "Griffin," Broker said, raising a hand, trying for calm amid the shattered wood, the lock and hasp, the scattered magazines on the floor. "We switched cars. He's coming to pick up more wood. C'mon." He reached for her arm again. She danced back in an instinctive fighting stance, and Broker wondered if it was finally coming down to a no-holds bare-knuckle fight between them. Practicality counseled him: No, her training was to kill. Go for the eyes, then the throat. She wouldn't use that on him. Grappling and restraint was his expertise. And he was encouraged by the quiver of indecision now trembling in her eyes, spreading down her cheeks into her lips. Her eyes getting wider. "C'mon," he said softly. "We'll have Harry sit with Kit. Take this down the road, out of the house."

But he still wasn't willing to turn his back on her. He waited until she stepped into the kitchen. Then he crossed quickly to the door, opened it. Kit stood framed in the doorway, clutching her bunny.

"What going on?" she said, close to tears.

"We're just having an argument," Broker said, with an awful forced calm in his voice.

Kit swallowed and stared at the rifle in his hand, the pistol in his belt. "With guns?"

"Go out and get Uncle Harry," Broker said. He left the door open. Then, keeping the island between himself and Nina, he picked the deer rifle off the floor, slid open the bolt. Empty. He leaned it against the wall, and his hand was still shaking, because the weapon slipped sideways and crashed to the floor. He ignored it, continued to the patio door, and studied the back deck. Two inches of swirling undisturbed fresh snow. Glanced at the shadowy tree line, indistinct in the horizontal blowing snow. He turned, placed the AR-15 on the table, and slid the wobbling operating handle in place. Put the magazine next to it.

Nina stood hugging herself, one thought recurring over and over, timed to a tick in her cheek: *Seeing things that are not there* . . . She watched Broker do his thing; being practical, cautious. Every methodical move he made, checking the deck, disabling the rifle, assuring Kit, sending for Harry, was an instant replay of the last three months.

She was losing light. Sinking. Hallucination was another way of saying "seeing things."

She watched Harry Griffin enter the kitchen, snow on his shoulders and cap, one hand guiding Kit. Heard Broker say something about a little 'domestic situation.' Could he keep an eye on Kit while they took a break to talk.

They were all so carefully normal . . .

. . . in the presence of the sick person.

Griffin's alert eyes scanned all present, the room. Broker had zipped his jacket to hide the pistol, but the rifle was still in plain view on the table. Griffin adjusted immediately, low-key. Said something about Kit could help him load the oak. Be fun in all the snow. Kit's eyes darting, confused.

Broker lifted Nina's coat off the hook by the door, stood waiting. Sinking, she crossed the room, grabbed at the pack of cigarettes and lighter on the island. Eyes lowered, she walked past Harry and Kit, took the coat, and followed Broker out the door.

Chapter Forty-six

Shank hunkered in the thick spruce maybe sixty yards from the garage, squinting into the blowing snow. He'd hoped to spot the wife, coming back from running. Couldn't see shit. Thought he saw some lights for a minute. Then a wall of whiteout erased the shadow of the house. The terrain had disappeared, the road, the woods, just this white plasma blob. Maybe Gator was right, should have broke in, waited in the house. Problem was, what if they came back and saw the forced entry? Scare them off. Better this way, he decided. He had his hood pulled up under the hood of the smock, one gloved hand on the cell phone in his left pocket, the other on the SIG in the right pocket. Not that uncomfortable, still warm from looking over the house, getting focused. In fact, he liked the harsh wind, working an edge off the storm charge in the turbulent air. And appreciated the way it banished the noises he started hearing when Gator left him. Those creepy *Wild Kingdom* noises sandwiched in the wind.

Fuck a bunch of wolves, just big dogs. Had to laugh, really; he'd killed nine men. Count 'em. Not the time to worry about animals. Still, every time he picked up a weird twist to the wind . . .

Then, faint headlights in the white gloom. Somebody coming up the driveway. Okay, let's get this show on the road. Okay, folks, what's going on here? Windows still dark in the house. Looked like. When he could see the fuckin' house. The minutes stretched like chilly ivory dominoes, clicking end to end. Then, finally, he saw the headlights again. Closer. The green Toyota had returned, was pulling around the back of the house, backing up to the side of the garage. Like it was before. Uh-huh, that's Broker, getting out of the truck. Impossible to make out his features in the blow, but the same brown coat and black hat. Hank's heart skipped a beat, seeing the smaller figure get out of the passenger side. Must be the kid, in a blur of green coat and hat, something, a scarf maybe, tied around the face. This'll be a first. He forgot, was it a boy or a girl? Fuck it. Green target. He hadn't seen the woman but assumed, given this weather, she was inside.

He watched them start loading pieces of wood into the truck bed. Now he was waiting on Sheryl to get back in position. More white dominoes. Then, finally, the cell buzzed in his pocket. He whipped it out, removed his glove, and punched answer.

"I'm back," Sheryl said. "But I can't see shit."

"Showtime. They're home. Start your drive."

He ended the call, replaced the phone in his pocket, then stuffed the glove in with it. When he looked up, he saw Broker and the kid climbing the steps to the back deck, going in the sliding patio door.

Okay. See better in the house. He was up, removing his other glove for a surer grip on the SIG. He unzipped the front of the camo smock, not liking the way it bound his chest and arms. Swung his arms—more freedom of movement. Shank pulled the ski mask down around his neck and stepped from the cover of the pines. No more detours, go straight in. Get it over with.

Kit stood at the end of the kitchen, by the basement door, unwinding her scarf. Griffin dusted snow from his hat, removed it. Seeing the frozen fix of her eyes, he went to her and gently brushed snow from her freckled cheeks. "Hey, honey, it'll be all right."

She looked up at him with an awful anger in her eyes. "You *all* say that. You *all* lie," she said in a measured voice.

He reached to hug her, and she stepped back, arms raised, warding him off.

Let her be, he thought. Then he turned, started for the cabinet next to the stove, glanced out the patio door. "Funny, huh. We take a break and the snow lets up. Should be some hot chocolate in here—"

Something. A snap of red in the corner of his eye.

Whipping around, he saw that it wasn't all right.

The figure of a man emerged from the trees, white camo flapping around something red underneath. One second he was obscure in the blowing snow. Then the wind stopped and the snow disappeared, and Griffin clearly saw the black pistol in his hand. The man started jogging toward the house.

Griffin didn't waste time with how or why. He dropped instantly into threat and response, judging time and distance. He was in the middle of the room, between Kit and the table with the familiar rifle and magazine on it. Guy was fifty yards out . . .

First get Kit free. Out of the line of fire. The basement.

"Kit, come here, fast!" he shouted. Galvanized by his tone, Kit hurried to him, her face shaking. "Take this." He whipped the cell phone from his pocket, opened it. "Now listen to me. Go in the basement. If there's shooting, unhook the window, crawl out and get into the woods. Punch in 911. A nine and two ones. Press this button, here. Send. Tell them a man with a gun is coming into the house. Go!" he shouted, spinning, lunging for the AR-15 on the table.

Shank came up the steps two at a time, swinging up the pistol, saw a flurry of movement in the lighted kitchen. Shit. Musta seen him. Broker picking something up off a table . . . Then Shank's boot slipped on the top step, and he skidded, righting himself, and his heart caught in his throat.

Broker was slapping a magazine into a serious military-type rifle, pulling the thingy in back, taking aim.

Nothing happened.

Close enough to see the look of surprise in Broker's eyes, jerking at the operating rod.

Shank fired twice through the glass, saw Broker go down through a splatter of shattered glass, flung open the siding door, and fired a wild shot at the wide-eyed kid who ducked down a doorway at the other end of the room.

Stepping over . . . wait . . . paused a second, looking down at the waxy face of the man laying on the floor. Hit him solid, twice in the chest. Then . . . Where's the fucking eyebrows? *Not Broker*. What the fuck? Blinked. Focused. Swinging the SIG, ready for the wife when she appeared. No sounds in the house. Immediately he sprinted for the basement doorway. Get the kid first, come back. Shank scrambled down the cramped stairwell, yelling, "All right, you little shit . . ."

Not sure why he'd lived, not knowing why he was dying, Harry Griffin opened his eyes and watched his killer step over him and dash down the stairs after Kit. Wouldn't you know, the same old familiar things; the brimstone scent of cordite, the copper taste of blood. He lay on his right side, right arm trapped beneath him. Couldn't move it. His left hand was detached. Couldn't feel it, sprawled there on the floor, tremoring, having its own local death. A foot away from his palsied left hand, along the baseboard, level with his eyes, he saw the .257 Roberts laying on the floor, muzzle pointed in the direction of the basement stairwell, bolt pulled open.

Heard a snarl from the basement, stuff crashing, thrown around.

Hardest thing he ever did, resurrecting that left hand, willing it to reach over and tug the rifle along the floor. Way too weak to lift it. He fingered a bullet from the sidekick bandolier on the stock; trembling, he inserted it in the chamber.

Heard the guy yell, raging, "Why, you little shit!"

Tasting blood, Griffin smiled. She got out. Good girl. Run. He slid the bolt forward, locking in the round. Second hardest thing he ever did, feathery, his left hand went off on a journey, searching for the trigger, nudging the muzzle along the floor, centered on the stairway. Found the trigger as the heavy footsteps pounded up the stairs. Something going through his mind shutting off the lights on the way out . . . *everything I ever did getting me ready for this moment . . .*

Lied, Kit . . . not all right . . . but maybe . . .

Craning his neck, Griffin managed to catch a glimpse of the guy's face and shoulders, clearing the top step; pale blue angry eyes, skin too white. Harry Griffin squeezed the trigger and rode the exhilarating crash of the bullet out of this life.

Shank stamped up the stairs, and the kitchen exploded in his face. He spun back, clawing at the handrail. The power of the needle pile driver that hit him promised a lot of pain to come. Hit him low in the left hip, it felt like . . . He touched the wound. There was a lot of blood. Not the hip. High inside the thigh.

He gathered himself, pulling on the rail, and staggered up into the kitchen. Saw the deer rifle on the floor next to the dead guy. Fucker had his eyes wide open, head contorted toward the stairs. Sonofabitch looked . . . happy. Shoulda shot him again . . . made sure . . .

The kid.

The kid had seen his face.

He lurched out the door into the garage, then into the driveway. Saw the open basement window, the scrambled snow where she'd crawled out. Different. Looking around, he realized the snow had stopped. Had stopped before he even got into the house. Just this huge white silence and the kid's tracks leading through it. Looking across the yard, he saw her standing at the edge of the woods, looking back at the house. A lump of shadow against the white trees. Maybe eighty yards. Too far, but he took a shot anyway. She disappeared into the trees.

Now I'm really pissed.

He dug through his parka pockets. Found his bandanna, tied it around his screaming thigh, knotted it, and limped along the trail of small boot prints, leaking blood.

Chapter Forty-seven

"We'll use the Jeep, Griffin needs the truck," Broker said, guiding Nina. His thoughts mirrored the flurries driving at his eyes. His mind seemed erased, full of white noise. Never been to this numb hopeless place before.

They got in the Jeep, and as he turned it around, they glimpsed Griffin and Kit appearing and disappearing, climbing into the Tundra. Broker drove to the end of the driveway and stopped. At a loss for which way to turn.

He turned left, made it maybe four hundred yards down the road, pulled over, stopped, and put the shift in neutral. They sat, eyes fixed straight ahead, and listened to the heater fan grind cold air.

Nina stared at the webbed maze of the dream catcher hanging from the rearview mirror. Then down the headlight beams pushing into the snow. The electricity struggled out maybe twenty yards and fizzled. White or black. What's the difference. She had lost the light.

She snuck at a look at him, slouched back, chest caved, snow shadows fluttering over his face, the muscles rippling in his cheeks. He grimaced, rose up, reached behind, removed the bolt for the AR-15 from his back pocket, and placed it on the dashboard like a compact steel indictment.

Still didn't look at each other. No words left. And no moves either. Cratered.

Someone had to make a start. "I got scared," she said.

He turned, looked at her, and brought up his right hand,

palm up, fingers curled, like he'd packed it all—their whole history, all his hoarded resentments—down into an ice ball he could grip in his hand. The hand shook. "*You* got scared? What about Kit? What about—" He was yelling now. More out of control than she'd ever seen him.

"You?" she yelled back, grabbing his shaking fist and yanking it hard. "Listen. I got scared, goddammit!"

Their hands parted, and they both took a breath. "Jesus, Nina, you stuck an AR in my face, in Kit's," he blurted, his voice still shaking, but lower, reeling in.

"I thought I saw—" She stopped, began again. "The reason I got scared is because I knew I had to tell you something, and when I did, I'd have to face it myself. Really face it."

They both looked up as a set of low beams materialized out of the gloom and a car slowly slipped past, this gray silent shadow.

She fluttered her hand, an explosion of nerves, and reached for her cigarettes. Clicked her lighter. "Christ," she said, blowing a stream of smoke, making a bitter laughing sound, "look at me, just talk about it and I start to panic . . ." Nina shook her head. "Must have tripped something. Call it what you want, post-traumatic whatever . . . scary how real it seems." She jerked her head back toward the house. Then tossed her hair, worrying her fingers through the sweaty ponytail. Turning back, she saw she had his full attention now. So she just said it. "Broker, this whole ugly thing we've been through. It's not about Janey and Holly. Oh, it's about loss, all right. A selfish, small loss. It's about me, goddammit." Her voice started to shake. "It's about *losing me.*"

"Okay, okay; take it easy," he said, his eyes deeply engaged in the sudden fury of emotion on her face. As Nina steadied herself, puffing on the cigarette, the windshield cleared, the world returned. The wind collapsed, the snow vanished. A pristine winter road stretched before them; spruce, balsam, and cedar decked in white. The low clouds unwound, almost electric with saffron light.

"See," Nina said. "When I call them at Bragg, I have to tell them it's over. They know. Just waiting for me to accept it."

"Over? What's over?" He drew himself up, like the jury was in and the verdict was about to be read.

Nina bit down on the cigarette between her teeth and slammed her left fist into her right shoulder. Then she thumped the fist on the black logo type across the front of her sweat-suit jacket. "The fucking Army. That's what's over. I'm coming home, Broker. There, you happy now?"

"Jesus, Nina, hey—"

"It's my shoulder, I got the shoulder of a fifty-year-old woman. It's wrecked. Irreversible tissue damage. I been faking it with steroids and narcotics for years."

Broker blinked, trying to take it in. Then he turned his head, squinted at her, like . . .

They both jerked their heads alert, "You hear that?" Nina wondered, looking around.

"Yeah," Broker said, gritting his teeth, sitting up. "Sometimes you can get this thunder snow—"

"There it is again," Nina said.

Broker waved his hand at the smoke filling the interior of the Jeep. "Crank down the window." As she did, he opened the one on his side. They listened, straining . . . the silence almost creaked, like this wishbone . . .

The snap carried through the icy air, pointed and resonant. Their eyes locked. Instantly, Broker jammed the gearshift, popped the clutch, and spun the Jeep in a giddy fishtailing turn, mashed on the gas.

"Small-caliber, about four hundred yards. Pistol; back by the house," Nina's voice rose, she flipped the cigarette. *Give it to me!* she shouted.

Broker never took his eyes off the road as he yanked up his coat and handed over the Colt. She was the handgun expert in the family.

Chapter Forty-eight

Kit Broker stood shaking at the edge of the woods, looking back across a field of new snow that glistened like a million sequins. She could see her boot prints stamped in that clean snow like a line of huge black ants.

She saw the bad man who shot Uncle Harry stagger into the driveway, inspect the basement window where'd she'd escaped the house. Then he started across the yard, following her tracks, and saw her. He yelled something and raised his hand. His hand twinkled, and then she heard a sharp crack. Branches snapped farther down in the trees.

Shooting at her.

People kept getting shot in her young world. Auntie Jane. Uncle Harry. She knew she should move. Get out of here. But she kept looking down the road, her eyes pleading for headlights, for her mom and dad. Go in the woods, and she'd lose the road. The cell phone Uncle Harry gave her made a lump in her jacket pocket.

The man was coming. With his gun.

Still she couldn't move. She was rooted in the snow, so far inside the shaking, she couldn't find a way out. She didn't understand what was happening to her. *What do I do? . . . I don't know.* Just some words Mom and Dad said: What goes up comes down; don't quit, don't cry . . .

Words.

He was almost halfway across the yard now, this lumbering shadow, coming to hurt her. Worse. Uncle Harry . . . And then, finally, she did know something. Balling her gloved hands into fists, she yelled at her pursuer: *"I am not a little shit!"* Galvanized by the sound of her voice, she turned and plunged into the forest, pumping her arms and knees, running zigzag through the trees and bushes.

Heard him behind her, crashing in the brush. Something else. Like a horn?

She fell headlong, plunging her arms into the snow, felt sharp things in the dirt tear at the palms of her hand; pushed herself up on her stinging hands. Lost her hat, branches ripped her face. Tasted blood. Got her feet under her.

A doe bolted in front of her, so close she could see the bulging white of the terrified animal's eyes. Just running like crazy.

Run faster. Have to run faster because . . .

Because he was running faster than her, because he was running beside her, this shadow flitting through the trees, against the clean sparkles. Then crossing in back of her, back and forth. But quiet, not crashing. Silent.

And then he was on the other side too. He was everywhere. She sobbed for breath and ran harder, but he stayed with her, and then she saw a long low shape that was too short to be a man. More than one. Running on either side, pacing her. Hard to tell. Looked like dogs. One of them bounded ahead of her and stopped, watching her with shining eyes. Then it raised its pointy head and howled.

Kit stopped running and stood absolutely still.

Not a dog.

Dumb little shit. Where did she think she was going? Blind man could follow these tracks. Shank pushed on, gaining ground, driven by a raging necessity to lay his hands on that kid. But by the time he made it to the trees, he knew something was seriously wrong. His left pant leg was stiff with frozen blood, crackling at every step. More disturbing was the deadening cold in his hands and legs. When he gripped the SIG, the pressure stopped in his palm, didn't make it to his fingers. Swung his eyes at the hostile trees. Not that cold out.

Was it?

He didn't know a whole lot about anatomy. Just knew he was bleeding way too much for a flesh wound. *Fucker. Musta got the vein . . .*

The cold was inside, not outside coming in . . .

All his warm stuff was dribbling out.

He blinked, and it felt like his eyelids were sealed, glued. Vaguely he realized he had stopped sweating. His breath no longer fogged the air. No heave to his chest. He lurched, reaching for the trunk of a pine tree. Pressed his cheek into the rough reddish bark. *Rest a second.* Squinting. Limbo light through the branches—clouds spun with amber in the tree breaks, like cotton candy. His eyes focused, and he noticed that the kid's tracks were crisscrossed with other smaller tracks. Lots of them. His left leg buckled, and he bumbled down, hugging the tree trunk until he collapsed heavily in the snow. Rolled over on his back.

A blur of movement against the snow, low, to the right. He swung the pistol and fired twice. When he tried for a third shot, he realized his numb hand was empty. He'd lost the SIG.

Amazed, as his kidneys released, he became fascinated with a tiny wisp of steam rising from his crotch. Warm there. His stiff right hand fumbled for the warm. Couldn't feel it. When he raised his hand, his fingers looked like they were covered with sticky oil. When he brought the oil to his lips, it tasted like blood. The hand fell to the snow and he couldn't raise it.

When the eerie summoning howl bounced off the trees, Shank barely heard it, just part of the rushing background noise draining from his mind.

He didn't see them gather at first, sniffing the blood trail, circling patiently in the creepy shadows. By the time he did see them sitting patiently in a semicircle around him, that's all he could do. See.

Last picture his brain took. Snapshot from the dawn of time.

Hot yellow electric eyes, electric fur. A flicker of teeth. Deep in his still chest his heart might have screamed. One furtive thump. He didn't feel the rough tongue lick at the bloody thigh. He was gone before the first tearing bite.

Kit found herself suspended in a strange breathing bubble inserted in the ocean of fear. Entranced, she watched the wolves sniff the air, then wheel and bound away. Slowly, soundlessly, she walked though the trees, putting distance between her and the snarls of the feeding pack. When the sounds faded, the bubble burst and the fear rushed in, but it was a hot fear now, angry. She broke into a run. Not sure what happened back there. But she hoped it was him they got. Hoped it hurt.

Then she saw the slow moving light tremble through the trees. Sprinting now, she dashed toward it, falling, getting up, breaking out of the trees, tumbling in a ditch, getting up again, running up the road shoulder toward the now stationary headlights. Screaming.

"Mom. Dad. Help!"

Chapter Forty-nine

After Shank called, Sheryl put the car in gear and crept down the white tunnel of County 12, alternately checking the odometer and the shoulder at the side of the road. Had the radio going on country-western, some guy crooning about a woman who only smoked when she drank. Something to keep her sane. When she got past 1.5 on the odometer, she saw a red Jeep Cherokee idling at the side of the road, waiting out the storm.

Her first thought: *Smart move. What I should be doing.*

Then. *Too close.*

A minute later she caught a break, and the snow stopped. Still creeping, she eased around a turn and saw the edge of the green cabin in the trees. Thought she heard something. Was worried she'd hit something on the road. She tapped off the AM. Kept going until she drew up even with the foot of the driveway. Stopped.

Was supposed to wait here till he came out and waved her in . . .

What the fuck!

Shank? Yeah, it was Shank. In that white-and-black branchy coat flapping on his back. What was he doing, running across an open field, away from the house?

She pounded the horn. Probably not a good idea. He kept going.

Shit. Now what?

She put the car in drive and accelerated down the road, past the woods where he'd disappeared, slowed down, trolling, peering into the trees. Made another turn, pulled over. Tried to think.

Decided she should turn around, at least get pointed in the right direction. After she carefully executed the turn, she switched the high beams on and off. Although it had stopped snowing, it seemed like the snow was still there, latent in the gray air, ready to jump out any second. Looking up, she saw the clouds had this weird orange glow, like something getting ready to bust out.

Dark everywhere she looked. Scary out here.

She forced herself to get out of the car and yell, "Shank, over here. Shank?"

Screw this. She hurried back inside.

Getting real nervous now, she palmed her cell, put it down, and flashed the lights again. Then kept them on. She lit a Merit. Waited. Turned up the heater.

Huh?

First she saw the branches shake along the road, snow flying off, then this . . . kid in a green coat . . . tumbled out and fell into the ditch not twenty yards in front of the Nissan. The kid scrambled to her feet and started running toward Sheryl. Arms waving. Yelling. Sheryl zipped down the window, heard the kid screaming, *"Mom. Dad. Help!"*

Oh, fuck me, now what?

Sheryl opened the door, got out, eyes darting up and down the road. The kid was now doing the same thing, wild eyes tearing around, looking at Sheryl, the car, the road. A girl, red hair coming out of a ponytail, stuff matted in her hair. She staggered the last few steps and threw herself on the hood of the car. Like it was a safe place. She was covered with snow, her trousers were torn, and she had a long bleeding cut across her cheek.

"Help. There's a man with a gun. He shot Uncle Harry," she panted.

Great. Who the fuck was Uncle Harry?

Sheryl moved forward and took the kid by the shoulders. Two powerful diametrically opposed emotions clashed in her chest; she felt an instinctive impulse to comfort her. And she wanted her to disappear.

"Jeez, kid, what happened?" Sheryl said, feeling the bone-deep shudders coming off the kid's shoulders, into her hands.

"He's in the woods. He's after me," the kid said, panting for breath.

"Okay, okay." Sheryl tried to think. "He's after you. How far away is he?"

"I don't know, they got him," she panted.

They?

"Hey, maybe we should get you out of sight," Sheryl said, eyes darting up the road, then at the dense hostile trees.

"We should call . . . ," the kid started to say.

"No, we gotta hide you first. Get you outta here, someplace safe." She turned, dashed back to the car, leaned in, and punched the trunk release. Saw the bottle of spring water in the dashboard caddy, plucked it up, and hurried back. "Here, drink this, it'll help calm you down." She thrust the plastic bottle into the kid's gloved hand. "Don't cry now."

The kid bunched her forehead, blew a strand of loose hair from her face with a fierce huff, and said, "I'm not *crying*."

"Okay, right." Firmly, Sheryl gripped the shoulder of her jacket and walked her around to the back of the car. The kid started to resist. "Look, you said a guy with a gun. We gotta get you outta here. If he sees you in the car with me, he'll be after me too. So you gonna hide in here." Sheryl lifted the trunk lid.

"No way," the kid said. She threw the bottle of water at Sheryl's feet and started to back away.

"Sorry," Sheryl said, pitching forward, throwing her arms around the kid, hauling her up, and falling forward with her over the edge of the trunk. Shit, the kid was strong. "This will be easier if—"

Then the kid punched her in the forehead with a soggy wet-gloved fist and almost staggered her.

"Fuck this," Sheryl grunted and pounded the kid right back, stunning her enough to stuff her arms and legs free of the lid and slam it shut. As the kid's feet beat a hollow tattoo on the inside of the trunk Sheryl ran back, yanked open the door, leaned on the horn. Listened to it echo into the still trees.

Tried yelling again, "Shank, Shank, over here!" into the gathering darkness. Wait a minute. Think. What if the person who'd been shot was still alive, was on the phone, calling the cops? Who's *they*?

Not the time to be jumping up and down yelling.

Sheryl jumped back into the car, turned on the dome light, and checked her face in the rearview, to see if she showed any damage where the kid punched her. Seeing none, if you didn't count the panic in her eyes, she drew her hand across her forehead, straightening her hair, and then, for one long second, she looked up and down the road. Reached for her cell, checked her slip of paper, and punched in Shank's number, listened to it ring. Got the fucking voice mail of the person the phone had been stolen from. Oh, great. She dropped the phone, put the car in gear, and drove slowly, scanning the trees to the left. Stopped, waited a minute. Nothing. C'mon. Where are you?

Then she crept farther down the road, right to the edge of the open lot next to the green cabin. She began to shudder. The shaking started in her belly and worked up into her arms and her throat. If she'd learned one thing living her life, it was not to hang around the scene of a shooting.

Then she picked up a flare of lights up the road. She killed the headlights, really shaking now as she saw the red vehicle sitting in the driveway of the target house. Two people. Running toward the house.

That's it. Sorry, Shank, but it looks like every man for himself.

Lights off, keeping her eyes straight ahead, not even looking off the road when she drove past the driveway to the green cabin. When she rounded the turn past the house, she switched the lights back on, accelerated, and reached for her cell and punched in the second number on the slip of paper.

Chapter Fifty

Keith Nygard sat at his desk in the sheriff's office in the corner off the courthouse, chewing a toothpick, his eyes drifting between reading an accident report and frowning at the snow on spin cycle in his window. He heard a knock on the doorjamb. Looked up. Saw Gator Bodine standing in the doorway. He looked different.

"Hey, Gator; you look different," Keith said.

Gator shrugged, brushed his knuckles along his cheek. "Just treated myself to a shave and a haircut at Irv's."

"What's the occasion?" Keith put the report aside.

"Barnie called me from Bemidji. Just sold that old 1918 Case Model 9–18, the one with the big steel wheels." Gator shrugged. "What the hell, thought I'd take a break, maybe go to the Anglers, have a sit-down meal."

"What'd you get for it?" Keith asked.

"After Barnie's commission, I should see about eighteen thousand."

"No kidding. I'm in the wrong racket. Grab a seat." Keith indicated one of the chairs in front of his desk.

Gator lowered himself in the chair. "Ah, reason I'm here—besides dropping in to see Mitch, down the hall"—Gator always visited his parole officer when he sold a tractor, offered to buy him a beer; Mitch always grinned and just shook his head—"is, ah . . ." Gator cast his eyes around.

Keith nodded, got up, walked over, and shut the door. Resumed his seat.

"Reason is, I ran Terry Nelson's kid out of the old Tindall

place the other night. He had all the ingredients. But he's pretty far gone. Had him an electric hot plate for a heat source. Check this, when I caught him, he was wandering around looking for someplace to plug it in. So, like that."

Keith shook his head. "Jimmy Raccoon Eyes. Christ, has that kid gone south fast. Can't believe he used to run the hurdles. He graduated high school just two years ago. Hot plate, huh? Christ. The electric's been off in that place for years."

"Uh-huh. So I hassled him some. Came up with some names." Gator withdrew a folded sheet of ruled paper from his jacket pocket, slid it across the table. "One of them's in high school. A senior named Danny Halstad. They been out at Tindall's cooking on a propane stove."

"How much?"

Gator shrugged. "Strictly their own use. A gram maybe. But if they keep it up, others will copy them."

"Okay." Keith slid the folded sheet across his desk and dropped it in his drawer. "What about the Mexicans?"

"They're keeping to themselves. Stay in that trailer on the building site. I think they got the message after you popped those guys."

Keith grinned. "You know, you got a flare for this snitching sideline."

Gator flashed on Shank's parting words: *What do we do with snitches?* "That ain't a term I like, Keith," Gator said evenly, but keeping his voice suitable humble.

"Yeah, well, you dumb fuck. You did it to yourself."

After letting an appropriate amount of time pass, Gator asked, "So what about that thing we talked about?"

"Forget it. You ain't gonna get your hunting rights restored, I don't care how many meth labs you help me bust. We'd need a pardon from the governor. And that just ain't gonna happen anytime soon. I checked with Terry"—Terry Magnason was the county attorney—"you should be happy with the local deal we worked with Mitch and Joey"—Joe Mitchell was the county game warden—"long as you hunt, quiet like, in the Washichu you can have your venison. You try going outside the county, even south of Z, Joe will stuff a walleye up your ass. End of story."

Gator accepted the lecture passively. It didn't really bother him anymore the way Keith harped on it—like he was mourning their high school friendship, like Gator had personally disappointed him or something. He glanced at the clock on the wall next to a mounted ten-point buck: 4:06. Then he stood up.

"Angler's, huh," Keith said, glancing at the snow boiling outside his office windows. "Watch it on the road going home. This could be a bad one. Howie's out on a three-car pileup on Two."

"You got a point," Gator said. "Maybe I'll drop in on Jimmy out at the garage. Looks bad, I'll stay over."

Keith nodded. "Good plan. You talk to Jimmy much lately?"

"Not really. Cassie called me few days back, whining about Teddy getting in a fight at school. Total bullshit."

"Yeah, Jimmy and the other kid's father went round and round. I had to get involved. Guess it did some good. Cassie called me, too, told me she got together with the kid's mother and they worked it out."

"Whatever," Gator said.

"Yeah, well. Congratulations on selling the Case."

Gator waved, turned, and left the office, walked down the hall, and nodded to Ginny Borck, who'd been two years ahead of him in high school and who now sat in a county uniform behind the dispatch desk with its bank of new radios and computers.

Strolling. He was strolling. Should be whistling. He went out on the street, turned up his collar, and strolled to his truck.

A few minutes later he was easing through the snow, approaching the Angler's, when the secure stolen cell phone rang. Relaxed, feeling complicit with fortune, he punched answer.

Sheryl's voice jumped at him; desperate, yelling, practically screaming: *"We got a problem!"*

Chapter Fifty-one

Broker braked the Jeep halfway up the drive in a four-wheel drift, left it idling. They were out, running toward the house. Ten yards out, seeing the garage side door open, Nina took the lead. Then she sidestepped and pointed down with her left hand while she held the Colt ready with the other.

Broker nodded, going numb. He saw the blood crystallizing, freezing in the snow outside the door, a lot of it. Then he saw the tracks. The basement window hanging open. Looked up. Nina was in. Started after her. She met him at the door to the kitchen. "Don't come in here," she said, looking him dead serious in the eye.

"Kit?" His knees buckled, then he recovered and surged past her. Saw Griffin sprawled on the floor next to the Roberts. Saw the AR-15 on the floor behind the body. Had a magazine in it. The operating handle angled back loose.

"I told you not to come in," Nina said. "Stay here." She darted away. He heard her dash up the stairs, rummage though the upstairs, come back down the stairs. Doing something in the living room.

"Kit?" he shouted.

"Not here." Nina reappeared, handed him the .12 gauge, a box full of shells.

"Basement," Broker said, pointing to the bloody steps as he jammed shells in the shotgun and racked the slide. Then old reflex kicked in. "Don't touch anything." He stuffed more shells in his pocket. "I'll be outside."

Nina skipped down the stairwell, avoiding the bloody steps. Broker turned toward Griffin. *Do something. Shut his eyes.* Shook it off. Totally on automatic. *Don't touch anything. Don't think.*

"Not here," Nina yelled.

"I'm outside," Broker yelled, going back out the garage. When Nina came out, he pointed to the tracks leading off across the lawn. "She got out the basement window. Those are her boots. The shooter's following her. Let's go." Then he froze, and his voice failed as it hit him. He swallowed to clear the roar in his ears. Through the explosions of their crystallized breath, he said, "He loaded the AR, Nina. I left him with a piece that didn't work . . ."

She pounded him hard on the chest. "Do your job! He did!" she shouted in that fierce voice, indicating the blood trail. "Now you do yours!"

They moved off in unison, running on either side of the tracks leading across the field. As he ran, Broker tore out his cell and punched 911.

"Nine-one-one, is this an emergency?" the dispatcher answered.

"This is Phil Broker. Fire number 629, on the lake. Harry Griffin is dead, shot by an intruder in my house. My eight-year-old daughter is missing. Put me through to Keith Nygard."

"Stay on this connection."

"Get Keith!" Broker shouted.

"Stay on the connection," the dispatcher repeated.

They were approaching the tree line. Nina shouted over her shoulder, "Griffin hit him hard. All this blood. This guy ain't going far."

They ducked into the trees. The dispatcher came back. "Hello?"

"Keith?"

"He's already in his car, on the way," the dispatcher said. "We're starting EMT . . ."

"Start *everything*!" Broker yelled.

"Calm down. We're sending all we got. Now, Keith wants you

to end this call. He has your number off our system. He'll call you back on your cell. Do you copy?"

"Copy." Broker ended the call, ran holding the cell phone up in his left hand, the shotgun like a dueling pistol in the other. They were moving fast, staying wide of the meandering bloody trail, with an eye for taking advantage of potential cover, aware that the bleeder at the end of these tracks was armed, had killed.

"Broker . . . ," Nina called out, a ragged edge to her voice. He saw what she was pointing at. More tracks, animal tracks, a lot of them. Too big for coyotes. When he looked up, he saw Nina sprinting ahead, arms pumping, charging headlong.

Broker tried to keep up, felt something, looked up, and swore, "Shit!" Not only were they losing light, but the top tier of the trees shivered and bent. Then the snow went off in his face like a white phosphorus round. Blinding.

Heard Nina's muffled scream. "I saw them. They ran. I can't tell . . . is it . . ." He ran forward to the sound of her voice. Found her dancing back and forth, peering down at . . . *Oh, no.* Without hesitating, he stepped forward, kneeling in it, checking the gristle of the face, clenched teeth showing two inches of bone top and bottom, the nose and lips chewed away.

Stood up, shook his head. "It's the shooter. Griffin got him. C'mon," he yelled, grabbing her as he went by. Dragging her away from the partially devoured corpse. His heart pounded hot as he pushed her forward. "See, look, look! There's her tracks. They keep going . . . leave *that* for the sheriff," he panted. Then he realized that Nina was crying, the tears freezing on her cheeks, yelling sweetly, "Harry!" over and over as she ran. Suddenly she stopped, raising her free hand cupped, like she was trying to hear.

"What?" he yelled.

"Phone," she yelled.

Christ, the phone was ringing in his hand. He fumbled with freezing fingers; neither of them were wearing gloves. Hit answer. Heard Nygard yelling:

"Broker, it's Nygard. Where the hell are you, man?"

There was a jagged adrenaline surge to Nygard's voice, but also a touch of deference. "Not sure," Broker stopped, looking around, trying to get his bearings. "Somewhere north of the house, in the woods between the lake and the road. Where are you?"

"At the foot of your drive. Tell me quick," Nygard said.

"We followed a blood trail from the house and found a body. Griffin fought . . ." His voice failed.

"Broker, you still there?"

Now stronger. "*Griffin got the guy*, he was following my kid, judging by the tracks, and he bled out."

"Where's your daughter?"

"In the woods, still running, We're on her tracks, but the snow . . ." Broker stumbled. Nina was dragging him by the arm, trying to stay on the fading tracks.

"I'm out of the car. I'm coming in," Nygard said.

"No. Give me lights and flashers north along the road. Maybe we can pick you up, talk you in. We need a search party in here."

"On my way. Stay on the phone."

Almost immediately they spotted the blue-red slap of lights blooming faintly through the ghostly swirl of trees and white.

"Good girl. Good girl," Nina yelled, pulling on Broker's arm. "Look. See. She'd headed toward the road . . . the lights . . ."

Moving at a jog, watching the lights move away up the road, Broker shouted into the phone. "Nygard?"

"I'm here."

"You still going north?"

"That's affirm."

"Turn around, you're about two hundred yards past where we're coming out of the trees onto the road."

They broke from the trees bent double, trying to see the tracks. Nina was going back and forth, frantic, searching. "They end here. They end here."

With the snow and the wind, they couldn't read the ground.

"I'll check the other side." Broker crossed the road, peered along the shoulder into the impossible mix of descending night and flying snow. Nothing. They needed lights.

Lights were coming, blue and red strobing the sides of the road as Nygard skidded the cruiser to a halt and jumped out. He paused for half a second, blinked once, seeing Nina standing oblivious to the cutting wind in the flimsy Army running suit, the big Colt hanging in her hand.

"We came out on her tracks. She came out here," Broker yelled.

"Okay," Nygard shouted, voice charged, swiftly walking along the far side of the road, holding up a service flashlight, scanning the shoulder. "We got people coming from all over. We got experts in this up here, winter searches. Take a breath . . ."

More lights, really coming fast. Jesus, *real fast*, like ninety-plus on the snow. They all instinctively moved to the side of the road as a maroon Minnesota State Police Crown Victoria slewed sideways in a not quite controlled skid, tires crunching to a halt in a shower of snow.

The female trooper bolted from the car; she was a powerfully built black woman, no hat, short-cropped hair like a woolly cap, no jacket. Service belt creaking with cold. Unfazed by the wild aspect of Broker and Nina, she shouted, "Keith, get on your radio, goddammit!" Electrified by the trooper's manner, they rushed with Nygard to his cruiser. Nygard hit the speaker box, and Broker sagged, hearing Kit's voice come through the static. Felt Nina grip his arm.

"I don't know where . . ." Kit was saying on the radio speaker.

"Just a minute, honey," the dispatcher said. "Stay with me, break, Keith, where are you?"

"Right here, Ginny. You found her?"

"Are her parents there?" the dispatcher said with obvious controlled intensity.

"Right here."

"Put them on. All this new stuff we got, I have her patched into the net. They can talk. Tell them to quiet her down."

Nina immediately grabbed the mike. "Kit, honey, it's Mom . . . Where are you?"

"I don't know. I ran out of the woods, and this lady put me in the trunk of her car. Uncle Harry gave me his phone, told me to call 911 before . . .

The mike trembled in Nina's hand, her chilblained knuckles blanched white, gripping. "Go on, Kit," she said in a steady voice.

"The car's moving. It's so dark . . ."

Broker took the mike. "Kit, it's Dad. Hold on, we're coming. You have to keep talking on the phone. Even if no one answers you, just keep talking."

Nygard grimaced, said, "Maybe you should reassure her . . ."

Broker shook his head, "No time." He turned back to the mike. "Kit. Leave the phone on. If they take you out of the car, hide it, look for something. A sign, anything at all. Try to talk when you can."

"Yes, Daddy." The signal faded.

"Kit. Can you describe the car?" Broker asked.

Static.

Nygard took the mike. "Ginny, stay on her, keep talking. I need this radio free for a while. Then I'll put her folks back on." He turned to Broker and Nina, who had stepped back from the cruiser to give him room. "She's close. If we keep hearing her, she's within nine miles of the towers. They go at nine-mile intervals between Highway Two and Little Glacier, remember, the skeleton house?" He looked up to the state trooper. "Ruth. You got the best radio, you gotta handle the traffic on the state net. Soon as I talk to my deputy and EMT, I'm going to keep mine open for the parents to talk." Nygard removed his hat and scrubbed at his thin brown hair with his knuckles. "All the roads in a fifty-mile radius, then work in. Let's shut it down. Gotta stop anything moving. We'll need everybody. I mean *everybody*."

"I'm on it," Ruth said. Starting for her cruiser, she gently started to put her arm around Nina. "How you holding up, ma'am? Maybe you should get in the car with me."

Nina looked right through the trooper, shook off her hand. Sergeant Ruth Barlow pursed her lips, observed the butt of the pistol stuck in Nina's waistband. Broker's shotgun. Drew herself up. "Keith, these people are armed; you on top of that?"

Keith jerked his thumb at Broker, "He's a cop, ex-cop. She's . . . okay. *C'mon,* Ruth."

"You say so," Sergeant Barlow said, continuing to her car. She got in and grabbed her radio mike. Nina thrust the Colt deeper into the waistband of her sweatpants, took out her cigarettes and lighter. Cupping her hands against the blow, impossibly, she lit the cigarette.

Keith Nygard watched her, red hair streaming, smoke tearing from her mouth and nostrils. Like some Celtic war priestess he'd seen on the History Channel. He turned to Broker, sagged briefly, clicked his teeth. "Harry, Jesus. Got a body in the woods, you say." Nygard shook his head, looked up. "How am I doing?"

"You're doing good. Call BCA in Bemidji, have them get the feds. It's a kidnapping. Find out the status of the Troopers—"

"State patrol helicopters, right," Nygard said.

"Get something in the air that can whip a radio direction finder on a cell signal," Broker said.

"Got it. Okay. Jesus, what's going on?"

"I don't know, goddammit; somebody got my kid," Broker said. His voice caught. He was accumulating a list of people whose names he couldn't bring himself to say. Holly, now Griffin . . .

"Okay. Later we'll talk about the why. Right now we'll work the problem," Nygard said. "Let me make a few calls, soon's people arrive, we'll start some searching right here. Then we gotta move back to the house. Secure the scene . . . but if she's in a car, moving—" Then he nodded at Nina." *You* tell her. One of you got to stay on the radio, talking."

Chapter Fifty-two

Sweat was dripping down Gator's freshly shaved jaw. It was all coming apart. Shank, the big shot from the Cities, had tripped on his dick. Sheryl said the kid said the man chasing her had shot Uncle Harry? And where the fuck was Shank? Wandering, lost in the woods somewhere? If he was out there in this, Gator hoped he was getting tired, that he would lie down and go to sleep. And die. *See. This is what happens when you rely on other people.*

That meant Broker was still on the loose out there. Knew his kid was missing.

Gator pounded the steering wheel as he drove. Shit. One minute he was winning. And now . . . He caught himself when he saw the blue flashers light up the blowing snow a block away, heading out of town, toward 12. Okay. Think. He contained his rage long enough to figure out he didn't want to drive his normal route home. Highway 12 in front of Broker's house would be jamming up with Keith, Howie, probably the volunteer firemen who had an ambulance and were EMT certified. Lost kid in a storm. Cops would be coming from other counties, piling on.

He swung the truck in a U-turn on Main Street and headed west out of town, turned north on Lakeside Road. Cut over the top of the lake. Pick up 12 above Broker's place.

He mashed his boot down on the gas, driving on pure adrenaline and instinct through the whiteout. Had the kid in the fucking trunk, Sheryl said. Tried to work it out in his head. Maybe strand the kid back in the woods. Make it look like exposure. Might work. I don't know. He pounded the wheel with his fist.

C'mon, Sheryl, don't screw up. Gator leaned forward, willing the truck through the storm.

His other cell phone rang. He checked the connection. Cassie. Shook his head. Dropped the phone. Kept driving.

"Shit, hell, damn."

Kit huddled, fetal, trembling, in the rocking black compartment. Swearing. They were the only three cuss words she knew. Mom let her sit under the kitchen table sometimes in the Stillwater house and swear, to work out her heebie-jeebies, Mom said. If Dooley was here, he could pray. But he wasn't. So she turned her face away from the phone and swore. Swearing, she'd discovered, helped keep her mad at the man in the woods and the lady driving the car. Helped hold off the smothering fear.

"Shit, hell, damn."

Her only other comfort was the bluish green light on the cell phone in her hand. Voices cut in and out like a bad radio station. Sometimes the 911 lady, sometimes her mom.

"Stay calm. We're coming," they said.

Desperate, she felt around in the dark, looking for anything. She was lying on a crinkly plastic sheet, all folded. When she probed her free hand under it, she found a flat metal box. Like they kept art supplies in at school. It took a minute to fiddle with the hasp, but she got it open and clawed around in this cold metal stuff. Tools. She selected a long screwdriver and clutched it in her hand.

"We're com . . . ay calm. . . ." the phone crackled in and out.

"When? When are you coming?" Kit pleaded to the blue-green wafer of light.

"We're coming . . ."

Kit gripped the screwdriver, clamped her eyes shut. She was gonna die and go to hell and burn forever because she never went to church.

"Shit, hell, damn."

♦ ♦ ♦

Sheryl hunched rigid over the wheel, staring in pure terror at the white freezing world that had materialized again out of thin air and battered the windshield. It was totally out of control. Any second it felt like the windshield would implode and this white wave would engulf her. Fuckin' Nissan handled like a boat, heaving though the greasy snow. Ice clogged the wipers, making this disconcerting clack, like two bones scraping on the glass. Barely make out the shoulders to either side. Could see maybe twenty yards, max.

Gator said, Take the kid to the farm, get her in the house, calm her down, give her some milk or something and find out what she knows.

Yeah, right. That kid? Good luck.

Finally, Sheryl saw a tiny smear of light in the blow, ahead on the right. Closer, she saw a red blur dancing in the white blast. The display tractor in front of Gator's shop. For the first time since she'd wrestled the kid into the trunk, she relaxed her grip on the wheel.

Slowly, she guided the Nissan off the road, past the tractor, orienting now on the yard light fixed to the barn. She jumped out and was momentarily stunned by the force of the wind. Leaning forward, she slogged to the barn, gripped the sliding garage door, and tried to yank it open on the creaky rollers. The heavy wooden door moved an inch and stopped. She didn't have the strength to break the bottom free from the snow jam. Frantic, she turned to the second door, on the left, where Gator kept the Bobcat. Room in there to park. Sobbing with exertion, aided by a surge of panic, she managed to move the door a foot and a half. It wasn't going to happen. She stepped back, panting, furious when she saw the seam split on the shoulder of her good leather coat, all this gunky paint rubbed off, abrading the sleeve. Let Gator open the fucking door.

She turned and faced the Nissan.

Gotta do it. He'll be pissed if I don't get her inside.

She opened the driver's-side door and hit the trunk latch, braced herself, and hurried around to the rear of the car. Lifted the loose lid.

"Hey. C'mon. Let's get you inside," Sheryl yelled, seeing the kid in the vibrating glow of the yard light, curled in a tight ball, eyes wide, angry; the cut across her cheeks streaked on her face like war paint. The kid didn't move. "I'm trying to help you, goddammit," Sheryl shouted.

The kid heaved up on her arms, looked around once, wild-eyed, then slumped back down. "Leave me alone!" she screamed.

"It didn't have to be this way," Sheryl screamed back, and she meant everything plus the storm that was driving her crazy. She lurched forward, plunging her hands to grab . . .

What? The kid rose to meet her, swinging something that gleamed. Ow, damn! Sheryl staggered back, clutching her left wrist, where it stung. Blood appeared in the white peeled-back skin between her glove and the cuff of her coat.

"Leave me alone!" the kid yelled again, reaching up, pawing at the top of the lid. Found a handhold and slamming it shut on herself.

"Suits me just fine, you little bitch," Sheryl mumbled, turning, running toward the house. To hell with this. Let Gator get her out.

"We stopped, we stopped," Kit, hyperventilating, unable to control her runaway breath, yelled into the phone, which she'd hidden beneath her when the lid opened. "I see a red tractor in a light. A red tractor in a light." Shouted it over and over.

Chapter Fifty-three

Police tape clamored yellow in the fifty-mile wind. An ambulance sat halfway up the drive. Glacier County's two police cars were parked at the foot of the drive. The state patrol cruiser was positioned at an angle across the road, to stop anyone driving by.

Nygard, Broker, and Nina were observing a local moratorium on bringing up Griffin's name. A BCA Crime Lab van was en route from Bemidji to work the scene. It was all about Kit's voice, patched through the radio.

They were hunched forward, holding hands, Nina in the passenger side, Broker in the backseat, listening to Kit's voice cut in and out. Nygard stood outside, talking to a fire and rescue guy; his deputy was in the house with another fireman; State Patrol Sergeant Ruth Barlow sat in her car talking on her radio. Two more volunteer fireman in heavy parkas were tramping across the broad lot toward the woods with flashlights, poking the snow, marking the faint blood trail with Broker and Kit's skis and poles from the garage. Going to locate the body.

Nina keyed the radio mike, spoke in a slow deliberate voice, "Stay calm. We're coming."

Just static.

The door opened, and Nygard jumped in behind the wheel. Removed his hat. Dusted snow from his neck and shoulders. Methodically, he removed his frosted glasses, took out a small plastic bottle, and squirted antifogging solution on them. As he cleaned them with a handkerchief, he asked, "Anything new?"

Nina shook her head. "Keeps cutting in and out. She's still talking."

"What's that?" Nygard grimaced at the speaker box.

"She's swearing," Nina said, gnawing her lip.

Nygard glanced back at Broker.

"Better than crying," Broker said, his voice awful.

Sergeant Barlow tapped on the window. Nygard zipped it down. She eyed Broker and Nina with restrained amazement. "I put out the APB with the description you gave me: Kit Broker, eight-year-old white female, red hair, four foot three, seventy-three pounds, cross bite on front teeth. Gave your names, said you were in contact with Kit by cell phone. Few minutes later the FBI in *St. Paul* called *me* back on *my* radio. Asked me if I'd met the parents and did the father have eyebrows. Was the mother in the Army. When I said, Yeah, about the eyebrows, the FBI guy says, in the clear: 'Prairie Island Broker and Nina Pryce, no shit.'"

Sergeant Barlow bit her lower lip. "I don't know who you people are, but the FBI outa Duluth is putting an Air Force Reserve Blackhawk up in this. Packed with electronics. BCA's coming from Bemidji *and* St. Paul. Something's going on in St. Paul, because half the troopers in northwest and central are shutting down the road—"

Nina cut her off, her open hand shooting up in a blur, signaling silence.

". . . stopped . . . red . . . I see . . ." The faint voice crackled in the speaker box.

Nina and Broker leaned forward, desperate.

"Shit," Nina said. "Can't—"

Then the dispatcher's stronger signal stepped on the static. Yelling with excitement. "Keith, got good copy on her last. She said, 'We stopped. I see a red tractor in a light.' You copy?"

"Copy. Ruth, saddle up!" Nygard shouted, slamming the Vic in gear, wrenching the wheel, and fishtailing the cruiser in a wheely, sending Sergeant Barlow jumping back out of the way. Nygard righted the vehicle and pointed it north up 12. Stepped on the gas.

"What?" Broker and Nina shouted in unison, lurching in their seats.

"Only one place in cell range I know of got a red tractor under a light. Gator's shop. He's Cassie Bodine's brother. Ex-con . . ." Then under his breath, "Maybe you ain't as rehabilitated as you look, you sonofabitch." He snatched up the mike, his eyes darting to the rearview. "Ruth, you with me?"

"Right on your ass."

"No flashers, no siren. We're going about twelve miles up this road to a farmhouse on the edge of the big woods. Place is just barely in range of the last cell tower. Gotta be. Okay. When I kill my lights, you do the same. We're going in blacked out."

"I guess," Barlow yelled back; her voice charged, building on Nygard's.

"And Ruth—"

"I'm here."

"Kick it. We're going in *real hot*." Nygard mashed down on the accelerator. He turned a quick eye to Nina, who was picking frozen snow out of the trigger guard of the Colt with the hem of the T-shirt she wore under the sweat-suit jacket. More blowing off tension than serious, he said, "If it gets rough, the book says I'm supposed to jettison civilians—"

"Drive," Broker said in a grim voice from the backseat, where he was wiping down the shotgun, checking the action.

"Yeah," Nygard said, doing 70 m.p.h., looking at maybe thirty yards of visibility, with Sergeant Barlow suicidally hugging his rear bumper.

Chapter Fifty-four

Gator wheeled into his driveway, saw the Nissan sitting in plain view with the lights on, vaulted out of the truck, and stomped toward the farmhouse. Coming up the porch steps, this inky streak zipped between his boots, nearly tripping him. Saw the kitten race toward the barn, get swallowed in the snow. *Great. And she let the cat out . . .*

He went in and found Sheryl standing at the kitchen sink. Her leather coat was ripped at the shoulder, and the sleeves were scraped with red barn paint. She was putting a Band-Aid on her wrist, with difficulty because her hand was shaking.

"You let the cat out," Gator shouted.

Sheryl stared at him incredulously, her face muscles jittery. "What?" she said. "*What?*"

Gator put the heel of his right hand to his forehead and pressed. Felt like something was busted in there, Spinning. "Where is she? And what's the car doing running, all lit up?"

"Slow down, goddammit," Sheryl hissed though clenched teeth. She held up her hand. "When I tried to get her out, she stuck me with something. She's still in there. And I couldn't get the garage door open. It's stuck."

"C'mon." Gator spun on his heel.

Sheryl followed him outside. He pointed to the car. She opened the driver's-side door and jumped behind the wheel. Then he approached the garage door, put his shoulder to it, and broke the ice jam. Shoved it open.

Sheryl gunned the engine and, wheels spinning, aimed the Nissan into the garage.

"Open the trunk," Gator said, striding toward the back of the car. Sheryl was out of the car fast, grabbing at his jacket. Hair flying. Face all scrambled, she shouted, "Just a minute. What are you going to do?"

Gator gritted his teeth and yelled back. "We," he corrected her. "What are *we* going to do. You're in this too."

Sheryl shook her head vehemently. "Uh-uh. No way. Not a kid."

Gator poked her in the chest. "*You* brought that idiot Shank in . . . from the big time . . ."

Sheryl pushed his hand away. "*You* sent me to get him."

"And you were supposed to be his ride out. So where the fuck is he?"

"She said he was chasing her. In the woods. I waited, I called him on his cell. Flashed the lights. Blew the horn. Yelled. I did a *lot*. Then I saw a car parked at that house, and I got the hell out of there."

They glared at each other, shivering, shoulders hunched, the snow frosting their faces. Gator thinking how cold was hard on machinery, harder on people. Affects judgment . . .

"Bottom line, Sheryl. Whatever happened to Shank. The way we are now . . . she's a witness," Gator said with finality.

"Oh, Christ."

"We find out what she knows. Then . . . I don't see any other way. You found her lost in the woods. They'll find her in the woods. Now *open the goddamned trunk*."

Moving like a sleepwalker, Sheryl reached into the car. The trunk lid popped. In the agitated shine from the barn light, Gator Bodine stared at Kit Broker, who was coiled back in the cavity, brandishing a screwdriver.

"Hey, now, girl; you look cold in there," Gator said in a reasonable voice.

"Leave me alone."

Damn kid coiled tighter, like an obstinate snake. "Can't do that—your mom and dad are on the way, with the sheriff. Heard you've had quite a night," Gator said.

At the mention of her parents, the kid's lower lip trembled. But the dark pockets of her eyes struck Gator as unyielding. He needed to get her in the light. See her eyes.

"Look, I'm not going to let you freeze. I'm taking you in the house." He extended his hand; she wielded the screwdriver. Gator struck fast, snatched her arm, plucked the screwdriver from her hand, and tossed it away. Getting pissed, he lifted her bodily, roughly, from the trunk and tucked her, kicking and flailing, under his arm.

When he got her in the kitchen, he released her. Immediately, she tried to run. He caught her easily and shoved her back into the room. She banged up against the kitchen table, arching away when she saw Sheryl come into the room. Gator could see her eyes now; hot, green, hostile over the smeared dirt and blood on her face. And Sheryl wasn't helping, walking to the corner by the stove, one arm folded across her chest, the other up, hand covering her face, fingers worrying at her forehead. Eyes downcast, Sheryl refused to look at the girl.

"C'mon, kid." Gator gestured awkwardly. "You want something to eat, some milk or something?"

She gave him such a look of utter pugnacity that he saw, uh-uh, no way. This was going nowhere fast. So Gator tried to think it through, to solve it like a problem. Put her back in the trunk. Couple hours she'd be unconscious, then put her in back of the truck. That way Sheryl could get the Nissan out of here. Ditch it in the Cities. Then he'd sneak the kid back, say two miles from Broker's house. Leave her in the woods. Be tricky, they'd be searching, but if the snow held, if he went on snowshoes . . . it just might . . .

"Gator!" Sheryl whipped around, alert.

He heard it too, a determined knock on the front door. "Quick," he said, moving to the utensil drawer, yanking it open, pulling out the Luger. To Sheryl, "Get her out of sight. In the bathroom. Keep her quiet." He glared at the kid. "Not a peep."

The kid stared wide-eyed for a moment, fixed on the Luger, then on his face. The hot hostile eyes refocused. Very distinctly she said, "When my mom and dad catch you, they're gonna shoot you right in the head."

"Get her out of her, keep her quiet," Gator muttered as Sheryl wrestled the kid down the hall into the bathroom, shut the door. He pulled his shirt out of his jeans, stuck the Luger in his back pocket, and flared the shirt around it. Then he walked to the door, moved the curtain aside, and groaned.

Cassie.

She stood in the porch light, wearing a white parka, bare-headed, hair whipping around, hugging herself, stamping her feet, face all bright and twitchy with craving of one kind or another. Gator opened the door. "What the hell?"

She stepped past him fast, shivering. "Cold out there. Crazy too. You hear . . ."

He stared at her. Un-fucking-believable.

". . . somebody shot Harry Griffin, killed him, at his place he's renting to that Broker guy. Except Griffin musta shot back, 'cause they found the guy they think did it. With a gun and everything. He bled to death, out in the woods. And you know what Madge Grolick heard from Ginny the dispatcher in the sheriff's office? She talked to Jeff Tindall who went out with Fire and Rescue and when they found the guy, he was all chewed up. Wolves, they think . . ."

"Cassie, you can't be here," Gator said. But he liked the part about Shank being off the board. Gave them some breathing room. Now if he could just get Cassie to shut up and go away.

". . . and now Broker's little girl is missing." Cassie grimaced. "I met them, in town. The mother was . . . nice to me."

Gator stared at her, mouth open. What the hell?

Cassie just continued talking, like she was gossiping over coffee. "There's cops showing up from all over. Madge said, Ginny said, Broker was some king cop in the Cities or something. They're bringing a helicopter, these special trained search dogs from Duluth . . ."

Gator gripped her arm, lowered his head, and marched her toward the door. "You gotta go."

"Why? You been trying to get me out here ever since you got out of prison," she said, her smile jerky.

"Where's Jimmy?" Gator said in a dull voice.

"Showing Teddy how to wash his favorite Canadian Labrie garbage truck at the garage. Where I was, and you never showed up like you said you would. To give me something. So here I am. Drove through a lot of crap to get here, too. Now what do I have to do, sing for my supper or what?" She ran her index finger down from his throat to his sternum.

Gator swatted the hand away. "I mean it, Cassie."

"So do I," she said, undeterred.

That's when the kid screeched in the bathroom: "Get your hands *off me.*" Stuff banging around, a struggle.

Gator sagged. Seeing Cassie react to the voice, obviously a child's voice, he sagged more. Wasn't falling apart. It was completely apart. Didn't matter now. None of it. Just let it happen . . .

"What the hell you got going on here?" Cassie said, suddenly frantically alert. "Christ, Gator, you can't have a kid around this shit you got out here." Her eyes flared. "Remember Marci . . ." He didn't answer, made no attempt to stop her. She pushed past him, strode down the hall, and yanked open the bathroom door.

She saw a woman standing in front of the sink with her hands cupped on a little girl's mouth, trying to hold her steady. Seeing Cassie enter, the woman reacted in a dazed spasm. Releasing her hold, stepping back. The girl had wild red hair, matted with burrs. Her green parka was filthy, snow pants ripped, and her face all red with scratches, bruises, and dried blood. The little Broker girl she'd met last Saturday morning in town, at Big Lake Threads, with her mother.

"It's all right, I'm Teddy's mom," Cassie said to Kit. Then she turned her eyes on the woman. Epiphany was not exactly in her vocabulary, but she was seized with a revelatory fury. There were things more powerful than the need to peddle her ass for a hit of meth. Than playing sick old games with her brother. "Who the fuck *are you*?" Cassie screamed at the woman, her voice exploding in the small dingy room.

Kit's mouth fell open, imprisoned in the close charged air, looked back and forth at their angry faces, their hair, their physiques. Then she looked up, away from the berserk tension in their eyes, and saw a corpulent gray leopard spider in a web in the corner next to the door. The spider uncoiled and flexed its legs.

Like a disturbed ghost.

Sheryl, having her own freaky prescient moment, yelled, "Gator, what's going on?"

Gator heard the incensed voices echo down the hall, through the kitchen to where he sagged against the peeling wallpaper next to the front door. Almost dreamy with the profound simplicity of it, seeing how they were all connected, this continuous piece of yarn. One loose end, and it all came unraveled.

"What's going on is, he's a control weirdo, that's what," Cassie shouted at Sheryl Mott. "And who's subbing in for who, I got no idea." Then she shoved Sheryl with both hands, hard, knocking her back so her calves caught on the rim of the bathtub and she fell backward, flailing her arms, pulling the shower curtain with her. Cassie gripped Kit firmly by the arm and walked her from the room. "Honey. You're coming with me. We're getting out of here."

Gator slowly shook his head. His rage was total, and his voice was so small. "No, you ain't," he almost whispered as, from the corner of his eye, he saw her striding down the hall, through the kitchen, escorting—that was exactly the word—escorting the kid, arm draped protectively over her shoulder like a mother hen.

"No, you ain't," he repeated softly, pushing though the terrible inertia, off the wall, placing one arm out, planting his hand on the far wall, blocking their path.

Kit watched it and listened to it, trembling. Confused at how the air kept getting thicker with all the scary, invisible adult bad stuff. She heard cursing in back of her, where the other woman was climbing out of the bathtub.

"You're in the way," Cassie said to Gator.

"Can't let you go. Just can't," Gator said in an almost helpless voice.

"Watch me," Cassie said, eyes flashing with disgust. "You stay here with your stand-in whore." They scurried past, out the door.

Gator shook his head. Years of work. Perfect plan. Perfect location. Belize. Boat engines. Never gonna see the fucking ocean. With tremendous effort, he pushed off the wall, started after them, Sheryl coming up now, grimacing, rubbing a bruised knot on her temple. Eyes like jelly. Shock maybe. Yapping, "What's going on? Who is she?"

"C'mon," he said, going out the door, onto the porch. Cassie and the kid were about ten yards out, ghostly in the blowing snow, starting to run toward the Jeep Cherokee Jimmy the moron bought her when he won the Moose lottery. Jeep was running, lights on. Why not. Everything else was in plain goddamn sight.

"I'm telling you, Cassie, you better stop," Gator shouted coming down the steps, bringing the Luger out, flicking off the safety.

"Run," Cassie shouted urgently to Kit, pushing her forward, shielding her with her body. "Around to the driver's side, I'll let you in."

The Luger drifted up. Gator, dreamy-eyed in the blowing snow, found Cassie's back, below her blowing black hair. Another Bodine. *And then there was one.* He squeezed the trigger. Kit screamed when Teddy Klumpe's mom pitched forward without making a sound, arms twisted, clutching behind at her back, bounced off the grill of the Jeep, twirled once in the headlight beams and fell face forward into the snow.

Gator shifted to the smaller target, but she was darting through the headlights, and with the snow, he briefly lost her. She reappeared, racing toward the barn. He fired again, but it was too far now, the light uncertain. Saw her duck into the narrow black vertical shadow of the ajar door to the left of the garage.

He turned and pounded Sheryl on the arm. Sheryl, practically useless now, had her hands up one on each side of her face. All freaked out and motor mouth, "Jesus, Gator, Jesus; when is this going to fuckin' *stop*?"

"Soon's we nail that little bitch. Now listen. You go in where she did, push her on through. I'll be around back, by the pens. Catch her when she runs out. Go." He shoved Sheryl toward the partially open sliding door. Took off running around the barn.

Kit wiggled through the door and ran on pure instinct, just a pounding heart and lungs wrapped around a bottle rocket of fright. Her boots skidded in the dark, collided with something hard, steel, some machine. She sprawled on the floor. Crawling, feeling with her right hand along a series of wooden panels. Ripe rotten grainy smells. She heard somebody take a sobbing breath as they squeezed through the door behind her. The bad woman who had put her in the trunk. Coming after her.

Kit scrambled to the end of the wooden thing and huddled, hiding behind it. She could hear the woman, feeling around in the dark, by the door. Kit swung her head. Eyes bulging, run-away heart; she saw that the back end of the enclosure was open to the storm. This empty floor dusted with white. And in the middle of it she saw a tiny familiar black silhouette arch up against the flickering snow.

Sheryl staggered forward—Jesus, what a bummer, talk about bad tripping on plain old real life—averting her eyes going past the prone figure under the Jeep high beams, the long black hair so like her own, rippling in the wind. She reached the barn, squirmed through the door, and tried to get her bearings. Their secret storehouse. *Okay. Where's the light switch?* Up on the wall to the right. Her hand fumbled in the dark. *There it is.* She took a step into the long room, her arm stretched back, fingers on the switch. Poised to flush the kid. *Aw right, ready or not, here I come. She snapped the switch.*

Chapter Fifty-five

Knowing the road, doing a hundred over the Barrens' flat, Nygard shouted adrenaline-spiked tactics to Barlow on the radio. "There's the barn to the left, then a cement-block shop and the farmhouse to the right, you know it?"

"Been by it, don't know it," Barlow shouted back in a crackle of static.

"I'll go in to the right of the house, you take the left. First one out of the car rushes the front door. We go straight in."

"Straight in," Barlow repeated in a throaty shiver. "No fucking around."

Another transmission, broke the static. "Keith, Howie; maybe you should wait, we're just ten, fifteen minutes behind you . . . got four cars on the road . . . more on the way . . ."

"Straight in," Nygard shouted back. "If it's for real, the last thing we want is Gator getting in the woods, figure he's got a deer gun at least." Nygard's face was working, staring into the snow. Then he yelled into the mike. "County Z, three minutes out."

"Three minutes," Barlow yelled back.

Broker and Nina sat silent, listening to the cops go back and forth on the radio. No communication between them. Past getting ready. Past tactics.

Almost three minutes to the dot, Nygard yelled, "See it on the right!" He switched off the headlights, and they hurtled through a spun gray tunnel. Then Broker and Nina saw the blur of the display light, the red of the tractor. Other lights, car lights. The shadows of buildings.

"Here we go," Nygard yelled, swerving off the road, sledding through a ditch, throwing up a cloud of snow as the cruiser stove through the drifts, skidding into the yard.

Nina and Broker leaped out before the car even came to a halt, were already bounding forward when the barn erupted in a sheet of fire. The confusion of snow disappeared in the roaring yellow orange plume of light. Instinctively they looked away, protecting their eyesight.

A few seconds later, Nina screamed in a voice loud enough to carry over the roar of the fire: *"Two o'clock!"*

Gator hugged the mudguard of an old rusty Deere at the edge of the tractor graveyard, where he had a good view of the open loafing shed in back of the barn. Caught movement, swung the Luger. Okay . . .

Huh? He held off, seeing the rabbit-ass cat running out from the shed. Cutting in back of the shop. He giggled nervously. No shit. Black cat crossing my path . . .

Then, just like hunting; let the doe go by, wait for the buck. He saw the kid dart from the shed, running like hell, *chasing the cat*. Saw her dive into the snow, wrap the cat in her arms. Get up, running clumsy now, arms out of play, clutching the cat. *Goddamn*, he thought, leveling the pistol. *Why didn't I think of that?*

No more than ten yards. Almost reach out and touch. Moving with her. All right, you little runt . . .

Just as he squeezed the trigger, the back end of the barn shuddered with a whoosh of flame, knocking him back, sending the shot wild, like he pulled the trigger and blew the fucker up or something. Scorched his face. Blinding him. What the . . .

Blinking, he saw the kid, sprawled in the snow, not fifteen yards away. His eyes blooming with spots, Gator couldn't aim the pistol. He stepped out from cover. She saw him, pushed up on her feet, and started running again.

Gator's breath came in a helpless giggle as he sprinted after her. Gaining on her going past the shop—clinging to the damn cat cut her speed. Rounding the house, reaching out now, feeling the tips of her hair whipping in the wind, grazing his fingertips.

"Got you," he yelled, grabbing a handful of her hair, yanking her roughly back as he skidded to a halt, grasping her hair at arm's length while she swung one arm, kicked at him. Her breath coming in fierce little sobs. Damn cat squirming in the crook of her elbow.

Heard someone yell over the rushing flames. Sheryl?

Stunned, he focused his eyes on the yard in front of the house, at the vision of two figures running in the hellfire blaze. Running straight at him. A man on the left with a shotgun and a woman on the right, in pajamas it looked like, with her arms outstretched, hands empty. Behind them he saw the county cruiser at the end of a trough of snow, somebody who could have been Keith, one hand shielding his eyes from the fire, the other raising a pistol.

Immediately Gator wrapped the girl in his left arm, pulling her in close, and jammed the muzzle of the Luger against her head.

"Everybody stop where you are," he shouted.

They didn't stop.

They were all in. Broker keyed on Nina. "Call it!" he screamed, running at the guy who was holding a pistol to Kit's head fifty yards away.

"Break left, draw fire," Nina yelled back.

Without slowing his stride, Broker swerved to the left, danced briefly, giving her time to close the distance. Then he raised the shotgun and ran straight at the guy, screaming, out-of-his-mind crazy: "Let her go, or I'll blow your fucking head off. Let her go. LET HER GO!"

Nina continued forward, plodding now, arms outstretched, pleading, hysterical. "Don't hurt her. *PLEASE*. Don't hurt her." Slowed her pace to a deliberate walk, out of sync with the frantic screaming all around, the rolling fire light, the crunch of a secondary explosion, flaming debris arcing up. Thirty yards . . .

Nygard's shaking voice calling out, "Wait, wait." Barlow

behind him, yelling too. Kit's screams topping off the bedlam. *"Mom, Dad!"*

Twenty-five yards . . .

Gator's heart was about to come right out of his chest like the tiny monster in *Alien*. He clicked his eyes on the bedraggled imploring woman for half a second, then quickly fixed his attention on the guy. It was him. Broker. His gaunt wolf face gone to mindless rage, running in from the right. Screaming. Loony. With a leveled shotgun. Keith back there, gun out in a two-handed grip. This black woman in a state trooper's suit, all tucked and neat like a painted toy soldier.

"I'LL DO IT!" Gator screamed, pressing the pistol against the squirming kid's head. Fucking cat clawing, going nuts. *"I SWEAR . . ."*

Broker coming on with the shotgun, irrational. Barely twenty yards away now. He'd lost it. Eyes pure psycho in the firelight. Gonna shoot no matter what. *"It's your kid?"* Gator screamed, astounded.

"Let her go!" Broker screamed back, coming on.

Even with the world blowing up all around, burning shit falling from the sky, instinct demanded that Gator protect himself from crazy people. He switched the pistol toward Broker, thrust his arm and jerked the trigger.

The instant the man holding Kit took the pistol out of line, away from her head, Nina's right hand flashed for the small of her back.

This time it didn't come up empty.

She smoothly drew the .45 jammed in the drawstring of her sweatpants, swept it up, set the stance, slapped her left hand over her right, and extended. The iron triangle formed in her heart and forked down her arms. Undeterred by the fire and blowing snow, she instinctively pointed, not aimed. Squeezed hard on the grip. Soft on the trigger.

Chapter Fifty-six

"What's Mom doing now?" Kit asked.

"She and Sergeant Barlow are putting a pressure bandage on her back," Broker said.

"What did you call it again?" Kit said.

"The bandage? It's called a flutter valve—"

"No." Kit knit her dirty forehead. "The way she's hurt?"

"It's called a sucking chest wound."

"But it's on her back," Kit said.

"Her lung's hurt, her lung's in her chest," Broker said in a calm voice. He stood on the road, oblivious to the raw carnage-scented smoke and fire; far enough back from the barn to be alternately chilled by the gusting wind and roasted by the flames. The night seemed softer, the barn burning down, the snow tamer, twisting on spiral zephyrs. The clouds still swirled with that orange glow, surreally enhanced, like Photoshop, by the blaze and rising smoke. But he couldn't really tell; he was drunk, on fire with adrenaline and relief.

So he just hugged Kit astraddle his hip and watched her face carefully in the flickering light for signs of shock. So far all she showed was an unwillingness to release her hold on the cat. And a voracious curiosity. Her wide green eyes were drinking it in; the burning barn, the body off in the snow, all the cops showing up, and her mom and the trooper sergeant working at strict combat speed to stabilize Cassie Bodine.

"What's that shiny stuff?" she asked.

"It's plastic wrapping from a bandage pack. They're taping it over the bullet hole and leaving a corner loose . . ."

"Why's that?'

"So Teddy's mom can breathe, honey," Broker said.

"Isn't she cold?"

"More important now to get her lung working; see, it was collapsed," Broker said.

Kit chewed her lower lip and scrutinized Nina and Sergeant Barlow, who knelt fifteen feet away. They held Cassie Bodine in an upright sitting position. They'd ripped away her clothes, and she shivered—eyes dilated, face waxy gray, naked to the waist. Her bare flank and lower back were splashed with orange Betadine disinfectant and frothy lung-shot blood. When they finished the tape job, they nodded to the two volunteer firemen crouching around them, holding a blanket as a windbreak. Nina and Barlow briefly discussed the bandage with one of the firemen, then scooted out of the way.

The fireman then covered Cassie with the blanket and lifted her carefully in a fireman's carry, keeping her upright while a third fireman gently fitted an oxygen mask to her face. Then they started walking down the road to where Howie Anderson stood, lit by the headlights of six police cars parked three by three on either side of the road. He held a mobile radio in his hand and was looking up into the fitful sky. Keith Nygard knelt next to a stretcher at Anderson's feet, where the woman who'd kidnapped Kit was swaddled in blankets, her head a loose mummy wrap of bandages. Right after Barlow discovered Cassie breathing, she'd found the other woman staggering from the barn fire; blind, her face and scalp a crisp.

When Nygard saw them bringing Cassie, he stood up, went to her, and put an arm lightly around her shoulder. He looked to Howie on the radio, said something to Cassie, then tilted his face up into the night.

Another fireman stood next to Broker with a blanket, wondered with his eyes if he should cover Kit.

"Not yet, we're good," Broker said quietly. He held Kit tighter as Nina approached, watching her stoop, wash her bloody hands in the snow, then wipe them on the thighs of her ragged sweatpants. Standing, she swiped her hands a few more times down the front of her jacket, leaving a dirty crimson stain on the black ARMY type.

Nina reached up and stroked Kit's cheek with her knuckles, the cleanest part of her hand.

"Is Teddy's mom—" Kit said.

"She'll make it. Needs a good surgeon, though. Think she's got some rib splinters in that lung," Nina said, looking up at the sky. "They'll have a good medic on the Air Force chopper. One of the EMT guys said the emergency room in Bemidji is alerted, should get them there in minutes. Got a couple surgeons reporting in." She smiled at Kit. Keeping her voice low-key with tremendous effort, she said, "You're gonna get to see a Blackhawk land in a snowstorm, Little Bit."

Broker and Nina working so hard at reassuring calm, they were almost moving in slow motion.

More urgently, Nina's eyes flitted up to Broker's. He nodded to her. *I got her. She's okay,* he signaled with his eyes, tightening his arms on their daughter. "Did you talk at all?" he asked, nodding toward Cassie.

"She told me she wanted to talk to us. But said she better get with a lawyer first," Nina said. Then she turned. "Look, honey, here it comes."

They stood on the road in a tight huddle and watched the helicopter descend like a ferocious electric-eyed steel insect. Broker shielded Kit's face with his free hand from the tempest of rotor-driven snow. Watched them load the casualties. Two guys jumped off the bird, in parkas; one of them was wearing a tie.

"Here come the suits," Broker said in a dreamy voice, still floating on flowing adrenaline. His voice was lost in the clatter of the chopper lifting off.

Nygard, fiercely protective, steered the two guys away from Broker, Nina, and Kit. He walked them over to the side of the house, where two more state cops and eight deputies from three counties had gathered to gossip about the relative merits of the 1911 .45-caliber Colt semiautomatic pistol, longest-serving hand-gun in the U.S. Army's inventory.

The new arrivals viewed Gator Bodine's brains scattered on the snow like red scrambled eggs. Then they observed the pistol Nina had left in the snow, slide locked open, magazine out. Broker didn't pay them much attention. Wasn't the first time he'd seen a bunch of men, mouths gaping, staring at his wife.

Gliding, holding Kit so tight he could feel her heart thump, Broker reconstructed it; Gator's jerked shot had passed a foot over his head as Nina drilled a bullet an inch above Gator's left eyebrow. Barlow had found Cassie and the burned woman. Nygard had yelled for help. Broker scooped up Kit. Nina ran to assist Barlow. Nygard had dashed into the burning barn, found the keys in the Nissan and backed it out.

Now the yellow tape was being strung. Procedure was setting in. Nygard escorted the two office guys over to the Nissan that was parked a hundred yards away. They huddled for a moment. Apparently having found something, the new guys started walk-ing toward Broker, Kit, and Nina.

Nygard and Barlow blocked their path.

"Mom, Dad . . ." Kit's voice suddenly shuddered with a release of tension. As they drew closer, Kit's voice trembled. "I'm scared . . ."

"It's okay, it's okay," they said in unison as the alarm in her voice started to burst the tight stitches of control in their own faces.

"I'm worried about Ditech, she's probably hungry being out in the cold in this strange place," Kit said, pressing her face into the bundle of black fur in the hollow of her neck.

"She'll be fine, just don't squeeze her too hard," Broker said.

"Got to hold her tight, so she don't get away."

As Kit said that, Broker and Nina's eyes met in the firelight. Tearing up, blinking, he lifted his eyes to the tall column of smoke towering up into the dark sky. That's when the adrenaline flamed out, leaving a terrible empty space in his chest. Griffin . . .

Broker raised his free arm, reaching out. "I . . ." The words faltered. His knees buckled.

"It's okay. I hear you," Nina replied softly, slipping under his arm; leaning in, taking some of the weight. A slender trickle of tears cut through the soot and blood on her cheeks.

Barlow jogged over, her hands gloved with smeared white latex, dark face shiny in the firelight. Her teeth flashed a smile that ended in a tense grimace. "They found some old pictures in the Nissan with you in them. The BCA guy thinks they might mean something," she said to Broker.

Broker just nodded.

Barlow looked around, planted her hands on the heavy leather service belt strapped around her hips, and shook her head briefly. Her eyes came back to them. "You need anything, anything at all, I'm here."

"Keep them off us a few more minutes, okay?" Broker said, hugging his wife and daughter. "We need a little more time alone together."